LUCK

—OF THE—

TITANIC

ALSO BY STACEY LEE

The Downstairs Girl
Outrun the Moon
Under a Painted Sky

LUCK

—— OF THE ——

TITANIC

STACEY LEE

putnam

G. P. Putnam's Sons

G. P. PUTNAM'S SONS
An imprint of Penguin Random House LLC, New York

Copyright © 2021 by Stacey Lee
Diagram illustration copyright © 2021 by Wenhan Shao

G. P. Putnam's Sons is a registered trademark of Penguin Random House LLC.

Visit us online at penguinrandomhouse.com

Library of Congress Cataloging-in-Publication Data
Names: Lee, Stacey (Stacey Heather), author.
Title: Luck of the Titanic / Stacey Lee.
Description: New York: G. P. Putnam's Sons, [2021] | Summary: After smuggling herself onto the
RMS Titanic, British Chinese teenager Valora Luck reunites with her twin brother and tries to
convince him that their acrobatic training could be their ticket to a better life.
Identifiers: LCCN 2020047365 (print) | LCCN 2020047366 (ebook) |
ISBN 9781524740986 (hardcover) | ISBN 9781524740993 (epub)
Subjects: LCSH: Titanic (Steamship)—Juvenile fiction. | CYAC: Titanic (Steamship)—Fiction. |
Brothers and sisters—Fiction. | Twins—Fiction. | Chinese—England—Fiction.
Classification: LCC PZ7.1.L43 Lu 2021 (print) | LCC PZ7.1.L43 (ebook) | DDC [E]—dc23
LC record available at https://lccn.loc.gov/2020047365
LC ebook record available at https://lccn.loc.gov/2020047366

Manufactured in Canada
ISBN 9781524740986
1 3 5 7 9 10 8 6 4 2

Design by Eileen Savage. Text set in Sabon MT Pro.

To my number one son, Bennett.
There are no cowboys in this one,
but there are a few sailors.

Of the eight Chinese passengers aboard the *Titanic*, six survived.

LIST OF CHARACTERS ABOARD THE *TITANIC*

THIRD-CLASS PASSENGERS

- Valora Luck
- James Luck
- Chow "Bo" Wah
- Wink
- Olly
- Drummer
- Ming Lai
- Fong
- Tao
- Heath Bledig
- Dina Domenic & Mr. and Mrs. Domenic

FIRST-CLASS PASSENGERS

- Amberly Sloane
- April Hart & Mrs. Hart
- Charlotte Fine & Mrs. Fine
- Albert Ankeny Stewart & valet "Croggy" Crawford
- J. Bruce Ismay, chairman of White Star Line
- Lady Lucy Duff-Gordon & Sir Cosmo Duff-Gordon
- Bertha Chambers

CREW

- Captain Edward Smith
- Andy Latimer, first-class steward
- "Skeleton," third-class steward
- Officer Merry
- "QM," quartermaster
- "Master-of-Big-Arms," master-at-arms
- Brandish, lead fireman
- Baxter, first-class porter

INSIDE THE
RMS *TITANIC*

1. Stern
2. Docking Bridge
3. Poop Deck
4. Aft Third-Class General Room
5. Third-Class Smoking Room
6. Aft Well Deck
7. Second-Class Library
8. À la Carte Restaurant
9. Second-Class Barbershop
10. Café Parisien
11. First-Class ("Tidal Wave") Aft Staircase
12. First-Class Promenade

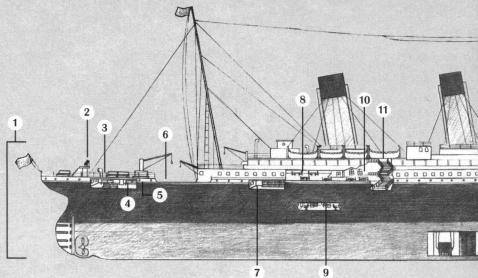

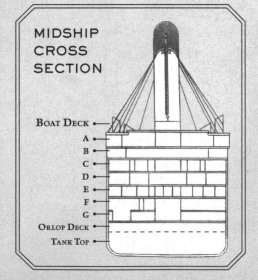

MIDSHIP
CROSS
SECTION

BOAT DECK
A
B
C
D
E
F
G
ORLOP DECK
TANK TOP

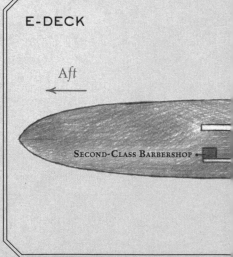

E-DECK

Aft

SECOND-CLASS BARBERSHOP

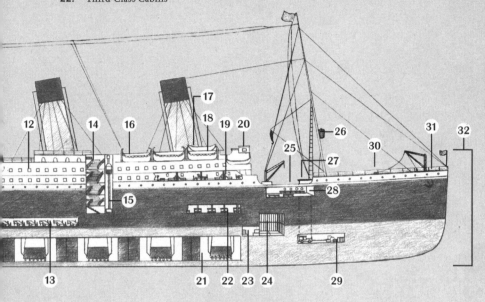

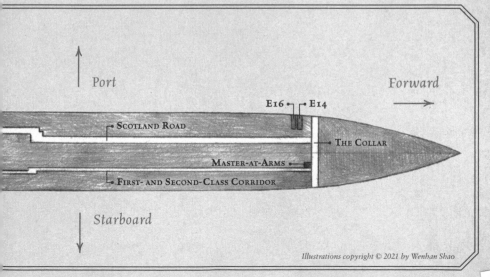

Illustrations copyright © 2021 by Wenhan Shao

Valor and Virtue

The captain paced his weathered deck,
A-talkin' to his boots.
They were his pride and joy, you see,
Anchored him like roots.
The right one he named Valor;
It always steered his course.
The left one he called Virtue;
'Twas steady as a horse.

Together, they had saved him from
Many a tottery fall.
Gripped the wood like tentacles,
In tempest, twirl, or squall.
He never took them off, did he,
Not even when he bathed.
Which wasn't very oft, 'tis true,
The same as when he shaved.

But even boots outwear their seams;
Their leather cracks and splits.
And one day Valor sprang a leak,
And Virtue's heel went quits.
When the captain surveyed, at the end of his legs,
The boots, like ragged jerky,
He cried, "Woe is me," threw them to sea,
Then pitched himself into the murky.

1

April 10, 1912

When my twin, Jamie, left, he vowed it wouldn't be forever. Only a week before Halley's Comet brushed the London skies, he kissed my cheek and set off. One comet in, one comet out. But two years away is more than enough time to clear his head, even in the coal-thickened air at the bottom of a steamship. Since he hasn't come home, it is time to chase down the comet's tail.

I try not to fidget while I wait my turn on the first-class gangway of White Star Line's newest ocean liner. A roofed corridor—to spare the nobs the inconvenience of sunshine—leads directly from the "boat train" depot to this highest crossing. At least we are far from the rats on Southampton dock below, which is crawling with them.

Of course, some up here might consider me a rat.

The couple ahead of me eyes me warily, even though I am dressed in one of Mrs. Sloane's smartest traveling suits—shark grey to match her usual temper, with a swath of black bee-swarm lace pinned from shoulder to shoulder. A lifetime of those dodgy looks teaches you to ignore them. Haven't I already survived the journey from London? A half a day's travel, packed into a smoky railcar, next to a man who stank of sardines. And here I am, so close to the finish line, I can nearly smell Jamie—like trampled ryegrass and the milk biscuits he is so fond of eating.

An ocean breeze cools my cheeks. Several stories below in either direction, onlookers crowd the dock, staring up at the ship rising six stories before them. Its hull gleams, a wall of liquid black with a quartet of smokestacks so wide you could drive a train through them. Stately letters march across its side: "TITANIC." On the third-class gangway a hundred feet to my left, passengers sport a variety of costume: headscarves, patterned kaftans, fringed shawls of botany wool, tasseled caps, and plain dungarees and straw hats. I don't see a single Chinese face among them. Has Jamie boarded already? With this crowd, I may have missed him.

Then again, he isn't traveling alone, but with seven other Chinese men from his company. All are being transported to Cuba for a new route after coal strikes here berthed their steamship.

Something cold unspools in my belly. I received his last letter a month ago. Time enough for things to change. What if Jamie's company decided to send them somewhere other than Cuba, maybe a new route in Asia or Africa?

The line shifts. Only a few more passengers ahead of me.

Jamie! I call in my mind, a game I often played growing up. He doesn't always hear, but I like to think he does when it matters.

In China, a dragon-phoenix pair of boy-and-girl twins is

considered auspicious, and so Ba bought two suckling pigs to celebrate our birth, roasted side by side to show their common lot. Some may think that macabre, but to the Chinese, death is just a continuation of life on a higher plane with our ancestors.

Jamie, your sister is here. Look for me.

Won't he be surprised to see me? Shocked may be more accurate—Jamie has never handled surprise well—but I will get him to see that it is time for him, for *us*, to move on to bigger and better things, just as our father hoped.

I think back to the telegram I sent him when Ba passed five months ago.

```
Ba hit his head on post and died. Please come
home. Ever your Val.
```

Jamie wrote back:

```
Rec'd news and hope you are bearing up okay.
Very sorry, but I have eight months left on my
contract and cannot get away. Write me details.
Your Jamie.
```

Jamie would have known that Ba had been drunk when he hit his head, and I knew he wouldn't mourn like I had. When you live with someone whose mistress is the bottle, you say your goodbyes long before they depart.

Someone behind me clears her throat. A woman in a

pinstriped "menswear" suit that fits her slender figure like stripes on a zebra watches me, an ironic smile wrapped around her cigarette. I put her in her early twenties. Somehow dressing in men's clothing seems to heighten her femininity, with her creamy skin and dark hair that swings to her delicate chin. She lifts that chin toward the entrance, where a severe-looking officer stands like a box nail, a puzzled look on his face.

I bound forward on the balls of my feet, muscled from years of tightrope practice. Ba started training Jamie and me in the acrobatic arts as soon as we could walk. Sometimes, our acts were the only thing putting food on the table.

The severe officer watches me pull my ticket from my velvet handbag.

Mrs. Sloane, my employer, secretly purchased tickets for the two of us with her dragon's hoard of money. She didn't tell her son or his wife about the trip, or that she might stay in America indefinitely to get away from their money-grubbing fists and greedy stares. After her unexpected demise, I couldn't just let the tickets go to waste.

"Afternoon, sir. I am Valora Luck."

The officer glances at the name written on my ticket, then back at me, his steep cheekbones sharp enough for a bird to land on. His navy visor with its distinctive company logo—a gold wreath circling a red flag with a white star—levers as he inspects me. "Destination?"

"New York, same as the rest." Is that a trick question?

"New York, huh. Documentation?"

"You're holding it right there, sir," I say brightly, feeling the gangway shift uncomfortably.

He exchanges a guarded look with the crewman holding the passenger log. "Luck?"

"Yes." In Cantonese, our surname sounds more like "Luke," but the British like to pronounce it "luck." Ba had decided to embrace good fortune and spell it that way, too. He'd intended the lofty-sounding name "Valor" for Jamie, and "Virtue" for me—after a sea shanty about a pair of boots—but my British mum put the brakes on that. Instead, she named my brother James, and I got Valora. It's a toss-up as to which of us is more relieved.

"You're Chinese, right?"

"Half of me." Mum married Ba against the wishes of her father, a vicar in the local parish.

"Then at least half of you needs documentation. Ain't you heard of the Chinese Exclusion Act? You can't go to America without papers. That's just how it is."

"Wh-what?" A pang of fear slices through me. The Chinese *Exclusion* Act. What madness is this? They don't like us here in England, but clearly, they *really* don't like us in America. "But my brother's on this ship, too, with the members of the Atlantic Steam Company. They're all Chinese. Did they get on?"

"I don't keep the third-class register. You'll need to get off my gangway."

"B-but my lady will be expecting me."

"Where is she?"

I was prepared for this question. "Mrs. Sloane wanted me to board first to make sure her room was ready." Of course, she had already pushed off on a different ship, one that wouldn't be making a return journey, causing me great inconvenience. "We had her trunk forwarded here a week ago. I must lay out her things." Mum's Bible is in that trunk, within its pages my only picture of her and Ba. At last, my family will be reunited, even if it is just with a photo of our parents.

"Well, you're not getting on this ship without the proper documentation." He waves the ticket. "I'll keep this for her for when she boards. Next!"

Waiting passengers begin to grumble behind me, but I ignore them. "No, please! I must board! I must—"

"Robert, escort this girl off."

The crewman beside the severe officer grabs my arm.

I shake him off, trying to muster a bit of respect. "I will see myself off."

The woman in the menswear suit behind me steps aside to allow others to go before her, her amber eyes curiously assessing me. "I saw a group of Chinese men enter the ship early this morning," she says in the no-nonsense tone Americans use. "Perhaps you can check if your brother was one of them."

"Thank you," I say, grateful for the unexpected charity.

A family pushes past me, and I lose the woman in a flurry of people, parcels, and hats. I find myself being squeezed back into the train depot, like a piece of indigestible meat. Mrs.

Sloane would've never stood for this outrage. Probably a rich lady like her would have persuaded them to let me on. But there is no one to speak for me now. I descend the staircase, then exit the depot onto the quay. The glare from the overcast sky cuts my eyes.

I figured the hardest part of this endeavor would be getting on without Mrs. Sloane. Never could I have foreseen this complication. What now? I need to be on that ship, or it could be months, maybe years, before I see Jamie again.

Something skirts over my boot and I recoil. A rat. They are certainly bold here, called by the peanut peddlers and meat pie hawkers. I shrink away from a pile of crates, where the rodents are making short work of a melon rind. The river slaps a rhythm against the *Titanic*'s hull, and my heart beats double time with the slosh.

Taking the American's advice, I make tracks for the third-class entrance farther down the quay toward the bow. Unlike in the first class, passengers crowd the gangway, tightening the queue as I near. I straighten my jacket. "I'm sorry, I just need to check if my brother made it through. Please let me pass."

A man with a dark mustache chastises me in a foreign tongue, then jerks his head toward the end of the line. Heads nod, cutting me suspicious glares, and people move to block me. Seems wearing first-class clothes will not gain me any advantage here.

Perhaps things would be different if I looked less like Ba and more like Mum. I exhale my frustration, a wind heated by a lifetime of being turned away for no good cause. Then I continue farther along the quay to the end of the line, passing dockworkers manhandling ropes and a navy uniform shining a torch into people's eyeballs. They don't check the first class for disease.

Beyond the nose of the ship, a couple of tugboats line up, ready to tow the *Titanic* from her mooring. Voices rise as people look up to a massive crane on the bow lowering a hoisting platform onto the quay ten paces away. A horn honks, and the queue shifts, making way for a sleek cinnamon-red Renault motorcar. It stops right before the hoisting platform.

It could take an hour to reach the gangway from here. But even if Jamie has boarded, they still won't let me on that ship without papers. Then the *Titanic* will leave, and he will be lost to me, possibly forever. His letters to me will be undeliverable at the Sloanes', and I will have no way of knowing which new route he was assigned. Jamie is the only real family I have left. I won't let him idle his time on a steamship when he is destined for better things. Great things.

A woman with large nostrils glances at me, then pulls her son closer, spilling some of the peanuts from his paper cone. A rat slithers out from behind a crate and quietly feasts. "Stay away from that one. I've heard they eat dogs."

Barely glancing at me, the boy returns his attention to the Renault.

A crewman gestures at the dockworkers positioned on either side of the car. "Easy now. Load her on."

I am getting on that ship, by hook or by crook. Jamie is

there, and I won't let him leave without me. As for the Chinese Exclusion Act, put out the fire on your trousers before worrying about the one down the street. But how will I board?

The hoisting platform sways on its hook, the stage just big enough to hold the motorcar. A crewman reaches up and guides it the last few feet to the quay.

By *hook*.

I flex my back, my muscles twitching. There are more ways onto the *Titanic* than the gangways.

2

I shade my eyes. The ride up stretches a couple hundred feet, with no walls and no safety net in case something should slide off the platform. I will have to stow away before the platform begins to rise. The car makes a poor hiding spot with its open design, but I can slide underneath and hope no one looks.

It'll be like the times Jamie and I snuck rides aboard the drays about town, slipping on and off without being seen. London is full of distractions. Of course, we usually only needed to distract the driver. The ship with its many portholes suddenly looms like a wall of prying eyes. More pressing are the hundreds of eyes right here on the quay.

I look wildly about for a ruse to distract everyone. Maybe someone is carrying a firearm and I can somehow get him to fire it into the sky. Right. And then maybe a flock of flamingoes will fly in from Africa and a marching band will appear.

Another rat sniffs around my boot, its tail worming behind it. I begin to kick it away but stop. I don't like rats, but they don't give me hysterical fits like they do Mrs. Sloane's daughter-in-law, who boxed my ears when she found one in the pantry. Of course, after this, they might.

Retreating to the train depot a few paces away, I put my back to the wall and tie the ribbons on my black hat tight. Mrs. Sloane gave the hat to me, saying its short brim made her look like a garden hoe. I pull a tin of milk biscuits from my handbag and set the handbag on the ground, wishing the joy of its contents—mostly traveling supplies—to the beggar who finds it. I empty the tin along the wall, crushing the biscuits with my foot.

The dockworkers push the car in place, and the crewman waves his arms. "Stop. Set the brake! Lash it now. Smartly!"

Come on, biscuits, work your buttery charms soon.

The men work quickly, lashing the wheels to the platform.

Of course, when you need a rat, there is none to be found.

Panic jabs at my heart. I abandon my post, searching the dark corners of the quay for the loathsome creatures. After several minutes of scurrying around, I spot a couple of rats feasting on a sausage—at least I hope it's a sausage. Something sour rises in my throat. I've done more repulsive things, but for the life of me, I can't think of a single one.

Slowly, I lower myself, flexing my fingers. Before any more doubts seep in, I snatch a fat one by its scruff. "Got you."

It wiggles and hisses, red eyes glaring, probably oozing poison and disease. Grimly, I hang on, my lips peeled in disgust. I hurry back toward the hoisting platform, casing the dock for a mark. I'll have to find someone with an open purse or a large pocket. A woman with pin curls stares openmouthed at the foremast staking the ship's bow, the hood of her old-fashioned cloak pulled back from her short neck.

Forgive me, ma'am, for what I'm about to do, and know that it is for a good cause.

I duck behind a bunch of men with long beards and burgundy caps heading her way. My rat jerks in my grasp. With light steps, I sneak up to the woman, and while saying a prayer, I release the rat into her open hood.

In four strides, I return to the platform, which has already started to rise.

"Stand back, folks." The crewman walks the perimeter of the platform, enforcing a two-yard margin. If my rat doesn't do his ratty thing soon, it will rise too high for me to scale.

The woman doesn't scream. Have I chosen that one-in-a-million mark who isn't scared by a rat down her back? Should I take a chance and climb on anyway, hoping to God that everyone blinks at the same time?

A scream that could separate the soul from one's body tears through the crowd.

At last!

The crewman glances toward the woman and the commotion forming around her.

I rush forward and hook my hands over the edge of the platform, which has lifted to waist level. Climbing onto it from the side closest to the water, I scoop up my skirts, praying my added weight won't topple the whole thing. I imagine myself light as a bird, the way I do when we walk the rope.

I flatten myself and roll under the car. But something is wrong. Something has caught me. My jacket! The back of my sleeve has snagged on a nail. I sharply yank my shoulder, and I hear the fabric rip. Then I scoot under the car, trying my best to melt into the rough wood.

The platform sways, and seagulls caw as they fly by. I heave in air. The scents of motor oil and my own fear fill my nose. At any moment, I expect the platform to stop. I listen for exclamations, or constables blowing whistles.

But the platform continues its ascent. So far, no one is yelling, except for my unfortunate victim. God save her from the plague. I press my cheek to the wood. From what I can see, no one is looking at me.

Then I see her. A child around five years old with stringy yellow hair and eyes as wide as planets is pointing at me.

I'm just an illusion, kid. Forget what you saw.

The steady pull of the crane snatches her from my view. New worries flood my mind as the platform swings over the *Titanic*'s well deck, ready for its descent into the cargo hatch. What if the shaft to the *Titanic*'s belly does not feature a wall ladder on which I can escape? I'll need to exit before reaching the storage area in the bowels of the ship, where surely men will be waiting to unload the car.

The platform slows as it nears the hatch, and my stomach turns loops. Glimpsing a crewman, I shrink back. He could see me if he thought to look under the car.

His face glistens with sweat and wonder as he walks the length of the platform, taking in the vehicle. "She's a looker. The French know how to make 'em. Thirty-five miles an hour—can you believe it?"

I close my eyes and hold my breath, as if that could hide me from view. Even my blood stops pumping.

He completes his circuit. "Bring her down."

The grinding of a motor and the clink of a chain unspooling herald my descent into the jaws of destiny. Sounds echo off the shaft closing around me, and the light changes.

Rolling out from under the car, I scramble to the edge of the platform and look wildly around for a ladder. It's on the *other* side. My wet fingers slip against the glossy car frame as I swing myself into the seat and scoot across. To my horror, before I can grab a rung, the wall ends.

The platform descends at a walking pace past a room with benches and tables filled with passengers—third class, by the looks of them. Some stare at me dropping from the ceiling, still clinging to the car seat. Nearby, a uniformed crewman chats with a woman, his back to me. Can't get off here. I hold my breath and wait for the platform to pass from view.

At the next level, the shaft becomes enclosed once again. I step up onto the seat, then grab the center chain. Clenching my boots around the chain, I use my legs to propel myself up, trying to climb faster than my stage is falling. The crane brakes, giving me a few precious seconds to scale higher, the chain digging into my hands. Then on it goes, rumbling to life again. I inch up, cursing my skirt for impeding my progress. Sweat blinds me. My limbs scream in anguish. I pass the large room. If anyone notices me, no one protests.

At last, the ladder appears and I hoist myself high enough

to place my foot on a rung. Grabbing the ladder, my skirt tears, but at least I'm no longer headed down. I rest, catching my breath.

Then I climb, rung by rung, until sunlight kisses my face.

I peek over the framed opening. Forty feet away by the base of the crane, the sweaty crewman who had admired the Renault has pulled back his navy beret and is looking up at a seagull. No one else is on the well deck. I imagine myself as invisible as the breeze, then hook a leg over the edge. As quietly as possible, I roll onto the pine deck.

With a loud caw, the seagull swoops in my direction, and the crewman wheels about.

Sod off, you screechy tattletale.

The crewman places a hand on the crane base to steady himself, then draws closer, his bloodshot eyes nearly pouring from their sockets. "Wh-where did you come from?"

I scramble to my feet, feeling a breeze through the tear in my skirt. The sleeve of my jacket collects around my elbow. I must look a fright.

Behind the crewman, the superstructure stacks up like the layers of a cake, at the top of which stands a man with a white beard and a proud bearing, the gold braids on his navy sleeves gleaming like bracelets. Even from fifty feet away, I recognize the face in all the brochures: Captain Smith, the king of this floating palace. He spreads his fingers against the rail and bends his gaze in our direction.

I squeeze a toe down on my panic, which, like a tissue-thin handkerchief in a strong wind, is in danger of cutting loose.

The crewman's nostrils put me in mind of the double bar-rel of a gun. "I said, where did you come from?"

As the Chinese proverb goes, the hand that strikes also blocks. Straightening my hat, I put on the haughty look Mrs. Sloane used with inferiors, eyes hooded, nose tipped up like a seal's. After months of assisting the tough old nut, I could do Mrs. Sloane better than she could. "My mother's loins. And you?"

Someone utters a short laugh. Behind me, leaning against a staircase up to the forecastle, I recognize the slender American woman from the first-class gangway. A fresh cigarette dangles from her red mouth.

The crewman's eyes narrow into slits. He points a thick finger at the cargo shaft. "No. I saw you come from the hatch. Else why's your jacket torn like that?"

"Are you suggesting *I* climbed out from *there*?" I snort loudly. "I can't even walk on this slippery deck without fall-ing. Look, I have ripped my jacket." I crook a finger at his bulbous nose. "You're lucky I didn't break my neck."

Lookouts stationed in the crow's nest halfway up the fore-mast peer down at us. I half expect them to start clanging the warning bell from their washtub-like perch. But then an offi-cer emerges from a doorway under the forecastle, his boots jabbing the deck, and I forget all about the lookouts.

A noose of a tie hangs from a severe white collar, and a jury of eight brass buttons judge me from a humorless field of navy. A uniform like that could have me thrown off this boat for a final baptism. "Something the matter here?"

The crewman mops some of the sweat off his face with his sleeve. "Officer Merry. She climbed out of the hatch."

Officer Merry folds a clipboard into his chest and glares at me. Shapeless eyebrows overhang a dour expression, perhaps caused by the pressure of living up to a name like Merry.

With my hand to my chest, I laugh, but in my nervousness, it sounds more like the honk of passing geese. "Of course I did. Right after I dropped in from my flying balloon."

"Who are you?" asks the officer.

He will ask for papers. The ruse is up. My leg shakes, but I clamp down on it, forcing it into stillness.

"Should I call the master-at-arms?" asks the crewman.

"For goodness' sake, I saw the whole thing." The American with the cigarette sashays up from behind me, her suit as fitted as if it were sewn around her. I'd nearly forgotten about her. "She was just taking some air, same as me, and the poor thing stumbled but caught herself on the lip of that hatch. Lucky for you, she has good reflexes. An accident right before launch could hardly be good press."

I try not to gape at her.

"Miss Hart. How nice to see you." Officer Merry affects an air of pleasant surprise, which is as effective as trying to spruce up a plate of spoiled meat with a sprig of parsley.

Miss Hart begins pacing, moving as regally as the queen's cat. "I must say, the layout of this ship is quite confusing. It's a wonder you don't have more people falling into the hatch. Obviously, you didn't get a woman's opinion on the design."

Officer Merry stares, caught in the fluttering trap of her

glamorous eyelashes. He clears his throat. "It was designed this way so that honored passengers such as yourself could enjoy their luxurious facilities without being disturbed." He glances up at the navigating bridge and, noticing Captain Smith, throws him a quick salute. The captain nods and turns away. "We would not want people to get confused about where they should be."

"So your answer is to confuse them further if they stray," she says brightly. "Interesting."

"You should be relaxing on the Promenade Deck, not down here with the third class. They are serving champagne. It's a good time to meet your fellow passengers. We have several notable guests traveling with us."

My ears get bigger. I learned from Mrs. Sloane's list of "distinguished passengers" that Mr. Albert Ankeny Stewart, part owner of the Ringling Brothers Circus, would be among those guests. When I received Jamie's letter announcing that his crew was being transferred via the *Titanic*, I knew it was a sign that it was time for me to finally get our family back together. We'd dreamed of going "big-time" in a real circus ever since Ba showed us a poster of P. T. Barnum and Co.'s Greatest Show on Earth. We'd even choreographed an audition routine that we called the Jumbo, after the great circus elephant. Somehow, I aim to show Mr. Stewart that routine.

"Mother doesn't care for my smoking." Miss Hart taps her finger against her cigarette holder, and ashes drop. "But I am ready to return to my luxurious facilities. I trust you know a more direct route back to B-Deck." She takes his

arm, nodding toward a small staircase that leads to the superstructure. I can't help wondering if she actually does know her
way around.

"Pull the gangway," barks a voice from somewhere in the
distance, lighting a fire in me. I make a hasty exit toward the
forecastle.

At last, it's anchors aweigh.

Officer Merry's gaze follows me, heavy as a boot on my
back.

3

escending a wide staircase under the forecastle, I find myself in the large room I passed while in the cargo shaft. Bright light from the open staircase gives the space an airy feel.

By the grace of God, I've landed on this stepping-stone, bringing me one step closer to America's shores. But before I search for Jamie, I need the grace of the lavatory. My bladder feels like a dozen butchers are whacking it with meat pounders.

I remove my ridiculous jacket and glance about for somewhere to do my business.

The words "General Room" are marked in gold letters on the wall. Seems they could've come up with a more interesting name. *Obviously, you didn't get a woman's opinion,* I hear Miss Hart say in her mocking tone.

I try to recall the ship's layout from the diagrams Mrs. Sloane requested so that she would be comfortable enough to make the journey. We reviewed them extensively, but it's hard to think when parts of you are under pressure.

Below the Boat Deck—the uppermost deck, where they keep the lifeboats—the decks descend from A to G and, for the most part, correlate to class, like how wool is rated for quality. This General Room, a gathering spot for the third class, lies in the forward part of the ship, on D-Deck.

No lavatory presents itself, so I hobble down another floor to E-Deck.

The stairway spills onto a wide corridor that runs from port to starboard, such that if the *Titanic* was a fish, this corridor would be the collar, the choicest piece to eat. I dub it the Collar, and I imagine Miss Hart would approve of the moniker, which is both memorable and practical.

Stewards in high-necked white jackets with gold buttons mill about the area, directing passengers to their destinations.

The sign for the lavatory is like a port in a storm, and I gladly take refuge within it.

Sinks face off against seven water closets, each with a dial near the handle, all marked "vacant." I throw my jacket onto the nearest hook and quickly smite my hands of any rat chiggers with a cake of soap imprinted with the White Star logo.

When I swing shut the door of the first water closet, an electric light flickers on. Even the third-class bathrooms here have class. Once I am blissfully empty, I lift a back lever, and the toilet neatly accepts my deposit. I wash up again, this time enjoying the cedar scent of the soap.

Now to find Jamie. If I ask one of the stewards for help, will they ask to see my papers? I've already made an unfavorable impression on those who needed impressing.

My ruined jacket hangs like a dead badger. I unpin the bee-swarm lace and hold it to my face. The black dots that give the lace its name certainly obscure my Chinese features. I could be anyone under this veil—the queen, even. Perhaps it will give me easier passage here.

I remove my hat and pin the lace to the band so that it overhangs my face to my shoulders. It's a fashionable curtain, of the sort wealthy women in mourning might wear. As for the rip in my skirt, I twist the garment around so that the tear hangs to one side and won't vent when I walk.

Back in the Collar, I case the area for a steward. Folks— mostly men—bustle around, carrying suitcases, looking for rooms.

From the ship diagrams, I recall that third-class cabins run along the port side on this level, with first- and second-class rooms on the starboard side. Mrs. Sloane didn't want to stay on this deck, or D-Deck above it, because of how the classes cohabit, even though the ship is designed so that upper and lower class will never meet. If she was going to ride an elephant, it would be at the highest end, not the rump.

"Only men here at this end for your protection," a steward tells a young woman with a straw hat. No wonder the lavatory was empty. "It's against the rules for men and women to visit each other's rooms. But you'll like your cabin at the stern. It's steadier back there, and closer to the poop deck, where the third class can take fresh air. Just follow Scotland Road." He points down a corridor that runs the length of the ship like the backbone of a fish. "Smartest way to get from bow to stern. You'll pass a slew of crew cabins, but keep going to the end."

If the single men are in the bow, I am close. "Excuse me, sir?"

The steward's eyes widen at the sight of me in my veil. "Yes, ma'am?"

"I'm looking for James Luck. Could you tell me which room he's in?"

"Let's see . . ." He runs a finger down his clipboard. "E-16. With the company of Atlantic Steam. Just around the corner." He opens a hand toward the port side. "But as I told the other lady, only men are allowed in the bow. I can leave a message for you, if you give me your name."

"Er, no, that's okay. I will find him later. Thank you, steward."

He bows, and I wait for him to leave. But the man stands his ground, as if waiting for *me* to leave. Before he gets suspicious, I duck back into the lavatory to wait him out.

Lifting off my hat, I smooth loose tendrils of hair back into my braided bun. My pounding heart flutters against my embroidered linen blouse.

I imagine how Jamie will take the news. He may play things casual, but I'll throw my arms around him and squeeze the casual out. But what if he's different now? Too old for my clowning around. What if the years have given him a vulture neck and a map's worth of lines on his face, and he rants at the world and spits when he talks?

Perhaps I should've warned him I was coming. But would the *Titanic* receive a telegram on a third-class passenger's behalf?

I replace my hat and arrange my veil. It's a good disguise. Maybe good enough to sneak into first class and discover the whereabouts of Mrs. Sloane's trunk.

After two minutes pass, I poke my head out again. A couple of kids running down the hall stop and stare at me. I shut the door again, waiting for their delighted shrieking to fade, then venture out. I quickly make tracks toward a small companionway on the port side. Room E-16 lies only a few paces down.

My heartbeat knocks double time as I rap twice on the door.

No one answers, but the men on the other side are speaking in Cantonese. Though the sound is harsh to Western ears, it reminds me of Ba's optimistic voice, and I feel my heart swell. I put my ear to the wood.

"Don't answer it, Tao," someone grumbles. "It's probably that skeleton steward again. Ming Lai already told him we're not interested in their 'sweepstakes.'" He says that last word in barely recognizable English.

"Maybe he is here to fill the water pitcher," says an airier voice, which must belong to Tao.

"Drummer already went to fill the pitcher. Sit down, old fool, and finish your meditation."

"How can one meditate with you breathing so loud?"

I knock again, and say in Cantonese, "Hello? I'm looking for Mr. James Luck."

The voices abruptly stop. The door opens, and a man with a braided beard that drips from his chin like an icicle tilts his thin face at me. A queue, like a grown-up version of the beard, hangs down his back. The front portion of his scalp is shaved clean. Chinese men wear this hairstyle to show fealty to the Qing dynasty, though since the Qing dynasty has fallen, some have cut it off.

The man's curious expression makes him look youthful, despite his many white hairs. "Who are you?" He must be Tao, judging from his airy voice.

"I am Jamie's sister, Valora Luck, Uncle," I say, using the respectful term the Chinese use for elders. "Is he staying here?"

I peer inside and see two sets of bunk beds. Four seabags hang on hooks, each embroidered with a different Chinese surname. To my dismay, none belong to Jamie. I'd stitched his myself from sturdy denim.

The second man holds the post of one of the bunk beds, peering at me through hooded eyes. Under his seaman's cap, his hair hangs oily and black around his round face, which is creased with discontent.

One is like water, and the other like smoke. They're probably in their fifties, though they look more like they're in their sixties.

Favoring his left foot, the grumpy man limps forward, blocking the bright light from the porthole as well as the cool ocean breeze. A top incisor tooth swings out a tad too far, like a single fang, and the knees of his sea slops are worn and patched. "Jamie never said he had a sister."

I cough in disbelief. "Well, he does. We're twins."

The sound of people cheering from the docks below mimics

the pounding of my own heart. So these men do know Jamie. I am close.

Tao tugs at his whale-blue kerchief, embroidered with the letters *ASC*. Atlantic Steam Company. Grumpy also wears the kerchief.

I lift my veil, and Tao's honest face takes on the look of one sighting a rare bird. He points with a finger that is missing its tip, and I try not to stare. "Same narrow ears as Jamie."

"Narrow ears doesn't mean they are related." Grumpy bats Tao's shoulder. "Why is she here? She probably wants money. Women always want money."

"She is wearing nice clothes. Why would she need money?"

"To buy more nice clothes, of course! She looks shifty. Women cannot be trusted." Grumpy pushes Tao aside and grabs the doorknob. A whiff of tobacco makes me wince.

"But I have traveled a long way to see him. Please, is he on this boat? Where can I find him?"

"He is not here." Grumpy closes the door in my face.

"You almost hit her, Fong," Tao protests. "Negative energy will return to you."

The lock snickers closed.

A heavy stone of dread sinks in me. "He is not *here* here, or he is not on this boat?" No one answers. "Please, Uncles, if you do see him, could you tell him his sister is looking for him?"

Tao begins to speak, but Fong cuts him off with a hacking sound. "Don't talk! You just encourage her to stay longer."

My face burns under my veil. Fong mentioned two other men—Ming Lai and someone named Drummer. Has one of them substituted for Jamie? If Jamie isn't on the *Titanic*, then I am in for one long ride.

Three stout notes, blown from somewhere above, form a chord that rumbles through my body. The floor begins to move as the ship sets sail. The trumpets that herald us out to sea remain in my ear, sounding more like the howl of the hounds when the fox slips through their grasp.

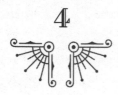

4

Chin up. I cannot despair until I have checked every corner of this ship. I shall start with the poop deck, where the third class air themselves. Perhaps Jamie is watching the ship depart.

I slog down Scotland Road—the spine of the fish—a brightly lit and bustling hall of slatted wood. The white enamel walls ring with a mishmash of languages, making my head hurt. I stop at a drinking fountain, and its cool offering is a tender mercy. Then I continue, nearly tripping on the raised sill of a doorway marked "watertight."

On my left, the humming walls bear signs that read "Boiler Casing"—from 6 to 1—and feel warm to the touch. Those must extend to the boiler rooms on the bottom deck, where the firemen feed the furnaces.

On my right, crew dormitories are arranged by pecking order—beginning with stewards by class, then engineers, cooks, dishwashers, and potato peelers. Then the dorms give way to passenger cabins. Doors open and shut, offering glimpses of families settling into serviceable rooms with tidy bunks, even a few with sinks and mirrors. The furnishings are nicer than one would expect in third class and fit perfectly in the cozy spaces. Everything belongs somewhere.

Except me.

I slow, watching two kids jump off a top bunk. Their mum whips around and pinches them by the ears. "Jump off again, and I'll have them lock you in the brig."

After what feels like miles, I reach the last staircase and follow the crowds toward the scent of the ocean.

Two decks up, people move in and out of the public rooms like bees to a hive. One, the Smoking Room, emits a pungent blue haze. The other, a second General Room, vibrates with the sound of a banjo player. No Jamie in either.

The ocean air blows its breath onto my face when I step out onto the aft well deck, which, together with the one at the bow, bookends the superstructure. I climb a final staircase to the rearmost deck, the ingloriously named poop deck. There again, a woman's opinion would've been helpful, as one cannot help but think of the toilet every time one refers to it.

I draw a horseshoe-shaped path around the deck. Folks bundled in their plain wool coats and thick sweaters step aside at my approach. Some men even tip their hats to me. It seems wearing a veil does improve how I'm treated.

A raised catwalk called the docking bridge spans the width of the deck, on which a crewman grips a steering wheel. When I explained to Mrs. Sloane that they steered from the docking bridge when the *Titanic* had to go backward, she declared herself sold. If a big boat like the *Titanic* could go backward, it was safe enough for her.

The crewman at the wheel spots me, and his short forehead crimps under a beret straight enough to cut timber.

I stop breathing. Has he seen through my veil? Or will he chase me away for being on the wrong deck?

But then he acknowledges me with a touch of his hat and begins polishing his brass instruments with quick movements of his short limbs.

Behind us, Southampton has shrunk to fit in a doll's house, chasing a thrill up my spine. I wipe the sea mist from the railing on my skirt.

Farewell, England. Farewell, *land*.

A thread of fear tickles my back. This is my first time on a boat. Suddenly, the idea of trusting a box of steel to float thousands of miles across water seems as ludicrous as flying by balloon. But people do this every day, don't they? Besides, I am on the newest—and, therefore, safest—ship on the Atlantic. And I have more important things to worry about right now, like finding Jamie.

I lower myself onto one of the benches arranged bow to stern and try to come up with a new plan.

"They charge a shilling if you want a room key," says a woman on the bench behind me. "That's banditry."

"We don't need a key," replies the man beside her. "What do we have worth stealing?"

"My mother's Spanish hairnet."

"As I said."

If they charge for keys, I could try every unlocked door until I found Jamie. Though I might not get very far before I was branded a deviant and thrown in the brig, if there really is one.

I twist to my left, glancing across the well deck toward the top of the superstructure and the lifeboats that ring the perimeter of the Boat Deck. If all else fails, I could sleep in one of those. Of course, I would need to grow a layer of blubber to protect me from the freezing nights. The Atlantic will be as cold as snowmelt, maybe even colder, once we reach the ice fields off Newfoundland.

My shoulders have pulled toward my ears, and I roll them back.

Below the Boat Deck on A-Deck, women in the latest seashell pastels and men in suits as slick and oiled as seals collect around a quartet of musicians. The view is less grand one level down on B-Deck, where the second class mingles. My mind skims to the bottom levels where the "black" gangs work, so called because of the color the coal turns them.

Ten decks in all, home to two thousand passengers.

Jamie, will I ever find you?

I sniff, on the verge of falling into the pity pit.

"This time, no cheating, Wink," says a voice with an accent like Ba's.

My breath catches. On the bench behind me, two Chinese lads and a young man with a deep scowl have replaced the couple and are playing a card game. The speaker sits in the middle with his cards held close to his nose. I guess he's around eleven or twelve years old. He has the shape of a matchstick, which is how Jamie looked at that age, with a big head and narrow everything else.

"I never cheat," the lad closest to me growls in the highly offended manner of someone who *does* cheat. He glances back at me. I put him at around nine or ten, and in danger of drowning in his clothes. A too-big cap droops to one side of his head, and his kerchief is so tattered, it's more like a tag around his neck. His delicate cheeks twitch in a way that makes his eye wink, probably the source of his name.

The scowling man, who looks about the same age as Jamie and me, stretches an arm taut as a bridge cable along the back of the bench. His ring catches my eye. It seems to be made from thick shell and etched with a circular design. I've seen the scrimshaw sailors scratch on whale teeth and bones, but never on a shell.

"We could get jobs showing people how to play Winds of Change," says the matchstick lad, his voice not quite that of a man but no longer that of a boy either.

My spine stiffens. Jamie made up that game. He loved cards, though after he'd lost our grocery allowance on High Card, he swore off gambling for money forever.

The scowling man snorts. "Your only job here is to stay out of trouble." Now, that is a man's voice. It's not heavy on the bass notes, but it exudes a quiet authority. Unlike the lads with their easy tongues, he speaks his English carefully, like a cat choosing where to put his paws on a slippery rail.

"But why do you and Jamie get to find jobs?" asks the matchstick lad.

I bolt up in my seat at the mention of Jamie's name.

"We are older, and White Star does not hire children."

"No, it's because you and Jamie bet the washing over who can make more money, and you don't want us to get in the way," says Wink in his growly voice, which is so at odds with his petite self.

"That, too."

A bet. That sounds just like Jamie, who was always challenging me. We did it all: contests to see who could hold their breath the longest, who could balance an egg on their forehead the longest, who could fit the most biscuits in their mouth.

Wink plucks a card from his hand. "Winds of Change."

"You can't call Winds of Change until an eight has been played," the matchstick lad objects.

The scowling man's gaze wanders to me and loiters, probably trying to see through my veil. The noble angle of his jaw challenges me to run a finger across it, like one might test the edge of a knife for quality. But then his eyes drift away, as if deciding I am not that interesting.

"Bo, Olly's making up rules," Wink complains.

"If you kumquats do not stop arguing, we play Old Maid."

"I'm afraid he's right. An eight must be played first," I hear myself say. If these are Jamie's mates, surely he is close by, though I don't see any other Chinese around.

"See?" says Olly, before joining Wink and the scowling

man, Bo, in staring at me. I scoot back to the armrest so all three are in view and no one is tempted to peek behind my veil.

"How does she know Winds of Change?" asks Wink, switching to Cantonese, which they naturally assume I cannot understand. His delicate cheek begins to twitch.

"Maybe Jamie lied about making it up," says Olly.

"Jamie wouldn't lie, you cow's butt."

Olly ignores the insult. "Why do you think she's wearing a veil?"

Wink's eyes grow large. "Maybe she has warts."

"Or maybe she doesn't have a face."

Bo turns forward with a snort, the ridges of his back flexing visibly even under his peacoat. "Maybe you should both shut up. She's first class. Too good for you to speak to."

"If she's first class, why is she on this deck?"

"Because first class can walk where they want. Stop looking at her."

The two lads continued gaping.

"I don't have warts, and if I didn't have a face, then how could I be looking at your funny mugs?" I say evenly in Cantonese.

Olly's jaw drops, exposing rows of crooked teeth. Wink slaps a hand over his mouth, as if to hide the state of his cutters. Bo quirks an eyebrow, and I revel in the small triumph of getting a reaction from him.

"I'm looking for James Luck. Know where I can find him?"

They hesitate, and I'm reminded of the two men like water

and smoke, Tao and Fong. I've heard that sailors are superstitious, but I had no idea they were so distrustful.

Bo's eyes drift to the well deck, where a crowd has gathered. He stretches up as if to see something, then nods toward the people. "Start there."

I cover the two paces to the railing and crane my neck. The crowd parts to reveal the back of a young man dressed in sea slops, kneeling as he pets a dog. Is it . . . Jamie?

He removes his cap and smooths his hair, a gesture I've seen a thousand times. It *is* Jamie, though he's broader in the back than I remember. My heart squeezes, and all the nerves kinked up inside me seem to shake loose. *At last.*

Olly blows out a thin whistle from where he, Wink, and Bo have joined me at the rail. "That's a poodle, the kind of dog you have to *pay* for."

"Jamie's always been good with dogs," I say, remembering how the neighborhood mutts would follow him around.

"I do not think it is the dog that interests him," Bo says cheekily.

"What do you mean by that?"

"See for yourself."

A young lady leans over and attaches a leash to the dog, spilling her minky hair into her face. Guess I'm not the only first-class lady slumming it with the poor. She's not dressed as flashy as the other nobs—a cheerful suit in butter yellow and pearl earbobs—but she has the kind of pretty face, with soft brown eyes and strawberry-pink lips, that causes men to drop their jaws and women to drop their stitches. Jamie says something, and her patrician nose crinkles becomingly. They're . . . conversing?

Olly stretches far over the rail. "Who's she?"

Bo pulls Olly back by his collar. "White ghost means trouble. Jamie should avoid her."

The Chinese can be suspicious of foreigners, who rarely do them any favors.

"She's a fetcher," says Wink, who then steals another glance at me. "I bet she smells like marmalade."

Olly breaks free from Bo. "And butter."

"Why would you think that?" I ask.

"Jamie said those are the best smells."

Clearly, they know him well. Mum made us biscuits with marmalade and butter whenever we had money to spare, which wasn't often.

Jamie climbs the stairs, not as spryly as I remember, but rather as if each step requires a separate thought. I marvel at how he has filled out his wrapper. New muscles mean better acts, faster moves. Acrobatics came naturally to him, unlike me. I always had to work twice as hard, especially after I started rounding out. Though he isn't tall by English standards, five eight at most, there is a brightness around Jamie that commands attention, even from first-class girls with poodles.

He bounds over to us, a high flush on his golden cheeks. He nods at me. "Ma'am."

I almost laugh out loud, but suck it back in. The first class does not waste their breath responding to commoners.

"Make a new friend?" Bo asks him.

Jamie gives his coat lapels a sharp tug. "Miss Charlotte Fine of New York City."

Miss *Fine*? I snort hard enough for my veil to ripple. Jamie glances at me, but Charlotte waves a pretty gloved hand at him, then makes her poodle wave its black paw. Jamie returns the wave.

"Her poodle slid off the deck during that one dip, but I caught her. She sure is clever. She can beg and play dead and everything."

This time, I can't hold back. "The girl or the dog?"

Jamie's eyes—narrower than mine but a richer brown, like Mum's—snap to me. He stares hard at my veil, but unlike the others, he knows the face on the other side. Knows its heart shape as well as his own, with our same tendency to stick up our chins as if perpetually checking for rain.

His mouth splits into a half grin, half grimace. "I don't bloody believe it."

I raise my veil long enough for him and his crew to get a peek. "Believe it, Jamie, because here I am."

5

Though I cannot afford to attract more attention than I already have, I embrace my brother. The familiar scent of milk biscuits and trampled ryegrass, now dusted with coal, puts a lump in my throat. "How about you? Shoveling coal shored you up." I give his solid shoulder a thump.

Despite his new density, his face is still youthful with fine bones and cheeks you can cup your hands around. He looks like a pretty boy, and I look like a boyish girl. "They said you were in E-16, but someone named Fong shut the door in my face, and I thought you didn't make it after all, and you have no idea—" It's hard to string words together when you're trying not to blubber.

"Sorry about that. Fong's a suspicious old boot. We exchanged rooms because he didn't want Room 14."

The Chinese avoid the number four, which sounds like the word for "death" in Cantonese.

"What are you doing here, Val? And why are you dressed like that?"

"It's a bit of a story."

His mates stand by, sporting various states of confusion. Olly stares openly, his eyes flitting to the short fan of feathers on my hat, which somehow survived my perilous journey aboard. Wink places a thin hand on the back of the bench and lifts himself up onto his toes, as if to get a better bead on me, his expressive eyes jittery. Bo leans his sturdy frame against the rail, chewing his lower lip. With or without his scowl, he charms the vision, his dark brows standing out against clear skin, his guarded eyes the color of oolong tea steeped to just the right smokiness.

"Jamie, how come you never told us you had a sweetheart?" Olly blurts.

I let go of my brother with a loud guffaw. Jamie slaps my back harder than he needs to. "Everyone, this is Valora. My twin *sister*. So no one get any ideas, because she's off-limits."

Wink and Olly snicker, proof that they are not the ones Jamie is worried about. Bo glares up at the docking bridge, as if he can't be bothered to look at me anyway.

Olly ties his thin arms into a knot. "Why didn't you ever tell us you had a twin?"

"Does no one know about me?" Well, that is a knife to the gut. I tie my own arms together.

"You never told us you were rich, either." Wink reaches out a finger and touches a bit of lace on my sleeve.

Jamie slaps his hand away. "We call this one Wink. He blinks a lot, but nothing gets past him."

Wink puffs up his bony chest and lifts his nose.

"And this eager fellow is Oliver. When I first met him, he didn't have two words to rub together, and now we can't shut him up." Jamie pushes the lad away by his bony forehead.

"They're our boiler monkeys, sweeping up coal, fetching water. But mostly they just get underfoot."

The lads protest, but Bo knuckles them on the head.

I'd imagined the men of Jamie's company would be, well, *men*, grizzled and hard-boiled, like Fong. Certainly not this young. Jamie rarely mentioned his mates in his letters. Yet, as I watch them horse around, I can't help thinking that these lads are more than mates. They're behaving like brothers. Why keep them a secret from me, and me a secret from them? I am not only his twin, but also his best friend. At least, I was.

"This classy gent is Chow Bo Wah." Jamie claps Bo on the back. "He's a fireman like me, but he shovels coal twice as fast. The muscles are all an act, though. Inside, he's a kitten."

Bo scowls. "You are a fool."

Jamie laughs. "Now out with it. Why are you here and not with the Sloanes?"

I muster a smile, despite Jamie having sidestepped *my* question. I will beat it out of him later. "Mrs. Sloane died, and her son and his wife went to Scotland to tour her ashes."

"Why didn't they take you with them?"

"They wanted to, but . . ." My mind flies back to when Mrs. Sloane's daughter-in-law launched a potted fern at me after I gave her my notice. Never mind that my main duty was to watch Mrs. Sloane and she no longer needed watching. I never told Jamie of the abuse I suffered there.

"But?" He cocks an ear toward me, as if trying to make my response come faster.

"But I quit. They didn't need me anymore. See, I read your

letter about your leaving on the *Titanic*, and with Mrs. Sloane departing and you departing, it all made sense."

"What?" He shakes his head as if clearing his ears of water, and his eyes take on the grippy look he gets when he thinks I've swiped one of his biscuits. "What made sense?"

"That it was time for us to go to New York together."

He wheezes out a laugh. "I can't go to New York. They're expecting all of us in Cuba, and I can't stop for a jaunt."

"I didn't mean a jaunt." I ignore the disbelief trampling his face. "Remember how Ba called America the beautiful country, where the air is always blue and fruit trees grow like weeds? And now here we are, going there together. You can't tell me you'd rather spend your time"—remembering his mates, I lower my voice—"shoveling coal than making our way in New York."

"Shoveling coal is hard work, good work. It's good for me."

"So we'll find you some good hard work in America, something that won't have you sticking your head in an oven every day."

"We don't stick our heads in the boilers."

"Then why are you getting a vulture neck?"

He straightens his posture.

"You want to end up like those men in E-16, crabby and missing fingers?"

Bo nearly smiles. He pushes himself off the rail. "Hey, kumquats, let's see the propeller." Catching the reluctant Olly and Wink by their arms, he hauls them away.

We watch the lads stop in front of a couple of young men

with plaid jackets tossing a strange oval ball. Back and forth it flies. Olly says something, and one of the plaid jackets shakes his head and grips his ball tighter. Bo pushes them along, taking one last glance at me.

Jamie sinks onto the bench and holds his head between his hands. "America doesn't want us. They passed a law to keep the Chinese out."

"But we're not from China. We're British. We write our letters better than our characters."

"British subjects, not citizens. England's only happy to be rid of us."

I carefully smooth my skirts before sliding in beside him. "If everything goes according to my plan, New York will be throwing a ticker tape parade for us."

His eyes narrow. "What are you on about?"

"I happen to know that Mr. Albert Ankeny Stewart, part owner of the Ringling Brothers Circus, is a first-class passenger here on the *Titanic*."

"Stop there."

But the barrel has already started rolling. "If we could impress Mr. Stewart, he could hire us as employees of his circus. Surely America would make an exception for an influential man like him. We've been talking about this since forever. Virtue and Valor, the Chinese acrobats. Come on, Jamie, you can't tell me you don't miss it. This is our chance!"

Before he contradicts me, I sweep ahead, the barrel picking up speed. "We can do the Jumbo routine and make sure he sees it. It'll be just like in St. James's Park. They loved us there."

St. James's Park was our stage of choice, with its wide expanses of green and constant stream of people. We'd make enough in one day to keep us fed for a week in the summer months.

"They didn't always love us. Sometimes they called us pinch-eyed mongrels." He twists his tricky wrist—the left one, which sometimes gets stuck in one position.

"Sticks and stones."

"Yeah. They threw those at us, too."

I watch the oval ball spiral in tight arcs from one plaid jacket to the other. A memory trickles in: a couple of college men, dressed in dark blazers and the distinctive red-white-and-blue neckties that marked them as Cambridge scholars. I had just climbed up Jamie's shoulders, in preparation for our four-hand six-egg juggle act. One of the Cambridge men jerked his chin at us. "It's a damn shame, all the litter filling our fine parks nowadays." He reached down to adjust his sock. Or so I thought. The next moment, a pinecone hit me in the collarbone. I fell, rolling like Ba had taught us to let the ground absorb the impact. Jamie was so angry, he threw all the eggs at the blighters. After the coppers arrested *us* instead of the Cambridge pair, Ba had to pawn his silver belt buckle to get us off the hook.

I bump my knee against Jamie's. "Let that go. We're here now, no worse for wear, and we have our future to think about. Family has to stick together, Jamie. That's you and me."

He sighs. "How did you get here?"

"By train."

"You know what I mean. Tickets aren't cheap, and neither are those togs." His eyes travel down my linen shirt to the silk jacket in my lap.

"Mrs. Sloane bought the tickets. She'd been wanting to visit her brother in America, but she hates—*hated*—sea travel. Then she heard about the new ship and decided it wasn't going to get better than the *Titanic*."

"How did they let you board without her?"

"They didn't."

He grits his teeth. "Keep going."

"I snuck in."

"Bloody snakes. You *snuck* in? Explain," he growls.

I summarize my ride up to the cargo hatch. His spine seems to contract with my telling, as if each statement is a hammer blow, driving the nail farther into the bench. By the time I get to the part about my rescue by Miss Hart, he is back to holding his head in his hands.

"Have you got straw in your attic?" he huffs, finally straightening again. "They'll figure it out. Then they'll send you back, either in Cherbourg or Queenstown, probably in some fish hauler with a bunch of smelly old sods."

"Cherbourg's in a few hours," I say of the French port where the *Titanic* will be taking on additional passengers. "The crew will be too busy to figure it out before then. And Queenstown isn't until tomorrow morning." The last stop before open sea. "I'll keep my chin tucked until then."

"You'll have to keep it tucked longer than that. Bollocks,

what are we going to do?" He whacks his cap against his knee. "This is so typical. Plans always half-baked."

"So I've had to improvise."

"You wouldn't have had to improvise if you had thought things through. You can't just"—he throws out his hands— "waltz into first class without your mistress. They'll catch you eventually."

I primly smooth my skirts. "Aren't you a nelly naysayer?"

"Better than a Jack the lad," he shoots back, calling me a show-off.

"Simple Simon."

He twists away from me and pounds a fist to his mouth. Clearly the naming game is not filling his nose with the perfume of brotherly love.

"All right, Jamie. I guess I could've planned it better. But the stars must have aligned, because here we are, together. This is our Halley's Comet. We'll find Mr. Stewart and show him our Jumbo act. He's our ticket into America."

"You're cracked. What makes you think a man like him will even see us, let alone employ us? You're starting to worry me."

"Because I dream of a better life for us?"

"No. Because you're reminding me of Ba."

I hiss in air, which feels cold against my teeth. "Ba was a visionary."

"If you say so."

He can't still be angry with Ba after all these years, can he? The day Mum collapsed, Ba had just brought her the news—his ratty top hat in his hand—that his bee farm had flown away, taking with it most of our money. Ba was that rare man with a head full of ideas and the courage to make them happen. Of course, they hadn't all worked out.

At any rate, that explains all the dreams I've been having about Ba lately. He's stuck in this life because Jamie's anger is keeping him here.

"Tonight you can sleep in my room. Then, tomorrow, you can get off at Queenstown. I have enough money to get you back to London. Aunt Susan would take you in. Find you another job."

I groan. Unlike her parents, Mum's sister visited us after Mum died. She helped me find the job with the Sloanes, and invited Ba and me for the occasional Sunday dinner when her parents would not be around. "Why would I want to go backward?"

"It's *illegal* for us to go to America. Who knows what could happen to you? I'd be half-mad with worry."

My jaw clicks in annoyance. America not wanting us worries me, too, but I know how to take care of myself. "I'm not going back."

The oval ball comes sailing at my head. I reach up to catch it, but Jamie snatches it out of the air a fraction of a second before me. He jumps to his feet. "Watch it, you clods."

I scramble to my feet as well, in case there's trouble.

The two young men with the plaid jackets run up to us. But instead of the wrath I expect, they doff their hats, exposing yellow hair thick as thistles.

"Beg your pardon, ma'am," one says in the flat accent they use in Birmingham. "Brummies" always sound like they have a mouth full of cheese. "Didn't see you there." His grimace looks more sheepish than cross, and his tone is apologetic.

My fists loosen. He thinks he's in trouble. I tip up my nose. "I'll say. You may have your ball back . . ." The Brummie reaches for the ball, which Jamie is spinning on his palm, but I sweep up a finger. "On one condition." Jamie pulls the ball away so fast, the Brummie nearly falls over. "You must pass along some generosity of spirit and let those two wee lads over there play catch with you." I nod toward the back rail, where Wink and Olly are craning their necks at something Bo is showing them in the distance.

"Sure, ma'am."

"Thank you, ma'am."

Jamie releases their ball to them, and they jog away. Shooting me a weary look, Jamie sits back down.

"Now don't you miss performing?" I crack.

"Not the kind of performing you want to do. I've moved on from that. I doubt I could even do a gunslinger, let alone the entire Jumbo."

"Sure you can. You just have to practice." The one-arm handstands we call gunslingers are our specialty.

"And even if all those things with Mr. Stewart happen, I don't want to go to America. Walking a rope is a hundred times harder than shoveling coal, and I only did it because it was the best way to keep us from starving. Besides, I have work to do. My contract won't be up for several months."

I expected resistance, but this is outright defiance. It was easier when it was just the two of us. Our plans always included each other. With his new mates, perhaps his loyalties have shifted. Maybe they've steered him in a different direction than he is meant to go. Especially that shifty ox, Bo.

The *Titanic* rolls and shifts, but I hardly notice. "Has all this salt water made you slow, Jamie? You were meant for better things. Think of this as a door to a larger world. You always wanted to study astronomy. With our talent, we can get into America, and then you'll have your chance."

"I study astronomy every night."

"I meant in the scholarly sense."

He lets out a frustrated groan, and a group of men cuts their eyes toward us from one bench over. "I like what I do."

"Fine. Do what you like to do. But I'm not going back to London. I'm going to New York, with or without you." I get to my feet, and a cold breeze slices through my thin blouse.

Dragon and phoenix twins are yin and yang opposites that usually create harmony together. But when we disagree, we won't easily stand down, especially the more masculine "yang" dragon, which in our case has always been me.

"Come on, don't be that way. Where are you going?" He follows me to the stairs.

"I'm tired, Jamie." Our footfalls clatter on the steps. "I thought scaling a crane or hiking for miles through this wobbly maze just to find you had wrung me out. But you know what really put me through the wringer? Talking to an ungrateful clod like you who wouldn't know a good opportunity if it bit his Queen Mum."

I let that sink in before crossing the well deck. Jamie tails me to a doorway into the superstructure marked "First and Second Class Only." Somewhere in there lies Mrs. Sloane's trunk, which I should fetch before they move it into the cargo hold. Plus, I'm getting cold, and I'm not asking my gobby goat of a brother for a coat.

"You can't go there," Jamie hisses from behind me.

"Watch me." Emboldened by my anger, I reach for the door handle.

A crewman appears on the other side, holding up a hand like a stop sign. Another stone in my path. "It's only the upper classes here."

Jamie's grimace burns the back of my head. But instead of pulling me toward safety, that damnable expression prods me forward.

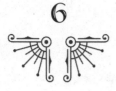

6

I summon Mrs. Sloane's commanding tone, ignoring the pounding of my heart between my ears. "I *am* a first-class passenger, and I seem to be lost. Which way to B-Deck?" I hold my breath, hoping my deception works at least long enough to retrieve Mrs. Sloane's trunk.

The crewman's face relaxes. "Oh. I'm so sorry, ma'am." Allowing me to pass, he closes the door behind him, cutting Jamie from my view. He stretches out an arm, directing me past a library. "Pass through that door and keep going until you see a grand staircase. B-Deck is one level up."

"Thank you." The door leads to an immaculate corridor floored with octagonal tiles. Can I really just waltz into first class? Every common bone in my body says "stop," yet my legs keep going. Gilded dome fixtures cast spotlights on me. Paneled walls that stretch twice as long between doors as the ones in third class echo my trespassing footfalls.

The excitement I felt upon seeing Jamie gives way to a gripping sensation at my temples that seems to squeeze my brain into the size of a walnut. It's a good thing I came. Spend all day in the bottom of a ship, and one might start thinking down is up. Well, I will get him to see the right of it.

After about forty paces, the corridor widens into an open space housing a tidal wave of a staircase, with wooden banisters that look too ornate to get a good grip. At the foot of the stairs, a cheeky cherub seems to sneer at me, as if to say, *I see through that veil, you faker.*

I sweep by it. *It takes one to know one, imp.*

People stare as I pass, and it occurs to me that the first class is no better at containing their curiosity than the third class. In fact, they stare even longer, as if it is their right.

One level up, the staircase empties into a populated reception area, where well-dressed people drift around upholstered furniture like exotic fish around blue coral, attended to by plainer fish in uniform grey and black. A woman slips off her fur coat and dumps it on her reedy maid, who nearly spills the wineglasses she is holding. Don't I remember those tedious days of being a human coatrack and side table?

People here sail around as if they have all the time in the world, unlike in the third class, where one is not wasteful even with time. Even the stewards, in their short black jackets, seem to drift as silently as clouds as they dispense moisture into crystal goblets. More people float down the tidal-wave staircase from A-Deck. A square clock on the half landing reads 2:25.

Two sets of felted doors—like billiards tables—flank the staircase. I choose the port-side doors, since the even-numbered rooms are on that side. Mrs. Sloane specially requested Room B-42 since she was born in 1842 and could easily remember that number. The first-class rooms probably come with keys, with more stuff to steal, but I hope not.

The noise of the lobby dampens as the doors swing shut. This corridor seems even nicer than the one I just rattled through. It's quieter, with an expensive smell to it, like roses and cinnamon spice. Is Mr. Albert Ankeny Stewart in this section? I will need to find a guest list.

I read the room numbers set in gold letters and numbers: B-86, B-84.

A steward approaches. "Afternoon, ma'am."

"Afternoon," I reply curtly, striding away. My heart pounds like a fist calling for drinks.

Another steward backs out of a room in front of me. "No, sir. I'm sorry, sir." He's an Irishman, pronouncing his long *i*'s like "oy's."

"These are not high-quality cigars," barks the room's occupant. "Don't you know your cigars?"

"Yes, I do. I worked in a cigar factory, and let me assure you, these are triple-A rated—"

"Silence. I expect better than this on my ship. Find me better ones, or I shall report you."

The steward bows. One tab of his collared shirt has flipped up, and his tie has pulled free from his buttoned-up black jacket. "Again, I apologize, Mr. Ismay."

I halt at the name. That must be Mr. J. Bruce Ismay, the chairman of White Star Line. Of course, the shipping tycoon is on the maiden voyage of the *Titanic* to take his bows. If he is staying here, these must indeed be the royal suites.

The door slams in the steward's face, knocking his tray off kilter. He keeps a tight grip on the tray, but the floor suddenly dips, and he falls. The contents of his tray—a silver bowl of cigars and another of nuts—spill everywhere.

I bite my lip, annoyed at Mr. Ismay for putting this stone in my path when I am busy trying to stow away on his ship. I quickly collect cigars and nuts. The sooner I help this man clean up, the sooner I can go about my business.

"No, no, ma'am, please, it's not your place."

Is he mocking me? The steward's plump cheeks flush red beneath his muttonchop whiskers, which are dappled grey and brown. Of course he isn't mocking me. He can't see who I am. I put on the posh accent that the Sloanes use. "It's no trouble."

As I help him gather up nuts, I'm tempted to store a few in my mouth like a squirrel for later. "At least it wasn't hot tea and your best china."

The steward smiles. "True enough, ma'am."

We put the last of the nuts back in the bowl, and I collect my feet, hoping to make a hasty retreat.

"Do you need help finding your room?"

I hesitate. If B-42 is locked, he might help me open it. "B-42."

"B-42? That can't be right. I just put a gentleman in 42. What's your name?"

Now you've done it. The question seems to bounce around the hall, making my ears ring. "I—I'll be fine. I believe I'm on a different floor."

"But I can help you with that, too. I insist. It's the least I can do." His hopeful green eyes are the color of clover.

Do I dare? Now it would be suspicious if I refuse. And how else am I to find Mrs. Sloane's trunk? I will have to ask *someone*, and this fellow seems the goodly sort, especially now that I've done him a favor.

His flat eyebrows round under his square hairline. "Miss . . . ?"

"*Mrs.* . . . Sloane. Amberly Sloane." The severe officer kept my ticket for the arrival of Mrs. Sloane. Well, she has arrived.

He hands his tray off to another passing steward, then pulls a paper from his jacket. His finger runs down the page, just like the moisture tracing a path down my back. "Ah. Here we go." A frown replaces the man's hopeful expression. "You hadn't checked in, so we gave your room away. We didn't think you were coming."

I snort, channeling my fear into indignation. "I was attending to"—I straighten my veil, which has bunched to one side—"er, funeral arrangements."

"Oh! I am so sorry." The man has the kind of pasty complexion that, like a cuttlefish, turns color with the slightest pressure.

"Well, where did they put my trunk?"

"I'm not sure, but I will get this sorted at once, ma'am. I'm Steward Andy Latimer, and I'm the chief steward here." He smooths his tie back into place and straightens his collar. Another man, this one in a simple white jacket atop black pants, emerges from a room. "Porter Baxter! See if you can locate Mrs. Amberly Sloane's trunk. Bring it to B-64."

"Right away." Porter Baxter, who can hardly be older than me, gives a curt nod and hurries off.

"In the meantime, I've got the perfect stateroom for you. It's even better than B-42."

"Y-you do? I mean, I certainly hope so."

His kind smile lifts me from my mourning. "Follow me."

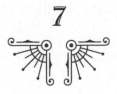

Steward Latimer opens the door marked B-64 with a quick turn of the knob.

A gasp escapes me. Panels of rich diamond-patterned crimson silk lead down a short hallway. On our left lies another door, which he opens. "Private bath."

A lavatory basin with a marbled counter neighbors a sleek enameled tub that is twice as big as Mrs. Sloane's old-fashioned slipper tub. A bar of soap smelling of bergamot has its very own dish.

"Hot and cold water." He thumps a finger on one of the taps. "Let us know if you'd like us to draw you a bath."

He pulls open yet another door. "Water closet." A personal toilet stands at attention and ready to serve. The room's occupant could go whenever and as many times as the urge called. We'd always shared water closets—or sometimes just outhouses—with other building tenants.

In the bedroom, a Persian rug tops wall-to-wall carpeting. The room is wide enough for me to cartwheel and flip over in one run, if not for the center table. Two beds—one a canopied double, the other a single—are dressed with cream skirts and topped with puffy quilts that seem to float. A chaise longue stretches along a wall, in case you need somewhere to rest as you travel from the bed to the square window. There are even two mirrors, one topping a vanity and another above a second sink. I figured the digs here would be fit for a king, but seeing it all laid out around me makes the bones float inside my body.

Ba, I've landed in the cabbage patch now.

He had dreamed of living in the most exclusive neighborhood in London—which he called the cabbage patch, where the richest soil is found. Mum had not. She considered mirrors sinful. But I won't waste my time gazing in the mirror—though I could waste it lying in that bed.

What am I thinking? Impersonating Mrs. Sloane for a few minutes to retrieve a few items from her trunk is one thing. But keeping up the charade for the entire trip? That is hardly keeping my chin tucked.

Steward Latimer presses his hands together. "I hope you will be very comfortable here."

"It is acceptable."

Then again, as long as I stay in my room, no one will be the wiser. The first class can stretch out on their chaise longues eating bonbons all day if they wish. This is the perfect hideout. Mum raised me not to tell fibs, but if Ba were here, he would be cackling with glee. If there was anything he liked better than getting something for free, it was getting it from someone who had done him dirty. White Star Line refused me entry, after all my expense and trouble, causing me to put my life and limbs in great jeopardy. By my thinking, they still owe me.

Steward Latimer pulls apart the lace curtains. "This room hasn't been aired yet. I'll crack the window." A gentle sea breeze filters in. Probably even the breezes here are more refined than in third class.

That done, the steward circles the room, pointing out the furnishings. "Light switches there, heating fan—just press this button—fresh towels in the cabinet. Further amenities include the Turkish baths, which are a feast for the eyes— aquamarine tiles, bronze lamps from the Middle East. We've got a swimming pool, a squash court, and a gymnasium."

I catch him trying to sneak a look behind my veil. "Do I look like someone who needs exertion?" I say, more forcibly than necessary.

"O-of course not." He glances at a writing table. "Dinner is served at six o'clock in the dining room on D-Deck. We didn't realize you were staying with us, or we'd have left the daily menu, but I make it a point to remember the fixings. Tonight, we have oysters, consommé Olga, salmon mousseline, chicken lyonnaise, roast duckling, chateau potatoes, foie gras and celery, Waldorf pudding, and vanilla eclairs. You'll hear the ship's bugler wandering the decks, calling out mealtime."

The alligator in my belly snarls, even though I didn't understand half of what he just said. I didn't eat but a few milk biscuits this morning. But a stowaway cannot socialize with the first class, even if the stowaway has never tried foie gras. Even Ba wouldn't be so reckless.

"I'm sure the food is exquisite. But I'm afraid I will not be in the mood for much socializing. Do you have anything more, er, private?"

"The À la Carte Restaurant and Café Parisien provide refreshment throughout the day. You may also order pastries and tea to your room. Pay the tab with the purser at journey's end."

Another opportunity for sinning opens her arms to me. A free line of pastry credit.

A knock comes at the door, and the young porter Baxter appears with Mrs. Sloane's steamer trunk, a sturdy chest with oak straps and metal hinges. The sight of it is like a reassuring pat on the back.

Steward Latimer takes the trunk from him. "Fetch Mrs. Sloane a welcome plate."

"Yes, sir." Baxter makes a hasty exit.

The steward hauls the trunk to a wooden rack and, in one smooth motion, heaves it up. But with a click, it pops open, and its contents tumble free.

A cloisonné vase containing snuff tobacco that Mrs. Sloane purchased for her brother drops onto the carpet and rolls. I'd wrapped the vase with twine so the lid would not come off.

Steward Latimer rushes to stop the vase from rolling farther. "Oh dear, oh dear. We must be making a terrible impression on you." For a first-class steward, he is all thumbs. But there is an earnestness about him, like a tuft of hair that refuses to bend to pomade. He holds out the vase, a horrified expression tightening his face. "Is this . . . ?"

It takes me a moment to understand. "Yes, it is. Set Percival there. He likes a good window view."

Steward Latimer sets the vase down and quickly steps back. "Both my first wife and my daughter passed the same year thirteen years ago, but it feels like yesterday."

"Oh? I am sorry." Guilt straddles my shoulders, as my deception grows thorns.

He nods, his Adam's apple rising.

I sweep up Mrs. Sloane's clothes, thinking of my parents. "It feels like you've been gulled when they're taken early like that."

His eyes go bright. "That's exactly how it feels." He sets the trunk properly on the rack. "If I hadn't found my Jennie, well, I'd be hiding behind a veil, too."

"I am *not* hiding," I say a little too strenuously.

The cuttlefish turns red again. "O-of course not. I only meant, I understand how you feel."

Baxter returns with a silver platter. On it, candied fruit glitters like the queen's jewels. There's also a dish of buttery cheese and a basket of bread rolls so airy looking you could probably toss them up and not worry about catching them again until the next day. Baxter sets the tray on a table, then slips out of the room again.

"If there's something else you'd like, please do not hesitate to ring this bell for service." Steward Latimer points to a gold button above my bed. At last, he gives me a kind smile, then backs into the hallway. "I'll be sure to inform the staff about missing your entrance and giving away your room."

"Please do not trouble yourself. All's well that ends well."

"Oh, but I must. Someone's head will roll, believe it."

I grimace. May the head in question not be the one on my shoulders.

8

After closing the door and locking it, I whip off my hat, glancing around in disbelief at the kingdom I've inherited. I nibble a gold coin of orange, cherries that glitter like rubies, and a slice of silvery pear.

The rhythmic hiss of the ocean sounds vaguely like the tsk of a tongue. *Don't you start, too.*

After washing down everything, including the bread and cheese, with a glass of lemon-flavored water, I wish I could do it all over again but slower.

At the bottom of the trunk, I find my belongings: two plain dresses that I wore as a maid, a flannel nightgown, a knit cap, wool stockings, and Mum's Bible.

I haven't gone to church since Ba died and Reverend Prigg told me it was God's will I join the convent before my feet led me down Jezebel's path. I told him that if God had such a lack of imagination, then I wanted no part of His religion.

Opening to the book of Ruth, which Mum had read often, as Ruth had married outside of her tribe, I pull out the only photograph I have of my parents. Ba, in his wedding suit, sits on a chair, grinning as wide as a crescent moon. Mum, with her curly hair puffed around her head, stands patiently beside him, her hand on his shoulder. Her big eyes, which always magnified her emotions, today look troubled.

"I know, Mum, you disapprove. But I have to stay *some-where*, and you don't want me bunking with Jamie's mates, do you? So it may as well be here, where—had they let me board—I would've stayed anyway. I'll be as careful as if I were walking a line of cobweb. And I'll keep what's left of our family together, I promise."

Drawing the heavy brocade curtains closed on the late-afternoon sun, I undress to my knickers. Then I lie on the bigger of the two beds, my hands resting on my full belly. With tonight's stop in Cherbourg, and tomorrow's in Queenstown, I told Jamie I would keep my chin tucked, and that's precisely what I'll do. Anyway, perhaps a little time to digest the shock of seeing me will bring him to his senses.

In case I drop off into a nap, I switch on the reading lamp by the gold call button.

The dark is an old enemy. It doesn't bother me so much when others are around, like the Sloanes' cook, with whom I shared a room. But when I'm by myself, the dark waits to ambush me, so I won't give it the chance.

Then I sink into the thick feather comforter, which is how I imagine sitting in a cloud might feel. It turns out the wealthy sleep higher than us, too. Before long, my eyelids grow heavy.

—————·•·—————

BA LEANS AGAINST *the trunk of a live oak, struggling. Bees are swarming him, enough to cover him with a buzzing coat of armor. They crawl out from his shirt and up his narrow brown face. They cover his thinning hair, a blurry, angry mob.*

Jamie perches high up on a branch, swinging his legs. He's always up there, lost in his own world.

"Jamie," I scream, "get down here and help me!" But Jamie just points his nose to the sky.

A horn rouses me from my slumber.

I sit up, trying to remember the end of the dream. I never remember. I only know that Jamie holds the key.

I flick a switch, and the ceiling lamps shine down at me like four eyeballs. I draw open the curtains, giving the evening a peek into my room. Sure enough, the tiny lights of a harbor are growing ever distant as we leave Cherbourg. One port down, one to go.

My stomach grumbles, and I feel thirsty from the cheese. Jamie must have had a good dinner with his mates. I don't know what I envy more, his having dinner or his having mates.

Loneliness, like a fledgling returning to an empty nest, creeps into my soul. The crimson walls strike me as too bright, and the gilded furniture, too pretty. Luxury is like good news, hard to enjoy without someone to share it with.

Well, how can I not be lonely, after all those years alone? Long days of toiling with no one to confide in, only a sad father who hardly acknowledged my presence after Mum died. But I muddled through it, didn't I? And all the while, I kept myself limber for the day Jamie and I would fly again.

I dab my eyes, my anger petered out. We never stayed angry with each other for long. Mum wouldn't let us. *Don't spend too long looking behind you, or you'll miss out on what's ahead,* I hear her say with a cluck of her tongue.

Despite promising to keep my chin tucked, I decide to pay Jamie another visit. I dress in one of Mrs. Sloane's boring brown dresses and tie on the garden-hoe hat.

Someone knocks. I steal to the door, not breathing.

"Hello? Is anyone there? It's April Hart. Don't be afraid. I'd like to talk to you."

It's the American who saved my Queen Mum on the well deck. A warning bell sounds in my head. There's no chance I'm going to answer this door.

"It's Valora Luck, isn't it?"

I cringe. She must have remembered my name from the gangway. She might as well bang the brass bell they keep in the crow's nest. Especially with Mr. Ismay right down the hall.

"Are you in there, Miss Luck?"

Before she calls my name a third time, I wrench open the door. "It's Mrs. Sloane. May I help you?"

Lime-green silk pours over Miss Hart's slender figure, interrupted only by a navy silk sash slung low across her hips. A headband with a single peacock feather cinches her short hair in place. What a simple but bold hair accessory. In her hand, she carries a suitcase made from some reptile's skin, probably one of those alligator monsters from America.

With an unimpressed tilt of her fine-boned face, she reaches out and lifts my veil.

I jerk back. "How dare you!"

"Oh, I dare a lot of things." She smiles. Her eyes glitter like two pieces of amber that trap more light the longer you study them. She marches right in with her suitcase as if she is boarding a train. The scent of her cigarettes and something musky follows her. She looks around her. "Nice. Very Empire-style. I prefer a more modern design, myself. Doesn't catch so much dust. Obviously, they didn't get a woman's opinion."

I close the door and hurry after her.

She slinks around the room like a fox, sliding out drawers, peering into the wardrobe. "That was a skillful bit of climbing you did. How'd your limbs get so bendy?"

"Is there something I can help you with, Miss Hart?" I ask, trying to be polite, though my face still stings from being unmasked. She knows my secret. She alone can undo me. Has the fox come to stalk a weak prey?

She glances at me fanning my face with my hat. "April, please. Don't worry. Your secret is safe with me. But I do have a little favor to ask of you." Setting down her suitcase, she lifts the vase of tobacco and sniffs. "Not bad. But a little too much tar for me."

I lean against the vanity, tracking her with my eyes. What could she possibly want from a beggar like me?

"You have a lovely shape." She looks up from where she was peering at the contents of Mrs. Sloane's trunk and winks.

"M-my shape?"

"Oh yes. Perfectly proportioned, strong limbs, good posture. Well, it's perfect for House of July."

I snap up. "I'm not that kind of girl."

She laughs, a hearty sound that is more like applause. "And

it's not that kind of house. House of July is my haute couture fashion label." She picks up one of Mrs. Sloane's more matronly dresses, olive green with generous pleats, and her face puckers.

"What do *oats* have to do with fashion?"

"Oats? Oh, you mean *haute*." Another round of applause. "*Haute couture* means 'high dressmaking' in French."

I'm getting a little tired of this woman who goes anywhere and touches anything she wants.

"I'd like you to wear my brand." She smooths her hands down her bodice and turns a circle. "It'll be fun."

I snort. "I'm trying to keep a low profile."

Rather than look insulted, her face bends into an amused grin. "Wearing a veil like that? You're drawing eyes, whether you like it or not. Might as well give them something to look at."

"I wasn't planning on parading about. I am a woman in mourning, after all."

April sweeps a hand over the chaise longue and pours herself across it. "Mrs. Sloane must be a woman of means to get a crib like this, and I believe that you are her maid. But why isn't she here?" Her eyes grow round. "Did you murder her?"

"Of course not. She . . . died, if you must know. Over a week ago."

"Aha. So you're a thief."

"No! I mean, not intentionally. We had already sent the trunk."

"Hmm. And did you find your brother?"

"Yes," I say around a grimace.

Her brow dents. "I hope he appreciated your commitment to seeing him."

I make a sharp noise in my throat. She certainly is presumptuous. But perceptive, too. Why am I telling her any of this? I don't want to be part of this woman's schemes. I have enough trouble as it is. "My answer is no. Now if you don't mind, I need to be going."

"So you *will* be parading about."

"Not in the way you want me to."

"I don't ask for much. Just wear my clothes whenever you go out." Retrieving her suitcase, she sets it on the chaise longue and unbuckles it. "They are scrummy, as you Brits like to say. Sinfully rich and tasteful. They will make you feel like royalty."

"I plan to be in my room ninety-nine percent of the time."

"I highly doubt that. A young woman who climbs cranes as easily as pulling on stockings is not someone who stays put for long."

She holds up a pearl-white crêpe de chine dress. The English love all things Chinese—silk, tea, plates—just not if it comes with a beating heart. A cloth panel like a wall hanging overlies the front, hand painted with a crane and bejeweled with tiny beads that catch the light. My jaw yawns open, like I've caught a gullet of fish. It's the most magnificent dress I have ever seen.

"You made that?"

"Yes, I did. A crane's good luck. This is your daywear for tomorrow. Touch it."

As cautiously as if the crane might take flight, I stroke my finger over the front panel. The fine fabric feels cool and slippery under my hot finger.

"I have the perfect one in mind for your meeting with the captain."

I snatch back my finger. "What meeting?"

"Everyone gets to meet the captain. It'll be your big moment. Everyone will be watching. Don't worry, they'll send along an invitation."

As if that is the thing I'm worried about. "B-but why can't you parade your own clothes?"

"The best way to sell your art is to let someone else do it for you. I'm trying to create a 'stir' around my line, and I can't do it myself. It would be uncouth."

She frowns at my black boots, which were made for a man with very small feet and could use a good scrub with a horse-hair brush. Draping the crane dress on the bed, she pulls a dainty pair of tan pumps with straps from her suitcase and dangles them from her fingers.

"No one takes American designers seriously." She closes the suitcase and sets the pumps on top. "All they want is Lucile, never mind that her overwrought 'creations' look like clown outfits. Those Merry Widow hats of hers—piled high with garden clippings—were abominable, a crime on the eyes and a pain in the neck."

She must be referring to Lady Lucy Duff-Gordon, whose fashions are all the rage. I remember how Mrs. Sloane's eyes became as big as chestnuts when I told her that the Scottish baron Sir Cosmo Duff-Gordon and his wife would be among the *Titanic*'s passengers.

"Say, *you* could be the Merry Widow, just like the operetta. You're a mysterious woman in mourning, but not even death will quell your allure." She puts a hand on her heart and holds the other to the ceiling, as if on a stage.

"That might work in the theater, but in real life, widows cannot be so flashy."

"Says who? Mourning dress is so passé."

"I wish I could help you—"

"The way I see it, we can help each other. Someone like you needs an ally, hiding up here in first class all by yourself. You never know when you'll need a friend." She sidles up to me and touches my nose, as if to prove she can. I shrink against the vanity, and she backs off. "Besides, I've got a good ear for gossip. How else did I find out where you were staying?"

Artists may not sell their own work, but she's doing a pretty good sales job on me. "Do you know Mr. Albert Ankeny Stewart of the Ringling Brothers Circus?"

She lobs her gaze to the ceiling. "No. But I could do some digging."

I have no doubt that with her persistence, even if Mr. Stewart is hiding behind the last boiler on the lowest deck, she will find him. But how exactly am I supposed to keep my chin tucked *and* create a stir? I sigh. "I'll wear the clothes, but I won't do any sales pitches."

"Of course not. Be as mysterious as possible." She lowers

her voice, as if we are conspiring to rob a bank. "Meanwhile, I'll be dropping a trail of bread crumbs behind you."

She extends her gloved hand, and though all the horses leading my rickety sleigh rear up, I take it. Unlike the dead-fish hands that wealthy women usually offer, her grip is solid, a grip that could open her own doors.

"I'll be back tomorrow night at nine. If you need anything, I'm in room B-47, right by the elevators. It's good to be in business with you."

———·•·———

I HEAD TOWARD the bow, quiet as a shadow in Mrs. Sloane's black coat, doing my best to look like I belong. Men and women favor me with nods and smiles, but keep their distance, which suits me fine.

The suites that make up the Cabbage Patch end at a well-populated Entrance Hall, which features another tidal-wave staircase. Unlike the aft staircase, tucked behind this one is a trio of humming lifts in an oak-paneled foyer. While I wait, I eye a set of rooms to the side of the lifts, one of which, B-47, belongs to April Hart. One of the boxes stops at our level, and a lift operator slides open a wrought-iron gate.

"E-Deck," I inform him, in the terse way Mrs. Sloane issued orders.

"Yes, ma'am."

Three floors down, the box opens, and I pass uncertainly into a hallway, which must be on the starboard side of E-Deck, where the first-class rooms are kept. Unlike the bustling

Scotland Road, which parallels it on the port side, this corridor is as quiet as a library, with decorative floor tiles and globe ceiling lights set inside ceramic roses. It's a notch down from where I'm staying, the engine noise louder, and the cabins closer together. Mrs. Sloane was right about preferring the elephant's highest end.

The hallway and first-class section terminate at a door that leads into the Collar. Just outside this door, a sign reads "Master-at-Arms." I edge away from that residence. Of course, law enforcement is berthed just around the corner from where I'll be doing my sneaking about.

Watching for stewards, I hurry across Scotland Road into the companionway and knock lightly on Room 14.

"Come in," says a voice in Cantonese.

The lads are tucked in, the room half lit. Wink sleeps tightly rolled into a ball, whereas Olly half hangs off the bed, snoring loudly.

A shirtless Bo kneels over the bottom bunk, his wet hair slicked off his face. His back is steep and contoured like the cliffs of Dover when golden sunlight falls upon them. He glances up at me, and a fire licks my neck. Haven't I seen my share of backs—dockers', Jamie's, though his is more like a slender ridge compared with the cliffs of Dover.

Bo fastens twine around a flat leather pouch and gets to his feet.

"I was just looking for Jamie," I inform him quietly so as not to wake the lads. The close quarters and the dim lighting make the room feel uncomfortably intimate.

He slowly draws a shirt over his chiseled chest, fueling the fire on my neck. "Jamie said his sister was a card."

"Oh?" So he talked about me with Bo, at least. "He never mentioned you."

"Maybe words cannot do justice." Even with his noticeable accent, his words swagger.

"I can think of a word for you. Wagtail."

"Wagtail?" he pronounces.

"That's right. A kind of bird with a long tail feather it likes to shake around for attention."

He shrugs with one shoulder, appraising me with eyes that seem to see right through the shadows. "Jamie never teached us that one."

"So, Jamie *taught* you English."

He blinks and draws back his head, probably the kind of head unaccustomed to being corrected by a woman. "Jamie *helped* us all. Better chance for work if you speak English. If you want the best for him, go home. Girls should not wander by themselves."

Despite the softness of his tone, my face begins to burn, as if I am holding coal in my cheeks. If he looked a few years older, I'd think he was born in the year of the ox. People born in that year are hardworking but often obnoxious.

"You've known Jamie now for, what, two years? I've known him for eighteen, if you count the year in the womb. I think I'd know better than you what's best for him."

"Maybe he has grown since he left. Grown enough not to take orders from sisters."

My expression hardens. "If you're not going to tell me where he is, then I'll be on my way."

"He did not say where he went. But since you are his sister, I bet you can guess."

I close my coat around me with more force than is needed. I'm about to spin on my heel when I notice that the blanket on the top bunk is missing, with Jamie's flannel nightshirt stuffed under his pillow. He isn't ready for bed yet. If Jamie studies astronomy every night, I have a hunch where he might be. Bo, still watching me, gives me a smile so brief, it could be a trick of the light.

Well, Jamie, maybe I do know you better than you think.

9

As I carry myself down the companionway, footsteps approach from behind. "Ma'am?"

I freeze. A steward with a grin like a well-oiled saddle inclines his head of black hair toward me. Protruding cheekbones pull his skin taut, giving him a rather skeletal appearance. Did he see me emerge from Room 14?

"Evening, ma'am. Lose your way?" he asks with a jaunty swing to his voice. "T'isn't safe here for a woman such as yourself."

"Yes." I remind myself that I am a fine English lady, and people here live for my comfort, not the other way around. "I seem to have gotten turned around," I say imperiously. "Please direct me to the lifts."

"Certainly." A dorsal fin of a nose takes an expansive sniff, as if he has a cold. He points a bony finger down the Collar. "Past Scotland Road about a dozen paces, you'll come to a door on the right. Continue through and keep walking until you see the signs."

I take unhurried steps away, sure that if I turn around, the man will still be watching me. I must be more careful to avoid being seen here, not just as a woman, but as a first-class woman, who certainly has no business in these parts. Without looking at the master-at-arms's cabin, I swing open the door to first class.

The lift takes me as far as it can, to A-Deck. The cherub standing at this highest leg of the tidal-wave staircase is even chubbier than the ones below. I climb past nobs in their finery toward the Boat Deck. At a half landing, more divine types loiter, including two angels holding in place an elaborate clock that reads 8:40. The afterlife certainly features prominently in the decorating here. But is a vessel in the middle of the ocean really the place to be constantly reminded of death?

A glass dome spanning the ceiling is a dark crown reflecting the light of the chandeliers. On a side table, a golden mermaid offers a clamshell full of fruit, including a pineapple. I've seen pineapples in the markets, though I can't imagine who would eat a prickly thing like that. I sniff it, detecting a scent that is not at all like a pine tree or an apple, but rounder and sugary.

After pocketing an apple, I pass through a lobby where a pianist churns out a melody. At last, a quarter of an hour after leaving Room 14, I reach the *Titanic*'s summit, the Boat Deck.

The air places blissfully cool hands on my cheeks. Mum's hands were always cold, and Jamie and I loved holding them in our too-warm ones.

The sky is freckled with stars, more than I've seen in all my days put together. And how those stars beckon, fancier than all the jewels in first class. Like clusters of tiaras, strings of pearls, dripping earbobs, all pinned to a swath of dark velvet.

The benches are empty with few people about, most finding better fun inside the ship. Electric lights cast an eerie glow around the smokestacks. The fourth and farthest one does not smoke. Perhaps it is only for show. The Chinese avoid the number four, but Westerners like even numbers.

The lifeboats stand pale and motionless, ghostly cradles held by skeletal arms. Four in each of four corners. I shiver. This deck is full of bad luck, and I bet Fong would steer clear even if he was allowed up here.

A couple tightly joined at the shoulders nod at me as they pass, leaving a trail of the woman's amber perfume. I stride more purposefully toward the stern, keeping a careful watch for Jamie.

Wooden chocks raise the boats to eye level. A system of hooks and eyelets secures the canvas covers. I peer more closely. The canvas over the third lifeboat has been partially folded back. I slip over to the boat and whisper, "Jamie?"

The ocean gulps and shushes, drowning my voice. "Jamie?" I say more loudly.

A head lifts. "Cats, Val. What are you doing here?"

"Looking for the mast so I can hoist my white flag. Truce, Brother? I won't try to persuade you to go to New York, and you'll button it about London." I hold out my apple.

The right half of his mouth shrugs. "Truce." He takes the fruit, then scoots over to make room on the floor where he's seated, a blanket pulled to his chest.

Peeking around to ensure no one's watching, I hike up my

skirt, then haul myself over the edge, unintentionally stepping on his foot before falling in place beside him. He stifles a curse.

I remove my hat and place my head on the bench.

He glances at me. "So where have you been? I've been looking everywhere for you."

"You must have skipped the first class."

"You didn't."

"Why not? The room was empty, and it's already paid for. Plus, I discovered an ally."

"A what?"

I give him a brief account of my meeting with April Hart, ignoring his groans as I try to put a more confident spin on it.

He blows out a breath that sounds as heavy as a rain barrel.

I sniff. "I've sacrificed a lot to be here." I spent every penny I had for the ticket from London to Southampton.

"I know, Val."

"Why didn't you tell your mates about me?"

"They ask too many questions. Bo and Drummer knew about you."

That rubs a bit of salve on the wound. I haven't met this Drummer yet, but expect I may soon.

A whiff of pine mingles with the scent of fresh paint. We might be the first people ever to occupy this vessel. "It's cozy, if a tad bare. Where are the oars?"

"Dunno. Seems crackers to keep them separate from the boats, but no one asked me."

Or any women, as April Hart might say.

"This is top of the line. Clinker-built, elm rudder. But there are only sixteen lifeboats—plus they store a few 'collapsibles' up front. That's only enough for about half of the two thousand–something passengers. Yet they say it meets regulation."

I whistle. "Good thing Ba taught us how to swim."

The only sound is the shushing of the waves against the *Titanic*'s hull and the rhythmic creaking of wood. Jamie sighs. "What did you do with the books?"

"Sold them off."

One of Ba's schemes involved collecting books from estate sales and peddling them off a cart, like *Astronomy Through the Ages* and the infamous *Bee-Keeping for Beginners*. That didn't work out so well, though. If there's one thing you can count on in London, it's rain, and books and rain are natural enemies. But on the bright side, *Astronomy Through the Ages* introduced Jamie to the stars.

"I wish you hadn't had to take care of things by yourself."

The stars seem to shrink back, as if giving me space. The memory of that dark morning blows a ghostly whisper through my mind. I found Ba in an alleyway a block from our house, dead from a drunken run-in with a lamppost. His top hat rolled haphazardly in the breeze, like a troubled animal.

I pick out the emotions knitting in me like loose threads: anger at his carelessness, guilt that I wasn't there, and sadness for the things he will never see, like elephants. And all of these seasoned with relief that he will no longer have to suffer.

Usually, when the "hounds of drink" dragged Ba to the

dark place, he wouldn't speak for days. But after Mum died, he stopped not only speaking, but listening. Ba tried so hard, but like all visionaries, the world was set against him. I hope his next life in Chinese heaven is easier.

"You laid him by Mum?"

I shook my head. "Her parents wouldn't allow it. But I found him a spot at East London Cemetery."

Jamie snorts. He shifts, and I can feel his eyes worrying me. "What's wrong?" he asks.

"Every night I dream that Ba's in trouble. It doesn't make sense. He should've already moved on to the next life. He's trying to communicate something. Something to do with you."

He scoffs, and I feel something close in my face, like a door on a traveling salesman.

I stick a foot in the door. "See, you're in the dreams, too. But you never help him. You're always staring into space."

With another scoff, he points his nose up.

"Exactly like that." I poke his nose, and he jerks away.

"What are *you* doing in these dreams?"

"Trying to help him. But it's not me he needs. It's you. Whatever you're miffed about, you need to forgive him."

He shifts, causing the planks to groan. "He never asked for forgiveness when he was alive. Why care now?"

I lean against his shoulder, which gives as much as a steel post. "Because he's stuck."

Jamie clamps his eyes as if to shut out my words. "She wasn't even a week in the grave when he pawned her wedding ring and used it on gargle juice." I wince at Ba's euphemism for his cheap gin.

"That's what you're on about? He needed the money to pay off our debts. Remember the bee farm?"

"How could I forget?" he mutters, nudging my head off his shoulder. "Sometimes you can't forgive because it cheapens the people you love."

"But Mum would want you to. 'Don't spend too long looking behind you, or you'll miss out on what's ahead.' Remember?"

"No way, Val. Don't ask me again."

A bitterness has crept into his voice that I don't remember hearing before. Jamie seems to have grown heavier, and not just from his new coal-shoveling muscles.

We were still grieving over Mum when he left, and I hoped the boiler rooms would at least give him a place away from the memories to heal. But perhaps down there, without enough air to vent them away, his troubles only compounded.

I decide to let it go for now. I'll keep tugging little by little, and like the boats that coaxed the *Titanic* to sea, eventually I'll get Jamie to budge. There are more time-sensitive matters that need solving, matters that require Jamie and me to be on good terms.

I point at one of the brighter stars. "What's that big red one?"

"The White Tiger to the Chinese. Westerners call it the Bull."

Isn't that like life? Two people look at the same object but see two different things. I look at shoveling coal and see a job. He sees a calling.

"So why do you like those boiler rooms so much? It's so dark down there." I shiver.

"How would you know?" he chides.

Jamie knows well my fear of dark, confined spaces. He's the one who found me after I fell into the coal hole, only six years old and spindly.

He shifts around again, pulling at his clothes. Finally settling, he sighs. "When Drummer bangs out the beats, and we get into a rhythm, I feel content, peaceful. Sometimes when the weather's good, we'll string hammocks on the deck, and I'll lose myself in the stars. I couldn't sleep all night when Halley's Comet came around."

I soak in all the constellations, like so many grains of spilled salt. "That is one savory stew."

"It's mad, right?" His voice becomes animated. "In London, we're lucky to see a few stars a month. But out here, they're everywhere. I still can't get over it. I feel like if I reached high enough, I could scoop out a whole handful, then blow them away like dandelion seeds."

When we were children, Jamie and I blew wishes off dandelions, like all kids. But one night, our parents were quarreling in the kitchen, and a dandelion just wasn't handy. Jamie, lying next to me in our half bed, said that if we blew anyway, the heavens would still hear us, even without the dandelion, and maybe grant our wish. He took my hand, and together we blew, just a puff. My parents quieted. Then just like that, Mum laughed. After that, we didn't need dandelions to wish. We'd just blow. And every time a wish came true, I'd hear Mum's sweet laugh.

More quietly, he adds, "I see her up there, too, you know."

"What's she doing?"

"Dancing with her shoes off. Remember?"

I smile. "Yes."

Mum loved singing bawdry tunes and kicking up her heels while the bread baked, though I never found out where the vicar's daughter picked up such songs.

"But sometimes, she's quiet. Like she's just watching us from the window." His sigh takes its time leaving.

Jamie and I competed for our mum's affections, but he adored her the most. We both picked her flowers whenever we passed a good patch, but he did it even in the pouring rain.

I squeeze his hand, and he squeezes back.

"Jamie?"

"Hmm?" His gaze is still pointed to the stars, but his brow is knitted in thought.

"There are stars in New York, too."

We'll fly the Stars and Stripes on our foremasts, leaving the Union Jack behind. A new start for us, and a peaceful ending for our parents. I reach into the sky as if I am grabbing some stars, then blow them like dandelion seeds off my palm.

10

*B*a is tied to a live oak growing in the middle of a wide, water-filled ditch. Jamie stands on the oak's highest branch, his shirt billowing like a sail moving in the wrong direction. The water rises, as if an underground spring has burst.

I wade to Ba, my movements sluggish. At last, I reach him. My fingers frantically dig at the knots. But the ditch is filling too fast.

"Help me, you goat!"

Water edges up Ba's thin chest, then laps at his chin. He stretches his neck, his sad eyes gazing at me.

"Jamie!"

My brother's head lifts. Something has caught his attention. But it is not us.

I sit up with a gasp, the feather comforter tangled in my legs and my nightgown sticking to my back. Drawing in deep breaths to still my trembling, I grasp at the wisps of my dream.

How had it ended? And why can I never remember?

The carpets grab my feet as I cross to the window and peer

through the curtains. Bright daylight slashes my eyes. The sun is nearly overhead. We are moving west, which means we already left Queenstown, Ireland, the last place to dump me before we cross the Atlantic.

Only six days until we reach New York. Six days to bring Jamie to his senses, prepare our routine, and persuade Mr. Stewart to watch it. There is no time to waste. There is also the matter of the Chinese Exclusion Act, a fire that is now one day closer. Surely Mr. Stewart could help us put that one out, being a man of influence and money. Isn't that how the world works?

I open Mum's Bible and gaze upon my picture of Mum and Ba. "Good morning, honored parents. Jamie's being stubborn, as usual. And he's not making sense. How can he like working in the bowels of a ship when he's so obsessed with looking up at the sky? Something's off. But don't worry, I'll get him to see the right of things."

April Hart's crane dress catches my eye from where it hangs in the wardrobe. A beggar like me isn't fit for such togs, but I can't wait to try it on.

Jamie isn't expecting me until lunch. Before dressing, I spend my time stretching my pins from heel to hip, then do side bends, handstands, and hand walking—the "wake-up drills" I do almost every morning. It isn't as easy with the floor moving around, but soon, the initial burn settles into a tingling warmth.

When I finish, I set down my feet and stroll to the facilities. The mirror forces me to reckon with my appearance. My uneven hair forms messy waves. Mum called my "lion's mane" my best feature. It's thick and glossy, an almost black that glints red in the sun.

Running the tap, I make liberal use of the bergamot soap. Then, with my wet hands, I knot my hair and smooth my tweaky eyebrows. At least my eyes look bright, despite my chewed-up mouth.

From Mrs. Sloane's trunk, I remove the "bubby-cubby" of my own invention, which I use to bind my chest for performing. If I'm going to dine with Jamie's company, I'll have to blend in using Jamie's spare sea slops, and the bubby-cubby hides my shape.

Once that is in place, I slide the dress over my head and shoulders. Somehow April cut the garment perfectly so that it doesn't need buttons. I pin the bee-swarm veil to the velvet toque April also left for me—trying not to disturb its fan of hackle feathers—then arrange the hat over my hair.

Despite resolving to ignore the mirror, I ogle myself, unsure who that royal lady is. The dress's waist nips in, and the skirt skims my hips. My carriage has always been unassailable, thanks to years of line practice, but wearing a fine dress like this seems to pull my spine even straighter, as if someone is pulling it up by a string.

From the photograph on the table, Mum seems to lift an eyebrow at me. "Sorry, Mum, it's the clothes. I can't help it." I sweep up the picture, wondering if I should show it to Jamie. But seeing Mum would sadden him, and he's still angry with Ba. It isn't the time. I tuck it back into Ruth and close the book.

Finally, I step into the pumps. They are two sizes too big,

and were it not for the straps, they would probably break my ankles. My own black boots would serve me better if I need to run. They are high quality, with real metal aglets, not glue or wax, on the laces. But even I know that wearing those clunkers with such a fine frock would cause heads to shake—not exactly the effect April intended. Plus, if I really need to run, I doubt I could do it in this dress anyway.

Even worse than wearing men's boots with an elegant dress would be wearing pumps with Jamie's sea slops. I look for something in which to carry my boots. In the wardrobe, I find a canvas bag stitched with the White Star logo containing a pair of black velvet slippers and a pair of white ones. Never in my life have I had so much footwear at my disposal. I add my black boots to the slipper bag, then collect a cashmere coat the color of vanilla tea cakes.

In the hallway, Steward Latimer holds a vase of stargazer lilies. He's standing so still—with not a single brown hair out of formation—that I wonder how long he's been there. "Ah, good afternoon, Mrs. Sloane. These are from White Star Line with our compliments. May I place them in your room?"

"Yes, of course." I step aside and follow him to the table. "Steward, could you tell me where Mr. Albert Ankeny Stewart is staying?"

A regretful expression rolls down his face. "I'm terribly sorry, but certain guests have requested privacy, and he is one of them."

"I see." The news drops like a coin into a dry well, tumbling and spinning before landing with a dull clunk. *This is so typical. Plans always half-baked,* I hear Jamie say. Well, at least the fire hasn't reached my trousers yet.

The lilies seem to cough at me out of their scarlet throats. The real Mrs. Sloane, with her limited vision, would've appreciated those heavy scenters, but they remind me of the cemetery.

Steward Latimer straightens and puts his hands behind his back. "Captain Smith invites you for a more private welcome with him tomorrow at two o'clock, in the Reception Hall of the À la Carte Restaurant."

So here it is. The meeting with the captain. I'm struck with the urge to flap my arms and fly away. But if I refuse, April Hart will lose out on her "big moment" for parading her clothes. And I need her help finding Mr. Stewart now more than ever. "I look forward to it."

"Also, in case you're interested, tonight there's a lecture on whales in the library." He bows and glides away.

Back in the hallway, a crystal bowl of wrapped taffies rests on a ledge, free for the taking. Not seeing any signs to the contrary, I grab a handful and stuff them into my bag.

The Merry Widow tries not to trip through the Cabbage Patch, even though her feet slide forward at every step and already the straps are strangling her ankles. I just have to bear down. Walk on my toes. Haven't my pins suffered worse for the sake of a show? Still, pain for the sake of fashion seems twice as wretched since no one will be tossing coins at me afterward.

Heads nod at me. But this time, they also turn. A group of women even stop, and I catch the distinctly round vowels of admiration that float from their mouths. I can't help preening a bit, tossing back my head and sashaying my hips. *Why, this old thing? It's just something I grabbed on my way out the door.*

While I wait for the lift, I angle a pose toward B-47, in case April Hart emerges. One of the lifts opens, and the couple inside stops talking.

"Your dress is remarkable, my dear," says the woman, a stout madam with a cabbage-rose hat wide enough to take out someone's eye. "Is it Lucile?"

"No. It is House of July."

"Oh," she replies thoughtfully.

I reach E-Deck and button on the vanilla coat. No need to advertise in the third class. Then I proceed to the Collar, glancing around as I remember the skeletal steward with the saddle grin. Seeing a few men but no steward, I take big steps toward the short companionway to Room 14.

The door seems to vibrate with all the noise behind it. I listen.

"Make a fist and line it up with the axis of the Southern Cross, and your thumb will point south," says Jamie. "No, your *right* fist. You'll end up in Timbuktu if you use your left."

I knock, and the door opens right away. Wink gives me a shy smile.

Jamie is holding a piece of paper to the porthole on which he has drawn five points in the rough shape of a kite. Olly stands next to him with his thumb pointing down. Bo is missing.

"Good morning. Who likes taffy?" I pour the taffies into the lads' hands, and their faces light up.

Jamie frowns. "Don't eat them until after lunch. You'll spoil your appetites."

"My appetite won't spoil," Wink grumbles, but he stops unwrapping the gold foil.

I scowl at my brother, whose hard forehead I can almost knock with my own at my new elevation. "Now you know which one is the fun twin. I also brought slippers."

I upend the contents of my bag onto the floor. Grabbing the four slippers, I give them a quick juggle, then catch them—the white pair in my right hand, the black pair in my left—and hold them out to the lads.

"Wow, where'd you learn to do that?" Olly takes the white pair.

Wink kicks off his shoes and puts on the black pair.

"Our father taught us." Ba made sure our hand-eye coordination was so tight, the two parts might as well be connected by a string. Does Jamie even do wake-up drills anymore?

Olly and Wink pace the floor between the beds, trying out their new slippers.

"I don't juggle anymore," Jamie proclaims.

"Of course not," I add smoothly. "What would be the point of juggling coal?"

Shaking his head, Jamie takes a step back and appraises my outfit. "If you sold those togs, you could buy a ticket back to London, maybe two."

I work off my coat and set it, along with my toque, on

Jamie's bunk. "I was thinking more a ticket to the Ringling Brothers Circus."

Jamie frowns as he runs a finger over the vanilla cashmere. I dust his fingers away, my annoyance at him making it hard to think. We could bicker for hours but come no nearer a solution.

"They look more like twins now," Olly whispers to Wink.

The door opens and Bo walks in, bringing with him the scent of the ocean and the heat of the sun. His eyes graze me, and he shuts the door behind him. "Found a job. Enough work for two."

Jamie runs his fingers distractedly through his hair. "What's the job?"

"Some deck chairs need fixing. Ship's carpenter has influenza. Good money, but we must keep quiet, because it is against White Star rules to hire us. But since I found the job, I win the bet, and you can do my washing."

I snort. Jamie loves his wagers. Hold the train. Maybe there's an opportunity here. I may not have persuaded him to perform for Mr. Stewart, but when has he turned down an opportunity to show me up? An idea stamps a bold foot in front of me.

"I have a wager for you," I say, hurrying my thoughts along to keep up with my mouth. My pinky finger, the weakest but cheekiest of the lot, wiggles at Jamie's nose. "I bet I can make more money than you before the lights-out bugle."

Bo makes a skeptical noise behind me, and my pinky circles around to include him. "Both of you, combined. If I win,

Jamie will . . ." For a moment, even the room holds steady. "Jamie will perform with me in front of Mr. Stewart." I cannot overplay my hand. Jamie will never agree outright to go to New York. But when you're onstage, you're both the magician and his hat of tricks. You have the power to cast spells that people will remember for the rest of their lives. I have to rekindle the wonder in Jamie. Once he remembers how it feels to perform, to *fly*, maybe he'll have a change of heart.

Bo's eyebrows drawbridge up, and Jamie's mouth goes crooked. "I can't wait to hear what I'll win if you lose."

Olly and Wink, now each wearing one white slipper and one black, watch Jamie and me as if we were playing a tennis match.

"If I lose, we go our separate ways." I stand perfectly balanced, though the room starts swaying around us.

Most of our wagers were for bragging rights or who got the bigger drumstick. Never for something so, well, titanic.

"Val," he says, his face suddenly weary, like Mum's when she found one of Ba's hidden flasks.

It occurs to me that Jamie might refuse me, walk out of the ring, no longer the brother I remember, but a blander, mopier version of himself. Though it saddens me to see him like this, it affirms that I'm on the right path. Our fates are tied together, so when he's unsteady, I must take a firmer hand. Didn't Ba always tell us that one boot leads the other, and when one lags behind, the other must pull its twin forward?

The ship rolls sharply. My feet shuffle for steadier footing, even in my pumps, but Jamie distractedly grabs a bedpost.

Stand too long in the same place and you'll get stuck, Brother.

He catches my scornful glance and grimaces. Noticing his mates, hung like mismatched laundry around the room, he grows taller, glaring at them as if to ask, *What are you looking at?* A cocky smile feathers his face, and he wiggles a finger at me. "We don't just go our separate ways. If you lose, you return to London. I'll get you the money."

I bark out a sharp laugh, waiting for a punch line that doesn't come. If I want Jamie to play, I have to risk something equally big. London is my past. My future is America. Can I afford to gamble with my own destiny? But how can I not? Once Halley's Comet is gone, you'll never see it again in your lifetime.

With two strides, I reach him and hold out a fist. He bumps his on top, a gesture that indicates the sealing of a bet. "Good luck, Sister. You take my seat at lunch."

"I thought we were having lunch together."

"An extra place setting would look suspicious, and I'm still loaded from breakfast." From his seabag, he pulls out an extra set of slops and tosses them to me with a grin. "I think I'll get started on those deck chairs."

At least he isn't going soft on me. I have half a mind to skip lunch and get cooking as well.

"Well, if you're that worried . . ." I toss out.

He laughs, not taking the bait. "Bo'll take you to the Dining Saloon. And lads"—he gives Wink's and Olly's caps a tweak—"stay salty." Then he slips out the door.

After Jamie leaves, an awkward silence descends between

Bo and me, punctuated by the swish-slap of the lads' slippers. From the window, a gust of salty air belches in my face. *What exactly was your plan again, you cocky-boots?* Bo and Jamie have the advantage. Not only do they both fill out their clothes, being actual men, but there are two of them.

Well, lads, I will be smarter.

"We wait outside," Bo grunts.

Wink lines up his slippers under his bed, while Olly throws his in a heap by the sink. Stepping into their shoes, they start to follow Bo out the door. But before exiting, Olly squats, his attention caught by something on the floor.

Glancing up at me, his humor vanishes, like it was knocked off his face.

"What is it?" On the floor is a feather. I pick it up, a small white quill I recognize from the toque. Probably I broke one of the feathers when pinning the veil to the brim.

Olly gives Wink the kind of look you use when you're holding a picnic hamper and thunder claps. "It was pointing to twelve o'clock," he whispers.

I twirl the feather in front of Olly, but he nearly trips over himself backing away and out the door.

Wink and Olly flank me, Valora the seaman, as we follow Bo to the Dining Saloon one deck below. Jamie said an extra place setting would look suspicious. But what about a different diner? Then again, Jamie thinks it's safe, and he's the conservative twin. I crank my seaman's cap lower on my head.

"We want in on the bet, too," Wink announces. The taffies in his pocket make crinkly sounds with each clomp of his oversized boots.

"Yeah, two against one isn't fair. And Wink and I count as another person."

The sight of the lads' earnest faces, turned up like sunflowers, squeezes my heart. "Well, what can you do?"

They furrow their brows as if they're looking deep inside their heads for hidden talents.

"Wink knows how to shine shoes," Olly pipes up.

Wink's boots tell a different story with their scuffed tips and a crack along the side that looks glued up. "Olly knows how to do armpit chuffs on the backs of his knees."

Stopping in the middle of the corridor, Olly snakes a hand up one of his trouser legs, then begins cupping the back of his knee, producing a symphony of musical flatulence. Wink adds harmony using the more traditional armpit.

Bo throws back a dubious glance. "Yes, do that. That will empty pockets for sure."

"Mind your own business," Wink growls.

"Oh!" Olly slaps his cheeks. "We can help you start a sweepstakes like they have here. You put in a shilling, and then you get a chance to earn a boatload of money."

I snort. That would be taking the express train to the crow-bar hotel. "People will think we're shaking them down. But I do like your enthusiasm. All right, you're hired."

The two start jumping like two ticks. Olly even clicks his heels.

"I'll let you know the plan after lunch. We don't want anyone overhearing our secrets."

Ahead of us, Bo shakes his head.

The Dining Saloon is divided by sex, with families filling in both sides. Long mahogany tables feature white tablecloths, real china, and individual chairs, not those benches you find in the pubs.

In the back corner farthest from the windows, four heads of black hair stand out against light sea slops. It doesn't surprise me that the Chinese are given the worst seats, though as someone who doesn't want to stand out, I should be thankful. I stiffen at the sight of rude Fong, shoveling in his food with gusto, while Tao takes cautious sniffs of his own plate, his queue rippling like a waterfall down his back.

Gazes follow us, with obvious disapproval, and I feel myself grow smaller. One woman even holds her napkin to her nose as we pass. It's not that different from what we experienced in London—more like taking a concentrated shot of bitters rather than having it fed in small doses. Yet, a vague sense of disappointment washes over me, and I screw my cap on tighter. Being in the same boat does not make us the same.

Two Chinese seamen I haven't met yet, both in their twenties, attempt to converse with the Russian family next to them, a couple with a rosy-cheeked daughter about my age. One of the seamen, a wiry man with laughing eyes, mimics the shoveling of coal while the family looks on. At least the Russians don't seem put out by our presence.

Seeing us approach, both men stand and make their way to us. I feel a pinch of apprehension. It shouldn't matter, but I hope these two don't reject me, like Bo and Fong.

The wiry man interlaces his knobby fingers together and bows. "I am pleased to meet you, honored sister Valora," he says cheerfully in Cantonese. "You look like one of us Johnnies." He says that last word in English, though I wonder if I heard right. *Johnny* is a dodgy term people use to refer to any Chinese man, no matter his name. "I am Drummer, and this is Ming Lai." He nods to his companion, a short man with a prematurely bald head and a clear, honest face.

"Jamie is lucky to have such a devoted sister," Ming Lai says in a deep baritone that reminds me of the sound a conch shell makes when you blow through it.

97

I relax a notch. "Thank you." If only Jamie saw things the same way. "Do you play the drum?" I ask Drummer. He's a ball of energy, shifting from foot to foot as if he hears music in his head.

"He plays anything with a surface," Ming Lai answers. His solidness is a perfect foil for Drummer's restless energy.

"Like this one," Drummer shoots back, slapping a few beats on the shorter man's scalp before he can duck out of the way. "I believe you have met Tao and Fong. They don't speak English."

"Neither do you," Ming Lai points out.

"Better than you."

Tao gets up from his chair. His icicle beard tweaks forward as he bows. "Nice to meet you, Little Sister. We are sorry we closed the door on you."

Fong, still seated and chewing, looks as sorry as a wood plank over which one has tripped.

"It is my fault, Uncle. You did not know."

Olly and Wink hop into seats across from each other, leaving Bo and me to sit at the end, awkwardly facing each other. I keep my gaze squarely focused on the table while white-jacketed waiters hastily set down plates of roast beef, corn, and jacket potatoes. It becomes clear that I needn't have worried over substituting for Jamie. The waiters barely glance at us as they serve, seeming more intent on getting away as fast as possible.

Meanwhile, the waiter at the next table, a man with a rectangular "door-knocker" beard and a rose in his lapel, wags his chin with its occupants. "I'll get you more bread at once." He snaps his fingers, catching another waiter's attention, and points at the basket. He must be the headwaiter here.

We don't have bread baskets at our table, though we do have butter stamped with the White Star logo, just like the soap. Maybe it is an oversight. I blink through the glare of the overhead lights bouncing off the enameled walls. Do the Chinese have smaller portions than the other diners? With everyone already working their forks, I can't be sure.

I should put my head to the trough. This is more food than I've seen in a long time, and it isn't as if our bellies will go empty. I'm supposed to be keeping my chin tucked, after all. But what good is butter without bread?

My hand shoots up, before I can stop it. "Waiter?" The headwaiter frowns at me, then advances toward us with short strides of his stubby legs. "We would like some bread, too."

Bo hefts an eyebrow. Beside me, Wink stiffens, and Olly puts down his potato. The diners within earshot spear us with disapproving looks, the kind reserved for sewer rats and unwashed feet.

Finding himself in the middle of a pileup of stares, the head-waiter angles his head in a mock bow. "I'll see what I can find."

Bo watches me with a mildly curious expression, as if watching a dog try to catch its shadow. I give him a satisfied smile. "Jamie would've asked, too."

He shrugs. "I doubt it." As he eats, he studies the framed

posters of White Star ships on the wall behind me. Probably he's wishing Jamie was here instead of me.

Glancing away, I catch Fong in the act of palming a pepper shaker. He slips it into his pocket, but Tao gives him a scolding look, and an under-the-table skirmish ensues between them.

It occurs to me that each of the seamen has a best mate. Maybe that's why Bo doesn't like me. If Jamie comes with me to New York, Bo will be all alone. But if Bo is Jamie's best mate, surely he wants what's best for him. Perhaps I can budge the stone by getting the stone next to him to move.

Olly puts his face up to Bo's. "How much are they paying for your job?" Despite the lads' preference for English, they speak Cantonese here, which they must use whenever the non-English-speaking men are present.

Bo rips a chunk of meat off his fork with his teeth, not answering.

Drummer leans in. "What's this about jobs?" His thin brown face is animated with chewing. "If there's work, share. My wife wants to attend the dragon boat races this summer."

"Go roll an egg," mutters Bo.

"Jamie bet Bo he could make more money than him, but then Valora bet she could make more money than both of them *together* by the lights-out bugle," offers Olly between bites. "If Valora wins, Jamie has to do tricks with her. But if Jamie wins, Valora has to go home."

Everyone steers their gaze at me. Even the fair-faced Ming Lai lifts his head from his conversation with the Russian girl, who is holding an apple from a bowl of fruit and teaching him the word in Russian.

Tao twirls his braided beard with his shortened index finger. "Big wagers. I believe sister will win."

"Then you will lose," growls Fong. He spears a pat of butter with his knife and eats it. "How can one girl make more than two men?"

Tao tugs his beard straight and gives me a serene smile. "Sister knows what she wants. She is very determined."

Fong makes a hacking noise, his prominent tooth stabbing the air. "Girls should not order boys around. They are weaker and should do as they are told. There is no contest."

My skin flushes, and a retort springs to my lips. But I clamp my mouth shut. The Chinese are taught to respect their elders. My bet with Jamie takes on more heft. I will show that old man who is weaker when I triumph.

When the last of my roast beef is making its way down my gullet, one of the waiters sets a basket before me. "Thank you," I say, despite the fact that most of us have finished our meals. He scuttles away without replying.

I lift the cloth napkin from the basket. The lads and I peer in, and my jaw goes crooked. It's filled with bread heels, all of them scorched. They are so hard, it would take days to soften them in soup.

Olly knocks his knuckles against one. "We could sharpen our razors on this."

"You don't shave," Wink scoffs.

"Cod's sake," I mutter. "That is some nerve." These heels could smash windows. I toss one lightly and catch it. Definitely good for throwing.

No wonder no one asked. Bo snorts, Drummer gives me an apologetic smile, and Fong, watching with keen interest, waggles an admonishing finger at me.

The headwaiter signals for quiet, and I stop myself from flinging a bread heel at his door-knocker beard. "Ladies and gentlemen, may I have your attention? It's time to draw the winner for today's sweeps, which—thanks to your generous contributions—totals two pounds in the kitty."

Applause breaks out, but I barely hear it as my face continues to cook. I can feel Bo watching me again. I throw him a fierce scowl.

"You believed they would give *us* good bread," he says mildly. "Maybe you are not ready for the real world."

I lift my nose. "It's a shame how working at the bottom of a boat lowers one's standards."

A man in a white steward's uniform enters the dining room, his grin like an oiled saddle on a face pulled tight over his bones. It's the skeletal steward who caught me in the hallway last night. In his arms, he carries a box with a crank, which he brings to the headwaiter.

Olly points. "That's Skeleton. He's our room steward, and also the one who collects for the sweeps."

The man sniffs, as if in confirmation.

"Kindly give the entries a final turn," the headwaiter directs. Skeleton cranks the box, pivoting his body so that everyone can see the good job he's doing. He unlatches a small door at the top of the box and holds it low enough for the nearest diner to stick her hand in. She draws a ticket, and he reads, "Ticket 412, belonging to Mr. Heath Bledig!"

A rousing shout punches the air, and a sturdy young man gets to his feet, cheered on by his towheaded mates. One yanks the stocking cap off Bledig's head, exposing his white-blond hair, which is slicked into a shiny helmet. Grabbing the cap back, Bledig moseys up to the headwaiter, pumping the man's hand hard enough to jar the rose from his lapel.

The waiter regains his arm and rolls out his shoulder. "Er, congratulations, sir." Skeleton leads the grinning Bledig away. "For the rest of you, better luck tomorrow."

That's right, we shall see who the better Luck is tomorrow. I turn a challenging eye to Bo, but his seat is empty.

12

Once back in Room 14, the lads immediately switch out their shoes for their slippers. Olly eyes my toque, which I had placed on Jamie's pillow so it would be out of the way.

"You have something against feathers?" I ask.

Olly jams his hands in his pockets, shifting from slipper to slipper. "The farmer's wife used to give me a slice of pork and some vegetables for scraping chicken piddles for her. She told me if I ever saw a hackle feather pointing to twelve o'clock, something was going to happen."

I've never heard of that one, but that doesn't mean it isn't true. Luck wears many faces. The number four for Fong, twins for Ba, a crane for April. Are we all just looking for the heavens to speak, to assure us things will turn out right? As far as I'm concerned, the best way to counter bad luck is to make some luck of your own. "Something's *always* going to happen."

"The first time I found one, someone gave me a whole bag of rock sugar. But the last time I found one, I saw a man gored by a water buffalo." Olly squeezes his shoulders together, as if trying not to get gored himself.

I poke his shoulder, and he relaxes. "Well, the good news is, I haven't seen any water buffalos around here, unless they keep them in the swimming pool."

Wink lets out a teensy smile.

"And while we wait for that something to happen, I'll show you how we're going to win that bet."

The lads watch me pull four bread heels and one apple from my pockets. I've chosen the heels from the basket with the most similar weights.

Olly works a piece of taffy off his back teeth with his finger. "How's that going to make money?"

Wink scratches his cap. "We're going to knock out a couple of nobs with those and steal their wallets."

"That's dark, Wink, and not what I had in mind. Now, who wants to learn how to juggle?"

The lads look at each other.

Olly lifts a slippered foot. "You mean what you did with these?"

"Exactly." Using the bread heels, I show the lads how juggling works, letting them see the pattern, then handing them the heels to practice throwing.

"That's it, toss it high, but not too high. Easy there. You're a natural."

Both the lads have quick reflexes and good balance. The room tilts unexpectedly, but Wink, focused on the heel he just tossed up, catches it without stumbling.

"Where'd you learn such good balance?"

"He climbed a lot of trees," Olly answers for him.

Wink glares at Olly, then takes off a slipper and starts whacking him with it.

Olly shields himself with his arms. "What? She asked."

I puzzle over what could make a boy self-conscious about climbing trees, but both lads have clammed up. "Jamie and I climbed a lot of trees back in London. Our favorite ones were these patchy giants in St. James's Park that were as tall as those masts up on the deck. Jamie loved it up there. He said we could see clear to America if we could find a tall enough tree."

Olly grins, wedging a smile out of Wink.

"Lads, do you have a pair of scissors?"

"Bo used to have a pair, but one of the other sailors pinched it."

"What about a knife?"

Olly's eyes grow round. "Jamie has one in his mess kit."

"Good. First, I have to fetch something from upstairs—the showstopper." I visualize the pineapple, prickly on the sides and spiny at the top, but with a bottom concave enough to balance on my head. I hope no one took it from the mermaid on the tidal-wave staircase. "Step out and let me get respectable again."

———·••·———

Two hours later, I'm back in sea slops. I unhinge Jamie's staghorn pocketknife and lift my hair off my neck. "Would anyone like to do the honors?"

Wink ties his hands behind him, his eyes twice their usual size.

Olly takes a step back. "Jamie would kill us."

I sigh. "He's much too concerned about hair."

Shearing off my lion's mane will be harder to do myself, and not just physically. But sacrifices are necessary. I can't wear a seaman's cap during my routine, and I need to score big. Jamie already has a lead on me. Plus, if I'm going to be impersonating one of his mates, I may as well look the part as best I can. Using the knife, I saw off my hair in chunks, committing them to the sea through the porthole.

At last, we are ready.

Scotland Road streams with crew and passengers. We head to the third-class decks at the stern, the bread heels, the apple, and the pineapple in my slipper bag. Olly and Wink keep looking at my newly shorn tresses, cut above my ear.

"It'll grow back," I assure them, wishing I sounded more certain.

A quartet of young men with baggy trousers eating from a bag of peanuts slice their eyes to us. I'm startled to recognize Bledig, the sweeps winner. With their flattened white-blond haircuts, the four remind me of the bottom cutting teeth, with Bledig the loosest tooth of the bunch. He must be riding high from his win, judging by his swagger and half sneer.

Noticing Wink and his clomping feet, Bledig snickers and, with a shoulder like an anchor, bumps him hard enough to knock him into Olly and Olly into me.

I catch myself on the wall. "Oy! Watch it, you blighter."

Bledig throws a peanut shell at us, though it makes it only partway before dropping to the floor. The men's laughter echoes off the corridor.

Wink attempts to storm after them, with Olly close behind, but I grab both of them by the collar. Those young men are not only older and bigger, but sport more scars on their hulls than the lads on their tender shells. I will take care of this myself.

When I set down my slipper bag, two bread heels roll out, and I reconsider. If I confront those bottom cutters, they might get violent, with me dressed as boy. There goes my juggling act, and I can kiss Jamie goodbye.

Wink straightens his crumpled jacket, scowling mightily after the men. "Ghost hair."

"Dumb eggs," Olly curses in Cantonese, all the friendliness gone from his face.

"Come on, lads." I hike my slipper bag over my shoulder. "We have better things to do."

With weightier steps, we set off again.

"So how did you two meet?" I ask, an obvious attempt to divert them.

"We were both runaways," says Olly. "Tao saw us begging by the docks in Victoria Harbor."

"Why'd you run away?"

Olly shrugs. "I just had people passing me along. I don't think anyone noticed I left. Wink had a father, but . . ."

Wink begins glowering again, his cheek twitching.

"Anyway," Olly hastily moves on, "Tao asked Captain Pibst to take us on as ship boys, and he did, except we busted a propeller in the Suez Canal. So then Atlantic Steam took us on, and that's where we met the rest of the Johnnies."

My nose wrinkles. "Why do you call yourselves Johnnies?"

"Bo was getting into fights every time someone called one of us a Johnny. So Jamie started calling us the Johnnies to poke fun at him. Then it became funny."

I can't help smiling, despite my annoyance at Jamie. He knows just how to save a cat without getting scratched.

Once, we saw a gent offer a hungry-looking man tuppence so he could buy himself a pie, but the man pushed the gent's hand away. Jamie took the tuppence and said to the hungry man, "Sir, your coins fell out of your pocket." The hungry man took the money. Jamie understood people. Me, I would've taken the tuppence and run. If that gent wanted to feed someone hungry, he had a willing person right there.

We reach the far staircase and climb to the poop deck. People crowd the rails, watching sea life pass below. The fresh air seems to shake the sand off the boys' foul moods.

Up on the docking bridge, the same crewman with the sharp beret as yesterday stands with his legs and elbows in triangles, looking out to sea. "Do they ever let passengers up there?" The platform's elevated position could provide a perfect stage for the upper-class passengers, who could see us clearly from across the well deck.

Olly glances at where I'm looking and stiffens. "No. That's the quartermaster's turf."

"The QM bites," adds Wink.

May we steer clear of him, then.

We descend back to the well deck with its lower profile—out of view of the docking bridge, in case juggling goes against regulations. At least it's closer to the superstructure, where three tiers of first- and second-class passengers move about, ready for the shaking.

The sun bouncing off the water plays a cruel game of daggers with my eyes. Passersby give us a wide berth, as if they're expecting trouble. A shot of nerves pours through me despite my earlier confidence. What if this crowd is not in the mood for entertainment? Unlike in St. James's Park, space here is limited. Folks could sour on those who take up more than their fair share.

Well, there's no turning back now.

"Ready, lads?"

Wink and Olly snap to attention, positioning themselves a few paces in front of me, one on either side. In the crowd milling about, eyes narrowed in suspicion begin to round, watching as I remove the pineapple from my slipper bag.

I exhale and roll back my shoulders. Then I hold up the pineapple.

"Afternoon, folks! I am Valor, the, er, Valorous." My voice quavers, but I force myself to continue. "Today, I'm going to entertain you"—I pass the ungainly fruit from one hand to the other—"by juggling."

A few people glare at me, as if to scold me for intruding on their afternoon, and I wilt a little. At least some from the upper decks peer down with curiosity. After everyone has gotten a good look-see at the pineapple, I toss it smartly from one hand to the other, back and forth, back and forth. "When it comes to juggling, I personally feel quality is more important than quantity."

That gets a laugh, and I feel my limbs loosen. As the laughter dies down, I place the pineapple on my head, holding it there with two hands. "My father, God rest his soul, said life is a balancing act, and the better you get at juggling, the better you get at living." Slowly, I let go with one hand, then the other. The boat sways, but I move with it, not letting the pineapple fall. "Of course, he never tried juggling on an ocean before."

More smiles. Good. Ba always said even the best performer in the world won't get a farthing if the audience doesn't like you. But the relationship is a fickle one, and an audience can turn on you if you don't deliver what you promised.

The deck heaves again, and the pineapple tips. With my hands held out, I slide in one direction, coaxing it back in place. A murmur ripples through the crowd. A lady in a seal fur coat covers her eyes, as if the sight of a crushed pineapple might be more than she can bear.

"But really, juggling is simply a series of throws and catches."

I glance toward Olly. Instead of tossing me the bread heel like we rehearsed, Olly can't seem to take his eyes off the pineapple. I jab him with another look, but he's still watching my crown.

Cod's sake. I shouldn't have put the lads in the routine. I forgot how easy it is for first-timers to freeze up.

Wink hisses at his mate. Olly snaps out of it and tosses me the bread heels: one, two. *That's it, lad.* I wink at Olly, glad his part is over.

I knock the heels together, making a clapping sound. "No, ladies and gentlemen, these are not chunks of granite. It's the bread they served us for lunch today in third class." A few disbelieving chuckles float from the audience. "I'm not sure why we haven't sunk yet." The chuckles take shape.

I begin tossing the heels up and letting them fall into the same hand. Up, down, nice and easy. Catch and throw, catch and throw. "Every day, life throws us . . . bread heels. The more we practice catching them, the more prepared we are when"—I begin tossing the heels across my center so that right catches left, and left catches right—"the heels change course."

I let a few cycles pass, to allow folks to see the pattern, then glance at Wink. He tosses his heel. It goes high, and my pineapple wobbles!

Hands cover faces. Breaths are sucked in.

Wink's heel falls into my hand. And just like that, the third player enters the ring. My hands move on their own, honed by years of practice with anything handy—shoes, rolled-up socks, tree pods, and, when Ba was on a winning streak, oranges, nature's gold nuggets.

The heels reach their apex in front of my nose, tracing a sideways figure eight through the air. I bring them down to chest level, moving faster and faster. People begin to clap, and the clapping grows.

I slow down the juggling by tossing the heels higher. "Of course, sometimes life throws you more than you expect." I glance at Wink, and more carefully this time, he lobs me his second heel.

Four heels whirl through the air. More gasps float on the salty breeze. "And you realize that what you were juggling before . . . wasn't actually so bad."

That gets a laugh. The size of the crowd has easily doubled since I started. Even a few of the crew have stopped their duties to watch. *Steady, girl. Don't let the crowd distract you, or you'll lose your flow.*

"With even more practice"—I switch my pattern, throwing the heels from the outside instead of from the middle, and tossing them vertically as well as horizontally—"you might find you can control them. Bend the heels to your will."

I change pattern again, tossing two heels at once up the center line so that four are used in a three-beat waltz. The applause becomes more animated, with cheering and laughter. A young lady on A-Deck bounces up and down excitedly, her arms wrapped around a black poodle. I nearly break my pattern when I recognize the girl Jamie spoke to, Charlotte Fine.

I shake myself free from the sticky trap of her gaze and find my place again. "Sometimes, a new heel is thrown. But if you've learned the tricks, you'll know what to do when that time comes." Wink, following my eyes, throws me the apple.

Incorporating an object with a different weight and shape into the set requires all my attention. I ignore the oohs and aahs, focusing on keeping the single apple spinning along with the heels. I throw the objects up in three columns, two heels in each outside column, and the apple bobbing in the center. "And if you're lucky, your effort is its own reward." I grab the apple when it nears my mouth, take a bite, then let it fall back into the pattern. Up, down, bite, juggle, up, down, bite, juggle.

That really pops the cork. People hoot and holler and clap their hands.

If Jamie were here, we could really make fruits fly. He has fast hands. He can throw a ball through a speeding train and have it come out on the other side.

The pineapple begins to teeter, forcing me into a simpler pattern. Sweat dribbles down my underarms, and juice streaks my chin. *Enough, you show monkey.* A professional knows her limits.

I toss the partially eaten apple and the heels, one by one, back to Wink and Olly. Then I bow low with a flourish, letting the pineapple drop and catching it just before it hits the floor. I bow in all directions—toward the folks on the superstructure, then toward the third-class passengers leaning over the rail of the poop deck.

"If you liked that," I pant, trying to speed things up, "my assistants will be on hand to accept your expressions of appreciation. And if you didn't, next time, cover your eyes."

Wink and Olly doff their hats and begin circulating, catching coins that fall from the first- and second-class decks, and even a few from the third-class passengers, bless them.

A voice grinds from behind me: "Hold you hard!"

It's the QM from the docking bridge, with a stare loud enough to drown out the applause. Another crewman, with the mien of an angry sturgeon, approaches from behind him, his navy coat seeming to swallow his neck. He folds his arms, which are so muscled, he can't get them all the way crossed. A set of heavy keys clipped to his belt catches the sunlight. It's the master-at-arms—or in his case, the Master-of-Big-Arms—here to haul me to the crowbar hotel.

13

Brackets appear around the QM's mouth. "Performances are not allowed, see?" He speaks in the North East accent, which sounds like the tongue is pushing the words up a hill.

I gulp. "Pardon me, Quartermaster. I wasn't aware." I wipe juice off my chin with my sleeve and furtively look around for Wink and Olly. They are still collecting coins. We can't go yet. Every penny counts.

The QM stands in his favorite triangular stance, knees locked inside his navy serge trousers, fists on hips with elbows stretching the fabric of his jersey. Even his chin is pointy. "Move along, or I'll have him do it for you." He ticks his head toward the Master-of-Big-Arms.

"Right away." Caught between their glares, it occurs to me that they haven't mentioned the lads collecting money. I try to catch Wink's and Olly's eyes, but a group of children have started up a game of beanbag toss, blocking my view.

"Seems to me," I continue before the men turn around, "entertainment will help the passengers pass the time. The band can only play so long, and it's nice to have variety. And if no one's complaining, where's the harm?" I attempt a teensy smile, but it crumbles under the weight of the QM's scowl.

"The harm's that you could be runnin' a dodgy scam, is how. So unless you want to take it up with the captain, work your legs, 'cause you're gettin' on my wick."

The Master-of-Big-Arms grunts his assent.

Wink finally notices me. His quick eyes assess the men corralling me, and I glance meaningfully at the stairs. *Make yourself scarce, boys! Smartly, before anyone makes us give the money back.*

Wink bows to the man who just dropped a coin into his cap. He signals to Olly, then both head for the stairwell, with Wink trying not to clomp in his too-big boots.

"Don't mean no trouble, sirs. I thank you for your indulgence. I'll just be on my way, then."

The QM's mouth becomes a gash. I can feel the men's eyes follow me as I stroll to the stairwell, taking big, unhurried steps to get me there faster without looking like I'm in a rush.

On the way back to our room, I stop at a water fountain to rinse my face, which is sticky with sweat and apple juice. That was too close. I can hardly perform for Mr. Stewart if I'm locked in a brig. From now on, I swear to keep my chin tucked.

The sight of Olly and Wink sorting a dragon's pile of money into neat stacks on their top bunk makes me forget all about the QM and the Master-of-Big-Arms. There's no way Jamie and Bo could've made more than that, short of holding up the purser's office.

"Are you in trouble?" asks Wink.

"Not yet," I mumble, running my fingers through a mound of change.

Olly holds up a gold coin. "Cats, someone gave you a sovereign!" He starts counting on his fingers, muttering numbers.

Wink takes the coin and bites into it. "It's real." His eyes narrow. "You sure you're not rich?"

I snort. "Rich in talent is what I am. When Jamie and I used to put on performances, we didn't have a boatful of millionaires watching us. We'd be happy to get a few shillings."

Olly slaps his hands against the mattress, and the coins jingle. "Two pounds, four shillings."

Wink takes a turn counting it, too.

A smile bends my lips as I imagine the looks on Jamie's and Bo's faces when I tell them. *Oh ho! You don't just send talent like this back to England, now, do you, Jamie!* "Seems that hackle feather brought prosperity. Stick with me, and you'll always have Luck." I wink at the lads.

I give them each five shillings, and Olly's face splits open. He pours the coins from hand to hand. "I'm going to buy a Panama hat." He glances at Wink's foot, hanging over the side of the bed. "And you should buy boots that don't look like they came out of a cow's butt."

Wink kicks him. "You came out of a cow's butt."

I rummage through Jamie's seabag for a pair of socks and peel one off for the boys. "This is for your money." I stuff my share into the other.

Wink puts his five shillings into their sock and hands it to Olly. But Olly closes his hand around his coins. "What if I want to buy something?"

"Like what?" Wink's face screws up, putting me in mind of an angry dumpling.

"I'd like to put in for the sweeps—"

"Waste of money," grumbles Wink.

"Or maybe get a souvenir. I hear they got spoons, pens, and wallets at the barbershop."

"Spoons? Pens? *Wallets?*" Wink turns a rosy shade of pink and begins cursing in Cantonese. "What makes you think you'll ever have enough money to put in a wallet?" He throws out his hands. "You waste all your money on stupid things. Candy, chewing tobacco—even though you don't like it— cricket races. Stupid, stupid, stupid."

While I marvel at all the unexpected words that just fell out of Wink's mouth, Olly's shoulders start twitching. "And saving up for a tree house isn't stupid?"

Wink's narrow chest heaves, and he squeezes his hands into fists. If he were still holding bread heels, we would have two piles of crumbs. "That's private."

"Not that private. You talk about it all the time in front of Jamie."

Wink slides off the bed and lands with a light thump. Olly must realize he's pushed his smaller half too far, because he hangs his matchstick head. "Okay, fine, I'm sorry. Look."

Wink grudgingly turns around, holding himself so tight,

one little swell could send him toppling over like a vase. Olly drops his coins into their sock, one at a time, as if each coin requires a personal farewell.

"That's a good lad," I say in the voice I would use to coax Ba into eating something when he was in one of his moods. "A penny saved is twice got." The familiar sound of Jamie's laugh grows louder from outside the door. "Grab the playing cards, lads! Time for a last trick."

14

When Jamie and Bo swagger into Room 14, their faces animated, Wink, Olly, and I pretend to be deep in Winds of Change.

Olly sets down an eight of diamonds. "Change to diamonds."

"Hello, Sis," Jamie nearly sings, pulling off my cap. "Cripes, your hair! Bald as a monkey."

Wink and Olly barely look up from their cards. Bo closes his mouth, dusting off his surprise like a bit of dirt on his lapel. Briskly, he removes his coat and washes up at the sink. Jamie reaches out to touch my head, but I dodge his hand.

"Lift your skirts and get over it. It's just hair."

"You didn't say that when I picked a hundred burrs from your head."

I bite back a smile, remembering the time we crawled through a thicket, our pockets full of stolen walnuts.

Wink lays down a diamond, and the lads side-eye me. I throw down my last card. "Eight of spades. Sorry, lads, but your last name's not Luck."

Jamie squats beside my bunk. "So fess up. Bo and I made out pretty good today."

Wink shuffles with zest, his elbows jabbing the air around him, and Olly makes the mattress bounce with his nervous energy.

"Is that right, Brother?" I ask, all starry-eyed innocence.

"The boatswain told us he'd pay us tuppence for each chair we fixed."

My lip trembles, and I make my eyes real big and fretty. "So how many did you fix?"

"Why, are you worried, Sis?"

"They do not look worried," says Bo, observing Wink and Olly through the mirror. Despite our plan to act casual, the lads look like two pipes about to burst. Bo wipes his face with a towel, but not hard enough to remove his scowl. "We fixed twelve each."

"Let's see, twenty-four chairs, at tuppence each, makes forty-eight pence. Divided by twelve pence a shilling . . . Four shillings is barking brilliant! That's more than your daily wage."

With a frown, Jamie crosses his arms, as if bracing for a hit. "What are you up to?"

"I hope you've been doing your wake-up drills, because we're trying out for the circus."

Olly whoops, and Wink gets so excited, the cards spill in every direction.

Jamie's jaw descends. "You made more than four shillings? How?"

Olly can't hold back. "She juggled four bread heels and an apple, while balancing that on her head." He points to the pineapple, which I laid on Jamie's bed. A consolation prize.

Bo leans against a bedpost, and a look of wonder crosses his face.

Olly scoops up cards, forgetting to arrange them facing the same way. "You should've seen all those nobs, throwing coins like birdseed. It was better than eating marmalade."

Wink snickered. "You never had marmalade."

"Snakes, Val. You could've gotten us kicked off this boat."

I tsk my tongue. "Where exactly would they kick us to? There's nothing but ocean for miles and miles."

"That may be, but they do have law here. Probably got a brig or something where they put the unruly passengers."

I remember the Master-of-Big-Arms's keys. Jamie could be right. His gaze probes me, as if he can actually see the close call I'm reliving in my head. I shut him out with a smile. "Well, unless they've got a brig where they put the jugglers, I guess we're safe."

Wink giggles, and Jamie's frown deepens.

"You're just miffed you didn't think of it." I slide off the bunk and come face-to-face with the tiny mole above Jamie's lip, which, according to Ba, indicates a considerate, thoughtful nature. You wouldn't know it by the way he's acting, though, scratching the ground like a rooster in a crate. Jamie can't refuse a wager, but he also never loses well.

"How much did you make?" Jamie asks.

I don't answer, enjoying all the clever contortions Jamie's face seems capable of making. The supper bugle calls, but no one moves.

"Five shillings?" Bo can't help guessing.

Wink sticks up his thumb.

"Six?" Jamie says.

Wink's thumb stays up.

"Seven?"

I guess Bo is taking odds and Jamie is taking evens.

"Eight?" Jamie blows into my face.

I push him away. "Have you such little faith in me, Brother? Try two pounds and four shillings."

Bo coughs and I give him a wink. "Sorry, Wagtail. Looks like you bet on the wrong team." I turn back to Jamie. "Now if you don't mind, I need to see a man about an elephant."

His jaw clicks. "The day's not done yet."

With that, he sweeps out of the room.

———·⁙·———

DINNERTIME APPROACHES, AND the lifts are busy. So the Merry Widow removes her coat and slowly climbs the tidal-wave staircase in her blasted pumps.

Without the mass of my hair, the toque sits lower—fortunately, hiding my shorn locks. My head should feel lighter, but heavy thoughts bow my neck.

Jamie still thinks he can outdo me. I shouldn't have been so eager to brag about my win. If you catch a big fish, carry it home in a sack, or don't be surprised if a bird carries it off. The lights-out bugle isn't until 10:30 p.m., so there is yet time. But Jamie won't be able to surpass me by fixing deck chairs. White Star Line would never pay that much for "off the record" labor. If he thinks to copy me with a trick, the fine members of the upper classes will all be tucked away in their libraries, lounges, or smoking rooms after dinner, places that are off-limits to the third class.

With my magnificent dress on display, stares and murmurs of approval follow me as I ascend. I am a one-woman show. A particularly bold lady even reaches out a gloved hand, as if to touch my beaded crane. I favor her with an elegant nod like the royals do. The adoration is intoxicating, like the liquor-filled chocolate balls Ba once brought home. One makes you hungry for more.

I reach B-Deck and cross the Entrance Hall to the Cabbage Patch, eager to free my feet from their torture racks. Near the felt doors, a news bulletin tacked onto a corkboard mounted on the bulkhead catches my attention.

THE ATLANTIC DAILY BULLETIN
The official newspaper of the RMS Titanic

APRIL 11

Weather: High 50s. Sunny and clear with moderate breeze. Expect cooling through the weekend. Possible ice.

Thousands of workers return to coal mines with end of miners' strike. New minimum wage proposed.

"Like the pineapple was glued to his head," I hear a voice say behind me.

My ears perk up. A few paces to my left, a tall man and an

older lady in a mink coat drift closer to me. I stare at the news bulletin.

"Really. He wasn't hired by White Star. I would know." The man must be six feet and some change, with an impeccably tailored wool suit that looks like it would never even dream of wrinkling. Close-set eyes interrupt a long forehead crinkled in consternation. A luxurious mustache droops from his upper lip like two squirrels' tails sewn together.

"Of course you would, Mr. Ismay. It's your operation."

So that's him, the grouchy White Star director. The top flag on this pole, the man to whom Captain Smith owes his position. He doesn't look pleased to have learned of a busker on the loose. He drains his wineglass, and a steward refills it even before Mr. Ismay holds it out for filling. "I will take it up with the captain. We don't tolerate troublemakers here."

Before he catches sight of this troublemaker, I hasten toward the door, plowing right into a young woman.

"Oh!" She catches me by the shoulders as if to steady us both.

The striking visage of April Hart stares back at me. An evening gown of violet silk somehow makes her skin look as luminous as moonlight. Her dark hair lies as sleek as a raven's feathers.

"I've got you, madam." Her eyelashes are so long, I feel a breeze when she winks. "Meet me back in your room in fifteen minutes," she whispers.

"April! Are you all right?" The woman in the fur coat bustles over, Mr. Ismay close behind.

"Just fine, Mother. We must have hit a swell."

"I'd say so." April's mother shines her own amber eyes at me, which fall to my crane dress. She spreads her short fingers as if waiting for an introduction to fall into her hands.

Mr. Ismay's eyes sharpen. "Madam, I don't think we've met. I'm—"

"Mr. Ismay, I have heard a rumor that you have quite a selection of cigars aboard." April wraps a hand around his arm. "How is a lady to get her hands on one?"

That's my cue. My heart skips ahead of my feet, and I make for the felt doors before the one-woman show gets booted from the stage.

15

I lock the door to my suite and put my back against it. But hearing no pursuers banging on the other side, I begin to feel slightly ridiculous. I hang my hat and coat, and unbuckle my pumps. I'll have to keep a sharp eye out for Mr. Ismay and hope he doesn't do the same for me.

The bed has been tucked and fluffed. A basket of fruit has been placed on a side table, including two perfect oranges, Ba's favorite fruit. Wouldn't he have been alit with glee to see me here? I imagine him pointing out the White Star logo embroidered on the napkins to Mum. "Look at that stitching, Penny. That's silk thread. Really fancies up the linens." He'd stretch the napkin between his veiny hands, the wheels turning. "We could embroider monograms. People love to see their initials."

Mum would take the napkin from him, her generous smile receding. "No one would use monogrammed napkins. They'd not want to dirty them."

But eventually, Ba would win her over.

They never would have thought Jamie and I would be guests on the maiden voyage of the Buckingham Palace of the Atlantic. I sink into a chair. Somehow being on the finest ship in the world makes our quarrel even worse. Part of me wants to find Jamie, throw a leash around his goat-y neck, and pull him to saner pastures, never mind that I'm the one frolicking about in first class. The chances of him finding his way on his own seem to grow slimmer with each day.

I peel an orange, reveling in the small triumph of getting the rind off in one continuous strip. The zesty scent perks my spirits, and the meat calms the gnawing in my stomach. I place the second orange in the wall tidy as an offering to Mum and Ba.

Ba raised us to care for our ancestors. We made regular offerings of cakes and rice wine on his teakwood altar and said prayers of remembrance to comfort them in their ancestral homes. Mum, who raised us Anglican, never joined in, but neither did she complain about it. I imagine she believed that when she married Ba, she'd married all of him, not just the parts she agreed with.

The grassy smell of the lilies jabs my nose from the center table. My eye catches on my photograph, and all my thoughts slam to a halt. I distinctly remember tucking the picture back into Ruth before leaving, the way I always do. The Bible has been moved to the far side of the table. Perhaps the photograph fell out when Steward Latimer was tidying. What must the man think? There's no reason why Mrs. Sloane might be carrying around a picture of a Chinese man and a white woman in her Bible.

I collapse onto a chair and try to force air back in my lungs. If he asks about it, I will simply have to shovel a bit more manure on the pile.

Next to the lilies, a tin of chocolates weighs down a card, which bears the official White Star logo.

> To Mrs. Amberly Sloane:
>
> Captain Smith will see you on April 12, 2:00 p.m., Reception Hall, À la Carte Restaurant.
>
> P.S. We hope you will enjoy these premium chocolates, our gift to you.

The words gather my stomach into a ball. I put the irksome lilies in the armoire and resolve to worry about the invitation later.

While I wait for April, I poke around for a place to store my money sock. Mum always stashed the money she made tatting her lace cuffs and collars in a cracked teapot that Ba had fixed using a glue of rice. He was clever at fixing things, like tying string to a leaky faucet so we wouldn't be driven mad by the drip, and rubbing soap on squeaky hinges.

The crimson seat cushions of the chaise longue catch my eye. I pull one off, exposing the slipcover buttons. Undoing a button, I push my money sock deep inside, then replace the cushion so that the bulge doesn't show.

A knock on the door makes me jump. "It's April."

I open the door and April bustles in, carrying yet another alligator suitcase. Her eyes jump around my shorn hair, and she combs her fingers through one side. "Interesting. Well, short is so much more practical."

"Is Mr. Ismay sending a hunting party after me?"

"If you are referring to Valor the juggler, I told Bruce to relax. The crowds need their diversions, and it sounds to me like the show you were putting on in third class was just as entertaining as the one you were giving in first."

"And what about the Merry Widow?"

"I admit he's curious. I told him I'd try to find out more about you."

"You . . . what?"

"Better me than anyone else, wouldn't you say?" She grins.

I have to admit, the fox is clever.

She fingers the reminder card for my meeting with the captain. "Aha! I knew this would be coming. Good thing I brought the kimono. It's a pièce de résistance." She sets the suitcase on the chaise longue and unbuckles the straps. "They were talking about you today at the Café Parisien. Come now, I'll help you change into evening wear."

"I wasn't planning to go out."

"Well, then, I'll just show you how this one works so that if you do feel like an evening stroll, you'll be appropriately attired."

"Why can't I just wear the crane dress? Not everyone saw it."

"The crane dress could be worn in the evening—I like clothes to be versatile like that—but it's expected that women will change into something different for dinner, and I can't have the Merry Widow making a faux pas. Quickly now, Mother's waiting for me." She grabs the skirt of the crane dress and smoothly pulls it over my head.

"How do you make it so it doesn't need buttons?"

"I cut the fabric on the bias. It uses more cloth, but the diagonal weave means the fabric will stretch."

I'm not sure I understand everything she says, but I nod, suddenly self-conscious standing in my underthings.

"Good heavens, what do you call that contraption?"

"My, er, bubby-cubby."

A laugh explodes from her. "Bubby-cubby. You made it?"

"Yes. It keeps the biscuits on the table. I even thought of some improvements, like stretchier fabric for the shoulder straps, and hooking it in the front."

"I like how you think." Her gaze becomes thoughtful as she shakes out a rose-colored dress.

I gasp at the rich color, which demands attention. The skirt is seamed down the middle, so it is more like trousers, and buttons climb up the back. "But everyone will look at me."

"That's the point," she says brightly. "Did you use the toilet yet?"

"Pardon me?"

"It won't be easy to make the bladder gladder in this number. But I'm in love with my trousers dress concept. If you're ready, step in like this."

I carefully work my legs into the garment. From behind me, she pulls the front of the dress over my torso, tying two wide straps into a bow at the nape of my neck and fastening the back buttons. I reach around but don't feel any fabric on my shoulder blades. "Is something missing?"

She laughs. "Taking risks gives fashion its passion. Wear the cape if you must, but please avoid red wine when wearing it. You don't know how hard it was to get the cashmere dyed this color. I stitched in sleeves to keep in the warmth." She holds out a cape in the same rose hue as the dress, and I slip my arms into it, wrapping it around me like a blanket.

My reflection in the vanity mirror reminds me of the elegant long-stemmed English roses found in the gardens of Kensington Palace. I begin to regret the bad haircut, which mars the rose like a clump of mud.

As if thinking the same thing, April fits a rose-colored hat with a rolled brim over my hair and helps me pin the veil to the sides. "I think I saw your brother fixing deck chairs." April's smile swings higher. "A handsome young man. Too bad he's not my type."

My temper flares. "Because he's Chinese?"

A wry expression settles on her face, like a robin on a perch. "No, darling. I rather like the Chinese."

"Oh," I say, because I can think of nothing else. "Well, right now he's a codfish."

She brings out a jeweled brooch from the suitcase and pins it to my cape. "You need to overlook whatever beef you have with him before it's too late. Trust me, I know."

"What if his beef is that he doesn't want me in his life?"

"Are you sure about that?"

"Our parents have passed on, and we're all we have. But he wants me to go back to England so he can go shovel coal." I am being overdramatic, but that is the long and short of it.

She stands back. "You do what you want and let him do what he wants. As I am always telling my clients, you must wear the color that suits you, and it may not always be the one you want, or the one others want for you." She appraises me. "That dusty rose color suits *you*. It's a shame you have to wear that veil."

If I looked more like Mum, I could go without the veil. Then again, if I looked like Mum, I wouldn't be in this situation. Rounded cheeks more like a robin's breast than a swift's, a weightier nose, lighter coloring. A one-degree shift in my appearance might've changed my whole journey. Mum gave up a lot to marry Ba—not just her parents, but the underrated power to be invisible.

Briskly April shakes out another gown, and I swear a waterfall pours from her fingertips. A thick swath of silk runs from jade green at the top to an indigo blue at the hem, just like the colors of a peacock. Beaded rosettes give the fabric movement and shimmer. "This is for your meeting with the captain tomorrow."

I snort. "Go'an. I can't wear that." A bit of Mum's Cockney leaks out.

"Why not? This style just slips on." She shows me both sides of the robe-like garment. It's a kimono with wide sleeves that hang to the elbow. "The easy fit paired with my sumptuous fabric perfectly blurs the line between day and evening wear."

"It's too fine. What if I step on the hem or, I dunno, stink it up?"

"You stink the same as everyone else up here. It's just a dress. You're supposed to wear it, not let it wear you. That's called style." She gathers the kimono close to her, as if giving it a hug, then hangs it in the armoire.

The English rose droops a little in the mirror. This trousers dress and the one with the crane demand attention, for sure. But that kimono is the kind of dress that demands not only attention, but also a carriage and four horses. I sigh, resigning myself to dealing with this "style" problem later. "Have you found Mr. Stewart?"

"Not yet, but I found a clue. My sources tell me he favors purple bowlers and likes to sun himself on the Promenade after lunch."

"Thank you." A rush of gratitude sweeps through my heart even though I know April and I are just business associates. My plan is coming together.

"Good night, darling."

After April leaves, I decide to take an evening stroll after all. Mrs. Sloane purchased rubber-soled boots for the walking she planned to do around the first-class Promenade on A-Deck. Even though I have to wear the pumps, I may as well get the lay of the land before hunting down Mr. Stewart tomorrow.

With dinner being served, the area is mostly deserted. The dimming sun bathes me with a last rinse of warmth and tints the sky a deep pink. Lady Sky wears rouge when she wants to be noticed.

Reaching the forward section of the Promenade, I look out onto the spade-shaped forecastle, which is crowded with bollards, winches, and spools of rope. A massive anchor lies at the end, an iron pulling us toward some giant magnet in America. Up the mast, one of the lookouts rubs his arms. Jamie said the crow's nest is the worst place to be stuck, always either too cold or too hot, and as tedious as stirring tea with your eyes. Those lookouts must have very good vision. Neither one even wears binoculars.

Spray mists my skin as the *Titanic* plows the ocean. The sun hovers breathlessly above the horizon, a sovereign held by invisible fingers. Without warning, the coin seems to instantly vanish into some deep pocket.

I rub my eyes. How did I miss the sun's fall? The heavens have played another trick on me.

My heart sags in my chest. First Mum, then Ba. And now Jamie. How can he reject me, the only remaining member of his family? We used to be inseparable, learning early on that two were better than one when one of us climbed out of the crib using the other as a stepstool. Ba and Mum taught us that family came first, but with them gone, maybe he's looking for a new one.

I sniff, my nose running because of more than just the sudden cold.

By the time I ascend to the Boat Deck, the sky is the blue-black of a crow's wing, lit by a feather of a moon. If Jamie is here idling with the stars, he'll never beat me. But the canvas on the third lifeboat is pulled tight as a drum.

Fine, Brother. Give it your best shot.

A rustling picks up my ears. It's coming from the next lifeboat down. I squint into the dark. A bit of the canvas is folded back, so neatly I almost miss it.

Jamie *is* here. I approach the lifeboat, my feet light. "Is the view better from this one?"

The canvas mostly covers Jamie's form, though in the dim glow of the electric lights, I can see his elbow sticking out from where his hands prop up his head. I lift the canvas.

But it's not Jamie's face staring back at me.

16

Bo's surprised face gazes up, and I bite my tongue to keep from screaming. "What are you doing here?"

"I ask you the same."

"Where's Jamie?"

He snorts. "Not here."

"Anyone else in there?" I lift the canvas higher.

Bo yanks it back and continues in his careful English, "No. Now go, Stowaway, before someone sees." He lies back again, re-covering himself with the canvas.

"When's the last time you saw him?"

His face becomes cunning. "Why? You worry he will win?"

"Of course not," I lie. "I worry about the bad influences around him."

The dark slashes of his eyebrows flex. "We had health inspections before boarding."

"Health inspections?"

"Yes. No one has influenza."

"Not *influenza*." My laugh cracks like an egg, and Bo blinks as if splashed. "*Influences*." I provide the word in Cantonese before continuing in English, "You and that old one-toothed geezer think girls shouldn't tell boys what to do."

He grimaces. "I only meant that Jamie may not want to take orders from his sister anymore."

I sniff. "What makes you think he took orders from me before?" The *Titanic* sways, and I catch myself on the smooth lip of the lifeboat.

"He told me about—how do you say?—*Christmas* tree."

A cold breeze seems to slice off my nose. "He told you about that?"

During one wet spring when we were eleven, I saw men clearing trees in Cadogan Place Gardens, a few blocks from where we lived in Chelsea. I told Jamie we should bring home one of the evergreens to cheer up Ba, who hadn't left our flat for twenty-eight days after being thrown out of a public tennis court, since "dogs and Chinese don't need to play tennis." If he couldn't use the public courts, he couldn't give lessons, and he'd already spent all our cracked-teapot money on rackets. Jamie refused to help me get the tree, saying it was a pigeon egg of an idea and that Ba should never have bought rackets in the first place. I told him he was a pigeon egg of a son for saying that. Eventually, he relented, but how could he share that story with a perfect stranger?

"Did you also order him not to tell that story?"

An indignant cloud of vapor blows past my lips.

"Do not get angry. It was funny." A dimple appears next to his mouth, a tiny star emerging from behind a cloud. "Whose idea was the donkey?"

I snort. "Mine."

Jamie broke his wrist when the donkey we borrowed to

haul the tree bolted, with the tree bumping along after it. Maybe he blames me all these years later for that tricky wrist.

"Half the branches had broken off by the time we got it home. Mum said, 'You got daisies for brains if you think I'm letting that rottin' piece of timber in here.'" I pour on Mum's Cockney accent. Bo grunts out a laugh. "Ba chopped it up for firewood. At least it got him out of the house."

The pod creaks as he shifts around. "Get in before you get a bad influenza."

I'm glad for the dark that hides my reddening cheeks. But the warmth lifting out of the lifeboat nearly makes me swoon. "Fine, but don't try anything."

"Try what thing?"

I don't bother explaining in Cantonese. Instead, I carefully haul my frozen limbs over the edge of the boat, sinking into the space he just occupied. It feels as nice as stepping into a bath, and the chilly bits of me are drawn even closer to his solid warmth. He covers us with the canvas, trapping the heat.

I try to hold on to some of my righteous indignation, but every part of me has begun to feel gooey, like butter melting across toast. "Look, Bo. We may not see eye to eye, but if you care for Jamie, you must want what's best for him. He's changed. Maybe you can't see it because you didn't know him before. But he used to be lighter, more carefree. Now he walks like he's caught in a thicket."

"What is 'thicket'?"

I don't know the Cantonese word. "A tangle of bushes. Like what rabbits live in."

"Oh. Maybe thicket is just life."

"Yeah, a miserable life full of muck, and thorns—"

Voices and footsteps sound from somewhere close by, cutting off my speech. We both fall still.

"Twenty-two knots at least," says a man in the hearty voice of one accustomed to talking over the roar of the ocean. "Mr. Ismay's breathing down Captain Smith's collar from dawn till dusk to up the pace." The leggy chairman steps into my mind. "Wants to take the Blue Riband from Cunard, those oily frigates. If we're the fastest, we'll get the Royal Mail contract. Then it'll be raining silver. You'll be able to get your girl a shiny stone for her finger."

Closer they come, their boots falling as loudly as the pound of hammers in a forge.

"Shucks," wheezes his companion. "She already said no."

"That's 'cause you're poor as piss," says the hearty man. "But our luck might be changing soon. Hold." His boots stop right beside our lifeboat. Bo has gone corpse-like beside me, but my heart bangs as loud as a drum beating to quarters. "Looks like a couple of"—does he see us?—"eyelets came unhooked."

My heart flattens against my rib cage, like a trapped mouse. Any second, they'll discover us hiding and figure us for stowaways, which is half-true. Images of me walking the plank or being keel-hauled across barnacles—the way Jamie said they punish sailors—bubble up in my mind. I'd be cut to ribbons, seasoning the ocean with blood and gore and brains—well, obviously lots of brains. Then we'd never get to perform for Mr. Stewart. At least Jamie would be sorry for making things so hard on me.

My breathing comes too shallow and fast, and I can't stop my limbs from trembling.

A warm hand slides over mine. Calluses line Bo's palm and fingers, interrupted by the smooth bump of his shell ring. Curled over mine, his hand feels like a safe harbor in a storm. His warmth spreads up my arm, interrupting the catastrophes reeling through my head.

The canvas jostles. I try to shrink further into my bones, the rush of blood in my ears sounding like a second ocean. But instead of peeling open, our ceiling stretches tight again as hands hook the fabric back in place.

A lifetime passes before we move. I'm not sure who lets go first. But when finally we open our nest to the cold air of reality, we can't scramble away from each other fast enough.

Bo clears his throat. "After you, Stowaway."

He shows me the staircase at the back of the deck where he snuck up. His plain peacoat hid his sea slops, and with few passengers afoot, no one stopped him.

He balls his hands into fists that disappear into his pockets, affecting a casual air. "Promised others I would meet them in the General Room." His face looks sheepish, probably a reflection of my own. "You want to join?"

"No," I say too quickly, still feeling the imprint of his hand in mine. "You go on."

His face relaxes as if relieved. "Good night."

———·••·———

APRIL 12, 1912

THE NEXT MORNING, I wake before the sun, my stomach moaning for food. The free box of chocolates I had no problem consuming for dinner—despite the obligation to meet the captain that came with it—are a sweet but distant memory. Remembering the pastries and tea, I push the button for service. Moments later, a female attendant shows up.

"How may I help you, ma'am?" She keeps her eyes away from my veil.

"I would like pastries and tea to be brought up in thirty minutes. Don't be stingy with the marmalade either. I shall be taking a bath. Please bring it in and don't pour the tea."

"Right away, ma'am."

I'm really settling into this role. How easy it would be to grow accustomed to having people jump when you tell them to. Maybe it's like breaking in a new hat. The more you wear it, the harder it becomes to keep the old shape.

While the bathtub fills, I pull the photo out of Mum's Bible, which I now store in Mrs. Sloane's trunk.

"Good morning, honored parents." I set the picture on the table and start wake-up drills. "Jamie's sore at me for winning that bet. But he'll get over it. He always does."

Then again, Jamie is still holding a grudge against Ba. And the Jamie I knew would never have been so eager to dump his family. I wrap up my routine and replace the photo in the trunk, my doubts circling like vultures.

Putting Jamie from my mind, I settle into the sudsy water. Getting clean even when I don't feel dirty is one of the best parts of first-class living.

The pastries are waiting on my table by the time I emerge smelling of bergamot. The kimono eyes me from the wardrobe. She's a saucy miss, asking if I'm woman enough to put her on. I take my time eating a sticky bun and a scone with marmalade, washing them both down with good English tea.

Fortified, I slide the kimono off the hanger. It seems to slink right over my shoulders, the little minx, making herself at home around me. Buttons hidden inside the garment keep everything together, and a deep toque in peacock blue provides a comfortable topper.

I shuffle to the mirror, not surprised that I look like a seal caught in a tidal wave.

It's just a dress, I hear April say. *You're supposed to wear it, not let it wear you.*

I wiggle back my shoulders and loosen my neck. Keeping my feet springy and my carriage high, I watch myself strut like a peacock. Not bad. Still, I cover myself with the vanilla coat. The peacock chooses its moments to fan its tail.

It's time to collect on my wager.

The sun still has not risen, and the hallways are dimly lit with the electric lights. I hold my breath as I pass Mr. Ismay's suite, as if he can detect my nervous panting through the walls or feel the rise in humidity. Thankfully, it appears he's not an early riser.

I take the lift down to E-Deck, marveling again at how buttoned-up the first-class corridor feels compared to its rollicking twin, Scotland Road, on the other side. The corridor empties me into the Collar, and I make my way toward Room 14.

Voices leak from the cracked door of a room I haven't noticed before, perhaps a storage closet. "Y'ar own bleedin' fault you got jackrolled."

I slow, recognizing the jaunty voice of the Johnnies' steward, Skeleton.

"You Bledigs don't got enough sense to pinch betwixt your fingers, gambling away the butter and the bacon in one night. Christ almighty." *Sniff.* "You're an embarrassment to the family."

A frown pulls at my lips. Bledig is the bloke who won the sweeps. Skeleton is the custodian of the sweeps box.

"He swindled me, I swear, Cousin," says another man. Could it be Bledig? Are they related?

"Shh, don't call me that. You want everyone to know how you won?"

"Sorry, Cous— I mean, sorry. Those Johnnies are shifty as sails. Got me on three nines. Nine is unlucky, you know that."

Johnnies. Something begins to pluck at my skin. I rub my arms, but the feeling doesn't abate. So Bledig lost his shirt. But to which Johnny?

A bloodshot eye appears in the crack of the door. I stifle a gasp.

Before Skeleton can get a good look at me, I hurry to Room 14 as fast as my pumps will allow. Without bothering to knock, I duck into the room and quickly shut the door.

Bo looks up from where he's sitting on his bunk, his bare feet flat against the floor. A ray of sunlight crosses his chin, where a bit of stubble has begun to grow. He gives me a questioning look, but I march right up to Jamie, who's sprawled out like he's in a hammock slung between two palm trees. I poke him in the ribs.

He jerks, and his eyes pop open. "Huh? Val, what the bloody hell?" He sticks his face in the pillow, but I wrangle it away.

"Did you gamble last night?"

He hoists up an eyelid, wincing at the sunlight.

"You gambled, even though you swore not to. I heard Bledig telling Skeleton he got swindled by a Johnny, and I know it was you. Just say it." My voice stretches taut, and even though I'm trying to keep quiet for the sake of the lads, my hurt has grown wings and a stinger. "You want to be rid of me."

Jamie rubs his eyes. "I didn't gamble, Sis," he says more gently. The beds rustle and squeak as the lads awake.

"Then who—"

"I did." Bo's words hit me just like the pinecone I didn't see coming.

"How much did you make?" Wink asks, all business, even fresh from the land of Nod.

Bo doesn't answer, but he doesn't have to. Bledig lost his shirt, a shirt worth . . . "Two pounds," I say wearily.

"So that's two pounds, plus their four shillings from yesterday. They *tied* us." Olly's voice goes round with amazement. Wink scowls.

Jamie, fully awake now, works his mouth but can't seem to find the right words. Bo stares guiltily at his feet.

"Well, Jamie, I hope you'll be very happy stumbling around that thicket."

"What are you on about, Sis?"

"Ask your mate."

The doorknob slips in my slick grip, but I give it a hard twist, needing out. And though a goldfish has as good a chance of outswimming its bowl as I have of fleeing this ship, I bolt.

17

I scurry down Scotland Road on the balls of my feet, tempted to remove the pumps and throw them out the nearest porthole. The drone from the boiler casings competes with the noise in my head. Why would anyone choose a job doing the same bone-wearying thing day after dreary day, a job that slowly pickles you with soot? Where's the creativity in that?

Acrobatics may be physically challenging, but at least you have something at the end of the day—a new routine, a new feat, some way to leave your mark. And Jamie is so naturally gifted, he nearly somersaulted out of Mum's womb, with me grabbing his ankle for a lift. In America, the opportunities will be endless. We aren't traditionally educated, but Jamie is smart enough to be a clerk. Maybe even a scholar.

Well, he can throw his life down the can, but he won't throw mine. I have five days to find and impress Mr. Stewart. Maybe fewer, if they're trying to break records for this "Blue Riband." My stomach contracts, feeling like an unripe lemon.

If Mr. Stewart is a dead end, perhaps I can bribe an official to let me into America. I'll need more pineapples to juggle. *Plans always half-baked.*

Passing one of the companionways off Scotland Road, I'm

surprised to see the seaman with the shaved head, Ming Lai, and the Russian girl half talking, half gesturing at each other, too immersed in their conversation to notice me.

The closest cabin door opens, and the girl's parents emerge. The mother is a slighter version of her broad-faced daughter, who inherited her father's sturdier build. Now, that is one father I would not want to offend, with his bulging muscles and thick neck roped with veins. All four head away from me, back toward the Dining Saloon.

It seems as if the threads of their friendship are continuing to weave together more tightly, despite the unlikely pairing. How nice it must be to have her parents' approval. Or perhaps knowing the acquaintance is only temporary relaxes the rules. Might as well make merry.

The brisk air slaps sense into me when I finally reach the poop deck. Few people are out this early. A different crewman—but just as puffish as yesterday's QM—paces the docking bridge, his gaze darting around as sharp as a Doberman pinscher's.

If Jamie had won the bet outright, would he have forced me back to London? Chinese tradition expects the oldest boy to take over the patriarchy, with duties like arranging his sister's future. But when have I ever taken orders from him? According to Bo, it's the other way around. Anyway, the Jamie I knew always valued my opinion. Like the time I suggested we pay a kid to bark up business for our show, which more than paid for itself. Or when I told him to stop wearing his pants so short because it made him look like a jack-a-dandy.

Maybe I did order him around a bit. But I never did it to be superior, only to make things go easier. I didn't want him to get his nose punched for looking like a dandy. Was that so wrong? But now he doesn't need me anymore. He has mates to make sure he keeps his beak out of trouble. And I have no one.

My mind returns to that bleak day when I fell into a coal hole while fetching Jamie from the widow's house where Mum sent him to help her pull weeds. Jamie found me hours later. He slid down the chute, and while I wept, held me close enough for me to feel his heart beating beside mine, just as in Mum's belly. He's always been there for me. But not anymore.

I bite down on my lip, which has started to tremble, and focus on the sky. A few clouds break up the blue. Trailing us, a lone seabird bobs and ducks invisible blows. I shall be like that bird. Whatever current life blows in my face, I will plow on to the next bit of sky.

"Little Sister," says a voice in Cantonese, startling me from my thoughts. The seaman with the quick hands, Drummer, slides in beside me. He removes from his belt a "whirling drum"—a double-sided cylinder with two corded beads on a stick. He twists the drum, and the beads lightly rap against the stretched leather. "There is much sorrow in your face."

I wipe my eyes with my sleeves. "Why aren't you eating with the others?"

"I finished already." He pats his stomach, which is so flat, it's concave. His laughing eyes are no longer bowed in merriment, but open and concerned. "When Jamie told us his twin sister was here, Tao was not surprised. He said twins always

150

come together like ginger and garlic. They can stand by themselves, but they are always meeting in the same dish." The sight of his grin tugs a brief one from me.

"The ginger and the garlic may be seasoning their own dishes from now on."

"I hope not, Little Sister."

My eyes grow misty again. I try to find the seabird, but it has flown away. Drummer is kind, but it's rude to burden others with our troubles. "Are you a fireman or a drummer?"

"Both. The foreman on our last ship knew that my drumming helped others work harder."

"That small thing?"

"I could not bring the big one with me." He shrugs. "There are many ways to make music. You do not need a drum to drum. Just like you can smile without smiling, and cry without crying."

A swath of brown-black hair falls from his cap, long enough to touch his peaky nose. Curiously, his face bears the dark streaks of those who work in the black gangs. He isn't employed by White Star Line, though, so there's no reason for him to be dusted with coal.

"Has Little Sister seen a boiler room?"

"No." It's hard to keep the bitterness from my voice.

"The ones here are much cleaner than the ones on Atlantic Steam."

"How do you know that?"

A sly smile draws up his face. He cocks his head back, as if to get the full measure of me. "I will show you. Come."

LUCK OF THE *TITANIC*

I FOLLOW DRUMMER back to Scotland Road, curiosity pulling me one way, unease pulling me the other. After falling down the coal hole, boiler rooms top my list of places to avoid, right up there with sewer tunnels and dark basements. But as distasteful as I find it, I want to see the hovel Jamie chose over his family. Over *daylight*, for cod's sake.

Drummer's eyes track the slatted road, and his arms swing like the corded beads of his whirling drum when he walks. The man is a ball of energy, like the sun, and just being around him warms me.

"Before I joined Atlantic Steam, I worked with the *Titanic*'s lead fireman on the SS *Viscount*. The night before we sailed, I ran into him at a bar, and we took a pint together. I told him I was crossing on the *Titanic*, and he asked if I would help him, well, soothe over the men, like I did on the *Viscount*."

"Why do they need soothing?"

"Catholics and Protestants do not get along. Music puts men in good spirits. Plus, work gets done faster."

"You mean White Star Line hired you?"

"Of course not. But it is my honor to help my friend. He will let you visit, too. But first, you need to put on sea slops."

I shiver as the memory of the coal hole looms larger. "Actually, I avoid dark and small places."

"Ah. Do not worry, Little Sister. The ceilings are very high, and there is much light."

I find Room 14 empty. Before anyone returns, I slip out of

my kimono and into my seaman's garb. Then Drummer leads me to a door into Boiler Casing 6 off Scotland Road.

He appraises my plain cap, then takes off his own, which is embroidered with the Atlantic Steam Company insignia. "Wear this one."

The cap droops over my ears and makes me look like an official Johnny.

A few passengers watch us disappear into the wall. We must look like we know what we're doing, because no one protests.

Inside, a small room houses a metal ladder that descends into a hole in the floor. I follow Drummer down the ladder, and a trill of anticipation runs up my spine. I'm reminded of my trip down the cargo hatch, only this time, I'm not trying to escape. The shaft grows warmer with every floor we descend, and the scent of burned coal mingles with the smells of working bodies, grease, and seawater.

I've lost track of how many decks we've passed when we finally reach Boiler Room 6.

From my perch on the ladder, I see four grinning black dragons standing shoulder to shoulder, their triple furnaces blazing like two eyes and a mouth. Trimmers cart coal in wheelbarrows for the firemen to feed the dragons, while others sweep the floor plates or monitor valves and pipes and pulleys and, well, things I don't have a name for. It's another universe made of iron and fire and sweat and sinew, and, yes, light.

Drummer jumps lightly down to the metal floor grates, and

I land beside him. "Welcome to Boiler Room 6." He spreads his hand toward the dragons. "Aren't they beauties?"

Our arrival causes a stir among the workers. Men of all ages size us up, though it's hard to tell their expressions under the grime. One shakes Drummer's hand, and others throw out greetings.

"Well, look what fell down the rabbit hole." A fellow with biceps the size of my head claps me on the back so hard, it's a wonder his hand doesn't get trapped in my ribs.

Drummer bows to him and introduces us in cautious English: "Brandish, friend."

Brandish pumps my hand. His hair is yellow, but the rest of him is coated in black, even his teeth. "Any friend of Drummer's is a friend of mine, mucker." His brogue is weathered and warm, the kind of voice that bounces children off knees. "Whenever Drummer's around, we all get along. So, you rattlin' our spirits today?"

Drummer, suddenly shy, waves him off. But then Brandish begins to stomp the floor and clap. *Stomp-clap, stomp-clap-clap. Stomp-clap, stomp-clap-clap.* Others follow, not just with their feet, but with shovels and whatever else they have free to bang.

Drummer's head begins to bob, and his fringe falls into his eyes. He rolls up his sleeves. All the blackened faces seem to watch him, even those still turned toward the furnaces.

With a grin like a slice of melon, he hands me his whirling drum. "It would be my pleasure if you helped me."

I give the instrument a tentative whirl. *Tat-tat. Tat-tat.*

"Faster."

I match the stomp-clap of the men. *Ta-tat-ta-tat-ta-tat-ta-tat.*

Intertwining his fingers, Drummer bends them outward, cracking his knuckles. Then he brings his clasped hands to his lips, blowing through the opening created by his thumbs. The notes of the shanty "Drunken Sailor" whistle from his hand flute, and after a few measures, the fellows join in singing.

Way hay and up she rises
Way hay and up she rises
Way hay and up she rises
Early in the morning!

Shave his belly with a rusty razor
Shave his belly with a rusty razor
Shave his belly with a rusty razor
Early in the morning!

Way hay and up she rises
Way hay and up she rises
Way hay and up she rises
Early in the morning!

Put him in the back of a paddy wagon
Put him in the back of a paddy wagon
Put him in the back of a paddy wagon
Early in the morning!

Way hay and up she rises
Way hay and up she rises
Way hay and up she rises
Early in the morning!

With every new verse, the stomping and clapping grow faster, and the shovels work more quickly, becoming metal blurs before my eyes. My own heart begins to loosen. I keep up my pace, feeling a strange elation at being part of this symphony.

Drummer begins jigging, hopping from one foot to the other. Then he is off like a windup soldier, threading past the boilers and emerging out the other side, where there are more furnaces and even more cheering men. By the time they hang that drunken sailor up to dry, water is pouring down Drummer's ears, and I swear the *Titanic* hums along a few knots faster than when we arrived.

Is it possible that Jamie has found peace here, a place that is anything but peaceful, especially with Drummer stirring the place up? Perhaps so much activity on the outside frees the inside to relax. It's work of the grimiest nature, for sure, but I have to admit there's friendship here, and family of a sort.

Somehow, descending to the bottom deck has given me a view from the top—like the lookouts in the crow's nest. For the first time, I can truly see Jamie and the life he has built from ashes. It's not how I'd expected it to be—dark, grim, and indifferent—but rather it's warm, even thriving. If he were to leave, he would never see his new family again. Though I still don't understand why he had to leave his first one behind.

Brandish, his face as shiny as a light bulb, brings a mug of water for Drummer's thirst. Drummer drinks, but his laughing eyes flatten when he sees my grimace. He offers his cup.

Propping up a smile, I push the whirling drum back to him and say in Cantonese, "The grain sheds its husk and comes forth."

He waves off the expression, which means a talent has been exposed.

Brandish scratches at the stocking cap restraining his yellow locks. "It's a grand thing you came down and woke the boys when you did. Captain's been pushin' us since six this morn. Wants us in New York a day early. Tomorrow, I bet he'll push us for two."

He wipes his face with his sleeve, and it's hard to tell if he's serious. But if he is, that's two fewer days for me to find and perform for Mr. Stewart.

Drummer's face bunches. "Why push?"

"He's lookin' to break some records. Wants to go out with a bang for his last voyage, methinks, which means puttin' her on the boil."

"I like to help, but . . ." Drummer glances at me.

"Please stay," I tell him. "I need to talk to Jamie."

He smiles. "Ginger and garlic. Good."

18

Instead of going to Room 14, I climb to the General Room at the bow for the soda water they keep there for the seasick. The thought that Jamie and I are on separate paths pinches my heart between two stingy fingers. I'm not ready. Maybe I'll never be.

A familiar cheerful voice reaches my ear. "There she is." Olly threads his way through the roomful of passengers, followed by an exasperated Jamie. "We've been looking everywhere."

Jamie takes in my greasy face. "Why are you wearing Drummer's cap?"

"He took me to see the boilers."

Olly's jaw unhinges, showing me a mouthful of sharp-looking chompers. "But how? They don't just let people in. How many boilers they got? Double-ended?"

Jamie nudges Olly and ticks his head toward the staircase, meaning, *take a powder.*

"Er, right. I'll see if I can find Wink and Bo."

We watch him return to the staircase, taking the steps two at a time until he is out of sight.

My brother turns a contrite gaze to me. Puffy half-moons—

which Ba called silkworms—underline his eyes, probably from a late night of watching Bo gamble. He passes me a bundle. "No heels. Heard about that."

I open the bundle and squeeze a chunk of bread, which is as soft as rolled-up socks. "How'd you manage this?"

"Dina Domenic, Ming Lai's Russian friend, asked for us."

One of the small tables opens up, and he scoots out a chair for me, then, with an awkward cough, takes the seat himself. I plop onto the bench opposite and remember not to cross my legs. At the table next to us, a couple of knee-biters stop pulling their mother's braids and stare at us, their brown eyes like juicy currants in cream scones.

Jamie smiles at me. "We used to pull Mum's braids, too."

"She'd never wear a single braid. Otherwise we'd fight over it."

Gesturing for me to eat, his gaze crawls back to the mother beside us, and a sadness shrouds his face. He rubs at a dark knot in the wood of the table, as if he can possibly scour it out. "She could've had a better life, maybe even a longer life, if she hadn't married Ba."

Mum avoided going out with us in public. Folks tolerated seeing a Chinese man with his Chinese-looking children, but add to that an English wife and you invited trouble. Jamie broke some fellow's nose once after the man called Mum a Johnny-tart.

"What are you on about? If she hadn't married Ba, *we* wouldn't be around."

"Who knows? Maybe we would be. Tao thinks each soul

keeps being reborn in different bodies until we reach enlightenment. But if Mum hadn't married Ba, she could've had
friends, company. She wouldn't have had to go crawling back
to the parents who disowned her."

"What do you mean, *crawling back*?"

Jamie tugs his scarf looser. "Remember when Ba blew
Mum's lacework money on those bloody rackets?"

"Of course."

"It was raining frogs that month. Mum didn't want us to
perform in the rain. She went back to her parents, begging
them for a loan."

The air flies right out of my lungs. We never met Mum's
parents, though we'd seen the stern vicar and his wife greeting
parishioners in the arched doorway of their church. "Did they
give it to her?"

He lifts an eyebrow. "Did we perform that month?"

"No." We hadn't starved either. "Did Ba know?"

He barks out a laugh, throwing his gaze to the ceiling fan.
It doesn't surprise me that Mum never told Ba. It would've
wounded him to know that she had demeaned herself because
of him.

"Why didn't she tell me?" I press.

"Why do you think?"

"Why can't you just answer a damn question?"

"Because you already know the answer. She didn't want to
spoil you on Ba. Bad enough that I already saw him for what
he was, a sorry sack of empty promises, the selfish bastard."

I slap the table, and the children's eyes widen. Their mother gathers them closer, shooting me a look of annoyance. "How could you say that?" I hiss. "He always tried to provide for us."

"You call what he did 'providing'? Each of his ideas was as ridiculous as brick shoes. Sometimes *we* were the only ones keeping us fed. You might've liked our acts, but I hated them. We were only kids." He slumps back and crosses his arms.

"What about the spiced peanuts?" Adding salt and pepper allowed Ba to sell the nuts for twice their cost to tourists. He'd made enough money to buy Mum patent leather boots with mother-of-pearl buttons.

"Sure. Then he invested the money in tulip bulbs. And how well did that turn out?"

I don't answer, remembering how the bulbs rotted before Ba could find someone to rent him a plot of land. "I know he wasn't easy to live with. But he loved us. He loved you. He always said you had a scholar's forehead. That you were destined to do great things."

"He was demanding and unreasonable. Besides, what makes a thing great or not great? Making a pile of money? Buying a posh house? Maybe I think it's pretty great to get out of London. To go someplace where you feel like you can breathe the air, instead of the air breathing you." His eyes follow a fly bumping uselessly against a wall. "When I finally got free and looked up, I realized what I'd been missing."

"What?" I snort. "Stars?"

His gaze finds mine. "Space. I needed space."

"From me." It's hard to hide the injury from my voice.

"Not you, Sis." His words have lost steam, as if explaining

himself to me has wrung him out. Unexpressed thoughts hover like the brown clouds that collect over London in the summer when breezes are in short supply. "Sometimes, it's enough to simply be at peace."

"What's that supposed to mean?"

"I mean, you're eating roast beef with real silver forks, and you're miffed about the bread. I know it's not fair, but you've got to lower your standards to be happy."

"It's not the bread I'm miffed about." To prove it, I tear off a good chunk and pop it into my mouth.

"I know. You're angry with me."

I chew without tasting and swallow hard. "Your friends here are like brothers. I respect that, though some of them are backstabbing adders." Bo's presumptuously handsome face appears in my mind, that wagtail.

"Bo's solid. He didn't want me to count his winnings in the bet."

"You mean, he wanted you to perform with me?"

"Yes, he did."

My skin flames at the knowledge that I misjudged Wagtail. "Then why *do* you count his winnings?"

"Even if you get in, America is as foreign as the moon. They'll eat you alive." His mouth tightens, as if he has tasted something sour.

I toss my half-eaten roll back with the others. It's true that I may have hung a big fish on a slender hook. Even if we get past the Chinese Exclusion Act, for all I know, a nest of hungry alligators lies on the other side. "You're worried I'll end up like Mum."

"No." He levels his gaze at me. "I'm worried you'll end up like Ba."

The statement squeezes the breath from me.

"Your whacky ideas. Hasty pudding plans."

"Hasty," I sputter. I yank off Drummer's cap and fan my hot face with it. "We've been talking about going to America since we were kids. And just because I know an opportunity from a spot on the wall doesn't make it whacky."

He glares at me. His eyes climb to my hair, and his expression softens. "Look, Val, you're my sister. I want a good life for you. I'd hoped a stable job in a fine home could provide that. But if you're hell-bent on going to New York, I'll perform for this Mr. Stewart with you."

"You . . . will?"

His cheek twitches with a hint of a smile. "Yes, I will."

"And I'm not ordering you to do it either, right?"

"I'm regretting this already."

"You're a sport, Jamie." I resist throwing my arms around him. *Finally.* A bit of slack in the rope.

"So when do we meet him?"

"Well, I haven't found him yet." I ignore the grimace screwing into Jamie's face. "But I know he wears a purple bowler."

A thought seems to cross in front of him, and a laugh floats from his mouth. "I've seen him."

"Where?"

He folds his hands in front of him. "Charlotte hired me to walk her dog, Strudel, around the Promenade Deck. I saw a man in a purple bowler reading the paper. Charlotte says he always sits in the same chair on the starboard side."

The fact that Jamie has seen Mr. Stewart nearly bypasses my brain. "She—Charlotte—*hired* you to walk her dog? I thought third-class passengers weren't allowed on the upper-class decks."

"She got permission. Apparently, I'm the only one who can calm that poodle. Dogs get seasick, too, you know."

"When does this walking happen?"

He glances at a clock on the wall. It's nearly one o'clock. "Soon."

"Does she know about your acrobatic ability?"

"We might have talked about it a little."

"Huh." He doesn't breathe a word about our acts to the lads he has lived and worked with, but when a hen comes pecking, the rooster's all crow. "Does she know about *me*?"

He lifts one of his well-shaped eyebrows. "Aye. What are you up to?"

"Would Charlotte help us with a little ruse?"

"Maybe."

"Can we trust her?"

"I think the harder question is, will she trust *us*?"

I guffaw. "She can trust *me*. You're a strange cove she just met. I wouldn't trust you."

He sighs and his face becomes serious. "Val, I need you to

understand. Even if we do get to perform for Mr. Stewart, I'm not going to America."

My spine bumps hard against the bench. I bite back my disappointment and nod gamely. If he thinks I still hold out hope for him, he'll take back his offer. "I understand." But even as I say it, I can't help but hope that once he remembers how good it feels to fly, to defy the laws of gravity in the space of a breath, he will change his mind.

19

Disguised once again in my kimono dress, tan pumps, vanilla coat, and hat, I stroll to our appointed meeting spot on the promenade, just outside the entrance to A-Deck. A small table features lemonade, free for the taking. I pour myself a glass.

Only a few stepping-stones remain for me to cross this river, and getting an audience with Mr. Stewart is one large but necessary leap. But he is a private man. What if he refuses to be baited? What if he doesn't have time for a two-bit circus act like us?

I chase away those thoughts. I've prepared hard for this moment, and I cannot watch the river rushing under me if I want to reach dry land.

Beneath an arched window, Jamie squats beside Strudel the poodle, stroking her ears. Charlotte stands on the dog's other side, twisting her heel into the deck and gazing at Jamie as if he's the world's last nut and she's the last squirrel. Her apricot suit with cream lace puts me in mind of the breakfast pastry I ate this morning. When she sees me, she stops moving about. "Oh! You must be"—she lowers her voice to a whisper—"*Valora*."

Strudel greets me with a yip-yip!

"Miss Fine." We stand the same height, though her arms and hips are rounder. She smells of sweet peas.

"Just Charlotte, please. The Merry Widow, they call you. There are rumors you're a young baroness and that you haven't spoken a word since your husband died falling off his horse."

Did April start that rumor? It is a good one. Tragic with a touch of mystery.

"Everyone is dying over your clothes," Charlotte continues. "I think you're very brave, going to America all by yourself."

Not all by myself, if I can help it. "We appreciate your assistance in getting me there." I casually lift my glass, only to realize I'd have to lift my veil to drink.

"So what's the plan?" Jamie gets to his feet and takes the leash from Charlotte.

Twenty paces behind him, a pair of women in fur coats stare at us. It must be me in my veil and kimono, which peeks through the open front of my vanilla coat and spills out the bottom like blue flames. But peering closer, I realize it's not me who has caught their attention, but Jamie.

Jamie cocks an eyebrow at me. "The *plan*?" he repeats.

I hope those women move along soon. "The plan is just play along."

" 'Just play along' sounds half-baked."

I inhale so sharply, the bee-swarm veil sticks to my lips. I blow it out in irritation. "If you have a better one, pipe up now. We're on a schedule."

"Yip!" Strudel chimes in. Her puff of a tail sways like a lady's arm powdering her face.

Charlotte combs her manicured fingernails through Strudel's curly hair. "Don't worry, Jamie. I'm good at play-acting. My great-aunt was an actress."

Some of my annoyance shifts to her, daring to play peacemaker between the dragon and the phoenix. Jamie needs to relax. How am I supposed to know what the moment will require? He's just trying to impress Charlotte by showing that he has things under control when he doesn't.

A crewman strides up from the direction of the women in the fur coats. He looks down his bean-shaped nose at Jamie, who's straightening Strudel's leash. "Oy, you ain't supposed to be here. Go on, now."

"He has every right to be here." Charlotte's buttermilk voice has become frosty. "He is my dog walker."

"Dog walker?" The crewman glances at the women in the fur coats, who have retreated farther down the Promenade but are still watching us.

A scowl mars Jamie's smooth face, and his chest moves as if a cinder block has been placed on top of it. Strudel stares up at him, her feet jittering, and I swear that little dog knows just what Jamie's feeling, too. It isn't easy having to be defended when your instinct is to defend.

"Are you so light of chores that you must stoop to harassing dog walkers?" I ask.

Charlotte tips up her nose. "Chief Purser McElroy himself assured me Jamie could be here as I required."

Jamie threads his arms tight, glowering ineffectually at the crewman's midsection.

The crewman coughs, and his kidney-bean nose turns even redder. "I'm sorry, miss. I didn't know."

Charlotte's smile swoops down on him. "Now you do. Good day."

I push my full glass of lemonade at the man. "Please take care of this for me. It's not to my taste."

"Certainly, ma'am." He takes the glass and makes tracks away.

"I'm off," Jamie says gruffly, avoiding Charlotte's eyes. "Good luck."

Strudel tugs him toward the bow. When he passes the women in the fur coats, he ignores them, though if it were me, I would've speared them with a good eyeball javelin. Jamie always outclasses me.

Charlotte leads me in the other direction. A deep alcove with deck chairs is beginning to fill with the after-lunch crowd, their gazes shifting between Charlotte and me. I can see the narrative changing with the observation that the Merry Widow has made a friend. We continue past the alcove to a spot with a single row of four empty deck chairs.

"He favors that one." Charlotte's gloved finger points to the chair at the end.

"Then you shall sit between us." I can more easily make my point by directing my comments toward the man instead of away from him. I raise the back of my deck chair as far as it goes and lower Charlotte's several inches. Then we wait.

Charlotte removes her hat and places it in her lap, where it rests like a brown turtle napping. A smile rides high on her face between two spots of pink. Crying fish balls, I hope she loses that look soon before she gives us away as mischief makers.

I should attempt conversation. But the things I wish to say verge on impudent, and I'm in no mood to discuss the fineness of the sunny day or speculate on when sea ice will appear.

To my surprise, it is she who opens the door. "It's so refreshing to meet someone like your brother."

"You mean, someone who can walk dogs?"

Her face breaks out in dimples. "Jamie makes me laugh. After Mother got sick, I thought I might never laugh again."

Who'd have thought Jamie could charm someone like her? Ba charmed Mum, but at least she'd been as poor as him.

"What do your parents think?"

"Father moved to Baltimore. The laudanum puts Mother out most of the day."

"Oh. I'm sorry."

She nods.

A middle-aged woman with a high collar of ruffles blossoming around her jaw plants herself right on Mr. Stewart's chair. She promptly reclines and closes her eyes.

Charlotte gives me a wide-eyed shrug. *Now what?* If Mr. Stewart sees that his chair is occupied, he'll leave. Then we'll have to wait for tomorrow to try again, and with New York just around the corner, we've already wasted too much time.

I clear my throat and say in a coarse and overly loud voice, "So when I saw the sign, 'Healer of Canker Sores, Warts, and

Other Burdensome Blemishes,' I had to go in. You know I've had these psoriatic patches on my cheeks for years." That will not help the Merry Widow's image, but the truth is a slippery bucket of water anyway, with all the rumors sloshing about. "She gave me an ointment of cod liver oil, pig liver oil, spotty toad liver oil, cuttlefish liver oil—"

Charlotte's face turns red, and she shakes her head, maybe telling me that cuttlefish don't have livers.

Behind her, the woman's eyes unshutter, and her small mouth opens into a tight ring. The feisty Mrs. Sloane had the same kind of mouth, just wide enough to poke in a soft-boiled egg, though she sure could raise a good fuss with it.

Charlotte's lips move indecipherably, and her eyes slide to one side.

"What?" I mouth back, then continue on with my monologue. "She said to smear it on the patches once an hour."

The woman scoots to the farthest edge of her chair. If she were a seal, she could just roll off and swim away.

"Pur-ple bow-ler," Charlotte whispers, making a pecking motion with her finger.

I glance behind me. To my horror, a man wearing a purple bowler ambles toward us from the bow, his attention focused on the folded newspaper in his hands. A jockey-sized man in a valet's black uniform trails him with a tray of tea.

I redouble my efforts. "Wouldn't you know, the pustules are crusting over just like blackberry crumble. Here, let me show you." I lean closer to Charlotte and pinch my veil with my fingers. "It's not contagious, usually."

With a horrified gasp, the woman makes a dash for it, her heels tapping with the fury of a typewriter delivering a shocking headline.

Charlotte lets out a heavy breath, and we share a relieved glance that surprises me with the pleasure it brings, like when a strange kitten cuddles up on your foot.

Mr. Stewart stops in front of his chair and tips his hat at us with barely a glance. He's clearly the kind of man who wouldn't notice women's fashion if it came up and danced with him. His valet sets his tray on a side table, then helps Mr. Stewart out of his chesterfield coat.

Mr. Stewart waves him off. "Tea, Croggy."

The valet presents Mr. Stewart with his tea, then stands like a potted plant beside him, his eyes hooded, the arm with the coat held straight as a towel rack.

Besides the purple bowler, the rest of Mr. Stewart seems ordinary. A plain sand-colored suit with a pinstriped waistcoat wraps his middling frame, and brown rubber-soled shoes look as faithful as a pair of beagles. It's clear the man values comfort as well as flair. His eyes are the unremarkable brown shade of Bosc pears. I put him in his fifties, with a round face that has begun to jowl. The Chinese believe that jowls are like "money bags," and the bigger they are, the more wealth they attract.

I switch my voice to Mrs. Sloane's forthright manner. "Never seen the like, juggling all those things with a pineapple on her head. The astounding part was how she managed to talk at the same time. I can barely walk and talk at once."

Mr. Stewart's eyes, which had been glued to his paper, lift.

Charlotte clutches her hat, her teeth snagging her lip. Maybe she can't walk and talk at once, either. "She?" she mouths at me.

Cod's sake. I messed up. Well, Mr. Stewart would have learned the truth sooner or later anyway. "Yes, Valor is a girl—Valora, actually. But don't tell anyone. She thinks people take her more seriously if they think she's a boy."

Mr. Stewart's paper drops a fraction, and he inches closer, his head tilted slightly toward us. Well, that's a happy mistake. Nothing catches ears like a secret.

Finally, Charlotte's tongue unsticks. "Well, coordination like that takes years of practice. She must be very disciplined. She was more entertaining than the Marx Brothers," she says stiffly. "And, er, the magician Ching Ling Foo. And Harry Houdini. Yes, she was better than all three daisy-chained together." Charlotte's voice goes unnaturally high.

"I gave her a whole crown," she adds more naturally, perhaps because unlike her prior statement, this one is the truth. "I would've given more if I hadn't stored it all with the purser. How long do you think that takes to learn?"

I nod, approving of her question. "I know for a fact that their father, God rest his soul, started them when they were toddlers. I've seen them perform in the park several times."

"They?"

"Yes, there are two of them. Twins. Both on this ship. They go by the stage names Valor and Virtue."

Mr. Stewart pulls at his whiskery jowls, staring out into the endless blue, though I hope his ears are on us.

I tuck my pumps under my skirts. "Their timing is impeccable, like two boots walking. They do these one-arm handstands and then grasp each other's hands with their free arms."

"That doesn't seem physically possible!"

"If I hadn't seen it myself, I'd agree. You should see what she and her brother can do on a tightrope. It's as good a spectacle as a royal pageant, but they fly."

Charlotte clicks her fingernails together. "I certainly would pay to see a flying royal pageant."

Mr. Stewart goes back to his paper. *Come on, Mr. Stewart, visualize the possibilities. Hear the roar of the crowd.*

"Well, once they hit America, someone big's going to grab them. Like the Hagenbeck-Wallace Circus."

At the mention of one of Ringling Brothers' rivals, Mr. Stewart begins fidgeting.

"There are certainly lots of opportunities in New York," adds Charlotte. "They'll be like two fat tuna fish in a sea of sharks." I grimace at the startling visual that conjures.

Finally, Mr. Stewart makes a throat-clearing noise. "Excuse me, ladies. I couldn't help overhearing your conversation."

At last. Charlotte slowly pivots, stretching her eyebrows as if she's peeved. "Oh?" Perhaps she does have a bit of playacting in her blood.

Mr. Stewart's deck chair squeaks as he angles himself toward us. "Did you say you know these performers?"

"Well, yes, I do." I flick imaginary debris off my coat. "Did you catch the show?"

"No."

"What a pity. But I'm told there's a good lecture on jellyfish tonight in the library."

The ocean sprays mist at us. Croggy wipes his cheek and shudders, glancing out to sea.

Mr. Stewart's bowler seems to frown along with him. "Unless the jellyfish can perform in a circus tent, I'm not interested."

"So, you're a fan of the circus?" I ask with mild interest.

"Albert Ankeny Stewart's my name. I'm an investor in the Ringling Brothers Circus, and I would love to see this Valor and Virtue perform."

"Mrs. Amberly Sloane," I reply. "But only Valor, the girl, is interested in acrobatic work at this time, not that it matters. I'm afraid that unless you have influence with White Star, you'll have to be content with jellyfish, Mr. Stewart. Official permissions are needed."

"The captain is a tough nut to crack," he mutters to himself. "How old are they?"

"Almost eighteen."

He taps his paper against his hand. "If I can get the captain's permission, might I impose on you to ask Valor and Virtue to give us a performance? No guarantees, of course."

I pretend to consider for a moment.

The *Titanic* sways, and Croggy braces himself, then shrinks farther away from the ocean.

"Good God, Croggy, it's just a swell," Mr. Stewart grumbles. To us, he adds, "If I'd known he was so fearful of sea travel, I never would've hired him. Imagine being afraid on such a magnificent vessel as the *Titanic*."

I'm reminded of how Mrs. Sloane sometimes talked about me, as if I wasn't there. *That pinhead Valora is always overwatering my pansies.* At least the eccentric Mrs. Sloane was usually by herself.

"We're all afraid of something, Mr. Stewart," I reprimand. I'm a crotchety old woman after all. "I myself am afraid of turtles. Nasty snapping beasts good for nothing but a tureen. I'd say you're lucky to have a servant loyal enough to face his fears for you." I nod at Croggy, who's back to impersonating a potted plant.

Mr. Stewart scratches at his jowls again. Before he turns sour, I continue with mock reluctance, "I am fond of those twins. If the captain agrees, I will let them know of your interest. You can leave a message with my friend Charlotte Fine here, and she will get it to me."

He switches his gaze to her. "I will do that, thank you."

Croggy clears his throat. "Sir, your two o'clock shave with the barber is coming up shortly."

Mr. Stewart pulls a gold pocket watch from his waistcoat. "So it is." He gets to his feet and touches his hat with his short fingers. "Ladies, it was a pleasure to meet you. I hope to be in touch soon." He moves off with more purpose in his footsteps than when he arrived, with Croggy following at an appropriate distance.

Something niggles at my mind. I have an appointment as well.

With Captain Smith!

Charlotte grabs my hands, which have gone clammy. "I think that went smashingly."

"I must run. I will find you later!"

The deck slaps my soles as I hurry away, scolding me for dropping a ball. May it not upset the whole routine.

20

Ba always kept a tin of peppermints in his pocket to reward us whenever we crossed the line. Now I'm so close to the end of this rope, I can almost smell the peppermint.

Perhaps I can use my meeting with the captain to my advantage. Mr. Stewart needs the captain's permission for the performance; I'm on the brink of meeting the captain. Here's a golden opportunity for me to soften him for the ask.

The guests milling around the Reception Hall of the À la Carte Restaurant glance up at the Merry Widow's purposeful descent down the aft tidal-wave staircase.

Captain Smith chats with a handsome couple in a discreet corner, looking anything but discreet with his ruler-straight posture and combed uniform. His striking white beard seems to glow against his sunburned complexion. The man to whom he's speaking stands several inches taller—he's at least six feet—but the captain's proud bearing seems to put him at the same elevation.

Nearby, the nobs drink and socialize on the carmine-red sofas. I pause, recognizing April Hart, who, despite her reed-like figure, seems to take up an entire couch. From under her flat beret, a cigarette wags like a teasing finger between her painted lips. She nods at me, no doubt having planted herself here for Mrs. Sloane's "big moment."

"I've no interest in the Blue Riband, and I don't know where the rumor started," the captain's voice carries across the room. "We are built for pleasure and luxury, not speed. People would riot if we pushed our guests out of the castle early." His audience murmurs in approval.

Soon the man's blue eyes wash over me. I draw closer and try not to breathe so loudly under my veil. At my approach, the tall man—a haughty-looking fellow whose dark hair is split into two stingy shares—peers down at me. He nudges his wife, and she raises her cultured eyebrows.

"My stars," she purrs. The triple loop of pearls in her auburn chignon bounce like a butterfly wing. A dress in the popular but boring color of taupe drapes her form, topped by a fox stole with its still-attached legs hanging as limp as four tiny gloves. I'm not sure why anyone would want to carry around a dead fox like that, except maybe to scare away birds or small children. She angles herself for a look under my coat.

Captain Smith presses his hands to his thighs. "Mrs. Sloane, I presume?"

"Yes. How do you do, Captain Smith?" I say in the stately voice Mrs. Sloane used to greet men of her same station.

Captain Smith snaps his heels together. "Sir Cosmo Duff-Gordon and Lady Lucy Duff-Gordon, may I present to you Mrs. Amberly Sloane?"

The woman doles out a smile as thin as a Communion wafer. "Please call me Lucy."

I suck in a breath. This is the famous dressmaker of the Lucile brand. I glance at April sitting thirty feet away, and she pulls her fists across her chest, miming taking off a coat. She even shimmies her shoulders. No doubt she already knows who this couple is.

Lucy extends a hand as limp as a leg of her fox stole, and I press it with my own.

Her husband lifts his wineglass and bends as if to get a closer look at me, but I shrink back. "Pleasure to meet you." His longhorn mustache flaps when he speaks, and a Scottish accent rounds his words.

"The pleasure is all mine." As casually as possible, I slide off my coat and roll back my shoulders. My kimono comes alive. Its tiny beads catch the light from the bowl chandeliers, spinning shadows onto the ombre silk. I shift my weight, and the fabric ripples like water during low tide.

Lucy clutches at her husband, nearly spilling his wine, her eyes taking huge bites of my dress. I hope April is enjoying this.

The captain's white eyebrows bend toward each other, like two hands praying. "Madam, I wanted to apologize personally for the mix-up with your room. I assure you, someone will answer for this grave, er"—the captain's skin blooms—"I mean, serious error."

My stomach does a backflip, knowing that someone might very well be me.

He gestures with broad sweeps of his arms, used to conducting crew and passengers alike. "If there's anything we can do to help put this oversight behind us, please let us know."

Here's my chance. It isn't going to get better than this. I remove a handkerchief from my coat pocket and sniff daintily into it. "I thank you for your kindness, Captain Smith, but I only require time and space to heal."

"Understandable. Lucy was just telling us about her latest—"

"Of course, Percival and I had hoped to enjoy our cruise together, much like"—I cast my mournful eyes toward Sir Duff-Gordon—"you and your lovely wife."

Sir Duff-Gordon pats his wife's hand, which is tucked into his arm, and she bats her lashes at him.

Captain Smith clears his throat. "Why, of course you did."

"We'd hoped to enjoy all the wonderful amenities the ship has to offer—the dining, the dancing, the Turkish baths, the squash courts . . ."

The captain opens his magnanimous hands. "If you'd like, we can arrange for you—"

"I would never dream of doing any of those things without him," I snap. "It would be an insult to his memory."

The captain's face deepens in color, and his smile disappears. He's a man unused to being interrupted, but I must have a bite if I'm to leave a mark.

Sir Duff-Gordon nods at me. Probably he's the sort who expects his wife to refrain from enjoyment when he goes off to his reward. Lucy frowns, she likely the sort who will continue doing whatever the bloody hell she likes.

The captain runs a finger around the inside of his collar. "Of course."

"If only there were some . . . spectacle that might comfort me."

"Er, spectacle?"

"Percy loved the shows. Horse racing, opera, theater. My life has been so colorless without him. Of course, I wouldn't expect you to have horse races or opera here."

"I love opera." Lucy presses a gloved hand to her heart. "The Royal Opera House used some of my designs for their latest performance of *Don Giovanni*."

"That docking bridge seems made for a stage," I throw in. May as well go big. I'll have to revise the routine for the narrow strip, but the docking bridge offers the most dramatic and eye-catching stage on the ship. "But alas! Perhaps no such diversion exists for a poor widow like me."

There. That should widen the hoop through which Mr. Stewart can toss his ball.

"Well, that's a shame." Lucy's head shakes lightly atop its alabaster pedestal. She crooks a satin-covered finger at the captain. "You really should have brought an act aboard. You said yourself the ship is built for pleasure. What could be more pleasant than being entertained?" My unexpected ally lifts her face to her husband's as if for confirmation, and he gives her an indulgent smile.

"I will certainly suggest it to my employers," says Captain Smith.

"I suppose I will retire now," I say listlessly.

"If there's anything else at all we can do, please do not hesitate to ask." The captain gives me a dutiful bow, and Sir Duff-Gordon also inclines his head. My eyes catch on the single rosebud in Sir Duff-Gordon's lapel, the same deep scarlet as the one worn by the cheeky headwaiter with the door-knocker beard who gave us the bread heels.

As usual, my mouth runs ahead of my head. "Actually, there is one very small thing. While I was boarding, a thief tried to snatch my purse. If it were not for the brave actions of a few Chinese sailors, who defended me and returned my purse, I'm not sure I would've made it aboard. I'm afraid I was too frazzled at the time to remember a tip. Could you arrange to send them some of those lovely candied fruits as a thank-you?"

Mum would be clucking her tongue. She swatted our hands with a wooden spoon each time she found us stealing, though she never "caught" us when we were really hungry. Ba would've requested a round of spiced rum in addition to the candied fruits.

Captain Smith scratches his temple. "Chinese sailors. Are you sure they weren't in on the theft?"

The air beneath my veil grows hotter. I remind myself that I am Mrs. Sloane, a woman who doesn't give a flying fruitcake about a slight to the Chinese. She would care about a slight to herself, however. "Are you implying that I don't know when I am being defrauded?"

"Of course not, madam." Captain Smith claws at his beard. "I'll see what I can do."

"Thank you. Good day." And I swear the man sighs at my departure.

But before I go, Lucy catches me by the wrist and squeezes my hand. "Oh, please tell me who your dressmaker is."

"Lucy," her husband chastises.

"House of July," I say in a clear voice.

"House of July?" Lucy unfurls a fan. "Never heard of it." Her fan picks up speed. If she stood on the bow, she could probably motor us to New York all by herself.

The grieving widow wishes for nothing more than to drift back into the shadows. But April is jerking her chin slightly to someplace behind me.

I sneak a look over my shoulder. The whole room has drawn closer, their gazes moving from the top of my peacock-blue toque to the bottom hem of my shimmering kimono. So, this is the moment April has been waiting for.

I remind myself to wear the dress, not the other way around, and walk in a small circle with my chin lifted, giving everyone a proper view of Mrs. Sloane's "style." A light applause sounds like the flap of birds taking flight.

Finally, I begin to make my way back to the Cabbage Patch. Glances trail after me, as light as balloons being dragged by the strings.

At the sight of a purple bowler traveling up the stairs, I hastily slip through the felt doors, then peer back through their oval windows.

Freshly shaven and with his chesterfield draped over his arm, Mr. Stewart crests the staircase and calls a greeting to

Captain Smith. The two men shake hands, and Mr. Stewart starts talking. Whatever he says makes the captain squint and grab his elbows.

Mr. Stewart gestures as if grabbing a star out of the sky, and then uses both hands to spread an imaginary banner.

Captain Smith frowns. His eyeballs grow twitchy. He glances around, as if searching the room for answers.

I duck out of view.

I shouldn't have made that last request for candied fruits. I overplayed my hand. Tested the limits of the captain's generosity. Then again, I showed myself to be a difficult, hard-to-please woman of means, the type most likely to get what she wants.

I peek through the window again.

Captain Smith is talking, back in command of the situation. Mr. Stewart shakes his head. The captain must be refusing his request.

But then the captain slaps Mr. Stewart on the back. He hikes up the stairs, leaving Mr. Stewart by himself on the landing. Mr. Stewart shakes out his chesterfield and slips his arms into it, giving me a good look at his expression. My knees nearly buckle when I spot the double smile of his hat brim and face, lit by the flush of victory.

21

Dressed in sea slops, I pace Room 14, waiting for Jamie. With each step, I start to worry that I may have misread Mr. Stewart. Perhaps Captain Smith told him no, and his elated face was only a trick of the light.

The doorknob turns, and Bo steps into the room, blinking when he sees me. "You found your circus man?"

"Yes. I think we might have a shot at performing for him."

He smiles. "I wish you luck." Stooping, he rummages through his seabag. His hair tapers to a curve at the nape of his neck, like a hook waiting for a wriggly finger to bait it. I watch the cliffs of Dover cord under his simple jacket, knowing I misjudged him but unsure how to express my remorse.

After locating a small tin of green willow salve, he catches me watching him. I feign interest in the porthole, listening to the papery sounds of his hands as he rubs them together.

"Bo? I'm sorry, well, for presuming that you—"

"Forget it. Jamie is a good friend." A frown puts a dent in his cheek. "But family should be together." His gaze drifts away and floats light as a feather to the floor. "I had a brother."

"Do you mean *have*? *Had* is for the past."

He nods. "Past."

"Oh, I'm sorry."

The moment rolls gently along like the *Titanic*. He leans back against the door and switches to Cantonese so he can more easily express himself. "He was like you, a dog who nips at the heels." He crooks an eyebrow at me. "Once we made enough money, An wanted us to return to the island where we grew up and build our own fishing boat—not a sampan, but a forty-footer, large enough to house our wives and all our sons."

"Sounds like a good life."

He snorts and returns to English. "You do not really think that."

"You're right. How do you stand living on the water?"

"I like the motion. Makes me feel I am going somewhere."

"Aren't you?"

He doesn't answer but instead fiddles with his ring. I realize the circle design is actually two teardrop shapes forming a perfect yin-yang symbol.

"Are those koi?" I ask. Koi represent harmony, as is created when positive energy balances negative.

He takes off his ring and hands it to me. Though I'm no expert, I can tell the artist employed a deft hand with his needle. The image is detailed enough to see fish scales.

"Where did you get it?" I slip the ring over my thumb, where it hangs loosely.

"This was An's. I made it for him."

"You *made* it?" I glance at his rough hands.

A wry smile crests his face. "Even a rock has its points. Sometimes men ask me to sketch their wives so they can remember them at sea."

Well, I never pegged Wagtail as an artist. Imagining his strong hands creating something so tiny and perfect fills me with a giddy sense of wonder. "How did you cut the shell without breaking it?"

"Rubbed it against a stone. It takes patience, and sometimes they break. Not every shell wants to be changed."

I can't help thinking that we are no longer speaking of shells. I hold out the ring, feeling suddenly conscious of the shape of him in front of me, tall enough to kiss the top of my head, and broad enough to shelter me on a windy day.

He takes it back, and his fingers brush mine. My skin grows rosy. The man is hard not to stare at, with his high cheekbones, clear eyes, plus the scowling mouth, which at the moment looks strangely tender. The cabin conspires with the sea to rock us closer.

The door opens. Without turning around, Bo swings a hand back and catches the edge before it swipes us.

"Hello." Jamie looks from Bo to me, and his eyes bend into inquisitive hooks.

"Where've you been?" I demand, as if I've been doing nothing but waiting here.

"Collecting the men."

Olly and Wink, both looking fresh and windblown, jump

up onto the top bunk. Tao and Fong slide into the bottom bunk. Opposite them, Ming Lai and Drummer, his face and clothes black with soot, fit themselves onto Bo's bunk, while Bo seats himself on a pull-down wall chair near the door.

Jamie's cheeks dimple. "Charlotte gave me the good news," he tells me. "Tomorrow on the docking bridge at eleven a.m., but only fifteen minutes. She said you were 'brilliant.'"

I squeal. I hope the QM will be on duty for our performance so I can dish some smug into his mug when I do cartwheels off his docking bridge. We won't be able to do the Jumbo, though. Could we hang a tightrope? Probably too risky on a moving ship, but . . . I snap my fingers. "We'll use the railing. It's sturdy, and there's a good twenty-foot drop to add drama. It'll be like the fence at St. James's."

In St. James's Park, an iron fence surrounded a grove of pink apple trees to prevent people from stealing the fruit. We'd cartwheel atop the railing, and its spikes placed a foot apart added a visual element of danger.

Jamie yanks off his cap, pulling up a comma of hair. "I said I'd perform with you. I didn't say I'd break my legs."

I bite back a response. After a bit of practice, he'll find his feet. One thing at a time.

Tao's face crinkles in concern. "Who is breaking legs?"

"I'm going to break legs soon if someone doesn't explain why we are here." Fong presses his fingers to the low ceiling of the top bunk. "Who stinks?" He glares at the sooty Drummer.

But as I cross the room to open the porthole, I notice the

chief offender is Fong himself, with the stale tobacco smell wafting off him.

Jamie loosens his shoulders and begins pacing between the beds. "Thank you all for coming. As you may know, my sister is trying to go to America."

Heads nod. Wink's brow furrows, and his cap slides down over his eyes.

Fong makes a phlegmy noise. "I wouldn't go to America. It is full of barbarians. They probably don't even have bean sprouts."

Tao bats Fong on the arm. "Shh, this does not concern your stomach."

Drummer raises his whirling drum. "How're you getting into America? You have papers?"

"Not yet," I say.

"That's why we need your help," Jamie says. "You see, Valora and I, well, we're acrobats."

Ming Lai, quietly listening, shifts to the edge of the bunk, a look of wonder crossing his strong face, which is shadowed with whiskers. "How come you never told us that, little captain?" he asks in his conch-shell voice.

Jamie shrugs. "It was another life."

Ming Lai grins. "You're not old enough to have more than one."

"So what's that have to do with America?" Drummer pipes up. "They need acrobats?" His leg begins bouncing. You could power a steamer with all the energy he gives off.

"Sort of." Jamie smooths back his hair and re-lids his

head. "See, there's this famous circus in America called Ringling Brothers."

"Bah. Girls should not be acrobats. They should be at home, performing housework," says Fong.

Jamie ignores him. "A very important passenger named Mr. Stewart might bring Valora to America as a member of the circus if we can impress him. He arranged things with the captain so we can perform for him tomorrow."

The men exchange surprised glances, and a murmuring starts up. Drummer gives an appreciative drumroll against Ming Lai's solid arm.

Jamie holds up his hands, and the men quiet. "That's where you all come in. We need each of you to help us, if you are willing." He bows to the elders.

So that's what Jamie's up to. I guess he has his moments. We *are* auditioning for the Greatest Show on Earth, after all. Now is the time to pitch all the coal into the fire. The other seamen can help us make sure the show goes smoothly, even add drama.

Tao interlaces his hands and shakes them twice, a gesture of appreciation. "Tell us what you have in mind."

Jamie glances at me, and I pick up the thread as easily as if we were sharing a brain. "Yesterday, I did some juggling and made more than two pounds off those upper-class passengers."

"Two pounds?" Fong coughs out.

That's right, old man. "Wink and Olly helped me, catching coins in their hats while I took my bow." I throw the lads a smile. "We'll need you to do it again, if you're willing."

"Count me in," says Olly.

"Me, too," says Wink heavily, as though the words have to be dragged out of his mouth. Is it my imagination or is he dodging my eyes?

"Also, spread a 'rumor,' " I add. "Those tend to travel faster than 'news.' "

Jamie plunks his elbows on Wink's kneecaps and grins up at him, but Wink still doesn't smile. "Yeah, and make sure to use words like *death-defying* and *shocking*."

"Drummer and Ming Lai, you'll be our barkers, letting people know of the show. Ming Lai, you'll also introduce us. Olly and Wink can help you with the words."

"I am honored, but why me?" Ming Lai asks.

"You've got the best face and a good voice on you," I reply.

"At least that's what Russian girls say," Drummer wise-cracks. "Oh, Ming Lai, do you like my apples?" He mimics a girl's soft voice, batting at his friend with his fingers.

Ming Lai kicks him. "I'll show you my apples, if you stop shaking your rabbit legs." All the men laugh.

"Rabbit Legs, I mean, Drummer"—I duck when he pretends to throw his cap at me—"I've seen you rouse a crowd. We're going to need some beats, if you can find a big drum."

"It would be my pleasure, Little Sister."

"Val tells me you have some connections to the men working downstairs," Jamie chimes in. "We'll need a space to practice, somewhere private. Could you ask around?"

"Somewhere with a good rail," I add.

Jamie grimaces, but Drummer nods. "Consider it done."

Tao lifts his serene face to me. "What about us? What can two old men do for you?"

Jamie's nose crinkles. "Well, we haven't yet figured—"

"Actually, we'll need you to acquire some props," I cut in.

Jamie's eyebrows peak, and Tao asks, "What props?"

"Two cups with saucers."

Fong's eyes light up, two glittery gems in a craggy landscape. Perhaps his taste for pilfering can be put to some use.

Tao's braided beard seems to stiffen into a dagger, and he gives Fong a hard look. "Only if we can put the props back afterward."

"Definitely," I answer.

Jamie purses his lips and shakes his head at me.

"What will Bo do?" asks Wink.

All eyes turn to Bo, sitting with his forearms on his thighs. He scowls at the men, an expression that I'm beginning to realize is only a shield. Unlike Jamie or me, he's uncomfortable with attention, despite pretending to be a wagtail.

Jamie claps Bo on the shoulder. "Bo's the boss, keeping all you clowns in line. Plus, Valora needs a haircut. Your hair looks like it was cut with a fork and knife, and it's too long on one side."

"It's fine."

"It's too damn distracting. Remember the blue stone?"

Once I found a pretty blue stone that I put into my pocket and forgot about. Later that day, I fell off the line and got a mouthful of dirt. Ba was livid when he found the stone in my pocket: "Every detail matters when you're up there."

I hardly think a bad haircut will unseat me, but if it'll upset Jamie's concentration, it's better to cut it. "Fine, but what does Bo have to do with my hair?"

Bo keeps his eyes tightly focused on the seabags swinging gently on their hooks.

"He's our barber. There's a barbershop on E-Deck near Charlotte's room. They don't lock the doors. The upper classes have a soirée tonight, so the halls will be empty."

My throat goes dry, and I gulp a few times to get the juices flowing again.

Olly scratches his nose with a cracker he's produced from somewhere. "Bo does all of us, except Fong."

Fong tosses his greasy locks. "I can trim my own hair."

I wonder why Bo doesn't cut Fong's hair. Of all the Johnnies, those two never talk or sit by each other.

"Just do not ask for a shave," mutters Bo.

The thought of Bo touching my head makes my stomach flip, even though it's just a silly haircut.

Jamie studies each Johnny in turn. "Men, whether we impress Mr. Stewart or not, whatever we make, we split evenly. It's how we've always done things."

The men protest. "But you're doing all the work."

"Keep your money for America."

"It's bad luck to profit off the sweat of another's back."

"Do I look like I need it?" says grouchy Fong, whose knee patches are nearly worn through. He needs not just new trousers but an entirely new outfit, and maybe even a new outlook, if they sell such things.

Jamie looks at me, and I nod. "Those are our terms. Take them or leave them."

Standing, Tao presses his palms and bows toward Jamie. "There is a saying: If you always give, you will always have. Thank you, little captain."

With that, the Flying Twins cross to the next stepping-stone. Only a few remain until we step onto the shore of a new world.

22

The men leave, each to his errands, and Jamie turns on me, his face grippy. "A rail is hard enough. But props?"

"I've seen Fong nicking the salt and pepper. Why waste talent?"

He gives an impatient shake of his head. "They were common thieves until Tao found enlightenment. What I mean is, why do you always make it so hard? We haven't done a show in two years."

"Where's the challenge in just walking across?"

"Routine can be peaceful. Like being a fireman is peaceful."

I snort. Still running that same racetrack. "It'll wear you down, eventually."

"Unless my sister wears me down first."

"If it's too easy, the audience knows."

"As long as you act like it's hard, they'll buy it. You're always out to prove something." He mashes his lips together.

I cough. "What do you mean?"

"I mean, why can't we just give a performance? You have to make it ridiculous, just like Ba."

Each of his ideas was as ridiculous as brick shoes. Well,

if Jamie thinks I'm ridiculous, I think he's ridiculous, too. "You're the one chasing a girl who's two leagues ahead of you."

His mouth wads up like a fist ready to punch. Straightening, I face him eyeball to eyeball. The phoenix may stand taller than the dragon by several inches, but he'll never cow me.

He crooks an eyebrow. "Remember how you thought it'd be a good idea to juggle eggs on the rope? You got egg all over that woman's head."

"She should've been wearing her hat."

A smile struggles to break free from his face. "I doubt the RMS *Titanic* will look kindly on us if we crack their fine crockery."

"So we won't break it. We'll practice, and if you don't feel good about it, we'll take it out." I whack him on the arm. "Let's do wake-up drills."

We run through the stretches, and then I clear the floor to let Jamie practice walking on his hands.

He carefully lifts one leg, then the other. Locking them together, he takes small steps with his hands. But then he sways, and his legs fall apart. He manages to right them.

"When's the last time you practiced?"

"It's the ship," he grunts. "It's like walking on jelly." Veering, he nearly kicks me in the chin.

"You're like a hog on ice."

He snuffles, then falls on his Queen Mum. "So maybe I haven't practiced as faithfully as you. There wasn't a point."

"Family traditions don't need a point. They're traditions."

"Wake-up drills aren't traditions. They're more like . . . chores." He rolls out his tricky wrist. Sweat laces his forehead and parses his hair into wet tufts.

"All the more reason to do them. No wonder you're a mess. Rusty as an old rake."

How will he get up to speed by tomorrow? We can't be out of balance. If he can't ramp up, I'll have to slow down, and then we'll look like common street performers.

Hauling him up, I push him into a lunge. I won't let this unseat us, not after coming this far. "Ready for the three count?"

"Aye."

I grip his shoulders for support, then step onto his calf. "Yut-yee-som," I count in Cantonese, then leap onto his shoulders, holding myself in a crouch. If I stood up all the way, my head would hit the ceiling. "Mind the drift, you goat!" The slightest wrong move can have great consequences for the person being carried.

"I am minding the drift. You've gained weight."

"That's rude. You've lost muscle."

"Don't insult the bloke holding your ankles. You and Bo aren't up to anything, right, Sis?"

"Of course not." My protest comes out too forcefully.

"Good."

"And what would be so wrong about it if we were up to something?"

"There's a reason you don't put a puppy in a cockfight."

"Who's the puppy?"

"It's not you."

I pinch his shoulder with my toe.

He jerks, and we both sway. "All right, all right! Bo's my best mate, but it wouldn't be a good match, Val. He's a fireman. He'll never be able to provide for you."

Just like Ba couldn't provide for Mum. Charlotte wanders into my mind. "Can a fireman provide for someone who probably stuffs her mattress with money?"

He snorts softly. "I would never even consider it. Her father owns a bank."

"There's a shocker." Despite my sarcasm, his words press two fingers into the soft clay of my heart. Who's the girl for Jamie? He'll never find her buried in the boiler rooms. There were few Chinese in England, and there may be fewer still in America.

Jamie's shoulder begins to tremble, and I jump off. He mops his head with a small towel that he must have swiped from the lavatory.

"So why's Wink so mopey?" I ask.

"He wants to go to America, too."

I blink at the idea of it. Well, why not? Wink deserves the chance to grow in the light of the sun, not the hot glow of a boiler room. Olly, too.

Jamie regards me the way a cat studies its shadow.

"Well, maybe I—"

"Stop there. You can't save everyone."

I fix a bright smile on him. "Don't plan to. Only the ones who need saving." *And that includes you.* "Let's get a drink."

Grabbing my cap, I swing open the door and come face-to-face with Skeleton.

He couldn't have been listening to us, could he? I curse myself, wishing I'd remembered to make my voice low like a man's. I also wish I'd put my cap on before exiting. I slip it over my head. "Er, hello?"

"Last call for the sweepstakes." The steward shakes the satchel, and coins tinkle. "It's a good sweeps, more than double the last. What do you say, fine gentlemen?"

His beady eyes linger on me longer than they need to, and his beaky nose sniffs. Does he recognize me as the person who overheard him with his cousin, the hapless Bledig? But I'd been dressed as Mrs. Sloane then. Surely, he hadn't seen through that disguise.

Jamie levels his gaze at Skeleton. "We're not interested. But since you're here, one of the men in E-16 asked to use the bath, and he said you didn't understand him."

That must have been Drummer.

"Oh, well, there are many foreign tongues spoken here. You can hardly expect me—"

"Next time he'll draw you a picture," Jamie says dryly. "A bath before supper would be ideal."

The steward inclines his head and leaves, passing Bo on his way back in. Bo closes the door and gives us a questioning look.

"I think he heard me talking like a girl," I hiss.

Jamie attempts a handstand. "Forget about that creeper.

It's a dumb rule, not letting men and women socialize in their rooms. Bet they don't have that rule in First Class."

"No. That would be too drear."

Bo pulls down the wall chair and drops into it.

Jamie lifts a hand. He still has the grace of a swan. But after only a few seconds, his arm shakes so much that he sets the other one back down again and then collapses onto the floor.

"Nice," I offer.

He makes a face. "You only say it's nice when it's not."

"It's your tricky wrist. You have to warm it up more."

He can't lose his nerve now. We haven't even gotten to the hard stuff, like shooting stars, which are ten times as hard on the rail. The distance between this stone and the next suddenly seems to widen before my eyes.

I shake out my hands, which have begun to fist. "Come on, Brother. It's all muscle memory. 'Tame the devil in your mind, and you can fly.'" I repeat Ba's old phrase. "Remember?"

"It's not my mind I'm worried about. It's . . . this." He gestures at himself.

"So you're no longer spindly. But we've been growing all of our lives, and we've always taken it in stride. Why can't you do that now? Practice and your body will figure itself out. Try the gunslinger again."

"I doubt I can manage a two-arm handstand up there, let alone one."

"You just have to work up to it."

"Stop pushing me. I can't do it all by tomorrow." He grips his temples, his knuckles whitening.

I cross my arms. I feel Bo's eyes on me and remember his comment about me ordering Jamie around. "I only push hard because I know what we're capable of."

"You know what *you're* capable of." Jamie glowers at me, and I glower back. Mum always said we were like the two sides of a railroad track; when one got hot, the other got equally hot.

"But I can't do it without you."

He sighs. Suddenly his glare loses its heat. Something has changed about him, a shift in attitude that leaves me feeling foolish and young.

"Want to know what I think?" Bo says quietly in Cantonese.

I'm about to say no, but Jamie says, "Yes."

"Either of you walking on that rail is enough to turn heads. I think Jamie should do the basics and leave the fireworks to Valora." Bo puts a fist over his mouth, the bump of his ring like a peeking frog's eye. I definitely don't notice how his arm muscles bulge. He catches me not-noticing them, and I quickly shift my focus to my big toe. "I bet she can handle herself."

Jamie swabs his forehead. "What do you say, Val?"

"So . . . no double shooting stars? No gunslingers?"

Jamie slips on that old smile, which fits his face as easily as his cap fits his head. "We'll think of something just as impressive."

23

Drummer finds us a space to practice in a cargo hold with a rail like the one on the docking bridge.

After much vigorous discussion, Jamie and I agree on a routine that, like Goldilocks's porridge, is neither too hot nor too cold.

Yet even after we've practiced enough to imprint it deep in our fiber, a feeling of unease settles over me, like a London fog that can't be blown away. Will it be too much for Jamie, after years of not practicing? Will it be enough for Mr. Stewart, who surely has seen his share of performers better than us? I hope I haven't oversold the act.

Tao says he wants to fast, and so I join the Johnnies at dinner, digging into sausages gleaming with jewels of fat. Again, we don't receive bread, and this time not even the pretense of butter. The headwaiter marches around the room with self-important strides, ignoring us. We ignore him right back.

I watch Jamie sling jokes and slip in and out of conversations with the Johnnies as easily as if he had known them all his life. The only one he doesn't engage is Ming Lai, who's deep in conversation with Dina Domenic, the Russian girl, despite lacking a common language.

Raucous laughter erupts from the other side of the room,

where the sweeps winner Bledig and the other bottom cut-ters are lifting their cups. Under his stocking cap, Bledig's face wears the ruddy sheen of one who has had a few drinks too many, yet he tosses back another and lifts his cup for more.

As if feeling my gaze upon him, he turns to me. His eyes lose their glazed look, and he elbows the man next to him, set-ting off a chain reaction. Suddenly, all four are peering at me, devilment in their faces. I can't look away. It's as if their eight eyes have become pins, trapping me like some insect specimen. The room seems to get louder and brighter, as if someone has raised a switch on the electricity, charging the air.

Jamie senses me stiffen.

"Those are the men who knocked us on purpose," Olly whispers.

Jamie and Bo cut the men a look, drawing their interest. With the practiced hand of an old fisherman casting a line, Jamie flicks out his middle finger, using his other hand to slowly reel it in. Bo snickers.

Bledig's eyes become two chips of dirty ice.

A door opens and out marches the headwaiter, carrying a silver platter of candied fruits as pretty as Christmas lights. Conversations shut off. Heads turn, their faces animated.

The headwaiter stops at our table. His lapel bears a fresh rose. "Sirs, one of our first-class passengers sends these with her thanks for valiantly defending her person and property from harm. Captain Smith commends you for your, ahem, *heroism*." That last word seems as hard to get out as a corn kernel stuck between his teeth.

Jamie's honest face wrinkles in confusion. "Oh, we didn't—"

I kick him under the table. "We didn't expect this, but we are ever so grateful," I cut in.

A murmur rises up as the news circles the room. The platter is set before us.

"What's this?" Fong sniffs a sliver of tangerine, then pops it in his mouth. "Tastes like the sunset over Lisbon." He smacks his lips at me as I gape. Who knew the old goat has a poetic streak?

Wink surveys the platter for the biggest fruit, a plum, and pinches it from the hoard before Olly can get to it. Using a tiny pair of silver tongs, Olly serves himself two cherries. Ming Lai holds the platter for the Domenics, who nod their thanks. Drummer chews his fruit with quick beats, and a smile crests his face.

The other diners return to their own now-diminished meals, though several sneak looks back at us. *Take that, all you Johnny haters.*

I hold up a cross section of lime to Jamie. "This one's for you, you limey. Mrs. Sloane is clearly a woman of exquisite taste."

Jamie gives me a weary look and doesn't take the fruit. "Congratulations. Now everyone hates us even more than they already did."

I eat Jamie's lime myself, then lick my fingers. "Go on, sourpuss. The captain called us heroes. Now doesn't that tune your fiddle?"

"Some here look like they want to break our fiddles," he says, eyeing a woman with a tight bun who casts us murderous looks as she wrestles her young daughter back into her chair. The girl points at our table and wails, her wavy dark hair spilling into her large eyes. Folks start staring at us anew. The mother unleashes a flurry of foreign words in a language that reminds me of the Syrian spice sellers in the Borough Market.

Jamie appraises our fruits, then cuts his gaze to Bo, who's chewing with an almost-baffled look on his face. Bo shrugs.

I know exactly what Jamie intends before he stands. He wants us to share the spoils, a gesture that makes the waterworks in my mouth dry up. We owe these folks nothing except for a good thump with a bread heel.

"Let's go, Mrs. Sloane, before your generosity gets us beat up."

"Leave it," I growl. "You're not the fruit fairy."

Jamie glances at Bo. With a sigh, Bo wipes his mouth on a napkin, then pushes out his chair. If Bo goes, then *I* will be the bread heel.

With a grumble, I grab the platter. I suppose it isn't the child's fault that the waiters gave us the bread heels. Still, why are we always called upon to show greater generosity of spirit?

The Syrian girl's wailing dries up as I approach, and her mouth becomes a red lifesaver.

"Hello, poppet. Which one would you like?"

The girl points to a cherry. Jamie picks it up with the tongs, but before the girl can take it, he flips it up into the air and catches it behind his back with the tongs again. Her face, which has gone from outraged to baffled, now lights up with delight. Even her mother smiles as Jamie drops the cherry into the girl's damp-looking palm.

Before moving on to a bunch of knee-biters at the next table, I can't help noticing that the Syrian group's basket is filled with bread heels, too. Somehow, it makes me feel better that we aren't the only ones who receive poor treatment, but also worse that something as mundane as a bread heel can have so much power.

A few turn their noses up at our fruits, and I feel snubbed all over again. But all the children, and some adults, too, gladly take what we offer. I hope goodwill is like bay leaves, where just a few are enough to flavor a whole pot of stew.

We breeze by the bottom cutters without offering them any. After Jamie flipped them off, it just doesn't seem sincere.

Once all our plates are licked clean, Jamie returns to the cargo hold to practice, while Bo and I hike to one of the enameled doors off Scotland Road marked "Emergency Only" that leads into the first-class area on E-Deck. I doubt needing a haircut qualifies as an emergency, but I can hardly beg off now.

"I'll give you a two-minute lead," I tell Bo briskly. "We'll be less noticeable if we travel separately."

Bo, watching a moth buzz around a light fixture, nods. When Scotland Road clears of people, he ducks through the door.

I hold my breath, not sure if I'm more worried that the door will open again and he'll be tossed out, or that it won't and

I'll have to go through with this bloody haircut after all. But when nothing happens after two minutes of pacing, I follow.

I try to walk as naturally as possible through the well-lit corridor. Jamie was right. The halls are empty.

Finding the barbershop, I slip inside and shut the door behind me. The bracing scent of musk and pine fills my nose. I feign an air of indifference, though my pulse clamors in my neck.

Bo leans against one of two patent-leather swivel chairs, his arms crossed, gazing up at an assortment of souvenirs hanging from the ceiling: pennants with the White Star logo, dolls, caps, toy boats. Against the wall, a display cabinet holds wallets, cups, and playing cards, tuppence a deck.

"Olly needs a new deck. And Wink could use one of those." I tap my finger at a bright orange kerchief, also tuppence.

Bo gestures grandly to a chair. "Have a seat. What can I do for you today?" He holds a hand toward a poster displaying a dozen hairstyles and a menu of services: sixpence for a basic trim, thruppence extra for a shampoo or sea foam, whatever that is.

"Curly top, please, with extra foam." I point to a picture featuring rows of waved hair that reminds me of a poodle.

The seat gives a stuffy sigh when I settle into it, and I place my feet on the rest. A dizzying array of tonics, combs, and brushes crowd the counter.

The thought of Bo's fingers in my hair sends zings of nerves through me. He approaches with a drape, and I'm seized with the incomprehensible urge to spin around in my chair.

Setting my cap onto the counter, I reach for the drape. "I'll do it." My traitorous fingers fumble the ties, as if I'm tying my own noose.

Bo selects a pair of scissors with all the care of a man choosing a dueling pistol.

"Don't take off too much. I'm hoping I don't have to be a boy for much longer." I never considered myself a vain girl, though Mrs. Sloane certainly has been wearing down her mirrors. But I miss my lion's mane. It'll take a decade to grow it all back.

Bo combs his fingers through my hair, and I nearly swoon.

Get ahold of yourself, you mooncalf. Those little tugs of his fingers are purely professional, and not intended to launch spikes of heat. Talk about something. Anything.

"So what do you think those are?" I jerk my chin toward a row of mini lifesavers the size of bracelets. "They must have some use. Pincushions?"

He turns me around to face him and holds my chin, his eyes moving from one side of my head to the other. A freckle and a tiny scar bedeck his upper lip, marks of imperfection that make his face even more interesting. He catches me looking at his mouth.

I'm certain he can feel the beads of sweat that break out over my scalp as he begins to cut. Who knew getting a haircut was so risky?

I retract the last thing I said, discarding it as blather, and throw out another miniature lifesaver. "Where did you learn how to cut hair?"

"My brother. He cut ours with a fishing knife. He did all the Johnnies, until . . ."

When he doesn't finish his sentence, I gently probe, "What happened?" I watch his face for signs that I have overstepped, but he keeps his focus squarely on my hair.

"A man drew a knife on our friend, who owed the man a gambling debt. An tried to help, but the man stabbed him."

"How tragic. I bet the friend felt awful."

A frown presses into his face. "Never apologized. But that is okay, because now, every time he sees me, he remembers what he did. Maybe one day, I will see him fall."

"Fong."

His scissors pause. "Yes."

I grip the glossy arms of the chair, feeling a little sick. So it isn't my imagination. Bo and Fong don't get along, and with good reason. I doubt I could forgive anyone whose actions harmed Jamie.

Then the only sound is the snip of the scissors, set against the dull noise of the engine.

Bo brushes his fingertips along my neck, and the sensation throws a wrench into my thoughts, preventing the wheels from advancing. Somehow, I've lost feeling in my feet, and all my nerves have rushed to the back of my neck.

Bo hands me a mirror, unties the drape, and dusts it off. The sides are evenly trimmed above my ears, and he left most of the length on the top.

"I look like a boy," I announce.

"You'd never fool me," murmurs his reflection.

His eyes appraise his work, but I can't help feeling that he's seeing something deeper in me. The first day I met him on the poop deck, when he heard me speak Cantonese, I bet he knew who I was and why I was there even before I lifted my veil. Can he recognize what's on my mind now?

I blush. "You didn't like me."

"I did not like the situation." He shrugs. "I knew how close you were, and I was not ready to lose another brother."

"Well, I guess you won't be losing him."

"I know you think I am a wagtail. But one thing I know about wagtails is that they must make their own lives. They need to wander to turn into men."

The words cut me. Jamie said he needed space. But we are a dragon-phoenix pair, two halves of a whole that functions best when we are together. Plus, I just missed him.

"I upset you. I am sorry. Haircuts are supposed to relax."

His eyes, dark as charcoal, catch me studying him in the mirror. I quickly return to my own guilty reflection, like a cove caught with his hand in the biscuit barrel.

I push up from the chair. The boat sways, and Bo grabs my arm to steady me. My feet don't seem to work well around him. I begin to pull away, but he holds on.

"Wait." Gently steering me around, he blows the clipped hair from my neck, setting off a rash of goose bumps.

I almost don't hear the click of the door as it opens.

24

Bo quickly steps away from me.

A man with a dressing robe over his suit appears in the doorway. "Hello? I was hoping for a service. Tried to stop by earlier, but there was such a rush." He puts on his glasses and peers at us. I wonder if he can see me trembling, or if he notices the flush on my cheeks.

I clear my throat. "Er, sorry, guv'nor." Mum's accent slips out. "We're just tidyin' up here." I grab the drape and shake it out. Bo, catching on, clutches a broom. "The barber'll be back tomorrow, and he'll clean you up right as rain."

The man shakes his head, which is fuzzy like a summer squash. There's hardly anything left to feed the clippers, but maybe when you're rich, you don't need a reason to spend money. "Ah well, I'll try back tomorrow, then. Say, you must know those Chinese boys doing the acrobatics tomorrow. It's the talk of the Dining Saloon."

"Right. It'll be one helluva show. Not to be missed. Tell your mates."

"Will do. Good night, gentlemen." And the door closes.

Energized by our narrow escape, we quickly finish sweeping. I slip a deck of cards and an orange kerchief into my pocket, then leave a whole shilling in the barber's tip jar, triple what the items cost.

"Close shave," whispers Bo as we hustle back to Room 14.

Once there, I place the kerchief and the cards on the lads' beds.

"Wink will like the scarf," Bo says.

"I hope so. What happened to him? He doesn't want to talk about his parents."

He leans against a bedpost, and a dent appears between his eyes. "Wink's mother died when he was born. His father beat him with a stick many times. He would climb trees to stay out of his father's way."

I grimace. A sudden urge to protect Wink makes me glance toward his seabag, the shabbiest of the lot. All children need their mothers, even ones they never met.

Can I take the lads to America? Perhaps if Lady Liberty opens her arms to me, her embrace will be wide enough to fit two more.

"You have left this room many times in the last second," says Bo.

"How do you think Wink and Olly would feel about going to America with me? I could 'adopt' them, like sons, or at least like little brothers."

His star-like dimple appears on the smooth plane of his cheek. "I think Wink would follow you anywhere, and where he goes, Olly goes."

His dimple seems to grow brighter at my surprise. I've only known Wink a few days. Perhaps I'm the first female influence on his young life, and never having had a mum, he somehow took to me. Something stirs deep within me. The bones of my spine align, and my feet take a more solid stance. As if I don't have enough compelling me to go to America already, two new reasons hitch themselves to my kite like tails.

The dimple dims. "But do not ask them unless you are sure you want the responsibility."

I nod. I have lived by the bright candle of hope. I know how it felt to have it snuffed out when Ba's winning streak turned sour. Caring for two charges is no small task. Stealing taffies and slippers is one thing, but in lean times, will I be able to find food for their bellies and a warm place to sleep? What happens when they begin to question me? They might resent me for being stern with them. After all, Jamie thought I was overbearing. Was that, at least in part, the reason he left?

The *Titanic* rocks as if exhaling a great sigh, and the shushing from the ocean is a strange kind of music.

"Would you ever go to America?" My boldness paints flames on my cheeks.

He holds himself still, and I wish I could suck back the words. Then his dark eyes laugh. "You want to adopt me, too?"

"No," I snap.

He stretches his back, his amused expression dipped in regret. "Even if I wanted to, I cannot go to America. I owe it to An."

"What do you mean?"

"Fong celebrates his sixtieth birthday next year." Mentioning the name of his enemy tightens his mouth. The Chinese believe sixty years marks the first full cycle of life. "I want to be there to remind him he has blood on his hands. Bad luck will follow him even into the next cycle."

Ba never made it to his sixtieth birthday. And neither did Mum. "If your brother cared for you as much as you did him, I'd wager he'd not want you to waste your time as a bad omen. Fong may not be a basket of water lilies, but he's not the one who killed your brother." It occurs to me that Jamie does the same thing, carrying around his anger toward Ba, even though Ba didn't kill our mum. They're both looking behind, when what's important is ahead.

Bo's scowl returns, and it's like watching a peony bud die on the vine. A coolness settles over my skin, and all my exhilaration seeps away, leaving only disappointment.

THE KNOCK ON my door comes just as I'm pulling Mrs. Sloane's warmest socks over my feet.

"It's April."

She sweeps in, wearing a simple emerald sheath with a cunning slit up the side through which black lace peeks. Long black gloves cover her arms. I never pay clothes much mind, but April Hart's clothes force you to notice them, the same as a tiger prowling down the street.

"Bedtime already?" she asks, eyeing my flannel nightgown. She strides over to the chaise longue and places her suitcase upon it.

"Early day tomorrow. Is your, er, plan working?"

She grabs my hands. "Forget the filet mignon. House of July was on the menu tonight." With a girlish shriek, she whirls me around, spinning a laugh out of me. Then we fall upon the bed and let the ceiling spin above us.

"So your crane *was* lucky."

She lightly snorts. "Someone asked Lady Lucy Duff-Gordon her opinion of House of July, and she said it wouldn't survive 'past summer.' "

"So, she has wit."

"Yes, but"—her eyes glint—"she didn't eat a bite of her dinner. Claimed she was seasick." April starts giggling again, and I can't help joining in.

A trickle of longing, like a sip of lukewarm tea, runs through me. Within the span of only a few days, I've felt the stirrings of kinship toward two young women, both of whom can never be more than acquaintances. You can't just climb a staircase to friendship. It doesn't work that way. But even friendships with girls occupying the same "deck" in life as me have been elusive. I relied on Jamie more than I should have. But isn't that the point of family? They're supposed to be reliable.

Sobered, I stand up and shake out the rose trousers dress. "I thought of a solution that will make visits to the lavatory easier in this."

"Oh?"

"Buttons down the front instead of down the back." I hold up the dress so she can visualize it.

"Buttons down the front imply you can't afford a maid."

"What if you concealed them, the way they sometimes do with men's shirts?"

She taps a finger against her red lips. "A hidden placket."

"Yes."

Removing a glove, she runs her pinky down the front of the trousers dress, as if drawing where the buttons might go. "It would take very careful cutting, and if the fabric is a print, there would be no margin for error." She grins. "Valora, you're making my bladder gladder. Say, you ever consider a job in haute couture? I could use a good mind like yours."

"Thanks, but I'm auditioning for the circus tomorrow on the docking bridge. Eleven a.m."

"I heard. But if that doesn't work out, look up House of July when you're in New York. There's always more than one color that suits." She winks.

I watch her unfold a black and yellow dress in a striking honeycomb pattern. "Why did you name your brand House of July?"

She lays the dress on the bed and picks off invisible lint. "It's named after my aunt July. She and my mother were like this"—she crosses her fingers—"until they weren't." Her eyes seem to dull for a moment. "The argument was over whether Aunt July had returned Mother's ivory brooch. Later, Mother found the brooch in her wardrobe, but before she could make things right, Aunt July died of a stroke." She picks up the dress and slips a hanger into it. "Grudges are like heavy skirts—

they're just extra weight. I design my clothes to be fluid and easy to move in, so that when life takes unexpected turns, you won't get stuck."

———·••·———

BA LIES IN *a cage hanging from the tree, looking like a pile of bones. His head has become more like a skull painted with skin, and his eyes barely have the strength to blink.*

Below him, keys of every size and shape litter the ground. Silver, brass, gold, wood, iron.

Jamie climbs to the highest branch of the tree, where he stands, gazing up at the sky.

I scoop up keys by the handful and listen as they clatter and clank back into the pile. Which one will unlock Ba?

25

APRIL 13, 1912

While we wait for the drumming to start, I pace the General Room with Jamie, sharing the details of my dream. Yesterday's intense practice left both of us sore, and we spent the morning limbering up. "I don't remember how it ended, but Ba's struggling in some higher plane, I know it."

Jamie sighs. "You ever think maybe he's not the one who's struggling? Maybe you're struggling."

Yeah, I'm struggling with you, trying to make you see the light.

I bite back my retort. I cannot pick a fight now, with our future at hand. We'll only get one shot, and after yesterday's hit-and-miss practice in the cargo hold, we'll both need our focus to be as tight as possible. Besides, if being overbearing caused Jamie to leave, I'll need to stop pushing so hard and hope he comes upon the light himself.

Drumbeats punch the air, and my heartbeat rises to keep time. Summoned by the noise, folks migrate to the well deck, where Drummer has rigged up a pair of oil drums.

After his bath, he spent all night hammering their lids into a concave shape, despite having worked a full day in Boiler Room 6. Mum always said God gave us two hands, one for helping ourselves and one for helping others. But as the marvelous *boom-badda-boom* shakes the walls, I can't help thinking that Drummer is the rare sort born with a pair for helping others.

I roll out my shoulders. "I wish our parents could see this."

"Mum never liked us doing the high stuff."

"But she did like our shooting stars. They always made her smile."

He shakes out his limbs, his jaw clenched. A wave of nerves washes over me. Jamie was always easy before performances, focused but relaxed. This Jamie is different. Older and more worried. I'm glad we simplified his part.

Just hold on, Jamie, and we will be okay.

Ming Lai's ponderous conch-shell voice trumpets over the drums. "Hear ye, hear ye! A most magnificent show is about to begin. Two of England's most faaa-mous aqua-bats"— Jamie and I share a smile—"are right here on *Titanic*, and they will perform for the enjoyment of all."

The drums crescendo. *Boom-badda-boom, boom boom boom BOOM! Boom-badda-boom, boom boom boom BOOM!*

Ming Lai waits for the drumming to quiet, then repeats his words, sounding farther away than before. We follow the crowd out to the well deck and survey the scene. Wink and Olly stand at attention below the superstructure, where the upper classes have begun to collect. Spotting me,

Wink grins, his bright new kerchief like a second smile on his neck.

At the center of A-Deck stand three men: Mr. Stewart with his eye-catching bowler, the White Star chairman Mr. Ismay, and Captain Smith, who surveys his ship with the sharpness of a roving hawk. His eyes stick on Charlotte, who looks both noble and tragic in the honeycomb dress and vanilla coat, topped with a black bowler and the bee-swarm veil. In her hands, she holds the cloisonné vase of "ashes" as I instructed her. The captain shudders.

I couldn't have asked for a better stand-in for the role of Mrs. Sloane. Charlotte is a good egg, and I can see why Jamie likes her.

The eleven o'clock bell rings at last. Jamie meets my eyes and nods.

We thread our way through the crowd, which, realizing we're the act they've come to see, parts to let us through.

Passengers fill every space on the poop deck, with some children straddling their parents' shoulders. Ming Lai's Russian friend, Dina Domenic, and her mother wave to us from their spot on one of the benches, and her burly father pumps one of his massive fists in support.

Eyes follow us as we climb to the docking bridge. When he sees me invading his turf, the QM's cocky expression curdles. I try not to look too superior, which will only invite fate to stick a foot in my path. Tao and Fong stand on either end, each waving a purloined White Star flag.

Jamie takes his position in front of Tao at the starboard

end while I cross to the port side, where Fong stands favoring his injured foot. He snorts, as if to make sure I still know he disapproves of me. Well, I disapprove of him, too.

At least six hundred people, the biggest crowd we've ever had, watch us from all angles, drawn by our enthusiastic merrymakers. I break into a sweat. My stomach feels like a troop of mini acrobats is rehearsing inside. I breathe in the salty air and try to relax into the present.

The sight of a familiar lean and muscled figure discreetly standing by a ventilation shaft places a strangely solid hand on my back. I touch my hair, which, thanks to him, lies as smooth as duck feathers.

Finally, the moment we've been dreaming of since we were kids has arrived. Sure, there are no gunslingers, and half our act has gotten lost in a steamer along the way. But as long as Jamie is still in my orbit, I can't help hoping my gravitational force will eventually bring him around.

Jamie raises an eyebrow at me, as if he senses my thoughts even from across the docking bridge.

"Ladies and gentlemen," cries Ming Lai, who will be very hoarse after this, "please to introduce to you Virtue and Valor, the Flying Twins of London!"

A polite applause rolls out, and Jamie and I wave.

Mr. Stewart holds up a hand, while beside him, the captain studies us with his piercing blue eyes. Mr. Ismay greets two women who have joined them—April Hart and her mother, holding her daughter's arm.

April's gaze slides toward Charlotte, and she coughs out a small laugh. She gives me an approving nod.

"Please keep voices down. On with show!" Ming Lai cries.

Clouds cover the sun like hands over a face, as if the sun isn't brave enough to watch.

Time to give them something they've never seen before. We shall strike our feet upon the wire, and light a fire in the sky.

I look at my brother and blow a dandelion puff of air. He blows back. We are ready.

26

Jamie, who will start us out, fills his lungs with a breath, then expels it. The ship cruises at a moderate pace, which feels as steady as a skate across ice—a few bumps here and there, but nothing to throw one off course. Today seems especially calm.

If you aren't walking on a rail.

A zing of nerves for Jamie shoots through my belly. Most people believe that we can captain only our own ship, but I've always believed I could influence him from afar, just like the times I would call him with my mind and he'd turn my way.

He climbs onto the one-inch-thick rail. A hush falls over the decks. With his feet spaced perfectly, he balances, averting his gaze from the twenty-foot drop to the poop deck.

I envision for him a path where there is no falling. Only lightness, air, and wings. Tuning out the gasps and murmurs, I focus on pulling Jamie toward me, like a kite on a string. *One step, two, three, four*—a bobble, but he holds on—*five, six, seven, eight, nine*—he smiles as he nears—*ten*. He hops off the rail and lands beside me.

People clap, but Drummer tosses off a few drumbeats, and the crowd silences again.

Now people know what to expect. From here, it will grow harder.

"Ready," I tell Jamie, and he nods. Climbing the rail again, he takes the first step.

I alight behind him, and we step in time. When we reach the middle, he sinks into a lunge.

Visualizing a brick staircase, I step onto Jamie's calf and place my hands on his shoulders. "Yut-yee-som." In one smooth motion, I leap onto his shoulders and hold my crouched position.

The ship rocks, or maybe it's Jamie, but we hang on, with him poised under me like a crane wearing a sunhat.

Below us, the QM sucks in a breath, his hand flying to his chest. I imagine him as one of the brass instruments installed on the docking bridge, a telegraph perhaps, with its open face and jaunty hardware.

"God almighty, they'll kill themselves!" cries someone.

Life is a balancing act, and the better you get at juggling, the better you get at living. You could be killed walking down the street, but you don't let that fear stop you. You just practice until the fear is no longer part of the equation.

Of course, to the audience, the fear is everything. People want to see you in jeopardy; they want to feel the terror they imagine you must feel and then experience the sweet relief when you reach the end without falling.

Well, maybe the fear isn't *everything*. Watching an acrobat is also just brilliant fun.

Time to move. I zero in on the rail, visualizing it as solid and wide as the quay at Southampton. After another "yut-yee-som," I finish the leapfrog over Jamie.

Light as a bubble, I land on the rail with my feet in a line.

More clapping punctures the air. I breathe, and we make our way back to the starboard end and jump off.

"Bravo!"

"How'd they do that?"

"Saints almighty, they must have wings."

Drummer drums, and we prepare for the next trick. Jamie gives me a smile. We never encourage each other out loud, because fate has big ears.

Tao hands me a cup and saucer, which I make an elaborate show of placing on my head.

"No! Is he going to?"

"Blimey, of course he's going to."

Still tucked into one corner of A-Deck, Charlotte Fine stands as still and resolute as a lady waiting for her sailor to come home from sea.

Steady now, Jamie. "Ready," I tell him.

Back up onto the railing we go, me one pace behind him again. My teacup rattles against the saucer with each step. When we reach the middle, Jamie lowers into the lunge, and I prepare to mount his shoulders.

Lightness. Air. Wings.

I give the count, then push off his calf onto his shoulders.

One foot nearly slips, but Jamie catches my ankle. He grips the rail with his toes as if gravity doesn't exist and we might fall off the world.

Gasps escape. A woman cries out. A child whimpers.

Now for the second part of the leapfrog. I give the count, willing the crockery to stay put.

And I leap.

The cup and saucer lift off my head a fraction. But as I land, they manage to stay on the saddle.

We make it back to the port side, then dismount.

Fong produces his teacup and saucer. This will be our last trick, the final test. I avoid looking at the audience, especially Mr. Stewart.

One more crossing and we'll have done what no one has done before, and not just because this is the *Titanic*'s maiden voyage. We'll have danced on air. *For you, Mum and Ba.* We'll have made everyone see not just a couple of worthless Johnnies, but Virtue and Valor, *your flying twins.*

Something glints below. My breath snags at the sight of the four bottom cutters, not twenty feet away, their backs against the outer rail and devilment in their eyes. Peanut shells fall from their hands. Bledig lifts a bottle of ale to me, and I blink as the glare off it blinds me for a moment.

Shut them out, girl. Don't you dare let them unnerve you. Not in your moment of triumph.

Filling my lungs, I let the air sweep the worries from my mind and the tension from my shoulders.

Jamie places Fong's teacup and saucer on his head. I square my crockery as well.

Carefully climbing back onto the rail, we make our way to the middle once more. I can almost hear the breaths held, almost see the eyes opened wide, as they wonder what we'll do next. Surely, not the leapfrog again, not with a teacup and saucer on *both* of our heads.

My legs shake with the tension of holding still. Sweat dribbles down my scalp and pools in my ears. I place my foot on Jamie's calf, feeling him tremble as well.

"Yut-yee-som."

I leap.

Jamie's shoulders hold steady, his teacup barely making a sound against its saucer.

I visualize a steady road in front of me, give the count again, and jump.

Something small, like a pebble, glances off my shoulder. My balance crumples, and my teacup and saucer fly off my head.

27

People shriek, even the QM, who gusts out a high note like a soprano.

I manage to land on my feet, though I wobble around for at least five seconds.

Guffaws from the direction of the bottom cutters reach my ears. One of them has taken a step away from the rest, his arm recoiling as if he has just thrown a pitch. Did *he* throw the pebble?

Not a pebble, but a peanut.

Somehow, I find my balance atop the rail.

I realize I didn't hear a crash. Only the rain of applause and hurrahs and exclamations. Out of the corner of my eye, I catch a glimpse of Jamie's hand. He caught my saucer *and* my teacup.

"Encore! Bravo! Eccellente!" they cry.

Well done, Brother. You still have the touch.

I can almost feel the glow of his smug grin behind me. Several female voices sigh loudly. He must be breaking a few hearts. I wonder if I'm breaking any hearts.

Together we reach the end of the line and jump off.

The clapping grows louder as we take our bows. I open my

arms wide to take it all in, feeling tears come to my eyes. The routine wasn't as flashy as the Jumbo, but something tells me it moved people. I exhale, relaxing for the first time in days. The hard part is over.

"That was close." Jamie rolls his wrist in front of my nose. "Good thing the last name's Luck."

"You've missed it, haven't you?" I gush, wanting to bark like a sea lion.

Jamie lets out a good-natured laugh. "I did, Sis."

Just as I thought. But before he notices my triumphant grin, I wipe the slate clean.

"Bledig's crew threw a peanut at me."

Jamie cuts his eyes at the men and hisses through his teeth. "Those dogs. They'll pay for that."

The applause doesn't end even after we've bowed in every direction, taking an especially long bow away from those bottom cutters to afford them a good view of our Queen Mums. Mr. Stewart claps with vigor, while Captain Smith and Mr. Ismay receive congratulations, as if they were the ones crawling on the rails. April yells and cheers along with the men.

Below us, Wink and Olly collect tips while Bo and Ming Lai help Drummer move his drums away.

Jamie is watching Charlotte, who seems to be watching him back through Mrs. Sloane's veil. With a nod, Charlotte begins to leave. But then the boat dips slightly, and as she tries to catch her balance, she stumbles. Jamie sucks in his breath.

To my horror, I watch the vase slip out of Charlotte's grip and crack. Tobacco spills, and the dry particles blow about in the breeze. A steward helps her up. I catch a glimpse of mutton-chop whiskers, and my jaw drops. "It's Steward Latimer."

"Who?"

The steward spreads his arms to divert people from the mess, and Charlotte, whom I'd warned not to talk to anyone, hurries away.

"Mrs. Sloane's steward. He'll know the ashes are fake."

Jamie watches the silent curses backing up in me. Steward Latimer has been nothing but kind to me, and the notion of him discovering my lie drops a stone in my stomach. I will need to follow the lie with another.

He shrugs. "So? You're an eccentric old bat. Don't worry about it."

The lunch bugle at last disperses the crowd, and Jamie, Bo, and I finally troop back to Room 14. Olly and Wink are chattering excitedly over the money on their bunk, the sight of which pushes worries over Steward Latimer from my mind.

Olly scoops up a pile and lets it fall through his fingers. "We're bleeding rich. We belong up there with the nobs now. Wink and I counted sixty-odd pounds here, plus a bunch of coins we don't know how to count."

The jangle of coins reminds me of the swingy rag "Opportunity." That's seven pounds per Johnny, a whole month's wages.

Olly bites down on a gold coin that doesn't look English. "If I was going to America, the first thing I'd buy is an Oreo biscuit. Heard tell it's like eating chocolate cake and hardtack in one bite. That or muscles the size of Mr. Domenic's."

Jamie chortles. "That's out of your budget."

"But you *could* get muscles the size of Bo's," Wink pipes up.

"Get in line," Bo mutters. We all laugh, and Bo pulls Wink's cap over his eyes.

Then Jamie does a handstand in the middle of the beds. Letting his legs spread, he carefully lifts one hand from the floor and holds his position, looking like a seabird flexing its wings. The lads clap and holler, and hope rises in my chest.

Jamie is remembering how it feels to fly.

———··———

THE HOUR APPROACHES when Mr. Stewart is due on his deck chair. Judging by his reaction, the man liked what he saw, but if he didn't, Mrs. Sloane will find out.

I don the honeycomb dress, vanilla coat, and bowler, which Charlotte sent to Room 14 in a traveling valise. Wrapping our treasure in two towel bundles so they don't make noise, I carry it in the valise to the safety of Mrs. Sloane's room, rehearsing what to say to Steward Latimer in case I run into him. Fortunately, he does not appear. After I add our earnings to the seat cushion, reserving a few coins for my pocket, I make my way to the Promenade.

Jamie and the banker's daughter are already deep in conversation next to the lemonade stand by the time I arrive. Charlotte wrings her hands as she speaks, a dress of dotted swiss swishing as she fidgets. Strudel paces between them, issuing a yip-yip! when she sees me. Charlotte sucks in air through her teeth. "I'm sorry for my clumsiness."

I fix my lips into a reassuring smile. "You did well today, and we appreciate it."

"I did?" Charlotte looks from me to Jamie.

He nods. "Absolutely."

Before they stare each other's eyes dry, I pipe up, "We'd better get moving before someone steals our seats."

Jamie and Strudel pad off in one direction, Charlotte and I in the other. We find Mr. Stewart's deck chair empty, and fortunately, so are the ones next to it. But after ten minutes of making small talk, the man still hasn't shown.

Charlotte watches me glance around for the dozenth time. "Maybe he's drawing up a contract right now. Or maybe he's sending a telegram to Ringling Brothers and telling them the good news."

I brighten at the prospect, but then my mind switches directions. Perhaps he's trying to avoid Mrs. Sloane. Maybe he enjoyed the act, but it wasn't up to snuff. Where would that leave Jamie and me? My bones sink more heavily into the chair. Without a way into America, Jamie will continue on to Cuba. I will have no choice but to return to England. A band of sweat collects around my forehead, and I stop myself from tearing off my hat and fanning myself with it.

Jamie appears a hundred feet away with Strudel tugging him forward. I shake my head at him, and he continues back the way he came.

Charlotte watches him leave. "If the news is good, is there any"—she licks her lips—"*possibility* that Jamie would go with you to America?"

I cannot see her face, but perhaps she doesn't want me to read it. "That's my hope, though he has other plans."

She points her delicate chin at me, and her soft eyes press for more.

The sea coughs up mist, and with it, a rainbow shimmers in the air, stirring a memory in me. "Jamie and I always wanted a pet. One day, during a break in the rain, we saw a rainbow, and that meant it was a lucky day. So, we decided to sneak a baby heron out of the London Zoo."

Charlotte gasps. "Oh, my!"

"We got halfway home before Mum discovered it in Jamie's jacket and made us give it back. You know how she punished us?"

"How?"

"She kept us apart—it was the worst thing she could do. We were as miserable as a pair of trousers torn in half." I draw up my knees and lace my hands over them. "We used to be inseparable. But now he wants to shovel coal." I lean my head against the back of the chair, grateful once again for the veil. "When your family falls apart, it's a knife twisted in slowly."

Charlotte nods, fiddling absently with one of the buttons that trail down her front like glittery ants. Her hands are as smooth as magnolia petals and don't bear a single freckle. I hide my own hands, suddenly feeling like the imposter that I am.

"I know that feeling. Father wanted Mother to be a socialite, which he thought would be good for business. He considered her work with the Home for Little Souls to be beneath her. But the more parties Father pushed her to attend, the more she resented him. He stopped pushing after she got sick, but they rarely talk now. And the funny thing is, she loved my father before."

Am I like Charlotte's father, wanting Jamie to be someone he's not? I know Jamie prefers the view of the sky from the ground, not up in the air like me. But the circus is a means to an end. If Mr. Stewart comes through, we'll get the chance to shoot the three balls of fame, fortune, and a future in America, all with one swift jab of the cue stick. How could anyone turn down such an opportunity?

Jamie pops up again, this time stopping in front of our chairs. At the sight of him, Charlotte's lips bloom like a rosebud unfurling.

"No-show," I inform him.

Strudel puts her paws on Charlotte's lap, and she strokes the dog's curly head. Without warning, the dog jumps down and begins scratching and growling at the floor.

"Hey, pups," says Jamie. "What's down there?"

"It's the rats." Charlotte's face still manages to look pretty despite the statement. "She has the nose of a bloodhound. Once, Mother's favorite gelding wandered off, and Strudel found it at the end of Central Park, two miles away."

Strudel stops growling and paces between the deck chairs, looking up at Jamie.

"Looks like someone wants to walk more." Jamie gives the dog a vigorous scratching. "Guess you've got twice as many legs, don't you?" He stretches his back. "We'll do another circuit, see if we can't find your Mr. Stewart."

"If you don't mind, I'd like to join Jamie." Charlotte's dark lashes flutter from me to him.

"Why should I mind? I'll wait here."

The two walk far enough apart not to attract attention but close enough to converse. Charlotte moves with a gentle sway, her hat dipping toward him often.

It could be my imagination, but I swear Jamie's walking taller than before, with a higher-held chin, even a little swagger. If Charlotte asked him to come to America with her, would he go? Or would the siren call of the boiler rooms drown out even her pleas? If so, he would definitely have taken leave of his senses. A fine lady with money and a backbone doesn't come along every day. And neither do sisters.

I count 117 passengers who pass in front of me, including three dogs, eleven children, and one baby—but no Mr. Stewart. Gazes still linger on me, but folks are less interested in the Merry Widow than talking about the acrobats. If I were less worried about finding Mr. Stewart, I might savor the victory of outshining myself.

To pass the time, I read the *Atlantic Daily Bulletin*, a copy of which has been posted on the wall of the deckhouse behind me, and consume two glasses of lemonade and four oatmeal biscuits under my veil. By the time the pair returns, my bladder is madder.

Jamie crouches by my chair. "I know it's not your favorite thing to do, but wait. If Stewart wants you badly enough, he'll find you. Come meet us for dinner. The men want to celebrate."

"What's there to celebrate?" I grumble.

"A successful and lucrative show. Bo won't be there. He's doing sketches for passengers, so there'll be an extra spot at the table."

"Fine." At least it'll take my mind off the man with the purple bowler.

———.•••.———

To my surprise, a new steward stands by the window in B-64, a folded towel over his arm. "Oh, Mrs. Sloane. I was just tidying your room." He clasps his hands and angles his head of thinning hair solicitously.

"Steward Latimer tidied it this morning."

"Wonderful. I shall be on my way, then."

"Is he . . . around?"

"I'm afraid Steward Latimer is now attending another floor."

"But why?"

"I'm not quite sure. Is there anything I can get you?"

"No. No, thank you."

The door thuds ominously behind him. Did Steward Latimer request the move, or was he reassigned? With the choicest rooms in the Cabbage Patch, why would he want to work elsewhere? On the other hand, maybe the choicest rooms come with the fussiest occupants—Mr. Ismay, for example.

And Mrs. Sloane?

Maybe his suspicions are adding up, and he doesn't want to be scalded when the kettle finally boils over. He knows Mrs. Sloane asked about Mr. Stewart. Does he also know Mr. Stewart is the man behind the show with two Chinese acrobats? He's seen the picture of my parents. Put that together with my strange arrival, and perhaps Steward Latimer saw a pattern in the bread heels being juggled. Was the fact that Percy's urn contained tobacco rather than ashes the odd pineapple that upset the whole routine?

The lemonade and oatmeal biscuits make a queasy gurgle in my stomach, and the air under my veil grows warmer by several degrees. Of course, if he thought I was an imposter, they'd have the Master-of-Big-Arms waiting for me. They wouldn't be tidying my rooms.

I take off my hat and wipe my brow. There could be a thousand reasons why Steward Latimer moved to a different floor. Still, I can't help thinking I'm reason number one.

28

On the way to supper, while Wink and Olly argue over which service they should attend the next day—Catholic or Protestant—I share my worries over Steward Latimer with Jamie.

His face acquires the same pinched look as when he's testing that a rope is secure. "Hard to know why he moved without more information. I can ask Charlotte to ask around. She'll be discreet."

I sigh, wishing I wasn't so dependent on the young woman. "Forget it. It's probably nothing."

"Probably. But let's keep our ears sharp."

In front of us, Wink elbows Olly. "Mary was a Catholic, so that's the one I want."

Olly laughs right in Wink's ear. "Ha! They didn't have Catholics back then, cow dung."

When we enter the Dining Saloon, faces follow us. Some of them wear guarded looks as usual, but I swear some actually smile. One man presses his palms together and nods at us.

"Do you see what I see?" I murmur to Jamie.

"Yeah. I see fresh bread in our future."

The Johnnies and the Domenics hail us with a rousing

cheer. Drummer drums the table, and Ming Lai's baritone urges, "Speech! Speech! Speech!" Jamie acknowledges the applause with a low bow, and I do the same.

The headwaiter with the rose in his lapel approaches and presents a bottle of champagne. "Sirs, a lady in first class sent six bottles."

I nearly trip over my chair. "A . . . lady? Do you know who?"

"I'm sorry, sir, no."

It isn't Mrs. Sloane. Charlotte? My eyes find Jamie's, who must be thinking the same thing, because his neck reddens, and he begins waging a war with his smile.

Corks pop, and soon, each member of our table holds a flute of sparkling liquid. Even the lads get a splash. I was never tempted to try the stuff after seeing what gargle juice did to Ba. But this wine, elegantly tipped from a long-necked bottle so that it pours out like a ray of sunlight, seems worlds apart from the jugs Ba swilled.

Rising, Jamie lifts his glass. I can't help thinking how much he resembles Ba on his good days—affable, happy, and up for standing where the pointer lands.

Ba could've been great if the beast hadn't dragged him away. His own grin could feed a hundred people, that upside-down archway through which his personality leapt and dazzled. Somehow Ba is in this room, watching his twins with a gleam in his eyes.

"Here's to a day we will always remember, with new friends"—Jamie steers his glass to the Domenics—"and old friends we will never forget." He acknowledges each of the Johnnies in turn.

Wink and Olly are pretending to be fine gentlemen, holding their glasses with an arm behind their backs and haughtily pursing their mouths. Ming Lai wears a contented smile, fist around his flute. Tao elbows Fong, who's already drinking his champagne. Fong grumbles at the spilled drops but lifts his glass.

Drummer swipes his eyes with his sleeve. "Thanks to you and your sister, my wife and I can see the dragon boat races this summer."

When Jamie gets to me, he murmurs, "To you, Sis."

We clink. As the fizzy liquid paints a warm stripe down my throat, I can't help feeling that that's the kind of speech you give before you say farewell. He's preparing to say goodbye to his mates. Why else would he tell his "old friends" he will never forget them?

Though the thought of separating Jamie from the Johnnies rips a hole in my sails, maybe the two boots are at last treading the same path.

———·••·———

AFTER DINNER, THE men take the lads to the General Room to hear music, while Jamie goes to find Charlotte. I make my way up to the poop deck, hoping to find Bo.

My heart floats in my chest, buoyed by the possibility that Jamie is coming around.

Folks, tightly wrapped, cluster at the rails, their laughter salting the air. The QM is not on shift, but another uniform stands as straight as a fin, watching the road of foam break from that staggering blue. With so much ocean around us, the commotion we cause seems insubstantial, a nick in the sand. The *Titanic*, for all her splendor, is really just a tiny fish swimming in a pond that won't remember her from the next one that comes along.

On the rearmost bench, a familiar figure sketches a toddler squirming in his father's arms while his mother watches. Though the toddy's face is twisted in outrage, Bo draws him with a mischievous smile.

The mother takes the portrait with a grateful nod. "It's perfect. Darling, look." She shows the picture to the child, whose watery eyes grow big. Before leaving, the father gives Bo a penny, and Bo nods his thanks.

I slide in next to him. "Have you ever drawn a self-portrait?"

He stretches his fists over his head, and his back cracks. "Pictures cannot do justice."

I grin. "Wagtail."

Something out to sea catches his eye. "See that circle? The bigger fish create a whirlpool, helping to stir up the smaller fish. Makes them easier to catch. We call that a kiss from Tin Hau, the goddess of shipwrecks and sailors. It means good luck is on the way. Maybe for you." He rubs his sooty fingers with a rag. "Tin Hau is generous, but quick to anger. Some believed she sent the monsoon to destroy our village because we had taken too much from the sea."

"Was that why you left home?"

"Yes." From his pocket Bo pulls a small carved wooden object, the size of a spool of thread, and holds the figurine to me. "I made this for you to remember your trip here."

It's a whale. I run my finger along the details of its underbelly, its eyes, its fins, and its wide mouth, all carved with an exacting hand, using even strokes and hashmarks. Just like with his shell ring, he transformed something ordinary into something beautiful—for me. Strange feelings press on my heart like cat paws on a windowpane.

I swallow down the tightness in my throat. "Why a whale?"

"A whale rules the sea. It goes where it wants without fear. And if troubled, it can become a bird"—he flaps his hands, his long fingers moving gracefully—"beating wings hard enough to stir up the sea. It means being in control of your destiny."

Am I in control of my destiny? My grip on the whale tightens. Maybe I am like the *Titanic*, motoring along invincibly, when really, one push of the ocean could easily change my course. Mr. Stewart could say no. Jamie could say no. Mr. Ismay could sniff me out like a rat and throw me off his ship. But I've done all I can, haven't I?

Feeling Bo watching me, I project a casualness I do not feel, focusing on the vivid pink dome overhead. "This sky reminds me of my mum's favorite shawl. Ba bought it for her to wear to the Chelsea Pageant."

The celebration of Chelsea's history was intended to draw people from all ranks of society, despite costing a pretty penny. Ba wanted us all to look our best. How we looked reflected on all Chinese. Plus, Ba took great pride in being a Londoner, even if the city didn't take pride in us.

Bo nods. "I know about the pageant, and the shawl, too."

"Jamie told you about the *shawl*?" It's such a personal detail. It seems strange for Jamie to mention it.

One corner of his mouth lifts. "We talk about the latest fashions." When he sees my stony expression, he shifts around on the bench. "I think, maybe, your mother did not love this shawl as much as you think."

"But she did. Ba said it made her look like a queen."

His nose draws up to where a navy curtain has begun to descend over the pink. "Did your mother like . . . attention?"

"Of course not. What are you getting at?"

He doesn't answer, and it dawns on me. Mum hated the stares that followed us every time the four of us went out. I remember how brightly Ba's eyes shone when he gave her the shawl. But when the day of the pageant came, Mum told him she wasn't feeling well, that we should go without her. But Ba begged her to go anyway, dressed in that vivid, eye-catching shawl.

Lady Sky wears rouge when she wants to be noticed.

A young couple approaches Bo. He studies me, his mouth gripped, the way we used to look at the beggar children living under Blackfriars Bridge in Cheapside.

I throw back my shoulders. "Thank you for the whale. You should see to your customers."

The floorboards fight me as I cross back to the stairs. Something inside me has broken loose, upsetting my balance. I can't decide which bothers me more, that the shawl I thought Mum loved embarrassed her, or that Jamie understood her and I had not.

29

Dressed again in the honeycomb dress and bowler, I opt for the lift back to B-Deck, resenting all the faces that notice me. The chatter and laughter of the nobs in their fashionable evening attire make my ears ring, a ringing that continues even after I pass into the quiet halls of the Cabbage Patch. So Mum only pretended to love her shawl. How many other times did she put on a brave face for my father's sake?

Once back in my room, I take out my picture of my parents and study Ba, his smile like a light bulb on his still youthful face. For the first time, I resent how little the photograph shows me. It's only a flash in time, with no glimpse into what lies deeper.

Ba always said our family was like the four fingers of a hand, and that they had to pull together for the hand to work. I'd figured Ba was the pointer, the leader, but maybe he'd been more like the thumb, doing whatever he pleased no matter what the other fingers wanted. Mum had been the pointer, keeping us in line. But for the hand to grab what it wants, the fingers must agree. How many times did she bite back her own feelings?

Jamie and I might've been as alike as two people could

be—born at the same time to the same parents, under the same stars. But it's clear we experienced our sameness in very different ways.

"Good evening, honored parents. I wish I had better news for you. But we've done our best, and—well, you should've seen Jamie. He was brilliant, and I hope . . ."

Suddenly, confessing my heart's desire—for Jamie to join me in America—grows too complicated. If he joins me, will it come at the cost of his own feelings? But at the same time, how can I let my only family go?

Someone knocks on the door.

"April?" I call.

"No, ma'am. It's Baxter. I've a suitcase for you."

Remembering the young porter who found Mrs. Sloane's trunk, I open the door and quickly take the alligator suitcase. "Thank you."

Inside, I find a marigold silk dress that's fussier than I expected from April, with too many buttons and ties on the wrists. I wish she had delivered the case herself, not just so she could instruct me on how to wear her creation, but because I enjoy her company.

Perhaps she no longer needs me, now that her fashion has caused the stir she hoped for. I guess I no longer need her either.

———— ·•· ————

APRIL 14, 1912

AFTER A RESTLESS sleep, Sunday morning bustles in with the call of a bugle. The ship muscles us forward, and the port of

New York grows brighter. Will it be a beginning or an ending for me? All the optimism I've felt since setting foot aboard this ship has steadily mixed with dread, as when a warm spring mingles with the cold sea, leaving an unsatisfying tepidness in my bones.

At least I haven't been arrested, which means no one is the wiser about the imposter in B-64. And surely, Mr. Stewart will tell us his decision today. We did our job, and now he's doing his, handling arrangements, sending telegrams.

I pull the comforter over my head, trying to fall back asleep. Jamie isn't expecting me for breakfast anyway.

———.··.———

A PINE BOX *rests in a field of hollyhocks. Is Ba at last gone?*

Jamie's tree stands empty, and the leaves have fallen off. He's run off for good. Flown away to that space he loves so much.

I approach the box with a lump in my throat. My hand trembles as I lift the lid back from its hinges, dreading what I'll see.

Suddenly, I'm in the box. The dark wraps around me, squeezing tighter and tighter, and I can't breathe, I can't breathe . . .

I flip the comforter off me, gasping. Someone's knocking at the door.

"Mrs. Sloane?" calls a female voice. "Mrs. Sloane, are you there?"

I hurry to the door, my nightgown, which is drenched in

sweat, grasping at my legs. My face feels like I've stuck it in a boiler.

"Just a moment," I say sternly. "Who is it?"

"It's Charlotte."

I crack the door to make sure she's alone. Her soft brown eyes blink at me. A nautical-style dress nips in at her waist, giving her a waspish figure. I quickly let her in.

"Jamie sent me to check on you. He hadn't seen you all day, and it's past three."

My stomach grumbles like a creature from the deep, and she eyes my damp nightgown. I hug myself and try not to feel like a hobo. "I didn't sleep well last night. Any news?"

"Yes. Mr. Stewart wants to meet with you and Jamie tonight after dinner!"

With a shriek, I clasp my hands to the ceiling and nearly fall to my knees.

"His valet will fetch you at eight thirty. I'm so happy for you!" With a squeal, Charlotte flings her arms around me, enveloping me in the scent of sweet peas. "I was thinking. If you do end up in New York"—her eyes drop to the carpet—"maybe you'd like to visit? We have horses and plenty of space. Half the rooms we don't even use. I wish we had more people to fill them."

"That's kind of you." Her offer touches me, even though I know it's Jamie she's thinking about. Still, this is good news. Surely she wouldn't encourage a friendship between us unless Jamie had given her hope of a future together. And if that's the case, Jamie's definitely headed toward America.

"Well, I'd better go. Mother's waiting for me to accompany her to the cocktail hour. Bottomless shrimp boats are the only thing that get her out of bed. I can't wait to hear what happens tonight."

After she leaves, I secure myself into the marigold dress as best I can, leaving the wrist ribbons loose, since I can't tie those one-handed. Then I lid my head with the provided hat—a grand dame with a wide brim that at least puts space between me and the viewer.

As I slip on the vanilla coat, I notice an object on the floor: a hackle feather, like a tiny white canoe. It must have fallen out of my coat pocket. I freeze, hunched like a heron over the feather. Its tip points toward twelve o'clock.

Something's going to happen. That's a weak superstition, refusing to commit either way. A superstition like that should just be called a "stition," because there's nothing super about it. Yet the hairs on my arms stand on end.

Crossing to the window, I open it and let the bloody thing sail into the wind.

Before slogging to E-Deck, I stop for a snack at the lemonade stand, which fortunately is deserted.

The late-afternoon sun has a subdued, almost glowy quality about it, as if it clocked out early and the moon is taking over. The ocean seems too quiet, the water a shifting palette of blues and greys. I strain to see a fish or any sign of life in the watery desert, but none appear. Suddenly feeling lonely, I run my fingers over the carved whale in my pocket. It feels warm, as if radiating an energy of its own.

A tray offers now-cold cheese scones. I face toward where a new *Atlantic Daily Bulletin* is posted and feed myself one under my veil.

—————————————— **APRIL 14** ——————————————

Weather: High of 50. Clear with moderate breeze to the northwest. Evening temperature to drop below freezing. Possible ice.

Nurse Clara Barton died, and a Royal Flying Corps has been formed. Glancing around to make sure no one's watching, I slurp down my glass of lemonade, then begin on a second scone. But when I reach the society column, I nearly choke.

Mr. Stephen Sloane made a sizable contribu-tion to the Royal Garden Society to be put toward a "Garden of Smells" in honor of his late mother, Mrs. Amberly Sloane.

I rip the paper from the corkboard, crumple it into a ball, and stuff it into my pocket. Maybe they're already onto me.

The money towels. A rocket flare lights inside me, and I have to stop my feet from racing in several directions at once. First, I'll retrieve the money. Then I'll remove as many of the dailies as I can find. It may be too late—the dailies have been up since morning—but I can't just leave them out for people to read.

Back to hopping on the balls of my feet, I hurry into the

deckhouse and down the tidal-wave staircase. The walls and ceilings have grown eyes. Every person I pass seems to look right through the veil to my guilty face.

In the Entrance Hall on B-Deck, a few people mill around the corkboard with the daily. I'll take care of that one right now. I wait at least five excruciating minutes before the area clears enough for me to snatch the bulletin.

"Excuse me." A man with sharp cheekbones points at the page I'm stuffing into my pocket. "I wanted to read that."

I draw myself up. "Wait your turn, young man," I say haughtily, pushing through the felted doors to the Cabbage Patch, hoping he doesn't follow. The doors close behind me, seemingly more reluctantly than usual.

"Mrs. Sloane!"

"Oh!" I cry, nearly colliding with Steward Latimer in front of Mr. Ismay's suites. "Why, hello." He catches me by the arm before I stumble. I shrink away, with crab-like movements of my legs. *Get ahold of yourself. You are a first-class lady, not a pastry-bumming street urchin.* I straighten my coat, which has slid off one shoulder.

"I trust your steward has been taking care of you?"

"Yes." I compose my features. "I was surprised to hear you had moved floors."

"Yes. I'm embarrassed to say Mr. Ismay wasn't content with my performance, but I'm still helping here when needed. Do you, er, need anything?" A pleasant smile lights his furry face, and he leans toward me solicitously. He doesn't look like someone who's worried about being scalded by the boiling kettle of scandal.

"Actually, I was wondering where the dailies are posted."

"There's one right outside those doors."

"Yes, but are there others?"

"I could have one brought to your room."

"Oh, no, please don't do that. Er, sometimes I feel like reading it in different locations." What a load of codswallop. But it doesn't matter. He already thinks I'm an eccentric old lady.

He studies the ceiling and counts off his fingers. "Let's see, there's also one on the Promenade Deck, the library, the restaurant, and the Smoking Room. Five, that's it. We don't have the capacity to print many, you see."

Mrs. Sloane, that tough old nut, feels herself soften in gratitude. "Steward Latimer, I know you must think me a loon for carrying around tobacco in place of ashes. But the thing is, Percy loved that particular brand, and, well, the smell reminds me of him."

"Please, no need to explain. I carried around my baby's sock for years after she passed. Whatever gets you through is what gets you through."

"Quite so." I pull a sovereign from my pocket and hold it out. Mrs. Sloane had said she would tip a sovereign, or ten shillings for each of us, at the end of the journey, and this is the end of my journey in first class.

"Oh, why, thank you."

"I am grateful for your kindness."

He bows, and as we part ways, I can't help thinking that even if the man knew the truth, he wouldn't hold it against me.

Reaching my cabin, I brace myself, in case the Master-of-Big-Arms waits on the other side of the door. But when I open it, only the citrusy scent of bergamot greets me, chased by the heavy odor of the lilies I stashed in the wardrobe. They're rotting along with all my plans.

I lock the door behind me and rush to the chaise longue, relieved to find the two towels and one sock of money still inside the seat cushion. Maybe they aren't onto me quite yet. But there's no sense in taking chances by staying here, with so much already on the line. I stuff the money in my slipper bag, along with Mum's Bible. Sweating, I remove my coat, which is weighing me down, remembering to remove the whale from the pocket. Then I hurry out the way I came.

A cramp in my foot stops me in my tracks right at Mr. Ismay's door. All this unnatural hot-footing in these torture racks has finally done my pins in, and maybe me along with them. Naturally, it would be here that I am discovered. One can only swim across a moat full of alligators so many times before eventually meeting a gruesome end.

Two women approach from the Entrance Hall, chatting loudly. *Wonderful.* I ignore them and look at Mr. Ismay's door, pretending that I'm waiting for him to answer.

"Oh, Mrs. Sloane, isn't it?"

I will my hat to swallow me as the well-dressed figure of Lucy Duff-Gordon marches up, her auburn hair in a curl down one side of her neck. A finely woven straw hat in peachy gold features an array of feathers and ombre ribbon. She looks like a tropical bird.

The second woman stands a foot shorter and wears a boat of a cabbage-rose hat. I recognize her as the woman who asked me if my dress was Lucile my first time on the lift.

I lick my lips, trying to keep the moisture going. "Why, hello, Lady Duff-Gordon. Nice to see you. Well, don't let me keep you—"

"Lucy, please. Mrs. Bertha Chambers, may I present Mrs. Amberly Sloane?"

"Ah. You're the Merry Widow. Did Mr. Ismay invite you for the wine tour, too?"

"Uh, no." I try to stretch my curling foot enough to get it to relax.

The brass knocker on Mr. Ismay's door ogles me with its giant orb, like the one-eyed squid Jamie and I once saw in a fisherman's bucket. To my horror, Lucy knocks.

"I was just, that is, I just remembered I'm needed elsewhere." I begin to hobble away, but Mrs. Chambers steps in front of me, peering at my dress.

"Is that House of July?"

"Yes."

Lucy crosses her arms. "No, that's not House of July. That's *my* dress." Her eyes bear down on mine like two cannonballs.

A trapped fly buzzes around my innards, making it hard to think. Why would April give me Lucile to wear? Well, now's not the time to get it sorted. Any minute, Mr. Ismay will open the door. "Ah, of course you are right."

Lucy's face loses its sharpness. "Marigold Fantasy is one of my favorites, but the ribbons are supposed to crisscross, like this." She tugs the ribbons on my sleeve and spends an eternity tying them in a crisscrossing fashion like a corset. For cod's sake, women have enough things to fuss over as it is. She starts on the other sleeve, and I have to stop myself from ripping it off and running down the hall. "I've got a new Strawberries and Cream dress that would look fetching on you. I would love for you to wear it."

So, Lucy wants to create a stir of her own.

"I shall think about it. Lovely seeing you both."

"What's there to think about?" Lucy sniffs.

"Bit of a recluse," Mrs. Chambers murmurs as I stumble off, praying there are no alligators around the next corner.

30

By the time I reach the Smoking Room and tear the fifth daily from the wall, I feel like I've sprinted across the Atlantic Ocean. It occurs to me that the crew might simply replace the missing pages with new ones. But with it being so late in the day, maybe not. The square clock on the staircase landing already reads half past five.

When I finally slip into Room 14, Wink and Olly are making the walls ring with a rendition of "Lamb of God," conducted by Jamie. The blankets have been tucked and the seabags hung straight as Christmas stockings. Bo sits on his bunk, wiping his carving tools with a cloth. I press my back against the door and exhale in relief.

Jamie drops his arms. "Where you been, Sis?"

"Overslept. Charlotte gave me the news."

"So why don't you look happier?" His eyes drop to the slipper bag of money I'm carrying. The lads stop singing, and Bo looks at me through the mirror, his eyes concerned.

"We have a problem." I pull out one of the dailies and point at the society column.

Jamie reads it aloud for the rest of them, then crumples the page and throws it out the porthole. "Rest in peace, Mrs.

LUCK OF THE *TITANIC*

Sloane. You'll stay down here from now on. I'll ask Charlotte to hide you in her room. She's just on the other side of E-Deck." The first-class side, he means.

Olly squirms, jostling Wink beside him. "Or Wink and I can share a bunk. We learned how to pray for you, too. Wink can do Catholic, and I can do Protestant."

Wink nods vigorously.

"Thanks, lads." It doesn't feel right imposing on Charlotte, but the thought of spending the night in the same room as Bo makes my chest flutter. I run my fingers through my clipped hair, wishing feelings could be trimmed away as easily as a few locks. As if sensing my discomfort, Bo stores his tools under his bunk and busies himself in his seabag.

"Charlotte's place will stink less and be safer," Jamie says. "How about you take my place at dinner?"

Wink and Olly launch themselves off the top bunk. I pull down the wall chair and sit heavily. "No. I don't have an appetite, and I want to stay put somewhere awhile."

He nods and hefts the slipper bag. "I'll see if I can store the money with the purser."

Bo gives me a brief smile before following the others out. "Lock the door, Stowaway. And congratulations on the meeting."

I've only known him a few days, but our brief moments together have already etched themselves in my mind. How long before time rubs them away? The less I think about him, the faster it'll happen.

A bright knock interrupts my brooding. When I open the door, Drummer's narrow face peers back at me. He's holding a piece of White Star stationery. He glances into the room. "By yourself?"

"Yes. Aren't you going to dinner?"

He shakes his head. "I am needed in Boiler Room 6." Fireman Brandish must need Drummer's help to put her "on the boil" again. "But first, I am writing a letter to my wife, Chin Chin. I want to end the letter with something"—he clears his throat—"poetic."

I force back a smile as Drummer fiddles with his paper, a sheepish look on his face.

"What do you think?"

I take the letter from his suddenly reluctant hands, smooth out the wrinkles, and read the last line.

Thoughts of you float across my mind like lotus petals on the pond.

The simple verse presses a tender hand on my heart. "I think it's perfect."

I lock the door after Drummer leaves so I can change. Marigold Fantasy sticks to me like damp seaweed. Pulling it off, I discover a label stitched to the waist stay that reads *Lucile, Ltd*. Why did April send me one of her competitor's dresses? Or maybe Lucy sent the dress. But if so, how did she get it into April's suitcase? I snap it out and hang it on a wall hook. I suppose her kind doesn't need to provide explanations to the likes of me.

I slip on Jamie's spare shirt and stick a leg in his extra set of trousers. The door latch clicks. I stumble backward, my legs tangling in the trousers. "Who—?"

Skeleton appears and locks the door behind him.

"H-how dare—"

With sickeningly quick movements, Skeleton pounces on me, knocking me to the ground and clamping a hand over my mouth. My head bangs against the linoleum. "Don't you scream, if you know what's good for you."

31

I try to scream anyway. But Skeleton weighs more than his skin-and-bones appearance suggests, and with his hand covering my nose and mouth, I can scarcely draw a breath. His red-rimmed eyes peer down at me, the reek of alcohol seeping through his pores.

"I know you're a lassie. I've got a beak like a shark." He takes a deep sniff, as if to prove it. "You reek the same, whether you're in fine dresses"—he cuts his eyes to the Lucile hanging on a wall hook—"or those sailor dregs your mateys wear. Like extra-fancy bergamot soap."

My limbs feel sluggish, but I grab at his arm, trying to pry it off. But it's like a steel post pinning me down, his crazed eyes promising violence.

"Now, I'll overlook your crimes, as soon as you bowf up all that money you got paradin' around the deck. Hand it over, and my lips are sealed. Blink if you agree."

My lungs squeeze, begging for air, and I blink my assent before he suffocates me.

His hand lets up, and I suck in sweet breath.

Then something depraved gropes at his face. His saddle

smile drips with venom, his gaze a lewd caress against my skin.

But I have not come all this way to be done in by him. Something growls within the caverns of my soul. I glance around for salvation, and under Bo's bed, I find it.

When Skeleton shifts, fumbling at his pants, I wrap my hand around the handle of one of Bo's carving tools—a gouge. I strike, stabbing the man in the side.

With a yelp, he rolls off me. I scramble to my feet. Collecting himself as well, he makes a grab for the gouge, but I kick him hard in the knee.

The dog only catches the cat by surprise. In everything else, the more agile cat wins.

Cursing and spitting, Skeleton falls back. Then the snake slithers out the door.

I fall to my knees, suddenly nauseated and unable to draw a breath. What now? He will tell his betters, and my lies, like loosely tied knots, will unravel. The room seems to slide one way, then the other, like a seesaw, but I fight against the urge to give up.

Get up, girl. Put on your trousers. Fetch your boots.

I only get one boot on before my insides roil, as violently as bottles of milk carted over a bumpy road. Holding my bucking midsection, I rush to the porthole, then empty the contents of my stomach into the sea.

Yelling and footsteps rattle the hallway. Catching sight of Marigold Fantasy, I hastily pull it from the hook and toss it, the oversized hat, and the pumps out the porthole, too.

"She's in there," exclaims Skeleton in his rusty voice. "A lassie, and she's been staying in the men's quarters, like a common whore. I had my suspicions, and now it's confirmed. Methinks she might even be a stowaway." The man's splotchy face invades the doorway once more.

Behind him, the Master-of-Big-Arms peers at me through a half sneer, his stout arms curling at his sides. "You again. So *are* you a stowaway?"

I try to speak, but nothing comes out of my swollen throat but a hoarse, outraged whisper. Fiercely, I shake my head.

The Master-of-Big-Arms glances at the bright spot of blood inking Skeleton's white jacket. "Get to the infirmary and make your report after."

Skeleton stumbles off, and the door swings closed behind him.

"Lassie or lad, you're coming with me till we get this sorted." The Master-of-Big-Arms clamps a hand as strong as the jaws of a mastiff around my arm. He drags me to the door, not even letting me grab my second boot. "Knew you were a scammer all along. Maybe your kind can't help it. Wait till the captain hears how you fooled him. Better hope he doesn't dump you over. The water's colder than ice. You'll freeze afore the devil calls your name."

"It isn't right," I croak. "The steward attacked me. He's the one you should take away. He's wicked. He fixed the sweepstakes."

"Didn't I tell them they should include a brig?" he mutters. "But no one listens to me. Now they'll be sorry."

I try to dig in my heels as he tows me down the Collar. People watch in astonishment. To my surprise, we pass his cabin, and he flings open the door into first class. Passing a short hallway, he pulls me down a narrow staircase.

"Where are you taking me?" I gasp, slipping off a step.

He yanks me back to my feet. "Oy, stuff it."

Fear gnaws the last remnants of my composure, like rats to a melon rind. My nose has begun to run.

At the bottom of the stairs, we turn a corner down another hallway and then another. Windows stretch down the wall on the right, revealing a spacious high-ceilinged room with a floor drawn with lines. It's a squash court.

But before I can get a good look, the Master-of-Big-Arms marches me down a second staircase. I'm beginning to lose track of where I am, but I guess somewhere on G-Deck. The light has become too dim for my comfort.

Finally, he unlocks a door to what looks like a small closet.

"Not ideal," he mutters. "Not ideal a'tall." He shoves me inside, so roughly that I spill onto the floor. The smell of wood and rubber rise up around me. "This will hold you till we figure out what to do with you."

He slams the door. Keys jangle, followed by the click of the lock, which to me sounds like the cocking of a pistol.

A thread of panic unspools within me. The dark, my old enemy, sharpens its teeth.

"No, please don't leave me here! Please turn on the light!

I can explain!" I cry, my throat still aching and my mouth rinsed with acid. "Please don't leave me." I pound on the door, blubbering. "I beg you, turn on the light."

The hall lights click off, one last insult, and darkness rushes in, as thick as the tide. Frantically, I grab at the walls, feeling for another switch. But I don't find one. Why put a light switch in a closet?

I bang at the door. "Help! Somebody, help me!"

No one comes.

After several more minutes of yelling, my throat feels like it's been scrubbed with a horsehair shoe brush, and my knuckles are raw from knocking. I let go of the doorknob and grope at what's behind me. Perhaps there is something here I could use.

The *Titanic* dips. Losing my balance, I knock into something flat and metal—a shelf—and grab at it to steady myself. My hands collide with a pile of wooden objects—rackets—and a stack of something soft—towels.

I fall into a heap, and hard objects rain down on me. With a shriek, I cover my head with my hands. The objects make hollow sounds as they bounce off the floor.

Steady, girl, they are just balls.

I scramble to my feet. But the rolling balls make the terrain uneven, and I stumble again, landing hard on my knees.

Jamie won't be able to find me down here. We'll miss our appointment with Mr. Stewart. All this work. All these dreams. Buried in the rock pile, just like the little girl who fell down the coal hole. Now what? There's no crane to pull me out, no chain for me to scale.

The *Titanic* hits a wave, and hysterical laughter sloshes out of me like tea from a teacup.

Without windows in the closet, the stuffy air begins to reek of my own sweat. I'm going to breathe all the air out of this room. The more I think about suffocating, the faster my breath comes.

I'm six years old all over again, trapped like a tiny mouse in a watering can. The coal chute was too high and slippery. I tried to climb it, but every time, I slid back into the rock pile, cutting my knees and palms. Black dust filled my nose and mouth, like gunpowder rammed into a musket. Two bullies named darkness and cold pinned me down, and the biggest bully, isolation, took punches.

I gather my knees to my chest, trying not to cry.

Ba always said life is for the strong. But I can't help thinking that he was wrong about that. There are moments to be strong, but there are also moments to be weak. And in those moments of rest, we find strength anew and challenge ourselves to grow bigger than we ever thought possible.

So I order my shaky pins to grit down and my panicked lungs to breathe. Focusing on the drone of the ship's engine, I close my eyes. I slow my breath, inhaling as if drawing a bucket of water from a well, and exhaling as if pouring it back.

I picture Jamie and myself, standing on opposite ends of a wire. Folks have come from all over to witness our feats of amazement. The band stops playing, save for a pattering drumroll. Breaths are held. Eyes widen. Jamie gives the nod, and we begin to fly.

Sweat trickles down my forehead. How long have I been here? I have to get out. Life is streaking by, and there's not a second to waste. I twist at the doorknob again, feeling for the keyhole under the knob. If only I had something to pick the lock.

I stand and roll my shoulders, my wrists, then my ankles, feeling the weight of my single boot. *My boot.* I kneel and pull out the shoelace with its aglets of high-quality metal, not glue or wax.

I work an aglet into the keyhole. What am I feeling for?

Several minutes, maybe hours, pass. I feel something catch. But no, it isn't the lock; it's the aglet. The bugger has gone crooked and is now unusable.

Biting back my frustration, I switch to the one at the other end. My arm has begun to lose feeling, but I keep working at the lock. I twist and tug the aglet, madly searching for the release, careful not to break it. But the road has become a twisted jumble in front of me, and I cannot find my way.

Breathe.

Mum taught Jamie and me the art of tatting. As with most things, he caught on faster than me. After working our shuttles, he'd end up with a pretty lace snowflake, and I'd have a nest of thread, soggy with tears. Mum said the trick was learning how to breathe. Slow and easy. Somehow, breathing untied the knots.

Click.

With a cry of relief, I turn the knob and swing open the door. Fresh air cools my face. I feel around for a switch, and light pours over me. Blinking hard, I try to adjust my eyes to the brightness. The narrow staircase rises before me.

Grabbing my shoelace, I climb to the landing, where another door blocks my way.

It is locked.

32

I rest my head against the door, feeling tears come. I'll have to do it all over again. But my aglet is in shambles, worn down to a frail nubbin.

A yelp on the other side of the door startles me. Another yelp follows that sounds more like a yip-yip! Then the sound of scratching. Strudel?

"Valora?"

"Jamie?" Tears well up. "Jamie, oh, Jamie!" I blubber.

"Sit tight, Sis. Tao's picking the lock."

Moments later, the doorknob twists, and my cage opens. Jamie, holding my second boot, grips me in an embrace.

"Oh, Jamie, it was dark, and I wanted to die."

"But you didn't. And I've got you. Come on, now, don't cry."

Tao tucks a simple hairpin into his braided beard. "Magic fingers." I guess finding enlightenment hasn't dampened the man's skills.

I find a smile, despite my tears. "Thank you, Uncle. Thank you, too, Strudel."

The poodle puts her paws on my leg and sniffs me with her narrow snout.

Jamie eases my foot into my second boot while Tao helps me relace my first one with his nimble fingers.

"S-s-skel—"

"We figured. The purser didn't let us store our money, so we came back and found that slop bucket and his dogs in the room, tearing the place down." The light glints off Jamie's sharp-looking teeth as he yanks my laces tight. "Skeleton's wishing he really was dead. Bo gave him quite a mousing."

"Tell me the lads didn't fight."

"I sent them to find the other Johnnies, but they brought back Mr. Domenic instead."

"Dina's father?" An image of the brawny man with his bulging arms and thick neck appears in my mind.

"You should've seen him toss those jackasses like sacks of straw. Ming Lai said he used to be a professional wrestler."

"Where . . . is Bo?"

"Probably in the stern. We split up to look for you. Bo took Wink and Olly. Ming Lai split off with Fong. Drummer's been in the boilers."

"What time is it?"

Jamie's mouth girdles. "Close to eleven."

We missed our appointment. "Maybe he'll still see us. We don't have his room number, but perhaps—"

"We'll figure something out, Sis."

I plod up the stairs after Jamie and Tao, then stop at a drinking fountain. While I quench my sore throat, Jamie stretches his left arm back, wincing.

"What happened?"

"Dislocated my shoulder. It slipped back into place. It's fine. Smartly, now."

When we emerge again on E-Deck, still on the first-class side, Strudel bolts down the hall and scratches at a door. It opens. Charlotte, looking like a princess in a green velvet gown and a tiara, scoops Strudel up and presses a kiss into her neck.

"Good girl. Oh, Valora!" She puts Strudel down and embraces me. "We were so worried!" She lets me go, then checks me over, perhaps for injuries.

"Sirs, you aren't allowed in these corridors." One of the black-jacketed room stewards who always seem to be hovering around in first class marches up to us.

"Steward," Charlotte says in a clear voice. "I'm afraid Mr. and Miss Luck have missed Mr. Albert Ankeny Stewart's valet, who came to fetch them earlier. Would you mind seeing them to his room? I would hate for him to be kept waiting."

The man's egg-shaped face cracks a little. "Er, Mr. Stewart?" He crooks one of his large ears toward Charlotte, as if perhaps she has spoken under duress and he's listening for the real message. She gives him a hard look, and he shakes himself out of his confusion. "If you don't mind waiting just a moment, I shall check on that."

Charlotte nods, and the man disappears down the hall.

"They have telephones here," Charlotte explains.

Jamie, seemingly at a loss for where to put his hands, jams them into his pockets. "Strudel was brilliant." The electricity running between Charlotte and Jamie could power the whole deck. "Er, this is Tao, our locksmith."

Tao bows, and Charlotte bows as well. The three make polite conversation, but I cannot think with all the worries sprouting like weeds in my head. The hour is already late, past the lights-out bugle. Mr. Stewart is the kind of man who adheres to a schedule. We'll have to make up an excuse for our tardiness. I can't exactly tell him I was locked in a squash closet for stowing away.

At last, the steward returns. "Please come with me."

Jamie and I follow him toward the lifts, while Charlotte takes Tao's arm. "Uncle, shall we?" With Strudel following close at her heels, they set off in the opposite direction, toward the Collar.

The lift takes Jamie, the steward, and me to B-Deck. So, Mr. Stewart is staying on Mrs. Sloane's level after all. I hope he isn't in the Cabbage Patch, an area I'm anxious to avoid. The lift operator opens the collapsible gate, and to my surprise, the petite man with the discreet bearing of a potted plant quietly greets us. "Mr. and Miss Luck."

"Mr. Croggy," I greet Mr. Stewart's valet, remembering too late that we've never been introduced.

One of his threadbare eyebrows crooks a fraction. "It's actually 'Crawford.'"

The blood leaches from my face. "Croggy" must be a nickname, possibly one only Mr. Stewart uses. Now he must wonder how a lowly acrobat he has never met knows it.

Jamie throws me a questioning glance, but I shake my head, hoping my slipup hasn't ruined everything.

"It's nice to meet you, Mr. Crawford," Jamie says smoothly.

The valet recovers his neutral face, then leads us in the opposite direction from the Cabbage Patch. Room B-47 catches my eye. I'll need to return April's clothes to her, somehow. Will she notice that the Merry Widow has disappeared? I wish her the best. She has done me a good turn here on the *Titanic*, and I won't forget it.

Crawford guides us through another set of felt doors to a quiet section in the bow. His slight figure moves at a pace that neither lingers nor hurries.

"Don't seem too eager," Jamie drops in my ear. "See what he has to offer before running off with the bone. And don't make excuses about being late. It begs too many questions."

"But—"

"Shh." He knocks my arm with his elbow as Crawford swivels his thin neck back at us.

Crawford stops and knocks on a door. "Sir? Your guests are here."

"Show them in," replies Mr. Stewart.

The room is half as wide as Mrs. Sloane's suite, with a single bed opposite a couch, a carved armoire on one end, and a mirrored dressing table on the other. The walls are wainscoted in cream, with crown molding gracefully flared to the ceilings.

Mr. Stewart sits reading a book on one side of the couch, which is intricately patterned in reds and golds. His bowler and chesterfield coat have been placed atop the finely crafted mahogany bed. Save for a little fuzz above his ears, the man is bald as a buoy.

He rises from his seat. "Ah, Valor and Virtue."

Jamie extends a hand. "You can call me Jamie, and this is Valora. We're very sorry for our delay."

Mr. Stewart cocks an ear. When an explanation doesn't come, he frowns, and little pouches appear around his mouth. This visit is not off to a flying start. As he gives Jamie's hand a curt shake, the chains of his gold watch swing out from where they attach to the pockets of his linen vest, and the forgiving pleats of his pants balloon, emphasizing his stocky legs.

"Please." He lifts a hand to the couch.

"Thank you," I croak, my throat still swollen from yelling. I slide onto the velvety upholstery, whose sumptuousness calls attention to my dingy sea togs. Jamie sits himself next to me, barely moving the horsehair seat cushion.

Moving soundlessly, Crawford sweeps up Mr. Stewart's hat and coat, freeing a spot on the bed for Mr. Stewart to sit opposite us. Above his head, a Tiffany lamp twinkles like a jewel set in the wall.

Mr. Stewart's eyes dart back and forth between Jamie and me as if not sure where to land. "Where did you learn how to perform like that?"

"Our father taught us," I say congenially, hoping to thaw the temperature in the room a little. "He was a man with more cream than pail. Always brimming with ideas."

"You said *was*?"

"He died a few months back," Jamie says without emotion.

Mr. Stewart's eyebrows climb toward each other, then flatten. "Ah. I lost my own father when I was about your age, and not a day goes by that I don't think of him." His shoulders relax. Finding common ground seems to ease the way forward. He unclips the chains of his watch and holds the timepiece up like a rare coin. "This was his. It reminds me to embrace the moment. Which is why I agreed to see you at this very late hour. Charlie—er, Mr. Ringling—has been looking for a top-notch act, and I think you're it."

"Why, that's brilliant news. Thank you, sir." A surge of energy runs through me, and I have to stop myself from bouncing off the couch. These boots are making tracks for America. I grin at Jamie, and he grins right back.

"Croggy?" Mr. Stewart flicks his eyes to the dressing table, where an ice bucket beaded with moisture holds a bottle of champagne. As Crawford pours, the fizzy sound seems to make the air sparkle, and soon we are all holding a glass.

Mum never got the chance to try champagne, and now here we are, sampling it for the second night in a row. *Well, aren't you putting on the top hat, poppet?* I hear her say.

Mr. Stewart lifts his flute by the stem, like a rose, and I shift my glass to imitate him. "To your future."

I take a too-large sip, and the liquid rises sharply in my nose, making my eyes tear up.

"I have to apologize for not getting back to you right away. But I had to chat with a friend here who employs some Chinese—Isidor Straus, the owner of Macy's, the biggest department store in the United States. I guess I don't need to tell you how hard it is to get past the Chinese Exclusion Act." He feeds his frown some champagne. "As far as I'm concerned, the less the government sticks their fingers into my business, the better for all of us."

"How will you do it?" I ask. Jamie fidgets beside me, touching his left shoulder, which must be bothering him.

Mr. Stewart nods. "There are exceptions in the act, including one for teachers. Charlie has been wanting to set up a circus school for a while now." He rubs his hands together. "Perhaps as part of your employment with the circus, you can instruct others in the acrobatic arts."

"Will it work?" asks Jamie.

"I think so. Especially with Charlie in the ring." He tosses up his watch and catches it. "If it weren't for him, his six brothers would still be doing pony tricks on the farm, not running the largest entertainment company in the world. He secured the right to transport twenty-six camels, sixteen elephants, and three hundred and thirty-five horses by train, by knowing which hands to shake and which shoulders to tap. But here's the thing, folks."

My blood stops moving through my body.

"The teacher exception only works for males."

"I can pass as male. You've seen the act."

"Actually, what I propose is that Jamie come as the 'teacher,' with you as his 'wife.'"

Jamie draws back. "But that wasn't on the table."

His words echo off some chasm of disbelief that has opened inside me. Jamie doesn't want to come? I misread him. The farewell toast at last night's dinner was for . . . me. The ship's dull vibrations seem to amplify, like a hive of bees has moved into my head.

"I'm sorry, but the act works because it's two of you. Valor and Virtue. Plus, it's too risky for Ringling Brothers to hire a single woman."

"Risky in what way?" Jamie asks.

Mr. Stewart grabs at his chin, pulling hard enough to sharpen the point of it. "For one, she might run off. It's the women who tend to get in the family way."

"I certainly don't have plans for that."

"No one ever does."

Jamie stiffens. "Is that a remark on Valora's judgment?" His eyes have grown bright, and his fingers grip the edge of the seat cushion, like talons. He rarely yells, preferring to scorn rather than scald. "She cared for our father by herself after our mum died. Buried him, too. Does that sound like a girl who would shirk her duties?"

There's outrage in his tone, not all of it directed at Mr. Stewart. I can't bear to look at Jamie's face, not wanting to see injury there, hurt that will cause me to drift off the line.

Mr. Stewart's face is a landscape of changing scenery and shifting planes—the flattening of the hill of his nose, the widening of the crag of his mouth. His gaze shifts to me and becomes thoughtful. "No, it doesn't. Still, it's not an easy life. Constant travel can be hard on the constitution. The women Charlie employs are as tough as alligators."

"Valora's tough, and she works harder than me. She can do

an aerial somersault on the tightrope, forward *and* backward. She was born for the stage."

Jamie's words trigger a surprising flood of emotions in me, which collect in a warm pool in my stomach. I flash him a grateful smile.

"If you came with her, there would be no question. But Valora alone? No offense . . ."

The only sound is, strangely, Crawford, stirring the ice with the bottle. I suppose a good valet knows when to be silent and when a little noise is needed.

A shield-shaped mirror reflects my worried expression, my lips a hardening drip of sealing wax, my eyes almost squinting. Here it is, the chance to pull Jamie through the door, to get what I climbed through a cargo hatch for. Jamie doesn't want to go, but he won't refuse, not with my destiny on the line. I feel more than hear him draw a breath, as heavily as if it were dragging an anchor. Finally, the key has been presented to him, not the key to unlock Ba's future as in my dreams, but mine.

But an almond twisted from the tree before it's ready will always be bitter. That bitterness will seep into our relationship, eating away at it until we're nothing but angry words and icy glares. Then we might lose each other for good. I could never let that happen to us. Maybe I have been acting like Ba. I thought what was best for me was best for him. I didn't listen to what he wanted.

Life is a balancing act, and the better you get at juggling, the better you get at living. But juggling is not an act of holding tight. It's an act of letting go—of giving the people you love the time and space to find their own orbit. And it's an act of catching. I'll always be there for Jamie, just as he'll always be there for me.

The floor shifts, and the walls creak, sounding like the screech of a stage curtain slowly pulling closed.

"I—" Jamie begins, but I put a hand on his arm.

"I'm afraid that isn't possible, Mr. Stewart," I hear myself say. My whale is a warm lump against my thigh, reminding me to take control of my destiny. "But perhaps I can offer another option."

33

If Jamie and I are truly charting our own paths now, the way for me must be forward, not back. Ringling Brothers still holds out a hoop, albeit a shaky one. I just need to find a way through it, Valor without Virtue.

Jamie has stopped breathing. Mr. Stewart is rubbing his pocket watch like a worry stone. The Tiffany lamp casts a shine over his scalp.

"We have two younger brothers traveling with us. Wink and Olly are their names. They were the two collecting coins on the well deck after our performance."

"Yes, I remember them." He sounds about as thrilled as if I'd offered him a hairbrush.

"Our mother wished that her sons would be sailors." I send a silent prayer to Mum to forgive me for the ridiculous lies I'm telling with her good name. Something tells me, though, she's having a good chuckle up there on her cloud.

Jamie coughs. "Where are you going with this?" he asks in Cantonese through his teeth, pasting on a smile.

"I'll tell you when I get there," I reply, before returning to English. "She wished to offer a sacrifice to the sea goddess Tin

Hau as a thank-you for the plentiful, er, mackerel harvest that kept her village back in China from starving one summer. So she dedicated her sons to the sea."

A sigh blows from Jamie's nostrils, but he props up his expression and nods, his face as earnest as a starched collar.

"Turns out, they have too much of their father in them. Olly has excellent reflexes and would make a good juggler. Wink is naturally small and agile, and with proper training, he could learn to walk the rope, maybe even better than me. You might not have Flying Twins, but what about a Flying Family?"

"But I thought you buried your father alone?"

Belatedly, I remember that Jamie said I took care of Ba by myself. "Er, I was alone. The lads followed after Jamie . . ." My mind stops spinning, like a pinwheel in a fickle breeze, and Jamie picks up the slack.

"After I found work for them with Atlantic Steam," Jamie smoothly cuts in, "I sent Valora a letter that she should send them along. After all, the work was honest, and they'd be fed."

Mr. Stewart's eyes shift to starboard as he digests our concoction. "Well, what about your mother's wishes?"

"Ah, well, she has me, doesn't she?" Jamie thumps his chest and points to the ceiling, as if acknowledging Mum up in heaven.

"Jamie's the oldest born, which means he's the most important one, and he loves the queasy seasies." I slap him on the shoulder a little too hard, forgetting about his injury until he makes a strangled sound.

He absorbs my blow with a good-natured smile that doesn't reach his eyes. "Sure do."

Suddenly, the ship seems to grip as if someone stepped on the brakes, and the room leans to port, tossing Crawford onto the bed.

Mr. Stewart raises his eyebrows at the valet. "At least you weren't carrying the champagne."

Crawford scrambles to his feet again. "Yes, sir."

The bed squeaks as Mr. Stewart shifts around. "Well . . . this Wink and Olly. They're not acrobats yet. At this point, they'd simply be extra mouths to feed."

"Your point is taken. But as apprentice acrobats, they'll work for free for the first six months to give everyone a chance to test things out." Thanks to our performance, we have enough money to hold us at least a year if we're frugal, with no rent or board to pay. "If, in the end, you are not satisfied, you will not have lost anything."

"Except the trouble of getting you into the country."

"You would've done it for the two of us." I glance at Jamie. "What's another name or two on the application?"

"Jamie is a more certain bet."

I snort. "I'm afraid my brother wants to see the stars, not be one of them."

Mr. Stewart rises, and we stand as well. He gazes at his bowler, now hung on the wall beside us, as if it were a crystal ball. "Ah, this is . . . quite irregular."

Crawford creeps next to him and murmurs something into his ear. Is he revealing that I knew his nickname? Maybe he put two and two together and figured out that I was the imposter, Mrs. Sloane.

I squeeze my fists, feeling something slipping away. The floors seem to thrum harder under my feet, a sensation that not even the thick rugs, nor our elevation, could dampen. Life, like this ship, continues to move forward. This tiny moment, like all the other moments happening on this ship, will transform, like ocean spray, into rivulets bearing us in new directions. But if I can keep my feet planted in this moment for a little longer, maybe it'll take me where I want to go.

Jamie nudges me with his elbow, and I follow his eyes down to his hand. He pincers his forefinger and thumb, and then makes a tiny plucking motion, as if picking a flower. A dandelion.

He glances at me, a smile lurking in his eyes. His chest lifts as he breathes. Then together, we blow a puff of air, as light as a sigh, but loud enough for the stars to hear.

Mr. Stewart wipes his palms on his trousers, and his jowls lift as he smiles. "Welcome to the Ringling Brothers Circus." He extends a hand to me, and Mum laughs sweetly in my ear.

———·•·———

WE SET A time for our next meeting, and then Crawford, who I can't help thinking played a role in Stewart's decision, leads us back to the lifts.

"That was a strange swell," says Jamie, making polite conversation. "Now it feels like we're barely moving."

"I'll be glad of a slower pace," Crawford returns. "Best to

tiptoe around giants is what I think, and the ocean's the biggest giant I know."

I think back to when I first saw him. Mrs. Sloane offered a mild defense of his fear of the ocean. Is that why the man helped us? But if that's the reason, then he must know that I am Mrs. Sloane.

Just past the felted doors, April's room again catches my eye. As Crawford and Jamie move toward the lifts, on impulse, I cross to her door and knock. To my surprise, the door opens right away. April's mother, wearing her mink, blinks at me. "Oh, it's you."

"Er, yes," I agree. "Good evening, Mrs. Hart. I don't mean to bother you."

Jamie hurries over. "What are you doing?" he hisses.

April's face appears behind her mother's. "Valora! And Jamie, I presume?"

"Um, how do you do?" Jamie says cautiously.

April grabs my hand. Unlike her mum, she looks like she's ready to turn in for the night, with an embroidered robe in chocolate brown over matching silk pajamas. "Valora, I looked everywhere for you. Do you have a moment?"

"Well, yes, but we're really not supposed to be on this level." I glance back at Crawford, who has glided up behind us.

"For heaven's sake. Steward, officer, whoever you are, I will take personal responsibility for any rabble-rousing Miss Luck might do."

Crawford angles his head deferentially. If he wondered if I was a rabble-rouser before, now it's been confirmed.

Jamie frowns at me. "Don't take too long." Then he and Crawford return to the lifts.

Mrs. Hart, who has been studying me, announces, "I'm going to see if I can find some soothing music. That swell made my stomach turn a loop." She pulls her mink tighter and sets off.

April pulls me inside and shuts the door behind me. "Is there good news, then?"

"And bad. Which would you like first?"

"The good, of course. Makes the bad more digestible."

"Mr. Stewart wants me for the circus."

"Hurrah!" She squeezes my arm, then crosses to a table with a decanter of golden liquid. "This calls for sherry. I hope you received the champagne I sent down."

"That was you? Thank you."

"You're welcome. Now, what's the bad news?" She pours a measure into two glasses.

"This morning's daily mentioned the demised Mrs. Amberly Sloane. I've taken refuge on E-Deck. But your clothes are still in Mrs. Sloane's room."

"Oh, don't worry about that. But I am sorry to see Mrs. Sloane go." She hands me a glass and lifts hers for me to clink. We both sip. It tastes like gasoline fumes.

April's room is laid out similarly to Mr. Stewart's, though an explosion of clothes litters every surface. Her trademark menswear suits seem to lounge over the beds, with beaded capes thrown over the backs of chairs. Bright scarves hang from the bedposts, like pennants. April scoops a dress off a chair, clearing a space for me to sit.

"I like to air my clothes. Makes them last longer. Maybe we can hide you in here?"

"Thank you, but the farther I am from the scene of the crime, the better."

"Hmm." Her mouth swishes to one side. "So your brother's not going with you?"

I shake my head and take another sip of the gasoline, which seems a good alternative to airing my emotions in front of her.

"The sooner you let people be who they want to be, the better for all." She tucks a strand of dark hair behind her ear. "When I told Mother I had no interest in men, she was angry for a good year. Every time we saw a child, she'd give me a dirty look."

She raises an eyebrow at me, and I shut my mouth, which has begun to gape. Well, that certainly explains her remark about Jamie not being her "type."

Overlooking my rudeness, she continues, "But one day, out of the blue, she said, 'I guess that's that, then.' And we've been fine ever since."

I nod. "I just thought I knew him." I focus on a stunner of a dress spread over a bed, which looks sunrise yellow from one angle and sky blue from the other. It's much cleverer than Marigold Fantasy. "Why did you send that Lucile for me to wear?"

"I didn't get a chance to tell you. I was trying to throw Lucy off the scent by having you wear that dress. She thought House of July had planted you to upstage her. Which is true, but I didn't want her to accuse you of being a phony."

Someone knocks.

"Who could that be at this hour?" April smoothly crosses to the door, still holding her glass. "Yes? Who is it?"

"It's your steward, ma'am. Please don't be alarmed, but it seems we've run into a bit of a snag, and we're calling all passengers to the Boat Deck."

Casting me a disbelieving gaze, April cracks open the door. "You can't be serious. It's the middle of the night."

"Yes, ma'am, and I do apologize for the inconvenience. I'm sure everything will be okay. But please put on your life belts."

She closes the door. "Life belts? Can you imagine?"

"It must have been the swell. You don't think we hit something, do you?" Perhaps it's just a precaution, but a clanging begins in my head, like the ash-collectors banging their drums.

"A big boat like the *Titanic*? You'd think everything would get out of her way." She sets down her glass and opens the armoire. Reaching up, she pulls down two life belts. "We'd better go find Mother."

"I have to go back to E-Deck," I tell her.

"No. If we did hit something, it's better to be closer to the lifeboats, wouldn't you say? Your brother will find you. Stay with me."

"It's not just him I'm worried about."

"Valora, wait—"

But I'm already out the door.

34

I hurry down the tidal-wave staircase, this time not slowed
by the tan pumps. Most people have retired for the night,
but the few late birds throw disapproving glances my way.
A steward passes, suggesting that folks return to their rooms.
Another directs them to the Boat Deck. No one seems to
know much beyond the fact that something is happening.

The hackle feather floats into my mind. *Something's going
to happen.*

My stomach clenches like a fist.

When I finally reach the first-class corridor on E-Deck, I'm
surprised to see Charlotte and Jamie hurrying to her room.
"Jamie!" I call after them.

"Valora!" Charlotte waves. The hem of her evening dress
peeks out from under her wool coat. Her tiara has gone
crooked, and her hair hangs in messy curls, the kind of curls
that look played in. From the way she's blushing, and the way
Jamie pulls at his ear, I can't help wondering what they've
been up to in the time since he left me.

"Jamie, what's happening?"

"Not sure yet."

The cabin door opens and Strudel emerges, followed by a

woman in a blue-grey duster who must be Charlotte's mother, holding a life belt as if it were a soiled baby's nappy. More clanging goes off in my head.

"I've been waiting for you, darling," Mrs. Fine says a little dreamily, her eyelids fluttering. "We were told to put these on and go to the Boat Deck. But at this hour? It's hardly the time for drills. Why, hello, dog walker." She blinks at Jamie, then turns her eyes to me. "Oh, and another dog walker?"

"I think it's best to do as they suggest," Jamie tells the women. "Let me help you with that." Jamie helps Mrs. Fine clip the straps on the life belt while she holds her silver-blond braid to one side.

One of the first-class stewards approaches. "Ma'am, miss, you must go up to the Boat Deck. Come, I shall accompany you." His grey eyes brush over Jamie and me. "And you should get back to your own cabins. Your steward will direct you."

Why can't he direct us to the Boat Deck as well?

The steward sets off, with Mrs. Fine in tow.

Jamie squeezes my shoulder. "Valora, go with Charlotte."

"But I—"

"She and her mum might need help getting to the lifeboats." The phoenix glares at the dragon, a vein throbbing in his neck. "Don't worry. I'm just going to fetch the others. We'll figure out what's what and meet you up on the Boat Deck."

The dragon withdraws her talons. "Fine."

Charlotte catches Jamie by the arm. "You'll be okay, right?"

"O' course. Strudel and I have a date for tomorrow, don't we, girl?"

Strudel pants happily between them. I begin to turn away, but not before seeing Charlotte place a kiss on Jamie's lips.

Jamie whispers to Charlotte, and she whispers back, something stubborn animating her features. A tense moment seems to freeze them.

At last, Charlotte nods. Then like the sun as it sets over a hungry sea, she slips from his grasp.

———.··.———

A CROWD WAITS for the lifts, so the steward leads whoever is willing to walk up the stairs. But Mrs. Fine doesn't want to walk. Dutifully, Charlotte waits with her, and I wait with Charlotte, though each moment that passes squeezes my accordion heart tighter and tighter.

"We paid good money for this trip," a man in a silk robe complains to his wife. "Why should *we* do these drills?"

Another man bites down on a cigar, his chest puffed with importance. "They'll sort it out. I heard it was an accident on the Orlop Deck. Probably some bloke was drinking on the job and blew out a boiler."

Judging by the smirk on his face, he's probably never seen a boiler before. A blown boiler would be catastrophic for the men working it—and for the ship.

I can't help thinking of Drummer. What if something happened in Boiler Room 6? He could be injured, or worse. And here I am, waiting in this stuffy lobby with these nobs who can't be bothered to climb the stairs to their own safety.

Charlotte and her mother don't need my help. Jamie only sent me here to keep me out of the way.

Charlotte squeezes my arm. "Once we get to America, I was thinking, maybe I can take in Wink and Olly through the Home for Little Souls. I want to help."

"We're joining the circus," I say, though the words suddenly strike me as childish.

"Of course. I only meant, just in case."

Just in case *what*?

I need to find out what's going on. Jamie will kill me for going back for the others, but he somehow tricked me into going with Charlotte in the first place. Well, he can rant at me later.

I force a smile. "Help your mother. I'm sorry, but I must go check on something."

"No, Valora, stay with us."

"I'll be okay." And with that, I hurry back toward the Collar.

Back on the third-class side of E-Deck, a crowd has collected where the Collar crosses Scotland Road. Most are making their way up the staircase, lugging bags or sacks.

A feeling of dread untethers me, pulling me in different directions. I collect snippets of conversations, and though I don't understand all the languages, I feel the worry in them as sure as I feel my heartbeat pounding in my head.

A woman with a red nose clutches a man in a dressing robe. "Did you hear that racket? It was like iron dragged over a thousand marbles. I knew we should've stayed in London."

We didn't hear a racket on B-Deck. Maybe they have a better idea of what happened down here. I strain to follow their conversation.

The man pats the woman's arm. "Maybe it's a shot propeller. Caught a whale or something."

"Whales know enough to stay away from propellers. Mark my words, it's ice."

Ice.

The word slithers in my head and lies coiled, waiting to strike. *Possible ice,* the weather reports had said.

The lights flicker, and people shriek. The lights return, but no one trusts them now.

Several paces down Scotland Road, the door Drummer took me through to reach Boiler Room 6 opens. I hurry over. A man emerges, and then another, their clothes wet and beards matted.

"Sirs. Have you seen Drummer? He's a fireman. Chinese, slim in build, plays a drum."

Both bend and put their hands on their knees, panting and looking dazed. I'm about to repeat my question when a third man emerges, this one with hulking biceps. His chest heaves as he catches his breath. Water drips from his yellow hair into his squinting eyes. It's Fireman Brandish, Drummer's friend. I gasp at the sight of the whirling drum stuck in the waistband of his trousers.

"That's—" I can't manage to finish the sentence, as my own heart becomes a whirling drum, beating rapidly out of control.

"Aye." He passes the drum to me. "Drummer fell when she hit, got his foot stuck. We tried, but the water in 6 was too high."

The door closes with a heavy thud, like the sealing of a tomb.

Brandish wipes his face, which is wet with more than just seawater. "He was a good man, and I'm sorry. Plenty more souls will rise afore the night is done." He strides away after his mates, becoming a dark blur in my vision.

The beads hang limply on either side of the whirling drum. Drummer's laughing eyes dance before me, the liveliest notes on an instrument made to be played. I realize I never learned his real name.

Little Sister, there is much sorrow in your face.

35

A woman whose clogs punch the floor drags her suitcase over my foot, but I barely feel it. I sink against
the wall of the too-quiet boiler casing, feeling lost and
small. Drummer is below. It doesn't seem right to leave him.

A steward passes out life belts to a group of men with dark
beards speaking a language of rolling syllables. One presses
his hands together. "Please. No English. Help understand."

The steward flaps his arm toward the stern and snaps,
"Decks! Go to your *decks*!" Then, having run out of life belts,
he sets off in another direction.

"Stowaway!" says a voice only a few paces away.

Bo appears beside me, his face still handsome despite a new
cut above his eyebrow and a bruise reddening his jaw, probably from his fight with Skeleton and the bottom cutters.

"He's gone," I gasp, showing Bo the whirling drum. "There
was a flood."

Then his strong arms are holding me, his chest a firm but
comfortable spot to rest my head. I feel the rise and fall of his
breath, and all the torn bits in me that still quietly inflict their
damage stop hurting for a moment.

Bo's chest sinks a little. There's a grim set to his mouth, as if he looked into the future and saw something calamitous on the horizon. Catching me watching him, his expression softens. "If Drummer is gone, he chose a noble destiny. We will mourn the dead later. Come. We don't have much time. They are gathering people by the lifeboats."

"Did you see Jamie?"

"Yes. He and Tao went to fetch the men. Wink and Olly went to the Halfway There Party in the General Room, but they must have left, because I did not find them there. I thought they might return to the room. Stay here. I'll check."

I watch numbly as folks tread by, many still in their nightgowns and digging sleep from their eyes.

Bo returns a minute later. "Not there. Let's try the other General Room." He takes my hand, tugging me aft.

The woman with the clogs runs back toward us, wailing something in Dutch, heedless of the other people in the way. Bo catches me against him. The woman trips, dropping her suitcase, which springs open, littering the floor with clothes. Her sobs scratch my ears like forks over bone china. A man drags her away.

A thread of panic slips through me. "How do boiler rooms flood? They can't all flood, right? Isn't everything on the ship watertight? What's going on, Bo?"

He places a reassuring hand on my back. "I am not sure yet." His dark eyes force my attention to him. "You and I are partners tonight. We need to find the kumquats. If something bad happened, then we find a boat that will take Chinese."

I grimace, already anticipating the resistance. There aren't enough lifeboats to go around, only enough for half the passengers aboard. And people who get served bread heels are more apt to be kicked off them than put on. But perhaps our acrobatic performance has shifted the scales in our favor. Maybe it's harder not to save someone after giving them a round of applause.

We reach the aft staircase, where the crowd has thickened. Their protests make my ears ring.

"Won't let us up," a voice calls down the stairs. "Says we should wait."

"Wait for what?"

"It's outrageous."

"Probably just a drill. Let's go back to our rooms and wait until the ruckus is over."

"Wink! Olly!" Bo calls up the stairwell. No one answers.

"There's another way up." I pull him back down the hallway to one of the emergency doors and throw it open, ignoring its prohibitive "Third Class Not Allowed" sign. This is an emergency, after all. "You can get to the Boat Deck this way, folks," I tell the closest passengers, gesturing in case they don't speak English.

Several cast us guarded looks, or maybe they're just scared. A dark-haired group in thick sweaters passes, and a woman with a tight bun stops. It's the Syrian woman from the dining hall, clutching her little girl to her.

I gesture through the door and point up. "Lifeboats. Come."

Bo and I take the first-class stairs two at a time, pulling

ourselves up the ornate banisters. When we finally emerge from the deckhouse—five decks up—my legs begin to cramp, and I lean over my knees to catch my breath. The Syrians exit moments later, and we lose them in the crowd.

On the port-side corner where we're standing, the Boat Deck crawls with people, most collecting around the quartet of lifeboats. We cross to starboard and find the situation the same.

Unlike my prior visits to the Boat Deck, all the lights have been turned on. At least the electricity is still running. But with no moonlight silvering the water, the ocean seems to have disappeared. If not for the liquid sounds of water sloshing against the hull, we might be performers on a stage in the middle of some play. A tragedy.

"What happened?" I say, mostly to myself, shivering as the cold bites at my exposed parts. I wish I hadn't left April's vanilla coat in Mrs. Sloane's room. Worse, I put Mum's Bible in the slipper bag. It'll be lost in all this commotion.

I'm sorry to lose your wedding picture, honored parents. But in case you're worried, don't put on the kettle. You won't see Jamie or me tonight, I swear.

Bo distractedly takes off his peacoat and pours the sweet warmth of it over my shoulders, then puts his cap over my head. Peering at something in the distance, he points. His shell ring gleams like a gibbous moon on a night that seems to lack one.

My eyes can barely make out anything in the darkness. But then a hint of white shows itself. I squint, trying to interpret the grey-and-black gradations of what's before me. Finally, I suss out the edges of the thing—it's a pale, jagged wall of ice.

"Ice mountain," Bo says quietly, translating the Cantonese word for *iceberg*.

I gasp as the pieces fall into place. So we did hit an iceberg. It must have breached the hull, allowing seawater to flood Boiler Room 6.

Rivulets of water sprint toward the bow, angling starboard. The ship is definitely tilted toward the head. Are we still taking on water?

"They have ways to bail out, right?"

Bo fills his lungs, but then says simply, "There are pumps, yes."

Did he stop himself from saying more? He's intimately familiar with how boiler rooms work. Surely he has a good grasp of the situation.

I suddenly find it hard to draw air. He isn't saying more because it doesn't look good. What are a few pumps against a leak big enough to flood an entire boiler room? *Plenty more souls will rise afore the night is done.*

"We're sinking, aren't we?"

Bo squeezes my hand, his eyes grazing me with concern. "Maybe, Stowaway. But worry later." He pulls me along like a farmer leading a stubborn mule.

Mourn later, worry later. How can I just set aside the enormity of what's happening to us, like mail to open on another day? But I must, because people are depending on us. People I can't lose.

I fling away catastrophic thoughts, glaring hard at my surroundings for Wink and Olly. Adrenaline floods my veins, honing my senses. The crank of the winches sounds like the screech of owls, and my nostrils fill with the iron scent of fear. Crewmen grunt, positioning davits so that the lifeboats overhang the sides of the ship, ready to be filled. From what I can see, not one craft has been lowered yet.

Bo steers me to the back rail, which gives us a view of the poop deck and the well deck. Dozens of people clutter these third-class decks, but none seem willing to bypass the waist-high gate to the superstructure.

Why the bloody hell don't they crawl over the gate? Who cares about the rules now? The crew isn't helping, so they better help themselves if they want to wake up tomorrow.

I strain to see Wink and Olly but don't spot their narrow forms. "They could've gone into the Smoking Room or the General Room where it's warmer."

Bo nods. The stubble that covers his chin makes him appear older and more solemn. "But let's make sure they're not here first, in case we have trouble getting up again." He's back to Cantonese only. I guess the nerves are getting to him.

"How about we split up? I'll look down there, and you—"

"No. If I lost you, your brother would kill me." He offers me his arm.

With a sigh, I take it. We travel up the starboard side, a trip made trickier by the press of confused people. A lady faints, and a crowd collects, forcing us to climb a bench to pass them.

Jovial voices lift from a group of men smoking cigars, as

if this were a party and the crewmen cranking the davits, the entertainment.

Orders are barked. More boats are swung to outboard. Some hang lopsided, their cables twisting and their ropes whipping about, with crewmen scrambling to right them.

One might think they had never practiced. A performance needs practice, or it will fail.

A woman slips on the iced-over pine slats, and Bo and I catch her between us. She shakes us off, hardly seeing us. "I don't want to die. Where's that Great Dane? I didn't mean to lose him, Phinny. I'll find him!"

Her words send a charge through me. Whoever Phinny is, he's not present, at least not in the flesh. Many ghosts are being stirred up by this crisis. I hope they leave the living alone. There's too much harm on this boat already.

Bo steers me clear of a developing brawl between an officer and a drunk fellow trying to board a boat before it's swung out. "Sir, you must stand back!"

The drunk man swings a fist, but other men pull him away.

Then, wiping the sweat from his forehead, the officer blows a whistle. "We shall load women and children first! Men, stand back. Let the women pass."

Bo casts me a worried look. "Maybe you should get on now."

An offended noise clears my throat. "I'm not leaving until the rest of you can board."

Bo scowls, and a shadow crosses his face. With a shake of his head, as if to cast off his worry, his eyes comb the crowd for the lads. "I only see first class here."

He's right. It isn't just their clothes, but their better-quality life belts, with thicker shoulder straps and ties, that give them away. Wink and Olly can't be here. Maybe they're bottlenecked in one of the stairwells, or stalled elsewhere in the labyrinth-like passages of the ship. They're clever boots, and as boiler monkeys, they must possess some sea sense. But panic can be a ruthless scamp, slashing the knees of reason.

People peer out of the arched windows of the deckhouse, their faces tight with worry. Some flit from the lounge only to return, like foxes reluctant to leave the safety of the den. Others appear not worried at all, like the spry young man in the gymnasium riding an exercise bicycle.

The boats on the forward end appear less crowded, per-haps because they lie farther from most of the staircases. I count four lifeboats, including a smaller cutter already swung out, plus a flatter boat still covered with a tarp. Maybe the flatter one is the "collapsible" type Jamie mentioned.

A couple pushes past, headed for the closest lifeboat, where an officer yells, "Newlyweds! We will accept newlywed cou-ples, in addition to women and children."

"What is a 'newlywed'?" Bo asks me.

"A just-married couple."

I'm not sure if it's my imagination, but I swear Bo's fingers grip mine more tightly, and despite the chill, my cheeks warm.

Past another deckhouse, marked "Officers' Quarters," we stop at a gate that blocks entry to the navigating bridge. The gate is half-open. We steal closer, unnoticed by the crewmen readying the foremost lifeboats on our right. On our left, an open doorway allows us a direct view into the command center. Brass instruments give the illusion of a populated room, though only four officers stand the watch, including Captain Smith. Their movements are jerky, their voices agitated.

"No one. Take 'em three hours to get here."

"Where are those damnable flares?"

"Someone call Bell. I need an update on the boilers."

"Six is underwater. They're pumping five, and four is flooding, too."

They're talking about Boiler Room 6. Only thin veils of vapor trail out from the closest smokestack, the chimney for Boiler Rooms 5 and 6. The one behind it still vigorously puffs away. I push aside thoughts of Drummer.

A walkway hung with lifesavers wings out from the navigating bridge, blocking access to the front rail and thus our view of the forward decks. Even I cannot bring myself to breach the command center. All our fates depend on those officers doing their jobs.

Bo points to a narrow staircase cut into the floor, surrounded by a bulwark to prevent accidental falls down the hole. "Where do these stairs lead?"

"What the devil are you two doing here?" An officer emerges from the bridge. "This is off-limits! Move along!" He shoos us away, nearly clipping Bo on the shoulder.

As we retrace our steps past the officers' quarters, Bo halts abruptly and tweaks his head toward a ladder attached to the deckhouse. "Maybe the view is good up there."

I climb first, and Bo brings up the rear. Once on the roof,

we skirt around the first smokestack, where two more collapsibles, one on each side, wait like giant sleeping turtles.

Whose idea was it to store boats on the roof? They look heavy and will probably throw out someone's back when they're lifted over the safety rails and lowered onto the Boat Deck.

Past the collapsibles, we creep onto an unrailed stretch of roof that covers the navigating bridge. Standing there, on the head of the whale, the bowing of the ship is unmistakable, with a slight list to starboard.

My breath jams in my throat. When the ship founders, there won't be enough room for the third class on the lifeboats. We'll be the last in line. And that water looks cold enough to freeze at the touch.

Feeling me tremble, Bo slips an arm around my shoulders. Without that anchor, I might blow away, as flimsy as a cigarette flicked on the wind.

Focusing on the decks below, I stare hard for our lads. Both the well deck and the forecastle crawl with passengers, but no one stays in one place for long. I rub my eyes, wishing Wink and Olly weren't so spindly.

"There!" Bo points.

Two small figures have emerged from a staircase. A snippet of orange fabric catches my eye. It's Wink, his orange kerchief a tiny flame in the dark.

"Wink!" we call together.

The lads glance up at us. Bo motions for them to stay put. He points to himself, and then back to them, communicating wordlessly, *I will come get you.*

Olly and Wink both give the thumbs-up sign.

I follow Bo back to the ladder, my feet lighter. Minutes later, he holds the door to the deckhouse open for me. Inside, a deadly warmth cradles me, as treacherous as a fog of opium. The thick oriental rugs grab at my feet, urging me to stay.

Too many people linger inside, the goats. Can't they see the angle of the floor? This gilded whale is too heavy to float much longer. Or maybe they're counting down to their fates. I want to rail at them not to give up, but I have a few other fates to worry about first.

"The lifeboats take women and children only," Bo says. He's back to English now. "That's you and the kumquats. But you must convince the crew you are a girl."

"Convince them? You mean flash my beacons?"

A blush creeps around his stubble. "No, but you look nice in dresses."

"Go'an, you charmer." The flirting eases my anxiety for a moment. But then the lights flicker again, and a collective scream strikes my heart like a flight of arrows.

Bo grabs my arm. "Remember the woman on E-Deck who dropped her suitcase? There must be many clothes around."

I didn't lock Mrs. Sloane's room, and the Cabbage Patch is loads closer than hiking back to E-Deck. "Follow me."

We dash down the tidal-wave staircase. On the carved wall of the first landing, the golden clock reads 12:25. Somehow we've slipped into the next day. Our show on the rails feels like a distant dream whose edges have frayed, unraveling thread by thread.

Stragglers move about, most headed up the stairs. A few haven't made up their minds. A man in a tuxedo comforts a woman clinging to the golden cherub.

"Saint Christopher," she wails. "Please, Saint Christopher!"

We reach the spacious Entrance Hall on B-Deck, where another cherub offers empty consolation. I'm surprised to see people resting on the embroidered settees.

"Get yourself into a lifeboat," I urge. "There's not much time."

They throw reproachful glances our way. It occurs to me that, for the first time, my looking more like Ba than Mum may hurt them more than me.

The lights flick off, and people cry out. I grasp Bo closer. We halt in our tracks, with only the burnt-in images in our eyes to guide us. After a clutch of heartbeats, the lights turn back on.

With no time to waste, I hasten to the felted doors behind the lifts. "Follow this hallway to the end, and you'll find the crew stairs that lead to the forward decks." If I hadn't seen April being led up those stairs on my first day, I wouldn't have known about them.

"I do not want to leave you."

"I'll be fine. We're running out of time." I return his coat and cap.

The lights flicker again, but this time stay on.

Bo nods. "I will meet you back at the 'newlywed' boat."

Then he brushes his lips against mine, giving me a kiss as sweet as I imagined. And I imagined it quite a bit.

And then he's gone, leaving the sure-footed Valora Luck trying to remember how to work her feet.

Before setting off in the other direction, I knock on April's door, in case she's still around. No one answers, and the door is locked. I hope she and her mother made it to the lifeboats.

Then I make for the Cabbage Patch, glancing around more out of habit than actual concern that anyone cares about Mrs. Sloane anymore. The alligators here have more important things to do than worry about minnows like me.

The bed in B-64 has been tidied, and the rotting flowers removed, but everything else remains as it was. From the trunk, I select one of Mrs. Sloane's matronly dresses, a pair of gloves, and a coat. I shove Drummer's whirling drum into a deep pocket, along with my carved whale. With the bee-swarm veil tossed out the porthole of Room 14, I put on a knitted cap and say a prayer that a woman who looks like me will still be worth saving.

36

I make my way up to the Boat Deck, stopping short at the sight of Fong, sitting at the bottom of a flight of stairs with his head between his knees. His lame foot sticks out and is missing its shoe. Jamie crouches by him, with Wink, Olly, and Bo standing alongside. I cry out, and all but Fong look up.

Jamie takes in my change of clothes and nods in approval. A makeshift sling has been tied around him, taking the weight off his injured shoulder. His cap is damp, and sweat runs down the fine bones of his neck.

"What happened?" I ask. "Where are Tao and Ming Lai?"

Fong holds his knees and rocks himself.

"Ming Lai is with the Domenics," Jamie says quietly. "Tao, well . . ."

"He left," Fong howls. "Stupid turtle. Said he wanted to give someone else his place."

Though I hear the words, they have trouble sinking in. "You mean he—?"

"He left to meditate!" Spit flecks Fong's chin. "I lost him!"

Only now do I notice how Olly rubs his eyes with his sleeves, and how Wink's mouth bunches into a tight knot, as if to keep his emotions from spilling out. Bo, the farthest from Fong, stands with his hands loosely on his hips, slightly shaking his head.

"Aw, lads," I manage, placing my hands on the boys' slumped shoulders. "We also lost Drummer." A pained look crosses Jamie's face, and the lads begin sniffing. "But we have to get through this. Tao and Drummer would want us to make it, so let's not disappoint them." I swallow hard and meet Bo's gaze. "We shall mourn later."

Jamie crouches by Fong. "Uncle, we have to go. Please, think of the lads."

"Nothing is left," Fong moans. "Leave me here with Tao."

"Uncle, please." Jamie's eyes plead, a look I've seen countless times, as when Ba refused to leave our flat and we feared he might disappear into himself.

Fong clamps his knees tighter. The lights shudder ominously again. But Fong still does not rise.

Jamie passes me a look that contains ghosts of the past. We know Fong's grief, the kind that freezes you in space and time. The kind that blindfolds you, then hangs you over a wire, with no idea how deep the drop is or how much farther you must walk to get to the end. Neither of us spoke for a week after Mum died. It was as if talking meant progress and progress meant she was part of the past. That was something neither of us could accept.

Bo, chewing his lip, studies Fong with a mix of distrust and maybe a little despair. Perhaps, after years of hating the man, a measure of sympathy has finally bubbled up, and he isn't sure where to put it, like receiving a gift for which you have not yet found the right drawer.

My nose and eyes grow hot with tears as I remember the serene Tao, the man who unlocks doors. I plant myself on the bottom stair beside Fong, but he shrinks away from me. "Leave me alone, girl."

Bo extends a hand, and I reach out mine in response. But when he doesn't take it, I realize the hand isn't meant for me.

"Uncle," he says, "I will look for him. But if he does not want to go, you must honor his wishes."

The sound of Bo's voice seems to startle Fong, and his head snaps up. His eyes, more grey than brown, squint, as if not trusting his ears.

"Tao." Fong's voice cracks. "Tao is like a brother."

"Yes. And brothers honor brothers."

In the soft clinking of the chandeliers, and the groans of the ship as she labors, a glimmer of hope works its way down the tidal-wave staircase to the Chinese huddled at her feet.

At last, Fong extends a hand, a hand that trembles as if offering it is the hardest thing he's ever done. Bo catches it in his solid grasp, and firmly pulls the man to his feet.

Fong's bad foot hangs like a bag of sand from his ankle, and he can't stand up all the way. Bo squats in front of the old pickpocket and, in one quick motion, hauls him up, so that the man is draped across his shoulders like a fox stole.

"Let's go, Stowaway."

Watching the cliffs of Dover take the stairs two at a time, I admit that, for once, I envy Fong just a tad.

37

At the top of the stairs, Bo puts Fong back on his pins, then squares his cap.

Jamie and Bo grasp arms. "Good luck finding Tao."

"Stay salty."

Their voices are hale, but the two hold their solemn shake longer than usual.

Then Bo's eyes float to mine, which suddenly feel hot and in danger of melting. I throw my arms around the fisherman, squeezing him tight, as if trying to leave a permanent impression. I loosen my grip, and he gazes down at me, like a sailor taking his last look at land.

"It is not the end of us, Stowaway. Not if I can help it."

I lift my face to Bo's, and he kisses me with a fierceness that speaks of survival and wishes for a future. A sliver of a smile appears on his face and sears itself into my heart.

Taking the wooden whale from my pocket, I press it to his fingers. "Return it to me."

"I will."

Then he's gone, like the last notes of a song that ends too soon.

Jamie herds the Johnnies to the door, and we step into the

night. The population on the Boat Deck has tripled, and so has the hysteria, some expressed in loud voices, some in silent tears.

A loud hiss precedes a streak of light that bursts into a shower of sparkles, momentarily shutting off the stars. People gasp and cry out. A child points. A man holds his praying hands to the sky.

Olly twists up his neck. "What was that?"

"Emergency flare," says Jamie, pulling him toward the closest lifeboat, the newlywed boat. "They're signaling our distress. Come on, lads."

I shiver inside my coat. I can't help thinking that the flare is a last cry of desperation. We're the only ones out here. Unless heaven holds out a hand for us to climb into, half the people here will perish. Then again, maybe the flare is a *good* sign. Surely the crew has used their wireless. Perhaps help has arrived, and the flare simply pinpoints our location.

As if to reassure me, music begins to play from somewhere. I recognize the swingy, plucking rhythm of ragtime. People smile. Maybe the situation is not so grave after all.

In the newlywed boat, about thirty people have already boarded, mostly women but also a few men.

An officer raises his hands at the crowd. "Hold! No more passengers."

Jamie scrambles over to him. "Can you take us, mate? We've got a woman, two children, and an injured man."

I frown at Jamie, sick at the thought of leaving him behind. But Wink and Olly squeeze in closer to me, and I know they need me more.

The officer glances at the lot of us. "No."

"But it's only half-full!" Jamie protests.

"Prepare to release the falls," the officer yells at the crewman tending the pulley.

I gather Wink and Olly, one in each arm, and push them forward. "Excuse me, sir?" I project my voice, trying to make myself heard over the din of people and the ocean. "These children are my charges. Please let us board. There's ample space, and—"

The officer looks at me square on, and all my thoughts halt at the sight of Officer Merry's dour face. He doesn't speak. He must not recognize me from that first day on the well deck.

"And we won't take up much room," I finish.

The crewman attending the ropes twists around. When our eyes meet, my breath hitches. It's the QM, giving me a peculiar look. I glance away, feeling a net drop over me.

The QM takes in Wink and Olly, looking as earnest as two well-spent pennies beside me, and then his eyes snap back to mine. "I know you." He turns to Officer Merry and jerks his head in my direction. "That's no woman, sir. It's one of the acrobats who turned my bridge into a circus. A wolf in sheep's clothing is what he is."

Grimacing, Jamie puts his face up to the QM. "It's your own fault you're so easily fooled, so how 'bout you do your job or get stuffed?" With his breath fogging out of his mouth, Jamie looks like an angry phoenix rising in the mist.

Officer Merry peers at me, his squint deepening in his face.

"You're the one who came up from the hatch. Knew you'd be a problem. Trickster, huh?"

"Officer Merry, I *am* a girl."

The QM plucks off my knitted hat, and a chorus of women gasp. "Why is his hair like that, then?"

Jamie's hands ball up. Usually he keeps his cool, but now his feathers have been ruffled. I hiss at him to back down. Aggression will only ensure we won't get on this boat.

I pull the hat out of the QM's hands and look straight into Officer Merry's narrowed eyes. "As an acrobat, long hair gets in the way. Dressing as a boy allows me to perform tricks that some might consider unseemly if done by a girl." I turn to the occupants of the lifeboat. "Many of you enjoyed our show. I beg you to speak for us."

A chorus of yays and nays erupt, somehow canceling each other out.

Then a familiar figure gets to her feet, one hand on her mother's shoulder for balance. "Officer Merry, I can personally vouch that she is most definitely a girl, as sure as your man is an incompetent baboon." April's red swing of a mouth stays in the shape of an O as if to draw out the last word.

"I can vouch for her, too, Officer Merry," adds another voice, this one lighter in texture but just as clear. Behind April, a young woman rises. My eyes bug out at the sight of Charlotte, still in her green velvet gown and hugging Strudel tightly. Mrs. Fine is sitting on the bench next to her. "Valora, come sit by us."

"Oughtn't we be on our way?" says a woman with the pushed-in face of a bulldog, sitting at the front of the lifeboat with her hands in a muff.

"Get a move on!" cries another.

The QM switches his hard stare between me and the lifeboat.

Officer Merry sighs. "Fine, you get on. But not those two. They're old enough to stay."

"They're only eight and ten!" I undershoot by a couple years and hope it's enough.

"I was ten when my daddy gave me a mule and told me to git," says a man from somewhere nearby.

A chorus of agreement comes from the men still waiting on the deck. "Ain't fair to give those beggars a place when good women are still waiting on a spot."

"Which women?" I look around and see none.

"They're loading more from the gangway doors," says another man.

Wink and Olly stand straight as pins. Officer Merry squats so that his eyes are even with theirs, and the hard lines of his face soften. "Look, lads. It's time for you to be men. There'll be another boat along soon that'll take care of you, but for now, we have to get the women and tykes away, okay?"

"Yes, sir." Olly's voice cracks. Wink nods, his cheek as twitchy as a firefly's bulb.

"No!" I insist. "They are in my care."

"Then you stay with them," says the woman with the muff.

Jamie belts an arm over Wink's shoulder, pulling him back.

"You go on, Val. Come on, lads. We'll find another boat."

I snort. How can he be so certain the next boat won't present the same problem?

Olly follows Wink, and even Fong shuffles back. Cold air rushes against my teeth. The Johnnies are ganging up against me.

"Hurry, do hurry!" cries a woman.

April's gloved hands beckon. "Come on, darling. We've got to stick together."

Strudel barks, and Charlotte's wet eyes watch Jamie and me silently fight.

But I can't abandon my brother. Damn him. Jamie is like water in the palm, which can only be held a few moments before slipping through the fingers. I should never have let him walk away two years ago, in sailor slops too big for his spindly self, his too-straight posture full of hurt. If I take this boat, I may never see him again. Worse, because of him, I've grown attachments to others that will feel like bits of my soul ripped out if they are lost.

Officer Merry ticks his head at me. "Put her in."

The QM and another crewman reach for me, but I step out of their grasp and lift my chin. "Lower away."

"Bloody snakes, Val!" If Jamie's arm wasn't in a sling, he might toss me into the lifeboat himself. "We might not get another chance."

Wink's cheek has stopped fluttering, but Olly's nose has begun to run.

"Well, then, let's make sure we do."

38

If we get out of this, remind me to wring your neck," Jamie seethes, storming off.

The next two lifeboats are already being lowered, barely half-full. Have they already launched the lifeboats in the other three quadrants? My leg muscles cramp from the effort of running while trying not to fall on the ice-slickened deck. Jamie dashes to the small cutter, the lifeboat closest to the bridge, where crewmen are still boarding passengers.

Working his mouth the way he used to charm audiences before a performance, Jamie engages an officer, gesticulating even with his injured arm. "There are five of us. You've got plenty of room in there." He points his nose toward the craft. I count two women among the occupants, their faces obscured by broad hats.

The boat begins to descend.

"Hold the falls, hold the falls!" Jamie demands. "Officer, let us board, mate. Look at all the people still here. Plus, we have an injured man, two children, and a girl."

My boots clap the floor as I stride to the officer, whose nostrils flatten at the sight of me in his face. "Officer Merry told us we could board this boat. Go ask him if you don't believe me." I doubt the man will take me up on it.

His serious eyes squint down the deck. I swear he would've let us on, but then one of the boat's occupants half stands and wags his finger at the officer. It's the haughty Sir Cosmo Duff-Gordon. "Nonsense, do not let those mongrels on!"

Even in the cold, the word slaps me smartly across my face.

Lady Duff-Gordon looks up sharply from under her large hat. Her gaze skims my face. Then Lucy, as she asked me to call her, scoffs. "Now they're wearing women's clothes."

"Lucy, it is I, Mrs. Sloane." I hold my hands out imploringly, remembering how her satin-gloved fingers so warmly pressed my wrist only a few days ago. "You asked me to wear your Strawberries and Cream dress, don't you remember? Please help us."

Lucy's top jaw rolls back like a secretary desk. "I—I—" Her eyes cast about wildly, as big as lifesavers, at last coming to rest on her husband's confused gaze. Her face becomes severe. "I do not know you, and how dare you speak to me as a familiar."

The denial does not surprise me, yet my mouth puckers like the time I accidentally bit into an orange rind.

Sir Duff-Gordon flicks his hand. "We must be off. I've paid good money. Now lower away, man. Do as I say!"

Remembering all the people in third class who haven't yet reached the Boat Deck, and for whom it'll be too late anyway, my temper flares like a boiler ready to explode. "Who gave him a scepter?" I seethe at the officer. "Neptune?"

Jamie spits on the deck. "You're a bunch of bleeding nobs." Rile up one twin and you get two for your trouble. "You've got room. You just won't let us on. It's like you're playing God."

And then it's my turn. "And one day—and it could very well be this day—Saint Peter's going to call you to task for sending a bunch of innocent souls to heaven before their time."

Lady Duff-Gordon wraps her fur coat more securely around her. "You see how coarse they are. A bunch of savages. They will sink our boat."

"Come on, Officer," Sir Duff-Gordon urges, his blue eyes hardening like spots of glue. "Time's a-wasting. Lower away, man!"

The harried officer throws up his hands, and the crewmen crank the davits.

Olly's eyes are wide enough to net butterflies. I'm winding up to throw another stick on the fire when I realize Wink is gone.

While Jamie continues to spout protests, I gently put my hand on Olly's arm, not wishing to alarm him further. "Where's Wink?"

"I—I dunno." He looks wildly about. "He was standing here a moment ago."

I see only men nearby. A group huddles on a bench, swigging from champagne bottles. Another couple of gents stamp the deck, their breaths curling like white ribbons. One of them stands a whole head above the other. It's Mr. Ismay, the chair-

---

man of White Star Line, with his crane-like legs and shrewd eyes.

Stooping, he glances furtively about. If it's true that his zeal for speed led to this catastrophe, he will have a long wait at the pearly gates, accounting for many lost souls. I stare him full in the face, knowing he has lost his power over me. He blinks, as if trying to remember where he's seen me.

I leave him to work it out and return to the crisis at hand: Wink. "Did he say anything?"

Olly's potato nose scrunches up, the poor lad. His whole face is red, whether because of crying or the cold, and I hug him to me. "It's okay, Olly. Tell me what he said."

"I—I wasn't feeling so good, and h-he told me to think about the tree house we're going to build in America, and the Oreos we'll eat . . . And I said we can't get those things now without money." His lip trembles. "And then I lost track of him. I'm sorry."

I pat his back. "You did fine, Olly. And I'm going to go fetch him. I need you to stay here and get on a lifeboat when they find you a spot. Don't worry about Wink. I promise I'll take care of him, okay?"

Olly swallows and nods.

A crewman hands out life belts. While Olly and Fong help each other with their straps, I grab one for myself and one for Jamie, who's now speaking with another officer.

The officer struggles to raise the sides of the collapsible stored next to the cutter. Jamie uses his good hand to hold the boat steady for him. "Five of us," he says.

I hurry over. "Three of us for now," I drop in Jamie's ear. "Wink is gone."

"Wink?" Jamie grabs at his head. "Bloody cats. Where'd he go?"

"I think he went to fetch the money. Where is it?"

"I gave it to Wink to hold while we took care of Skeleton and his mates. Then we all went to look for you. I'm not sure where he put it."

"My guess is somewhere in the room."

"Oh, this is grand."

"I'll be right back. Go on ahead."

"No way." He grabs me by the elbow. "*We'll* go. Fong, take Olly. The crew are in a rush to drop the boats. We'll figure something out."

The old trimmer nods.

We tie on our life belts. I unhook one of the lifesavers, just in case we need it, and wear it like a necklace. Then we descend the crew stairs from the bridge. This time, no one protests our use of them. We tread carefully on the heavily slanted staircase.

"Stinkin' codfish," Jamie mutters. "When we find that minnow, I'm going to wring his scrawny neck and serve him with a wedge of lemon."

Reaching the well deck, we move carefully over the icy planks. Jamie sucks in his breath and adjusts his injured arm. He'll be of more help to Wink if he's not in so much pain.

"Let me fix your sling. Smartly, now. I dunno why you

didn't just stay up on the Boat Deck. You're dragging us down as always," I say irritably as I untie the sling and help him reposition his left arm so that it lies comfortably outside of the life belt. Somehow being crabby eases my anxiety.

"Stop fussing over me, for cod's sake."

"Stop getting into scrapes, you codfish."

He grunts, and for a moment, he feels as far away as the moon. "Do you remember what Ba would say whenever he'd wake from one of his spells?"

My ears perk. Jamie rarely brings up Ba. " 'Family saves family.' "

He stretches back his shoulder, and a shadow crosses his face. "But he was always the one putting us in jeopardy."

I begin to protest, but the truth stares me in the face. Ba *had* put us in jeopardy—our savings, our home, Mum's health. His intentions might have been good, but even when his schemes profited, catastrophe always seemed to wait around the next corner, like a thief with a bludgeon. And every time he got into a tight spot, *we* had to save the family, slipping our takes into the cracked teapot, bandaging each other up when the going got rough.

"I wish I could've done better by her," Jamie says quietly.

"What do you mean?"

"Stuck up for her more. Stood up to Ba. I'd see him take the money from the teapot when she wasn't looking. Why didn't I ever say anything?"

No wonder Jamie is so angry. *Family saves family,* but we

couldn't save Mum. As I watch him biting his lip, hurting from somewhere deeper inside, I sway, but not because of the movement of the ship.

The person Jamie can't forgive isn't Ba.

It's himself.

"We were just kids," I say.

The shadows hide his face, but I can smell his ache, as sharp as the briny sea.

"Well, if you're going to blame yourself, you'd better blame me, too, you guilt hog. In fact, why don't we throw some extra lifesavers around our necks, just to make it extra hard to move? Because I could really use more things to weigh me down. What about you?"

He glowers at me, and I reflect it back. Then I finish re-tying his arm, and we set off again.

The rush of the water snarls in our ears even before we get to E-Deck. By the time we reach the Collar, seawater has already filled the corridor, at least waist high. Room 14 lies just around the corner.

I cry out at the cold, and Jamie hisses.

"Think about, I dunno, summer," I grumble, pulling the lifesaver down to my waist. We move as if walking in thick mud, each step requiring the whole body. Holding up our arms, we slog forward as if we're coming to Jesus.

Most of the doors are closed. Objects float by: a child's cap—fortunately, not Wink's—a ball like the sort I saw in the barbershop. A roiling scrap of white grabs at my waist—a towel. I quickly pluck it off as if it were a dead animal, and let it sail away.

"Summer in London isn't exactly warm."

"Fine, imagine the desert."

"Hard to imagine a place you've never been to."

"Well, aren't you a nelly naysayer, rabbitin' on, all gloom and doom."

"You always mouth off at the worst times."

"Best times are always the worst times, china plate," I shoot back, strangely grateful for my foul mood, which at least keeps my mind off the questions clawing at me. Will we be too late? Will this dip in the sea be our first taste of a long and bitter drink to come?

Jamie grins at the Cockney term for "mate," one we consider especially ours, even though we never like when others use it. "Well, china plate, I guess you must regret not getting off at Queenstown."

"What I regret is having such a moody-pants for a brother. If you hadn't had so much to prove, we wouldn't be on this barge in the first place. *See the stars, be a man*," I say, affecting a mocking, masculine tone, and am gratified to see him wince. "Freezing our bloody cheeks off herding minnows what dunno how to take care of themselves short of wiping their tails."

He blows out an annoyed breath, but then he cracks a smile, wedging one out of me, too. "I'm sorry, Sis. I didn't think it would be so . . . *hard* on you. I thought you knew we'd always be together, even when we're not."

Some warm emotion rises in my throat, but I swallow it back down. Now is not the time for sentiment but for action.

We reach the cabin, and the door is shut. I stick my fingers into the water and grip the handle, which is so cold, even through my gloves, that it feels like a burn.

Dreading what I'll see inside, I put my shoulder to the door.

39

Inside Room 14, the water has risen to chest level, and one of the seabags is floating in the middle of the room. The ceiling light bulb blinks, somehow managing to stay lit. Water sloshes around like punch in a bowl. It grabs at my eyes and snakes up my nose. I don't see the youngest Johnny anywhere.

That grey morning when I found Ba in the alley, I knew no life remained in him, that his spirit had departed soon after he'd suffered the fatal injury. Mum's death had already pulled him into that murky space between life and death, his body in one place, his mind in another. And in that moment, his face looked almost tranquil, his body curled in a last slumber.

Unlike in that deserted alleyway, a pulse still beats here, even with the water tearing the place apart like a gang of thieves. I feel it, as sure as I feel Jamie splashing behind me. Wink is here. Somewhere.

Filling my lungs, I plunge underwater, trying to see in the dim light. A tangle of blankets billows like white seaweed. Another seabag materializes, this one . . . jerking?

I grab at the object, which feels solid, and not like a seabag at all. With my heart a frantic drum, I haul up the body.

Wink's not breathing. His face is blue, and there's a bump on his forehead. Something's twisted around his neck.

Jamie digs his finger under the ligature, untwisting it, and hauls something up from the water—the slipper bag!

At once, I understand what must have happened. Wink hung the slipper bag filled with the money around his neck, probably to make it easier to carry. He opened the door, and with the water pressure building on the other side, it clipped him on the head. Down he went, the bag acting like an anchor.

"Move him to the bunk," Jamie growls.

We haul him up, then scramble after him. Jamie kneels by his chest, with me at Wink's head. The water has not yet crested the top bunk but climbs as surely and steadily as a rising curtain.

"What do we do?" I peel off my gloves and feel for Wink's pulse, wishing his arm didn't feel so rubbery and cold. But I saw him jerk. It can't be over yet.

Jamie places his right palm over Wink's chest and pumps with a series of quick beats. "A man fell off the steamer a few months ago. We brought him back to life doing this."

"What if it hurts him? Don't make it worse."

"It can't get much worse than this. Come on, Wink." He rests a beat, then starts pumping again.

Not feeling a pulse, I open Wink's mouth and listen for breath. "Your time's not up yet, lad." My voice comes out sounding too tight, and I try to relax. "Your best mate's waiting for you. Olly needs you, or he's going to have trouble. We're going to America, remember?" A sob rises in my chest.

But as it reaches that tight spot in my throat, I growl it back. "We're depending on you. Don't you let us down."

Jamie continues to pump. He's lost his cap, and a blue vein jags like lightning across his forehead. Water streams down his face. He flips his hair back with annoyance.

"Let me take over," I tell him, scooting to take his place. My two hands will be better than his one.

With one palm over the other, I pump with quick beats, blinking away tears. Wink's chest bends and flexes, but he doesn't breathe on his own.

Jamie grabs Wink's hand. "Come on, mate," he orders. "Do this for your mum. Think of how proud she is of you. She's up there in heaven right now, sipping tea, and waiting for you to build that tree house. But you have to make it. Hear that, you stinkin' minnow? You have to make it." His voice cracks, chipping off a piece of my heart.

I keep pumping. The water rises to the mattress, pooling around Wink. The light bulb wanes, like a pale winter moon.

"Val," Jamie's voice tiptoes to me. I avoid his eyes.

My tired hands have gone numb, but I can't stop. I'll stay here, pumping Wink's chest, until my own chest stops. Wink's still in there, and he won't die alone, like Ba. I'm not a leaver. People can leave me, but I'll never leave them when I'm still needed.

Jamie puts a hand on my arm, and I look up. But just then, the water churns up a playing card. The eight of spades. The card that changes the wind. Surely it's a sign I must keep going.

With renewed vigor, I pump again.

At last, Wink coughs.

I gasp. "That's it, Wink, that's it."

Jamie turns Wink on his side, and he spits out the briny, poisonous seawater. His eyes roll back in his head, but he's alive. Hot tears paint warm stripes down my cheeks.

We help him to sitting, and soon he's blinking and twitching and hurling out his guts. It is a blessed sight.

"We need to hurry. You ready to move, mate?" Jamie asks.

Wink nods, wiping his mouth on his sleeve. "I'm sorry."

"None of that now." I swim for the lifesaver, which is floating near the other bunk. Wink shrugs it over his head and arms, holding it weakly.

With the boat sinking from the bow, we're forced to swim down Scotland Road toward the stern. Jamie takes the lead, doing a sidestroke with his good arm. The life belts keep us buoyed while we motor Wink along. Too tired to speak, I focus on kicking and not on the ceiling, which is only four feet above our heads. I also try to ignore the groans of metal coming from somewhere deep within the hull.

We're like three rats being flushed down a sewer pipe.

Scotland Road stretches for an eternity. Wink clings to his lifesaver like an octopus to a clam, trying to keep his legs from bumping me as I ferry him along. The sprint leaves me gasping, and I slow to catch my breath.

Jamie takes over, grabbing Wink's lifesaver with his good arm and pushing him ahead in fits and starts. When that becomes too awkward, Jamie flips onto his back. Resting his head on the edge of the lifesaver, he paddles his legs while gulping in air.

Jamie is slowing. The water is rising too quickly, and with no end in sight, we aren't going to make it.

"Let go." Though my stomach clenches at the salt water I've swallowed, I grab the lifesaver and dolphin-kick forward— past the remaining boiler casings, past the crew dormitories, past the endless passenger cabins. Wink kicks his legs as well, though after accidentally kicking me in the chest a few times, he stops. The ceiling now hovers only two feet above our heads. I push harder, scrambling to get us out before E-Deck is completely underwater.

My lungs heave and sputter. The air feels too thick, like breathing in oversalted soup. Is this what it feels like to drown?

A sudden swell makes my stomach drop. This is it. Jamie's gaze connects with mine, as if the same bleak thought has occurred to him as well. He blinks, an assurance that whatever happens, we'll be okay.

I prepare to hold my breath for as long as possible, even if it only prolongs the agony.

But then another swell muscles us forward with a watery shove that fills my ears and nose. The sea tosses us like bath toys, sweeping us down the long corridor. My head hits a doorjamb, and stars spark in my vision. Still, I manage to hang on to Wink. We're yanked forward once more, and then the water breaks, as if we've reached a wall.

I pop up to the surface with a wheezy gasp. The aft

stairwell rises around us, its glorious ceiling extending for several floors. Somehow, we've reached the end.

My knees hit stairs. I struggle to pull myself up by the rail while Jamie hauls Wink to his feet.

Wink's hands still clutch the lifesaver in a way that seems permanent. His eyes are glazed. Has the strain been too much for him? But then he spits and honks loudly, spraying seawater from his mouth and nose.

"You okay?" Jamie pants.

A shiver travels through Wink's small body. "Still salty," he says with a ferocity that surprises me.

Jamie grins. "I know *you* are. I was talking to her."

"Oversalted," I gasp, catching my breath.

"Let's get upstairs before we freeze."

Or drown. I take Wink by the elbow, but he doesn't budge, standing with the solemnity of a church pulpit.

"I saw Amah," he says, using the Cantonese word for *mother*. "When I was drowned. I saw her, and she said the Catholic priest was right."

Vaguely, I recall that Wink attended the Catholic Sunday service while Olly tried out the Protestant one. "About what?" I ask gently.

A drop of water slides down his cheek, and then another, and I realize it isn't from his wet hair. With a sniff, he uses his arm to wipe his eyes. "My ba said I killed her. But the priest said, babies can't kill."

I give his wet shoulder a squeeze. "I'm glad you got that

squared away. There's no baby on earth who could hurt their mum, and that's just how it is."

His hunched shoulders seem to loosen. For one so tiny, he sure is casting a heavy shadow.

Jamie's mouth is set into a line. As he pulls Wink up the stairs, I can't help wondering if he's thinking about more than just the water creeping up to our feet, but about Mum and the monkey on his own back.

At the landing on D-Deck, we squeeze out our clothes as best as we can, but Wink's teeth are chattering so hard, I expect to see shards breaking off. "Let's try the rooms."

We fling open cabin doors and find dry coats for each of us. Mine has a big enough pocket to keep the whirling drum secure. Jamie sets a pair of girls' patent leather Mary Jane shoes on the ground before Wink's bare feet. "Just put them on," he growls.

Wink, his cheek twitching like an angry click beetle, stuffs his thin feet inside. I thread his arms into a coat, then ring him with the lifesaver again. The extra fabric helps the lifesaver stay up. Last, Jamie pulls a stocking cap over Wink's head.

Then I help Jamie button his coat. "Let me redo the sling."

"Forget the sling. That ice bath has my shoulder feeling good."

"You mean numb."

Water splashes up from E-Deck, licking at our feet.

"March," Jamie orders us. "We don't have much time."

40

From the Smoking Room, I'm shocked to hear the sounds of people singing and the tinkling of piano keys. I shake out my waterlogged ears. Sharp cheers also burst forth—the kind that accompany a dice throw or shots of whiskey. In the adjacent General Room, someone is giving a vigorous sermon.

"Water," croaks Wink.

Though there are drinking fountains in both rooms, Wink chooses the one with the preacher. He takes a long draw, sucking in water with his whole body.

The preacher raises his hands. "It's never too late to be saved! Our heavenly Father welcomes even the newest convert."

When I put my lips to the fountain, the sweet-tasting water feels warm on my tongue. If these people want saving, they should get to the Boat Deck.

After he drinks as well, Jamie herds us back to the exit, edging past the clergyman, who's pressing palms with the woebegone. The preacher reaches a group of men sitting shoulder to shoulder, their white-blond hair nearly glowing, set off by their purpling faces. I nudge Jamie, recognizing Bledig and the bottom cutters. One of the men begins to bawl.

Jamie frowns, but his frown lacks true annoyance. If any-one has a chance of getting on a boat, it's probably not them, with their shabby dress and mean looks, made even meaner by Bo, Jamie, and Mr. Domenic. Resignation sits like a heavy log over their bent necks. I long to tell the poor wretches to get up and fight. Then again, they might take that the wrong way.

Outside, the well deck hums with passengers, most crowded around a rather flimsy staircase to the superstructure.

Only a few days ago, I juggled a pineapple on this very deck. My wager with Jamie and Bo was a simple one, the players evenly matched. Somehow, it feels like a wager is still on. Only I'm no longer a player, but a prop, along with two thousand other souls. The ship has laid a wager against the sea, and it's clear who's favored to win.

At the top of the stairs, the gate to the upper decks remains locked. A middle-aged gent scales it, uses his life belt as a pad, and swings his legs over. He grips a woman under the arms and hauls her over, too. Others crawl along the jib of the cargo cranes, bypassing the gate altogether.

Why won't they open the gate? It's as if they've locked us in a cage and hung the key just out of reach. Will there be a line in heaven, too, with the tin plates barred from the table until the gold ones are set? If so, the Chinese at least have an advantage. In Chinese heaven, there's no line, only stars, which, through forces of push and pull, regulate when you are born and move you back to heaven when you die.

Sometimes I picture Mum up on that terraced hill with Ba and the ancestors, where I hope she can visit when she pleases.

An afterlife without one's loved ones doesn't seem like a place I'd want to go. Maybe that's why Jamie likes to study the stars. Whatever the answer is, surely it's written up there.

Beyond the gate, the rearmost lifeboat is being lowered, occupied by a dozen men and women. The scrape of hull against hull as it inches down reminds me of a spoon against an empty bowl.

As we maneuver to a spot at the bottom of the stairs, Jamie stares out to port, where others are beginning to look. A tiny prick of light flashes from somewhere on the horizon.

"'Tis a boat," a young mother behind us tells the babe in her arms, her voice high and cracking. "And 'tis comin' ter save us, me love."

I hope that's true, and that it makes haste.

The gate finally breaks, and I hold Wink as close as his lifesaver will allow. People press in toward the lifeboat, held back by shouting crewmen.

"Women and children only!" cries an officer. "Men, stand back!"

Some of the men do as they're told, but others, whether because they're afraid or because they don't speak English, still manage to board.

"Hold boarding!" a crewman with the darkened complexion of a fireman bellows from inside the lifeboat. "We're at limit. You'll have to wait for the next boat."

"There is no next boat!" wails a man. "They're all gone!"

The news sets my heart rattling against my rib cage. If this is our last chance, we'd better make it good.

"Act helpless," I drop in Wink's ear. "Maybe cry. Can you do that?"

His eyes become flinty, and he nods.

"Smartly," Jamie orders hoarsely.

"Please let us through!" I cry, pushing Wink along past a couple of men, Jamie at my back. "I got me baby brother!" The Cockney wench bangs to be let out, apparently sensing a charade brewing. So I let her take over, careful not to overdo it.

Last time I tried to get Wink on a lifeboat, I was too polite, too quick to play by the rules, and that won't happen again. This time, I'll be as pushy and streetwise as the gangs in Cheapside, who'll beg, barter, or beat the shadow off you if they want something badly enough.

The officer in charge, a pale young man with a haunted face, holds up a hand to me. My feet halt, but my mouth keeps going.

"He's a wee one, barely seen life, and it's been hard, with Mum gone belly-up." I glance at Jamie, who quickly transforms his astonished face into one of mourning. "She dropped her teeth looking over the pier and fell in trying to catch them. Drowned right in front of his eyes. Come on, sir, give us a chance."

Wink, whose face has begun twitching, squeezes out a tear, a good fat one that takes its time rolling down to the tip of his nose, where it bravely hangs on.

The officer scratches his blond whiskers. From the boat, a man with a paunch like a bag of flour puts his hands to his mouth and bellows, "We're at capacity. Any more will sink—"

"You wanna let a child what seen his mum drown in front of him go down the same way? That would just be evil. Come on, sir, have a heart. Take us with you." I grab Jamie's arm. "We're family. You can't break up family. Please, we're no trouble. You won't even notice us."

"Officer, lower away!" a man calls down from the Boat Deck.

From the back of the lifeboat, a figure rises, someone with the stocky build of a trimmer, and a shaved head. "Wink!"

"Ming Lai!" cries Wink, maybe blubbering real tears this time.

Beside Ming Lai sits Dina Domenic with her parents squeezed in next to her.

"Blimey!" I cry. "Another of our bruv'ers. It's a sign from God Himself, a sign we should be on this boat. Hallelujah!" I clasp my hands and shake them over my head, like a high roller on his last throw of the dice.

The young officer twists at the whistle around his neck. "I can't let all three of you."

"How about just the deuce of them, guv'nor?" Jamie cuts in.

I grimace, and not just because his Cockney is as tragic as burnt chicken. The first two boats in this quadrant are already in the water, and the third is on its way down. This is the last lifeboat here.

"You said birds and babes," Jamie keeps on. "Far as I can tell, you got mostly blokes in your bucket. What do you say?"

The officer swivels between the boat and us. I keep my praying hands in front of me, nudging Wink with my elbow.

Wink squeezes out another tear. He begins to whimper and squeak, escalating to full-belly wailing. Now the tears are really starting to flow.

"I won't be no trouble, sir!" he hiccups.

"Let them on. For God's sake, man!" cries another voice.

The officer crosses himself. "Very well, the wee one and the girl. I'm sorry, sir, you'll have to wait for the next one."

With a nod, Jamie steps back. Wink legs into the boat, still wearing his lifesaver, looking like a cloth napkin pulled through a ring. Quickly, he works his way back to Ming Lai.

As I step onto the gunwale, a baby cries, a wail too thin to carry far. The young mother who was behind us fights to keep her bundle from slipping. A tiny leg sticks out, attached to a tiny foot that has yet to stamp a print on the world. The mother shrugs up a shoulder, wiping away her tears. They won't make it.

Jamie sees me eyeing the pair and shakes his head no.

"Ming Lai, take care of Wink," I call to him in Cantonese.

"Of course, Little Sister," he calls back, his deep voice as reassuring as a warm coat.

"Guv'nor, I'd like this lady to have my spot. That baby needs a chance."

The paunchy man lifts his hands. "That's two more people!"

Something pops in my chest, and this time, my boiler explodes. Why should he get a place while dutiful men, like this young officer and my stalwart Jamie, stay behind? "Sir, you've got a beer baby on your lap that's twice the size of the one she's holding, so shut your piehole!"

Paunchy begins to stand, his face twisting into something ugly. But in front of him, Mr. Domenic also rises. The Russian is so big, he could row the boat even without oars. Paunchy sits back down.

The officer nudges the woman forward, steadying her as she climbs aboard and sits. Then he throws a salute toward the leaving vessel. "Good luck, all. Lower away!"

With the boat descending, Wink stares up at me, his face open, his eyes no longer leaking tears. His cheek twitches, and his gaze wavers between Jamie and me. He nods once, as if to tell me he understands.

My eyes fill. *Goodbye, Little Brother. I may not see you again, but I will hope for it.*

41

J amie herds me farther up the deck. No other lifeboats remain on the starboard side of the ship, and according to rumor, none are left on the port side either. My mind flashes to Bo, who I hope found Tao and managed to get a spot somewhere.

Please, God, I haven't been the most faithful sheep in your flock, but let him make it, wherever he is. And Tin Hau, if you really are the goddess of shipwrecks, it's time to stir up some miracles.

We pass through a European-looking café with ivy trellises and rattan chairs, most overturned. Flower centerpieces lie broken on the tilting floor.

"Have I mentioned how annoying you are?" Jamie growls, stepping over a vase.

"Yes, but I always hear it as 'You *are* a clever boot, aren't you, Sis?'"

"You could've been on that boat. If you had just minded your own business, you would've been home free. But no, it's like you're one of those stewards handing out life belts, but you can't stop. Why?" He grabs at his cap before realizing he's no longer wearing one.

"Because family saves family."

"Those people were not your family."

"Wasn't talking about them, you goat. Mum and Ba are up there, like those stars you like to stare at, and they're pulling for us to help each other. Can't you feel it?"

His eyes flit up to the latticework ceiling, and then he yanks open a door leading to the aft tidal-wave staircase. "I'd just be happy to feel my feet right now."

"Me, too." My wet boots seem to have frozen around my pins.

The hands of the simple square clock on the landing stretch toward 2:00. By my estimate, we've been sinking for over two hours. Another of those ineffectual cherubs throws me a help-less gaze, as if to say, *I'm just as tired as you, Sister.*

"If we do manage to find a boat, they might not take me." Jamie slows to crook a finger at me. "Promise you'll go if there's a space. Promise."

I almost laugh. Does he really think I could do that? After coming all this way. But he looks so brittle. "I promise to do the right thing," I assure him. "Maybe we should get you a dress."

"Why?" he mutters, slapping at his head, though I think the question is directed at someone with more influence than me.

I use the banister to help me up the last few steps. The angle of the tilt to head is so severe now that climbing the stairs seems to defy physics.

We exit through a port-side door onto the Promenade Deck. The water churns with wriggling flashes of white that remind me of a shoal of mullet.

340

But they aren't fish. They're people. People who are freezing right in front of us. How did they get down there? Did they jump? Perhaps they planned to swim toward one of the lifeboats. But once that icy water touches you, it's a race against time. Our frigid swim through E-Deck was balmy compared with the open sea, the water slightly warmed from having passed through the boiler rooms.

At the rail, a man in a baker's uniform flings deck chairs into the ocean.

"Need help, mate?" With his good arm, Jamie helps the baker throw the last of the makeshift floats, then nudges me forward. Up another staircase, we top the Boat Deck again.

I cry out, though my breath only vents as a hoarse whisper. Most of the bow has sunk. Water engulfs the forecastle and is steadily creeping up to the bridge. Oddly, the ship no longer tilts to starboard, but to port.

The davits are empty, their ropes swaying in the risen water. Several lifeboats are rowing away, despite being half-empty.

No wonder people jumped into the water. The *Titanic* will soon founder, and like barnacles on a diving whale, we'll all be going along for the ride if we don't bail out soon. At least in the water, we can make for a lifeboat—until we stiffen up like icicles.

"Move," Jamie growls, cradling his left arm. "The collapsibles might still be there."

A terrier streaks past us, followed by a dachshund and a pair of sheepdogs. "Where did they come from?"

"Dunno. But they're headed to higher ground."

"Maybe we should follow them." I watch as they climb toward the stern.

"No." Jamie tugs me away. "Any collapsible would be this way." He nods to the sunken bow.

I plant my feet. "But I don't see any boats. We'd be jumping into the pot."

"Move your damn pins," Jamie orders.

We pick our way down the sloping deck, every step a pain. But at least moving forces the blood to circulate.

The lights have grown dimmer, the yellow glow fading to orange and casting grim shadows on Jamie's face. Steam fogs out of our mouths, reminding me that at least a few parts of us are still warm.

People fly by, headed to the stern. I throw Jamie a scowl. "Are you sure we're going the right way?"

Jamie pushes on, even though any nitwit could see that all the craft on this side have left.

The water seems eager to meet us as we reach the forward part of the deck. Waves hiss and slither like a nest of reptilian beasts, cold-blooded and dark and everywhere at once.

"Look!" Jamie points to an oblong hump, like the underbelly of a giant fish, floating thirty yards beyond where the water pools in the well deck. It's an overturned collapsible. Two ropes tether it to the railing on the roof of the officers' quarters. People crowd the sides of the boat, trying to climb the hull before it breaks free of its leashes.

"We're getting on that," Jamie says flatly.

"You mean swim?"

Two men scramble past us, almost knocking me down, but Jamie grabs my arm. "This way." He marches to the ladder leading up to the roof.

"Wait! Where are you going?" I pull myself up the ladder after him.

The roof over the officers' quarters sweeps before us, empty of people. Past the first smokestack, water has begun to flood the bridge. I can't help thinking about the proud Captain Smith, whose career will surely plummet with his ship. Even if he lives, there can be no surviving this.

On the starboard side, another collapsible is barely visible, growing smaller as its occupants row it away. Ahead, the foremast has sunk so low, the crow's nest appears to float on the water, its brass bell swinging like a lantern. To port, the tiny light that might have been our savior has grown no bigger, still just another cold and unreachable star.

Clammy beads of sweat prickle my skin. We're alone out here in this jungle. Who will save us but ourselves?

Jamie reaches the part of the railing where the two ropes connecting to the collapsible have been knotted. A strong current stretches the ropes taut, as if the lifeboat and the *Titanic* were engaged in a tug-of-war. "We'll walk across these two lines. It'll be a cinch, two tracks to the end just like a railroad. The less time we spend in the water, the better."

"But, Jamie, I can barely feel my feet. How am I supposed to—"

"You won't fall in. I'll be right behind you. Quickly, before the boat breaks free or they cut the line. You can do this."

He helps me up to the rail. He's done it a thousand times, but this time feels like the first.

My heart flip-flops like a landed fish, and my pins have become pillars of ice. I doubt I can make it even one step before falling in. In theory, walking two lines should be easier than one. But not in the middle of the barking Atlantic Ocean, with ropes that can go wavy at the whim of the current. And not when you're trembling so hard, you could shake all the bones clear of your body.

Below me, still holding my hand, Jamie's face clouds with worry. Somehow, seeing his distress knocks mine down a notch. Fine. I'll do this. If only to stop him from looking like his face might crumble off.

I blow a puff of air at him for luck. He blinks, then blows one back, giving me a lopsided smile.

Taking a deep breath, I reach out a numb foot and test the line. It's hard as a rail. Balancing, I reach out my other foot. Only about ten inches separate the lines. I'll have to make this fast, letting my momentum make me light.

Life is a balancing act. You could be killed walking down the street, but you don't let that fear stop you. You just practice until the fear is no longer part of the equation.

I let go of Jamie and begin to move.

The ocean spits and hisses just a few yards under me, rising higher with each step forward. Squinting to keep my vision clear, I muscle the fear away, the devil that must be tamed.

As my foot slips off one rope, I alight to the other. Back and forth, light as a mosquito.

Men shout. Some cry. Bodies flail in the water, their fear like crab claws, pincering my attention from every angle. Wrenching my eyes from the chaos, I focus on my footing. The collapsible takes shape before me, but I dare not look at it directly. As if sucking in a breath, I draw my mind inward, where there is only lightness, air, and wings.

The road wobbles. A drowning man has grabbed the rope on the left. Brackish curls obscure most of his face, except for his crooked nose. It's Skeleton!

My right foot clutches at its line, and I teeter, trying to keep from falling.

Quickly, I bring my left foot to join the right, levering my arms.

Skeleton loses his grip on the rope. With a wail that rattles my soles, the ocean snatches him away.

I don't spare another thought for the man's wretched fate.

But then my right rope begins to slacken, and I feel myself fall.

An outstretched hand grabs me. "Gotcha, miss!" says the man, hauling me onto the overturned boat. "Though I scarcely believe me eyes."

"Thank you," I gasp, breathing so hard, the air must be punching holes through my chest.

Seven or eight men have managed to clamber onto the collapsible's hull, sitting, standing, or crouching as if undecided either way.

The ropes tighten again, and Jamie starts down the tracks.

I balance on the hull, focusing all my attention on my brother. "Come on, Jamie."

His feet move quicker than mine, bouncing from rope to rope with the confidence of the *Titanic*'s cellist plucking his strings. The water has risen so much that it almost looks like he's walking on water.

"He's doing it, too, just like her. They're cracked as eggs."

"Work of the devil. Bet they're Catholics."

"You mean Protestants, you fish friar."

He's halfway there. *Come on, Jamie, just a few paces more.* I envision for him a clear and easy brick road that even a toddler could walk.

A loud screech like twisting metal lifts my head. Something shifts behind Jamie, a piece of scenery moving out of place. My horrified eyes take in the first smokestack as it sways off its base. The tethers holding the tower break, whipping and cracking, and setting off a chorus of screams. Then, like a giant tree at the fatal chop of the ax, the smokestack begins to fall toward us.

"Jamie, watch out!" I scream.

42

The smokestack belly flops in a cloud of sparks and soot just to the right of us, sending powerful waves that wash me right off the collapsible. And, oh, that murky has teeth! The cold sets deep into the bones. It chills the blood and makes everything sluggish, even thoughts.

I flail, trying to keep my head above the water. "Jamie!"

Another wave crashes over me, tossing me around like a piece of flotsam.

The waves eventually lose their anger, and I pop up, right next to a white tub. It's the crow's nest. Grabbing on to the lip, I hike one leg over, then the other. Water floods the nest to knee level, but at least it's a port in the storm while I dig through the dark for Jamie.

He surfaces with a loud gasp, forty feet to starboard.

"Jamie!" I cry, trying not to sob. "Jamie!"

The ocean sweeps my voice away. He looks around, disoriented.

One of the cables attached to the foremast drifts loosely around the crow's nest. But to my relief, unlike the smoke-stack, the foremast still feels securely planted, even with its cables snapped.

"Jamie!" I wave an arm.

He's drifting farther away. I lean out as far as I can, but something hard knocks against my ear. The lookout bell.

You ninny goat! Quickly, I grab the clapper and ring it.

Clang-clang! Clang-clang!

Jamie's head turns toward the sound. Finally he spots me and begins to swim.

I gather the drifting cable and wind it as best I can around my arm. Then I throw it hard. It goes wide, but at least it lands closer to him than he lies from me. He lunges toward it.

Working together, I haul him arm over arm toward me, while he kicks, speeding our progress. Soon, he scrabbles aboard, panting and shivering.

As soon as he's able to speak again, he gasps, "We have to clear out. Once the boat sinks, the water will suck us under. Look for something we can use."

From our vantage point, I spy bits of debris roiling about, along with a few people still bobbing around in their life belts. The collapsible has been pushed far to port, so far that it's barely a fingernail on the horizon. The ocean is a moving stage of props that don't belong: tablecloths, trays, broken posts. I point to a large piece of furniture. "There?"

"Good, let's go."

"But what if it's not—"

"It'll do. Smartly, now!"

We launch ourselves from the crow's nest. The water seems to have warmed a few degrees, perhaps a gift from the falling smokestack, but still it stabs my skin with a thousand needles.

After an endless swim, we finally reach the raft, which turns out to be a chaise longue, of all things. Its cushions have floated away, leaving only its wooden platform and single raised end. We latch on to the foot of it and use it as a kickboard.

"Kick!" Jamie orders, though my legs are so stiff, I'm not sure I can bend my knees. "Kick, you goat."

"Who you calling goat? You're the goat."

"No, you're the goat. Stubborn as all get-out. Kick!"

"Pig trotter."

"Cod belly."

"Pigeon egg."

"Stop wasting your breath," he pants. His legs, which are longer and more powerful than mine, slow to meet my pace so we don't go in circles.

A keening starts up, growing sharper and more frantic by the moment.

"Don't look," Jamie says. "Keep kicking, and don't look."

A vision of the shrewd-eyed Reverend Prigg, thundering on about how God saves the righteous, inserts itself into my head. But if that's truly the case, why are those people—most lowly immigrants just like us—screaming so loud, I swear even the stars pale at the cry?

Another metallic shriek and corresponding crash sends out more waves. It must be the second smokestack, fallen just like the first. That means there are two left. Only two.

I close my eyes and focus on kicking.

There were four of us when I took my first breath—Mum,

Ba, Jamie, and me. The number four sounds like death, but Ba roasted a pair of suckling pigs to celebrate our birth. After Mum got her first taste, she declared she'd bear Ba another set of twins just to have that special dish again. There were four, and now there are two.

Before the impact of the second smokestack finishes vibrating through my bones, another sound starts up, this one even more terrible. Metal screeches, accompanied by the clamor of wood, tile, glass, and steel, all being thrown together. It sounds as if a giant pair of hands has taken ahold of the ship and twisted her in the middle, slowly breaking her apart. Everything in me comes to a crashing halt—muscle, blood, breath.

With our cheeks pressed to the board, Jamie and I stare at each other in horror. For the first time, I notice that his cheek is smeared with something red, and a bump has appeared on the side of his head.

"Jamie, you're bleeding."

"Something hit me when that first smokestack went down. Don't worry, I've been applying ice."

"Not funny. You need medical attention."

"I'll be sure to call an ambulance as soon as I find the telephone."

The lights flicker out, and I hear myself whimper. This time, they don't turn back on.

Then the giant hands become fists that pound the ocean like a thirsty man calling for drinks. Water begins swirling around us, sucking us backward.

Jamie begins to kick again.

"I can't . . . I can't . . ." I gasp.

"Yes . . . can . . . a little farther."

I move my legs, wondering if it's possible to freeze mid-kick. I focus on counting—yut-yee-som, yut-yee-som—over and over again in my head.

The screams had tapered off, but they begin anew, as if everyone still aboard that doomed ship has taken a collective breath, filling their lungs for a fresh wave of torture.

I know I shouldn't, but I peek.

Without her electric lights, the *Titanic* forms a black outline against the starlit sky. But everything's gone pear-shaped, and for a moment, I wonder if my head is twisted on wrong.

The ship lies at a steep angle, her back half poking up like a duck that's bobbed under the surface to snatch a fish. The last two smokestacks have broken off, gone like the others, committed to the sea. People brace themselves on whatever they can—benches, rails, even ventilator shafts. But that doomed elevator will only move in only one direction now. If they don't step off in time, those riding it will be sucked under, the air squeezed out of them.

Jamie looks back, too, his kicking ceasing as well. "Bloody hell." His voice is barely a whisper.

I say a prayer for the Johnnies. For the peaceful Tao and the stubborn Fong. For the cheerful Olly and the sweet and salty Wink. For the romantic Ming Lai and the faithful Drummer. And most of all, for the complicated Bo, who made a promise to me that I worry he cannot keep. Let this nightmare be over soon, and may all wake in the finest first-class sheets, whether on this earth or in heaven.

The *Titanic*, or what remains of her, begins to sink, her giant propellers putting me in mind of a windup toy. At first chugging down slowly, she picks up speed as she plunges. Final screams erupt and burst, as useless as the flares that were launched from the bow.

Then a black hood is slipped over the stern, and the outraged cries abruptly halt. The ocean roils and gurgles as it devours the ship. Four big explosions shake the water, and the unmistakable sounds of a boat being crushed breach the surface.

We feel ourselves being pulled back toward the wreck, like a saucer on a tablecloth.

As if by reflex, we begin to kick once more. We kick with all the jelly left in our jars, powering forward as if heaven is closing her gates right in front of us, and the flames of hell are licking our behinds.

I close my eyes, which are so full of salt, I wonder how they haven't shriveled inside their sockets.

Bees are swarming Ba.

Jamie perches high on the oak.

It's up to me.

I blow fire onto a tree branch, igniting a torch. I run, and the bees follow.

"Climb up," Jamie says, sounding far away. "That's enough."

Enough. A soft, treacherous word. A word that means stop,

rest. A word that means you've done everything, but makes you doubt it all the same.

Inch by inch, I heave myself aboard, as awkward as an injured seal on a thin floe of ice. Every wiggle and twitch fills me with dread. If I roll off, this tired old bucket isn't hauling herself back up the well.

I center myself on the float, curled up so that my lifeless feet don't hang in the water. Jamie scoots up after me, flopping over my side and waiting for our board to settle before moving again. Our raft squirms underneath us, but Jamie, through some last act of balance and strength, keeps us topside.

Ba is in a ditch that's quickly filling with water.

Jamie's shirt billows like a sail.

I lead a circus elephant—one with a golden tiara on its head and crimson velvet on its back—to the ditch. The elephant dips its trunk into the water and drains it.

I can feel Jamie cradling me, passing me whatever warmth remains in him, just as he did in the coal hole. Moving slowly, he drapes his left arm over my waist and closes his hand over mine. His ragged breaths warm my neck. His shoulder must be in agony.

"You were the right boot, going fore instead of aft with the dogs," I tell him.

"And you were . . . right boot," he stammers out the words, his teeth clattering loudly. He's been in the water longer than me, and every second counts.

"About what?"

"Built it up in my head . . . how much I hated it. But you reminded me that . . . it wasn't so bad. When we flew together."

A half sob, half laugh bursts from my frozen lips. "We're going to make it, Jamie. This is a tough line. But we'll cross it."

A soft grunt reaches my ears.

I must keep him talking. "That Charlotte sure thinks you're the stuff."

"Wh . . . ?" Somehow, even with only half a word, he still manages to sound annoyed. But he doesn't say anything else. Even the chattering of his teeth has lessened.

"Jamie! Don't nod off, you sod!" Angrily, I flex my spine and feel him stir.

"Tired, Sis," he whispers.

"What were you two arguing about?" I ask, trying to keep him from falling asleep. He can't fight if he's sleeping.

"Told her . . . I could never fit . . . into her life."

"And what did she say?" My words slur.

"Said . . . she could fit . . . into mine."

My thoughts move as slowly as feet through heavy snow. What were we talking about? "You love her. She loves you. Why don't you see?"

"You're always . . . sticking your nose in."

Ba lies in a cage.

Jamie gazes up at the sky.

I lead an old man with an icicle beard to the cage. With a turn of his hairpin, he unlocks it.

Icy water splashes my face, rousing me.

"Jamie? I remembered how all of my dreams ended. I saved him. I knew what to do."

At least a minute passes before he answers. "Your dreams weren't about Ba . . . or me. They were about you. But I always knew . . . you could fly on your own."

"What made you so sure?"

His words are too quiet, despite being spoken only a few inches from my ear. "They're close."

"Wake up, Jamie," I say hoarsely. "Don't leave me. What made you so sure?"

"Your last name's Luck."

And then he goes still.

"Jamie? Jamie!" My tears flow freely, and a sob chokes my throat.

But my cries go unanswered. There's only the ghostly sounds of the breeze whistling across my ear, and the ocean slurping at our raft, its appetite sated but still craving a taste.

I search for the words of our old sea shanty. Singing warms the body, and the more heat I can give Jamie, the less he'll have to give me. Maybe he'll stay longer.

> *The captain paced his weathered deck,*
> *A-talkin' to his boots.*
> *They were his pride and joy, you see,*
> *Anchored him like roots.*
> *The right one he named Valor;*

It always steered his course.
The left one he called Virtue;
'Twas steady as a horse.

I sing, willing my warmth to flow backward into my brother's quiet limbs. I sing until the notes peter out, and my song passes through my lips like dry air through a flue. He doesn't move. In my heart, I know he's nearly gone. But I sing a song to keep him near.

Ba's spirit had long flown away by the time I found him, but Jamie's lingers. As tears blur my vision, I feel him hover, shielding me from the cold for as long as he can.

Long minutes pass, and hope rises and fades. Still, Jamie's spirit flickers like a candle, as if to sear the memory of him into my waxen body. As if I could ever forget.

A book opens in some dusty corner of my mind, the best in Ba's collection, a tender ode to lives barely lived. In the beginning, two babes take their first breaths together, their first shaky steps across a threadbare floor. As each page turns, the years pass, and their steps become steadier. Steady enough to cross railways, fences, and ropes as thin as clotheslines. Steady enough to walk through fire and ice—until a storm blows one away.

I thought you knew we'd always be together, even when we're not.

But without you, Brother, I am a beat without a heart.

A lady calls my name, her voice like the soft lap of waves against a hull. She presses her warm lips to my forehead.

We call that a kiss from Tin Hau, the goddess of ship-wrecks and sailors. It means good luck is on the way. Maybe for you.

The lady smiles down at me, her fair face glowing like a paper lantern.

Jamie, wake up! Tin Hau has come. Our rescue is at hand.

The dip and gurgle of oars reach my ears. But then the lady fades, and a lamp intrudes on my face.

"Help," I whimper.

But my throat produces no sound.

"Please," I try again.

But the sound is swallowed by the waves.

They are too far away to hear.

Something bobs in the water. The whirling drum has worked itself loose from my pocket, a bit of Drummer's spirit thumbing his nose at the ocean.

I reach for the object, my hand sluggish. Twisting my wrist, I let the corded beads speak on my behalf.

Weakly at first: *Tat-tat. Tat-tat.*

Then more strongly: *Ta-tat-ta-tat-ta-tat-ta-tat.*

Heads turn our way. Voices start up.

"There are two of them," says a man. "Look, one's moving!"

"Leave 'em," barks another. "They're Japs."

"Help us," I rasp.

"Is that a woman?" says the first man.

"No," the barker replies. "Look at his hair. That's a man wearing women's clothes. See how sneaky they are?"

"Well, Japs or no, shouldn't we take them?" says a third man, this one with a tremulous voice.

The first man curses. "Come on, man, you're wasting time."

"We only have room for one," the barker grumbles. "Two might sink us all!"

"Then let's take that one."

Hands reach for me.

If they only have room for one, they will leave Jamie behind.

"No," I spit, feeling one last fire spark in my belly. Words, which have frozen on my tongue, at last begin to thaw. "Take him. I beg you."

A whale means being in control of your destiny.

"But that one's not moving," says the tremulous man. "He might already be gone."

"No, he *is* moving. Look," says the first man as Jamie stirs beside me.

The barker groans. "Fine. At least he's bigger. He can help us row."

Hands reach for Jamie. He moans softly, his frozen hand clutching mine.

No, Brother. It's your turn for the leapfrog. Trust me.

With a collective grunt, they lift him.

Up the phoenix rises, and unlike at our birth, I don't grab his ankle for a lift.

"Val . . . ?" he moans, his voice thick.

"Don't look behind you anymore, Jamie," I manage to get out, though the ache of our parting stabs me like a dull knife through the gut. "The best . . . is ahead."

"Val . . . ?" he murmurs again.

He's covered in a blanket, and the oars are set to rowing. Soon, the lifeboat becomes a white blur, its wake moving me farther away.

When my twin, Jamie, left, he vowed it wouldn't be forever.

But this time, I hope he doesn't hurry home.

I rest my cheek upon the float, ready at last to let go. Heaven is thick with dandelion seeds, close enough to touch.

The fire in me grows cold. But something deeper begins to stir.

Troubled by all she has seen and felt, the whale turns into a bird, whose wings churn the water. And when that great seabird meets the wind, I feel my spirit take flight.

Look to the sky, Jamie, and you will always find me.

EPILOGUE

April 30, 1912
My dearest Charlotte,

*I expect it will be several weeks before you receive
this. I am posting this letter from our ship in Cuba,
and it may be weeks before the mail service comes
to collect it. By then, I hope Wink and Olly will
have settled into their new life with you, and you
with them. I thank the stars every day for placing
you in their path, our path. Your adopting them
through the Home for Little Souls was a pinch of
sugar in a very bitter tea, and I know their lives will
be changed for the better on account of it.*

*As for the rest of us, we are muddling through as
best we can. It is only Ming Lai and me now, as Bo
promised Tao that he would see Fong back to his
daughter in Hong Kong. May that old geezer live
out the rest of his years in whatever peace he can
manage. Bo will rejoin us in Cuba. The loss of my
sister—it hurts to even write her name—has cut us
both deep. As for me, I intend to embrace life the*

way she would've wanted me to. She'd always had enough life in her for the two of us, and now I shall live for the both of us. As I understand, there are exceptions for students in the Exclusion Act. But my dearest, even if that path does not open for me, as long as there are stars in the sky, I will look for the one that leads back to you.

I enclose letters for the lads.

Yours truly,
Jamie

Author's Note

Of the seven hundred survivors of the *Titanic* disaster, six—of an original eight—were Chinese men, probably seamen of some sort. But little is known about them. Unlike the rest of the survivors, their stories were not reported. While every other survivor was welcomed into America and given succor, these six were shipped off within twenty-four hours of arrival. The rare mentions of the Chinese passengers vilified them as cowards who took seats from women and children or dressed as women in order to sneak aboard the lifeboats, all of which were unfounded rumors.

A culture of discrimination against the Chinese, codified by the Chinese Exclusion Act, ensured that they would be written out of the story. Yet it's remarkable that six of the eight—or 75 percent—lived, when the overall survival rate for third-class passengers was 25 percent. It's likely that none of the eight spoke English, so they would not have understood orders easily. Stationed in the bottom decks, the Chinese would've had to grasp the situation and react quickly.

Of the eight Chinese passengers, five survived by boarding lifeboats, four of them on the last lifeboat to leave the *Titanic*, Collapsible C. Collapsible C was the same lifeboat on which

White Star chairman J. Bruce Ismay escaped. Faced with criticism about his legitimacy on the vessel, Ismay testified that the four Chinese men were "hiding" under the benches, maybe hoping to reinforce his own status as a gentleman. The sixth Chinese survivor was found floating on a door to which he had attached himself. Lifeboat 14 (the only one to return to the scene to look for survivors) was reluctant to pick him up because they thought he was a "Jap." Fortunately, they did, as he helped to row the lifeboat to safety.

Efforts to uncover these men's stories are underway, though after being shamed for surviving, many of them did not even share their stories with their own families. *Luck of the* Titanic is a tribute to the great place these men hold in history.

Author's Further Note

The wonderful thing about writing a book about such an
infamous historical event as the sinking of the *Titanic*
is the bottomless well of information available. In the
wake of the disaster, inquisitions were held. Scientists and
engineers endeavored to understand what had gone wrong,
so as to prevent future tragedies. Countries developed regulations. And newspapers reported on the events for years. In
addition, people with curious minds did their own investiga-
tions, trying to understand exactly what had happened. Many
are still investigating to this day. (There's a highly informative
discussion board at encyclopedia-titanica.org for anyone with
questions about the *Titanic*.) Some things we will never know.
Some questions will be answered in time.

The challenge of writing historical fiction lies in creating
a fictional story within the confines of the historical record
without doing too much damage in the process. Where I felt
it was important, I used the names of actual passengers for
my characters, mostly to invite the reader to discover their
lives. Of course, some of the more well-known citizenry had
to remain: Captain Smith, J. Bruce Ismay, the Duff-Gordons.
The *Titanic* would just not be the *Titanic* without them.

Additionally, Albert Ankeny Stewart was a real man with business interests in the Ringling Brothers Circus, a man named Crawford was his bedroom valet, and Bertha Chambers was a first-class passenger staying on E-Deck. Exploring these lesser-known characters was a way to honor their memories.

More often than not, I created entirely new characters to give me the flexibility to tell the story. May you enjoy each and every one of them (perhaps with the exception of Skeleton), but most importantly, may *Luck of the* Titanic provoke a discussion about which of these characters society considers "worthy" and which it does not.

Acknowledgments

I get motion sickness in elevators. For the longest time, I thought the poop deck was so-called because that was where the seagulls did their business. So I guess you could say I never thought I'd write a book that takes place on the sea, much less aboard the infamous *Titanic*. And I'm grateful to all the people who supported me while I wrote the thing I never thought I'd write.

Just as it takes a crew with many hands doing many different things to steer a ship, so it took a bucketful of amazing talents to see this story off. Thank you to my agent, Kristin Nelson, and her entire team at Nelson Literary Agency, especially Angie Hodapp, for steering my early drafts toward the right currents; my editor, Stephanie Pitts, and editorial assistant Matthew Phipps for working with me up in the bridge, providing your insightful advice, and helping bring this story to life; my publisher, Jen Klonsky, for your stewardship; and all the amazing folks at G. P. Putnam's Sons for pulling your oars with me.

Thank you as well to my friends and readers: the wondrous Stephanie Garber for rowing my lifeboat with me; Jeanne Schriel for your clear-eyed critique and for thinking so deeply about this story and making me think deeply, too; Ida Olson for your incredible structural and character insights; Kelly Loy Gilbert for helping me grapple with the harder stuff, which you're so good at; Abigail Hing Wen for your smart reading and constant enthusiasm for my work; Kip Wilson and Megan Bannen for your helping me bring it home. I. W. Gregorio, Parker Peevyhouse, Mónica Bustamante Wagner, Bijal Vakil, Adlai Coronel, Angela Hum, Chenyi Lum, Karen Ng, Susan Repo, Yuki Romero, Maureen Medeiros, Kristen Good, you are all first class.

Special thanks to Sherri L. Smith and Hedgebrook, where I was lucky to spend a transformative week thinking about this particular story, aided by their librarian Evie Lindbloom. Thank you also to Bruce Beveridge, Steve Hall, Daniel Klistorner, Scott Andrews, and Art Braunschweiger for your aggressive research for Titanic *the Ship Magnificent*, without which I would be adrift.

Last, thanks to my home crew: Laura Ly, Alyssa Cheng, Carl and Evelyn Leong, words cannot describe how profoundly I and my work benefit from your presence in my life; Dolores and Wai Lee, for your patient and wise instruction on our cultural heritage; Avalon, my wise-cracking and intrepid co-explorer in London for research; my buddy Bennett, for giving me all these laugh lines while I drafted and for being so patient in waiting for a book written especially for you; Jonathan Lee for poring over blueprints with me in our senior reading glasses and for being as passionate about my work as I am. You are my shelters in place and ports in the storm.

STACEY LEE is the critically acclaimed

author of the novels *The Downstairs Girl*, *Under a Painted Sky*, and *Outrun the Moon*, the winner of the PEN Center USA Literary Award for Young Adult Fiction and the Asian/Pacific American Award for Literature. She is a fourth-generation Chinese American and a founding member of We Need Diverse Books. Born in Southern California, she graduated from UCLA and then got her law degree at UC Davis King Hall. She lives with her family outside San Francisco.

*You can visit Stacey at staceyhlee.com
or follow her on Twitter and Instagram
@staceyleeauthor*